WINTER'S FIRE

WINTER'S FIRE

96-1948

JANICE MILLER

MOODY PRESS
CHICAGO

To my father, Irby Howard Miller.
His love of northwestern Colorado formed the basis
for my own love of the land, and this book is
as much his as mine, though he refused a coauthorship.
Thank you, Dad. For everything, but most of all
for your wisdom in settling in beautiful Colorado.

ISBN: 0-8024-7921-9

1 3 5 7 9 10 8 6 4 2

Printed in the United States of America

1

By October it was clear that the year of 1886 was going to offer up a violent winter. The elk and deer had been moving down from northwestern Colorado's high country for nigh unto a month already. The beavers had gathered twice their usual number of willow and quakie limbs, the smaller varmints had grown fur more than twice as thick as usual. The insects were already frozen up or burrowed deep into the earth. Even the birds that usually weathered the cold winter winds had left for parts unknown.

My ranch hands and I were at the tail end of the fall roundup, moving the herd down to winter range. Come sunup, I rode out of cow camp for the high country, to cut sign for a dozen or so missing beeves.

I had a good mite on my mind that morning. My wife of six years was expecting our second child. She'd been having a hard time of it. Last evening I'd left camp and ridden down to the ranch house to check on her and my two-year-old boy.

Caroline was usually more than levelheaded, but she'd puzzled me when I arrived. She'd been right frosty up until I was getting ready to leave, then she looked square at me, and said, "Courtney McCannon, do you think I'm ugly?"

I stared hard at her. "What in thunder has gotten into you, woman? I've never seen you more beautiful."

And it was true. Her rounded belly was a miracle to me, her long, soft chestnut hair was brushed to a shine, her face was peaches and cream. She'd readied herself for bed in a loose white flannel gown with soft lace at the throat. She and that canopied featherbed looked a whole lot more inviting than a cold bedroll by a half-dead campfire.

I thought about staying, then riding out about 3:00 A.M. That would just give me time to get back to cow camp before the boys came awake. I turned and looked at myself in the

5

oblong mirror, thinking I might step into the newfangled bathroom I'd put in last year and shave some of the red-brown cactus off my face, see if I couldn't get some of the trail dust out of my backbone and the tired out of my muddy blue eyes.

But Caroline wasn't thinking about romance. Before I could suggest a change in plans, she said, "I'm getting big as a barn, and I hardly ever see you anymore." She planted her feet firm and squared her chin, and her green eyes blazed. "I think sometimes that the fire has gone right out of our marriage."

I tried to talk to her, tried to hold her, aiming to prove her wrong. But she was in one of her stubborn moods—wouldn't so much as let me touch her, much less kiss her ornery mouth. "Look at you, Courtney!"

I looked at myself again in the mirror. I was a sorry sight to be sure. My shoulders slumped as though they were plumb worn out, and my face was thinned down by too many days of hardtack, beef, and beans. I was still wearing my range clothes—Levi's and a flannel shirt, boots that were more or less run over at the heels. All the same, I'd earned my poor condition fair and square. Six hard days of herding and chasing strays was enough to put any man under the weather.

Anyway, Caroline got in a mood, and that was that. The conversation put a powerful lot of extra strain on me. In the middle of fall roundup I had no time to spend at the house. She knew that—we'd been ranching ever since our marriage. I couldn't for the life of me figure out why she'd gotten so consarned difficult.

And she had been acting peculiar lately, no two ways about it. In a way it was somewhat of a relief to have her finally come right out and say what was on her mind. At the same time, it troubled me to see her so restless and unhappy, and me with no time to sit down and tend to her concerns.

I'd been thinking about her and my other troubles all the way up the mountain. Worrying, though I knew there was no point to it.

6

Now I crested the ridge. Old Brownie and I rode into the timber, and I let my mind move on to my problems with the missing beeves. Even though the bottom had just fallen out of the cattle market, I was bound to find those mavericks. It was looking more and more like I would have to borrow money to make it through the winter, and if it came to that I'd need my herd for collateral.

I had just reached the edge of a high meadow we used for summer pasture when distant thunder rolled off the Flat Tops to the south. I reined in as the echo cracked around us, but Brownie skittered in spite of it, and her flank muscles rippled with fear. I stroked her neck and muttered, "There, old girl, it ain't nothing. There now."

But as I turned to look back over the valley and toward the mountains beyond, I saw thick storm clouds piling up like dirty fleece, and I knew that this was the day the first real snow would fly on the lowlands. We were going to have our hands full with the branding. The cold night rains had already turned to snow up here in the high country. The plateaus above me had been barren yesterday. Now they were swirled and marbled; the green spruce trees just below timberline were plastered white.

Yesterday the bawling and hoof dust of nigh unto five hundred head of cattle had mixed with the cursing and shouting and hoorahing of a dozen cowhands, as we hazed the herd down to lower pastures. But today the high country silence was broken only by the cold mountain wind as it moaned through the timber and the rim rocks on the plateau.

I shook off a gut feeling of dread and loosened the reins. Old Brownie and I moved farther on into the timber.

We moseyed along into virgin forest thick with pine and blue spruce. Here and there a stand of aspen shivered in the wind, their faded orange and red leaves rustling against one another, then swirling to the ground. Banks of red scrub oak tangled up out of thick undergrowth and deadfalls. But there were grassy glades here and there, brown and mustard-colored from the frost. And I knew of a dozen or more streams with

7

wide, grassy banks where a renegade critter might find a hideout.

The sun was higher now, burning off the last of the night's frost. I took off my leather jacket, rolled it up, and tied it behind my saddle alongside my rain slicker.

I was some fifteen miles to the north of my own ranch buildings by then, some twenty miles to the east of Moses Skettering's M-Slash-S ranch, a spread he'd proved up some five years back, the same year my pa had died. An old cabin known as the Duke homestead lay some five miles to the west, lower down the mountain at the base of the forest. A family by the name of Hearne, with a couple of young'uns, had moved in there from back East last spring.

But in spite of all these newcomers cluttering up the terrain, it was plumb lonesome up here in the high country. I felt as though there wasn't another soul around for a thousand miles.

And I was as skitterish as my saddle mare. I had ridden these mountains most of my thirty-two years, ever since Pa settled the ranch back in '66. Back then, only a handful of other white men were in northwestern Colorado and most of them trappers or Indian traders. More often than not I'd been alone on my rides, even as a youngster. But for some reason a tinge of foreboding kept crawling up my backbone today.

I tried to shake it off. There'd been recent rumors of a good-sized grizzly marauding the high country, but I wasn't eager to believe them. Anyway, any bear worth his hide was already in hibernation. As for mountain lions, for the most part they favored the sandstone and rough rocks of the lower regions.

Still, my hide stayed edgy as I rode along. I got to feeling that something was watching me.

I tried to chalk it up to the cracks of thunder that boomed and then echoed now and again through the mountains. The storm was coming in fast. If I didn't find those strays today, they'd likely starve to death in the freeze-up that was blowing in on the icy wind.

I rode in and out of the trees for the better part of an hour, looking for fresh sign, worrying and thinking and trying to figure things out. I had a heap to worry about, that was for sure. Enough to finally drive my earlier trepidation clear out of my mind.

I finally came upon a stream that cut out of the timber and snaked off across the frost-browned meadows. The banks were muddy. Chopped into that mud were fresh, clean hoof-prints where several head of cattle had milled about. I reined in to have a look. At one place the cattails and joint grass had been crushed where a critter had lost its footing and stumbled in, then dragged itself back out again.

I nudged Brownie forward and to one side, then gave her her head so that she could follow the trail the cows had made through the belly-deep grass. Finally the tracks left the stream and veered off to the right and into a small clearing, where they divided. I reined up there to rest for a minute while I decided which set of tracks to follow.

The glade was wide, and the wheat-colored Johnsongrass was still tinted through with green in some places. A pond off to one side was choked with cattails and moss, with a beaver dam holding the green-brown water. The biting wind howled softly here and tried to pry my Stetson from my head. I pushed my hat down hard, near to my ears, then hauled the sheepskin jacket out, put it back on, pulled the collar tight around my neck, and started to button it up.

A sound cut through the wind.

I froze with my fingers on the last brass button, hunching into a bitter gust, not sure I hadn't heard only the wind itself. But the sound came again. A cow was bawling. Off in the distance.

I jerked my Winchester out of the saddle scabbard and laid it across the pommel in front of me, steadying it with my right hand as I touched a knee to Brownie and turned her toward the sound. The cow bawled again, louder.

I rode through timber, around back of a thick copse of spruce, then broke through heavy undergrowth. There she was, a fat two-year-old heifer who'd managed to get herself tangled up in dead branches and rotting, fallen logs. She was good stock, well fleshed, one of the yearlings with a good mix of Holstein blood that we'd bought from Ora Haley's spread down on the Lower Snake River last spring.

We'd had to rebuild our herds after last year's die-off, for the bitter cold had frozen any number of them stiff. We'd run out of feed just before spring breakup, and that had cost us a few hundred more. Likely to lose more this year too, if the weather held up to its miserable promise.

The heifer was clay red with a white face and black spots like the shadows of leaves scattered across her back. Her eyes were rolling now with fear, so that just the whites showed. She bawled harder, frightened by my closeness and trying to struggle to her feet. But with every move she made, her fore-legs got pinned even tighter. She paused to rest for a minute, her tongue lolling out, and then she set to struggling again and in desperation bawled even louder.

I shook my head in disgust, dropped my rifle back into the scabbard, and swung down from the saddle. Brownie was bridle-wise, and she stood there, right where she'd stopped, reins draped around the saddle horn.

The heifer bawled some more, and her thrashing got more desperate. She was trembling all over. I stepped up and put a hand on her forehead, then left it there for a minute so she could get used to me, as I said, "Easy, girl, easy now. We'll have you out of there and safe before this storm sets in."

That set her thrashing again. I waited while she wore herself out, and when she fell quiet, her eyes still rolling, I squatted down beside her and looked at the cottonwood log that had her pinned down. Then I tilted back my hat, frowned, and scratched my head. How the blazes had she squirmed in under there so as to pin herself?

I reached in under the log and got hold of it, slid it over to one side a bit, and then I saw. Her front legs had been hog-tied with rope. Someone had bulldogged her, then hitched her legs to that heavy log and pinned her there neat and tidy.

Rustlers!

The minute I realized it, I saw the boot prints in the drying mud, coming then going, right alongside the creek. I was suddenly madder than a peeled rattler.

I bent down quick to lift the log, and at that instant something smacked into a tree dead ahead of me, tearing the bark and sending splinters flying. The report came right on the heels of the shot, then echoed and cracked off the ridges around me. Reckon the good Lord was riding with me. If I hadn't ducked just then, the bullet would've caught me square in the back of my hog-blind head.

I hit the dirt and rolled over the log and away from the heifer, then came up into a crouch with my Colt sidearm in my hand. I got off a quick shot of my own in the direction of the bushwhacker, and as a second bullet whizzed past my head I flew into motion and hit the trees at a dead run, slid in under a deadfall, and lay there silent, waiting, my eyes squinted up to try to see the varmint.

After a moment a flurry of cold wind rode through. Some bright gold and rust-colored leaves set to dancing above me, then spilled to the ground. I squinted harder, but I couldn't see a thing back in the tree shadows.

It hit me suddenly and caused a shudder, as if a diamondback had just crawled up my trouser leg. Whoever lay back in those shadows meant to kill me, and no mistake about it. This was why I'd been so uneasy these past couple of hours. There was something evil waiting up here. Brownie had sensed it too. My guts laced through with rawhide, withered tight.

In spite of my awkward circumstances I was able to hold my gun aimed steady. I peered into the sunlight, watching and waiting. I kept trying to swallow the lump in my throat, but the blamed thing wouldn't move. Whoever or whatever was back in those trees didn't move either.

I thought about Caroline. For a second I saw her in funeral black at our little Windsor church, a veil over her face, her belly swollen with my child, Little Johnny clinging to her

11

hand, and I wondered how she and the children would make it with the ranch in trouble and my Maker deciding it was time, right here and now, to call me on to glory.

I pushed that thought aside and spent another minute wishing I had my trusty Winchester—it was still in the saddle scabbard, and Brownie had run over to the edge of the clearing when the first shot was fired. She stood there, skittish, ready to bolt again, her bridle reins dragging to one side now.

The heifer had quit bawling and thrashing. She'd felt the death in the air, and she lay there frozen, as if she were dead herself, only her rolling eyes still showing fright.

I thought about my predicament. I figured I could bide my time. I'd landed so that I was well covered by the brush and downed timber, but I could still see the thick copse of pine, spruce, and aspen from which the shots had come. Above me the frost-crisped leaves made little death rasps as the wind scratched them one against the other before they floated to the earth. I watched one spiral in the air above me like a tiny rust-colored rowboat caught in a downdraft. Then it landed on my face. I blew it off and waited some more.

I expect I'd surprised the bushwhacker by ducking at just the right instant. Reckon I'd surprised myself too, when I stopped to think about it. At any rate, the shooter and I were at a dead standoff now. I was hidden from him in the undergrowth, while the tree shadows hid him from me.

Time passed. The sweat on the palms of my hands made my gloves damp inside, so I pulled them off. The wind sifted through the piles of leaves beneath the trees. Distant thunder still boomed now and again, cascading echoes through the crags and cliffs of the mountain. I glanced up. Clouds heavy with snow had lowered and drifted so close above my head that I could almost grab a handful. But I didn't waste much time on the weather. I was busy watching the shadows back in the trees.

Suddenly the varmint shifted. I held my breath and took aim at a small portion of his head and shoulder that was now outlined against the quaking aspen leaves.

I bit down on my lower lip, made sure my aim was square in the center of his forehead, then I jerked my gun up just a slight bit, aiming to flush him out, maybe even graze him. I fired.

He was ready for me. He returned my gunfire fast, flames licking out of the shadows.

I fired again, the gunfire ringing in my ears. Then suddenly he was gone again, the thick trees swallowing him back into their darkness.

I scooted on my belly silently through the underbrush until I found a new position, then I waited again. A new gust of wind stirred some leaves off to my left with a sudden whoosh that brought me up so fast I almost drilled them with my peacemaker. I was plenty nervous.

I could imagine that bushwhacking varmint working his way back towards his horse, which I had seen from my earlier position. It was a fine-looking sorrel with a white star on its forehead, tied back in a quakie grove a few yards away from him.

The buzzard would have the advantage should he choose to take it. Brownie had bolted again at the last gunfire, and she was even farther away, though a thick stand of pines had stopped her from galloping all the way into the forest and vanishing completely. All the same, the bushwhacker was as good as mounted, for he could reach his horse any time he wanted, and I was now afoot.

I considered that a minute. I needed to even up the odds some if I was going to make it out of this predicament. I had to get back to my saddle mare without being seen.

I eased through the damp, loamy undergrowth, careful to keep well back in the trees. The smell of decaying leaves and mulch was strong. I scratched myself on some chokecherry bushes but finally worked my way around to Brownie, who had calmed down some and was nibbling on the cured grass at her feet. I managed to keep some large boulders and fallen timber between the bushwhacker and me as I eased out of hiding. I unfolded my six feet plus till I was standing, then I reached out, careful not to spook her, and took Brownie's reins. That done, I recoiled into a clump of brush and edged backward.

Hunkering down like a two-legged bobcat, I led Brownie behind a thick patch of service brush near the edge of the clearing. Once I knew I was fully hidden, I mounted her carefully. I checked the Winchester and placed it lightly inside the scabbard, handy for when I'd need it. Then I reloaded my six-gun from my gun belt, kept it in hand, and waited.

There was another long, dead silence, and I figured the bushwhacking buzzard was waiting back there for me to make my move and show myself. But then I heard a heavy rustling on back farther in the undergrowth and the sound of a horse blowing.

Every hair on my body stood on end. I was tensed up so tight that I about leaped out of my backbone when, in a sudden flurry of movement, a mounted horseman charged out of the timber off to my right, a small man with a black scarf pulled up high to cover the bottom half of his face like a cowhand in a dust storm, a battered gray Stetson pulled low, and a muddy black riding duster covering him from his neck to his boots.

I jerked up straight, got off one quick shot, aiming high so as to miss both him and his mount. The buzzard veered to the right, swaying to avoid a fallen log, and the horse fishtailed back and forth so that the varmint almost lost his balance. But he was more of a horseman than he appeared at first, for he caught himself, then swung back upright in the saddle. The horse slowed and gave a little buck, then came to a near dead stop as the rider regained full control and yanked on the reins.

Slowly, carefully, I'd followed his movement with my Colt. As he came to that stop, I was aiming square at the back of his head.

I had him. My finger tensed, and I stopped breathing. All of a sudden everything in my range of vision was crystal

14

clear and stark, and I felt my finger squeeze, squeeze against the trigger, but just as I almost dropped him, my finger froze.

Just froze up stiff. I couldn't pull the trigger all the way back to save my own skin. With a sudden burst of frustration, I jerked the gun barrel a hairbreadth downward, and at that same moment my finger curled all the way back, and the gun fired just as my target yanked on his reins and started moving again.

The shot spun him partway around. He yelped high and shrill, like a hog being stuck, and his head jerked about so I could see him better, though his black scarf still hid the lower part of his face. He'd lost his Stetson, and his hair was sandy and appeared to be stiff with dirt. And there was something about the cut of him that I recognized now, something about the way he sat that horse.

Keyed up as I was, I didn't quite put it all together right at that moment, though I sure did recognize the cut of him.

He'd been hurt but evidently not too bad, for he caught his balance right quick, gave a low hiss that carried on the wind, whipped up his pistol and got off another wild shot that went far wide of me and whined off into the trees.

Then he reined in his horse, swung full around in the saddle, and stopped dead, the better to get me in his sights.

My finger was itching, and my Colt was aimed, but I didn't shoot. Instead, I heard myself yell, "Drop that gun so's I don't have to plug you, you no-good wildcat."

I wanted to shoot him in the worst way. He'd rustled my cattle, he'd tried to drill me. But I couldn't for the life of me make myself pull that trigger all the way back and send that bullet flying into him.

I reckon I was waiting for him to put me in a position where I had no choice but to drill him good.

But instead of shooting me, he did a mighty peculiar thing. He leveled his gun at my horse, fast-like, before I realized what he was up to, and shot old Brownie square in the neck, about six inches behind her ears.

Her cry cut through the cold air, and she began to buckle beneath me, and I leaped wide of her, cursing the rustler, cursing myself for being so foolish as to hold back. And as I leaped free, Brownie folded to the ground, blood spurting from her wound, and I felt a black, poisonous rage well up inside of me that I'd never known before. If I could have gotten my hands on that man's throat, I'd have torn his head off with my bare hands, but it was already too late for that.

The varmint put the spurs to his mount, and he was gone, swallowed already by the thick blue spruce and aspen that covered the mountainside outside the clearing, all down the slope.

I looked down at old Brownie, and tears welled up as I saw her suffering, though I guess a tear or two came out of the plumb, pure mad I still had on. I'd ridden that horse for nigh unto eight years, and a better piece of horseflesh had never been born or ridden by any man.

She was hurt bad. Her front legs seemed to be paralyzed. I checked it out, moving her legs this way and that, trying to get her to move them on her own, and all the time her eyes just got wilder, and she began to tremble, and I could smell the pain and fear on her now.

I swallowed hard, brushed the water from my eyes, then pulled my Winchester out from under her, aimed it at the side of her head, and fired—twice—looking away the second time as tears welled up to blind me. She was already mostly dead, even before I fired, and now a great shudder went through her body, and she made not so much as a whimper, though her muscles twitched here and there. She went limp.

I heard a sob roll up out of my throat, then catch there. I would never ride my friend again.

I took out my old blue bandanna out of my chaps pocket and wiped the tears from my eyes. And in that instant, for the first time in my life, I desperately wanted to kill a man.

Odd thing was, I *could* have killed him a few moments before. And when all this was happening, I couldn't have told you for the life of me why I hadn't killed him or why he hadn't killed me instead of shooting my horse.

He'd bushwhacked me, rustled at least one and probably more of my range cattle, and by every law of man I had a right to kill him on sight.

But I'd never killed a man before.

Oh, I'd shot a few—winged them—and beat more than a few within an inch of their lives with my fists when I was backed up in a corner. Northwestern Colorado is hard country. My pa had settled here right after the Civil War, and I'd been mostly raised here, where a man who won't fight won't last.

But I'd had it drilled into me every waking day of my life, it seemed—*Thou shalt not kill.* Pa had come back from the war with those words on his lips. He claimed it was because he'd learned something about killing during that war that he never wanted to see me have to face—nor ever face again himself. Well, there was a lot I didn't understand yet way back when the whole thing began. Reckon I've learned a good deal since that day.

I know that the good Lord's Ten Commandments are not to be taken lightly. Still, doesn't He also say that it's always right to root out evil? And the evil that was about to flood into the Yampa River Valley started with my failing to stop that bushwhacker that very day. And old Brownie wasn't the last to die on account of my unwillingness to take that varmint's life.

Well—I reckon there are more kinds of killing than one. And there's been many a night when I've lain awake and wished I had it to do over again—that I would have pulled that trigger and shot that rustler dead right then and there, no matter if it had taken my own life to do it.

2

I woke up Caroline when I got in at midnight. I'd walked halfway down the mountain, boots burning my feet and my face burning with the shame of what had happened. After thinking over my actions during that long, trying walk, I decided that I'd all but killed old Brownie myself.

She was upset when I told her what had happened. "Did you walk all the way home?"

"Met Banty Brewster about halfway down," I said. "He was herding some stock from the western slope, and I rode double with him to high camp. Skunkweed was still breaking down the gear, and there was an extra mount in the pole corral."

"Why didn't you come home and get Dancer?" This was her thoroughbred, and she was in a mighty kind mood if she was talking about letting me take him out to cut cows. I figured maybe she was feeling sorry for the way she'd treated me last night.

"Too much work to do," I said. "Snow's about to fly."

"Did you go back up the mountain?"

I listened for some hint of chastisement in her voice. I'd expected her to still be on her high horse, but all I heard was concern.

"A couple of the hands went back up with me to look for the missing beeves. We buried Brownie."

She chewed on her lip and didn't say anything.

She surprised me again by helping me pull off my stoved-in boots, then fixing me a late supper of cold roast beef and fresh baked bread. While I was shoveling in the food—I hadn't stopped to eat since breakfast—she leaned her elbows on the white-and-red checked oilcloth on the kitchen table, put her hands under her chin, and gazed at me with a look of pure love.

The kerosene lamp made her eyes sooty, the shadows in her cheekbones deeper. It made me think of the first year she'd spent on the ranch. Then I thought of our wedding pictures. She'd been so youthful then, the smile on her face came so easily. As for me, I'd been a good-looking young colt with reddish brown hair and a bewildered look that pretty much reflected the way I felt most of the time back then.

I thought about how life had changed us, and a frown knit her eyebrows together as if she sensed my thoughts.

She shifted, restless. "What will you do about it?" She meant about the rustler.

"Don't rightly know."

She looked at me a long time, quiet. I tried to figure out what she was thinking, but I couldn't read her eyes. Then on a sudden she smiled. "You make me happy, Court. Did you know that?"

"Glad to hear it," I said, pleased and surprised. I wanted to ask her about her mood last night, but I was cautious about bringing it up.

"Six long years," she said. "And I don't regret a day." She nodded, as if to affirm it to herself.

I was silent, unsure what she was getting at. We had a deep and abiding love, but we seldom talked about it. Thinking about that, I realized that we'd gotten comfortable over the past few years. Maybe too comfortable. Maybe I'd gotten to the point where I sometimes took her love for granted. I wondered suddenly if I'd forgotten our anniversary or a birthday, but immediately I realized that wasn't it at all. What in thunder was on this woman's mind?

She seemed to sense my discomfort and decided to explain. "I just get tired of being alone," she said. "I'm sorry I snapped at you last night. I know you have more than you can manage without me fretting like that. But—I don't know, Court, I think I'd like to have my mother come from Denver until after the baby's born."

"Fine by me," I said, relieved that it was going to be so easy to make her happy. It would take a load of worry off my shoulders to have someone with her all the time. Virginia Ledbetter lived in one of the houses we'd built to accommodate our hired hands, along with her cowhand husband and young'uns. She'd been helping Caroline some, but she had her hands full at home.

And Mother Johnson hadn't visited us for a spell. She still thought we were forlorn and forsaken way out here in northwestern Colorado with not even a railroad running through. But she was always more than welcome anytime she cared to visit—or stay, for that matter.

Caroline was from back in Denver, which had blossomed into a full-on city in the past thirty-some years. I'd met her eight years ago, when Pa and I were there for a stockmen's meeting. I could still recall her sitting in the pew of the church we attended that Sunday, her chestnut hair in a fancy getup and her frock looking like pale strawberry ice cream.

It turned out to be easy to meet her. I asked right away and learned that our families had mutual friends. I knew right off that she was going to be my wife. I told her that very week too, awkwardly, at a picnic with the other young blades vying for her attention and cutting in so that she laughed and sailed away with her friends before I'd hardly spoken my piece. But I found excuses to go to Denver over the next two years, and she'd finally agreed to be mine.

As a young man, her father had made and lost a few fortunes throughout the West. But like a good many of us, he'd met a woman who could settle him down, and he'd stayed in Denver, married her, opened a haberdashery. Then he'd surprised himself more than anybody else when some of his investments in Leadville's silver mines paid off during the seventies' boom. He had died soon after he'd made his fortune, leaving his wife and two children—Caroline and her brother, Marshall—well cared for. Marshall had gone to a fancy school back East and was practicing law in St. Louis. Mother Johnson was content to spend most of her time now traveling, socializing, or visiting her children.

When I'd brought Caroline to northwestern Colorado for the first time, it had been late spring. The sky lay like gray flannel, spitting late flurries of snow and cold rain all the time she was here. I'd thought she'd hate the land, but she'd loved it right off.

She and her family came back that summer so they could meet my pa—Ma had been dead and gone for two years by then. I don't think I've ever been so proud and happy in my life as when I drove them down through the Yampa River Valley, the cottonwoods bursting with fresh-made leaves, the river long and lazy, and the greening meadows spattered with wildflowers that seemed to have bloomed just for them. "Penny for your thoughts," Caroline said.

I smiled. "I was thinking about the day I first brought you here. I'll arrange a train ticket for your mom. Banty or one of the boys can go pick her up as soon as we're done with roundup."

"How many more days?"

"One or two. Depends on when they manage to get the last of those strays."

"Thank you, Court. It will make a different woman of me, you'll see."

Later, after I'd bathed and shaved, we lay in bed, I on my back, Caroline spooned up next to me, my arm stretched behind her neck. Our old grandfather clock ticked in the darkness, and I was grateful for a chance to stretch out my bones in a nice soft bed and feel her warmth beside me. There was just a hint of moonlight coming through the window. The hills beyond rose huge to the sky, melting into the mountains that suddenly seemed a thousand miles away.

I thought Caroline had gone to sleep. She was quiet and not stirring. But when I started to move my arm, she came up on her left elbow and looked down at me, her face milky in the moonlight, her long hair dangling down, her eyes huge and deep as a mountain lake.

"Court, why didn't you pull the trigger on the rustler? You could have stopped him right there."

21

"Don't rightly know, Caroline. Reckon maybe it seemed that a man's life was worth more than a side of beef."

"But Brownie? Was some rustler worth more than dear Brownie?"

"Not to me. But maybe in God's sight."

She was quiet for a minute, looking out the window and into the night. Then she said, "If you'd known what the rustler was going to do, would you have shot him?"

"Can't say."

She shifted again. "It's hard, isn't it, to understand why some things have to happen? Innocent people hurt, innocent animals—"

"Reckon some things just aren't going to get dealt with in this lifetime," I said.

"Yes, but all the same—"

"Maybe the good Lord is going to wait till later on to sort some of it out."

Caroline lay back down. She was quiet again. But I knew she was still wide awake.

I felt bone-weary now, aching in every part of my body. I started to drift off in spite of myself, and I felt her lips gently brush my cheek. "I'm glad you weren't hurt, Courtney. I don't know what I'd do if I ever lost you."

"Not likely to," I murmured, halfway asleep. "I'm too dagnabbed careful to get nailed by any rustler."

But my last thought before drifting off was of me hidden in those trees up on the mountain, waiting for that cow-thieving varmint to lay buckshot into me and send me to kingdom come. And I knew that sometimes, no matter how careful you try to be, bad things just have a way of happening.

3

Spring roundup was finally done. Mother Elizabeth Johnson had arrived, rested up, and more or less settled in.

It was midmorning, two days after I picked her up in Rawlins, when a rider like a bat out of hades's front furnace came tearing down the hill to the back of the ranch house, his horse's hooves churning up mud and chewing up sagebrush. I knew trouble when I saw it. I left off mending the horse pasture fence and headed for the house at a dead run.

A four-inch snowfall from the day before had already melted off, leaving a crystal-clear day filled with golden sunlight.

Caroline and our two-year-old were on the back porch enjoying the warmth of Indian summer. She was wearing a warm calico frock, blue and gray, specially made to accommodate her swollen belly. Her shoulders were covered by a warm blue woolen shawl. Her peaches-and-cream face had more color in the cheeks than usual these days. Her long, sleek chestnut hair was drawn back in the newfangled knot she called a chignon, held in place by a blue net. She was sitting in a rocking chair, knitting a pink, blue, and yellow crib blanket for the expected baby. Little Johnny was playing beside her on the scarred-up rocking horse I'd had as a child.

As she spotted the frenzied rider approaching, Caroline stood up and shielded her eyes against the bright sunlight. I could see now that the rider was small as a banty rooster. Caroline and I watched from our different angles as he wheeled his sweaty, excited mount through the front gate and slid to a stop in front of the porch.

I was just a few steps behind him as he leaped from his swaybacked roan. It was only then that I realized I was looking at a gangly young boy of perhaps ten or eleven years of age.

The nag was bareback, and the young boy's dirty, calloused feet were likewise bare. His ragged denim trousers and scrap of a shirt scarcely covered his skinny body, and his trouser legs were cut off mid-calf. The boy was unkempt and haggard. His thin face had a grimy look to it. His shaggy, sand-colored hair might have been trimmed with a fence-cutter, and he wore no hat.

He hit the top of the steps at a dead run, then screeched to a stop. "Mrs. McCannon, ma'am, you . . . you gotta help me, please, oh, please—" Uncontrollable sobs exploded out of him, wracking his frail frame and drowning the rest of his words. He hadn't seen me behind him.

I moved in, knelt beside him, gripped him gently by his shoulders, and turned him toward me. "Now, son, take it easy. Slow down. We'll help you if we can, but you'll first have to tell us what's wrong."

He gulped back a sob, then shuddered with the effort of swallowing another one. Finally he managed to stutter out the problem. "It's my . . . my ma, sir. She needs help pretty bad. She'll . . . she'll likely die—" Another sob caught in his throat and closed it off to further speech.

"Ain't you one of the Hearne boys, moved in up at the old Duke place?" I asked him.

I'd seen the family once, down at the Tucker store in Windsor when they first came through town. I'd heard then that they were moving onto the old Duke place, which made us their closest neighbors. The four of them had been on their way out as I came in, and I'd tried to stop and say howdy. Mr. Hearne, a stubby man with a mean face, had cut me short as he sized me up, then he'd herded his drawn-faced wife and two boys past me. The older son appeared to be in his late teen years, though he wasn't a good deal larger than this scrap of a boy who stood before me.

"Yessir, Mr. McCannon. Name's Bobby. Please hurry. My pa is . . ." He suddenly ducked his head in shame.

"Is your pa with your ma?" Caroline asked sharply.

"Yes'm, but he's powerful drunk. And my ma is hurt bad."

Caroline and I exchanged an alarmed look.

I turned to the boy. "Come on into the house and have a dipper of cold water. We'll need to get the buckboard hitched up."

Caroline's rosy-cheeked face had turned stiff with anger. Her green eyes were snapping fire. But when the boy looked up at her, she swiftly hid her outrage and gave him her sweetest smile. "I expect you haven't eaten for a while, Bobby. Let me fix you a bite while Court gets the team ready. You'll need strength to help your ma once we get back to her."

"Yes'm," he said meekly.

I'd have sworn I heard his stomach rumble.

She took the boy into the house, Johnny tagging along with his hand in hers, a bewildered look on his cherubic face. I took the Hearne boy's nag and led it down to the barn, where I tied it up so it could reach a feeder of oats and hay and a trough of clear clean water.

Then I went into the barn and asked Banty to get the buckboard ready. It was the only transport outside of a horse that would handle the rutted roads back up to the old homestead, and if Mrs. Hearne was hurt as bad as the boy said, we'd likely need to bring her back with us and send for Doc Clayton.

While Banty readied the buckboard, I loaded my Remington 742 .30/06 and filled my cartridge belt. It was a new weapon, and I hadn't used it much, but after my experience in the high country three days ago I was of a mind to carry some heavy firepower. I put the rifle in the buckboard, strapped on my Colt handgun, then threw a couple of pitchforks of timothy hay in the back of the buckboard to make a comfortable pallet in case Mrs. Hearne had to be hauled back to the ranch.

I went into the house and pulled a half-dozen warm blankets out of the linen closet and loaded them into the buckboard as well, along with tarps, slickers, and some bandages and such. Then I went into the kitchen to find Caroline, Mother Johnson, Little Johnny, and the Hearne boy sitting around the oak table.

The boy's thin face and sandy hair had been washed, and he was wearing one of my gray flannel shirts, which nigh unto swallowed him, even with the sleeves rolled up to the armpits. He was gnawing on a fist-thick beef sandwich as if he hadn't seen food in a year.

"Buckboard's ready," I said. "Bring your grub—you can chaw on it while we travel."

Bobby nodded, blinked, and instantly stood up.

Mother Elizabeth Johnson was a ball of energy. She'd already packed a basket full of vittles for us to take along. Now she packed Bobby's sandwich in a piece of butcher's paper and handed it back to him, then grabbed up the wicker basket and followed the boy and me out to the buckboard, Caroline right behind us.

I lifted Bobby onto the spring-supported driver's seat, so that he could ride comfortably.

Banty had tied the boy's nag to the back of the buckboard. Far as I was concerned, the boy and I were ready to pull out when Caroline surprised me by picking up Johnny and giving him a kiss, then handing the child to her mother.

"Where you reckon you're heading?" I said as she stepped on the undercarriage and made to hoist herself into the back of the buckboard. For the first time I realized why she had donned her gray wool cape and was carrying her work bonnet.

"I'm going," she said, looking at me in surprise.

"I reckon you ain't," I said. "That's a bumpy ride for a woman who's heavy with child."

Caroline's green eyes smoldered. "Courtney McCannon, don't you start trying to tell me what I can and cannot do. Help me up this instant."

"It's plumb foolish," I said, standing my ground. "I ain't going to be much use to Mrs. Hearne if I'm busy helping you foal."

26

"Foal?" A spark of anger helped her hoist her own way up and over the side of the buckboard, then she sat down with a flounce atop the hay and stacked-up blankets. "Let's go, Courtney. That poor woman is waiting on us."

I wanted to argue some more, but these arguments had a way of turning on me like an addlepated steer. This one was likely to boil down to my climbing out of the buckboard and physically setting Caroline down on the ground, then leaving with the sting of her outrage on my back like a snow squall, only to return to a full-on blizzard that might easily last the full winter.

I calculated the dangers in the journey, calculated my wife's spunk, then admitted defeat. I hunched forward and shook the lines. The fast trotters headed out the gate and up the bumpy wagon road that led to the Hearnes' miserable old homestead shack.

The afternoon sun was warm on our backs as our rig bounced up the dim trail. We were all silent for a time, thinking our respective thoughts, the boy sitting rigidly beside me after finishing his sandwich, Caroline still in the back, hopefully comfortable atop the blankets and hay.

We'd reached the top of the hill and were trespassing a flat space when I glanced again at the boy, whose head had been turned away from me for most of the silent journey. He was staring dead ahead now, and tears were streaming down his face.

I said, "Whoa, now, young man. We're going to see to it that your ma's OK. Just settle down there." I was hoping a little palaver might loosen him up a bit, but my words just drew a sob from him. I spoke over my shoulder to Caroline. "What exactly happened to her anyway?"

Caroline explained that Bobby had told her and Mother Johnson that his ma wasn't exactly sick but had been hurt bad in an accident. She spoke to Bobby then. "What exactly did happen to her?"

Bobby's shoulders hunched up, and he shivered. "Don't know."

"Where is she hurt?"

He was still shivering. "Just . . . all over. She's just bleed-ing, that's all."

"Her head? Her nose? Other places?"

"Just . . . just all over. Her head and everything."

Caroline kept her voice light as she said, "Well, we'll be there to help her soon enough. Why don't you come on back here and finish up another sandwich? Mother Johnson packed one special for you inside this wicker basket."

He gulped down the sob and looked up at me as if for permission. The pain in his eyes nigh unto broke my heart. I nodded, then he turned and climbed into the back of the buckboard.

I kept my eyes dead ahead on the terrain.

I was thinking some about the owlhoot I'd run into the last time I'd ridden up this general way. After that rustler shot my horse and took off running, I'd walked all the way back to cow camp—which had taken the better part of the morning—and I'd been glad to find it still there. Banty had run into a snag with the chuck wagon's brakes and was still working on replacing the wheel.

I'd borrowed Banty's horse, ridden down to the pole cor-ral, then saddled a fresh mount and brought Hank Ledbetter and Stoke Mathers back up to the high meadow where I'd had my run-in. We buried old Brownie there beneath the quakies, then freed up the heifer I'd left hog-tied to the log.

We'd cut more sign and tracked it to a small meadow to the south, where the rustler had built a rough log pen around some thirty-three of my best beeves. He'd put some effort into his thieving ways. We could tell that he'd been at it for a while. We had recovered all but four of my cattle and herded them down to the valley, but old Brownie was gone forever.

Now we came to a turn in the rutted road, and all of a sudden I was looking off toward the eastern terrain, toward the high timber and the outcroppings above it where Brownie lay buried. I felt the tears well up as I thought about my lost horse. The feeling was clipped short though by that black rage boiling up again like bile in my throat. I swallowed and set my jaw. Sooner or later I'd get to the bottom of what had happened up there.

Caroline spoke to the boy, bringing me back to the present. "You folks have been having a hard time of it, I know. We'd like to help. Maybe some clothing for the winter and a side of beef, a few other supplies now and again, if you think that might be all right."

"My pa don't want nobody coming around, and he don't cotton to charity," the boy said. It sounded like he was talking around a jawful of roast beef, and his voice had firmed up some.

"I see. Well, perhaps we can talk it over when we get there. There's not a person in the county who didn't have a hard time getting started. Maybe your father will understand and let us help."

"How many more in your family?" I asked. I was wondering if there were more than the four I'd seen down in Windsor that day.

"I have an older brother—Jimmy—who just turned eighteen, and Henry, who's fourteen, but he's got the consumption, and he stayed in Kansas City with my grandma. Me and Jimmy and Ma and Pa makes up the family now, Mr. McCannon, sir."

"Two boys ought to be enough to keep things livened up at your house," I said friendly-like.

"Yes, sir, Mr. McCannon, but Pa don't allow any monkey business or carryin' on. He makes us toe the mark most times."

"I hear Ora Haley is hiring over at the Two-Bar, though that's a good mite distant from here," I said. "Right at fifty or so miles as the crow flies. Or I might be able to find some work for your older brother if he'd care to come around—though I couldn't pay as much as Haley does, seeing how he runs some forty thousand head to my six thousand."

I could use an extra hand to make ready for winter, though after the snowfall I'd have to make work for him.

We'd finished branding yesterday and had all the cattle settled on the lower range. But I could understand a man who didn't want charity, and there was no harm in helping them keep their pride and eat at the same time. Even though I was having financial trouble myself, I could manage that little bit.

"Jimmy's done found him work," the boy said. "He already bought Ma some supplies and promised me new shoes." There was a hint of pride in his voice for the first time.

"He riding for one of the ranchers or working in town?" I was trying to make polite conversation.

The boy's voice turned sullen. "I don't rightly know, Mr. McCannon, sir. He ain't never said."

I thought that was odd but held my peace, and as if my mood was catching we all fell silent for a spell.

My team of fast trotters had already covered most of the miles to Slide Mountain, the rocky slopes where Grisham had proved up his homestead. Soon we were cresting the rise above it, the high mountains and foothills making a crescent behind us and to our sides, the lower sagelands sloping off and opening up to the west.

I pulled the team to a stop. We were looking down on dilapidated, weathered gray buildings set amid rocky fields and the beginning of a long slope of hardscrabble terrain.

"Darlin', I want you to sit tight here in the rig. Keep your hand on that Remington. Me and Bobby will ride his horse on down to the house and see what's happening. Then when I'm sure things are safe, I'll signal for you to come on ahead."

Caroline frowned. "Why wouldn't they be safe?"

I turned to Bobby. "Your pa have a temper when he's drinking?"

He ducked his head as if he'd been slapped. "Yessir, Mr. McCannon."

I turned back to Caroline. "Considering your delicate condition, I'd just as soon see what's up."

Caroline bit her lip, but I knew she and I had been thinking along the same lines about the drunken Mr. Hearne, and I reckon she felt she owed me one, because she nodded her consent. She grabbed my .30/06 and climbed onto the driver's seat as Bobby and I climbed off.

When we had untied Bobby's swaybacked horse from the buckboard, we stood for a few moments and surveyed the house, the ramshackle barn, and the threadbare yard. All seemed quiet enough, except for a couple of half-starved chickens pecking in the dust and a couple of hounds sleeping alongside the house. There was a small cottonwood corral, and I saw a brown flash of movement there, but the pen was mostly hidden by the barn. The storm of two days ago had hit here as well as the valley, but it had mostly melted off. There were occasional dirty snowbanks in the shadows and overhangs.

I turned and looked along the barren ridge some two hundred feet to where a single gray slab of shale was set beneath a solitary leaf-shorn birch tree that had been bent half over by the mountain winds. I knew what the letters chiseled into the gray slab would say, for I had watched my pa carve them in:

Grisham Andrew Duke, Born 1800, Died 1879
May God Gladly Receive His Cantankerous Soul

Pa had put that memorial there to mark Old Man Duke's grave. As if sensing my interest, the wind whined through and stirred the barren limbs. I took a minute to remember the man who'd built this lonesome place.

Grisham Duke had been a mountain man who'd traveled West while still a lad. He'd trapped beaver down in the Brown's Hole region with the likes of Jim Bridger and Jim Baker, and they'd sold the pelts to the trading post called Fort Davy Crockett, back in the 1820s. My grandfather, Corrin Brevard McCannon, trapped with Duke for a year or two before returning to the more civilized climes of the Carolinas, where my pa had been born and from whence he had also come West after the war. But my grandfather was opposed to slavery, even though a good many of his family owned slaves. When

31

the war broke out, he defied the lot of them by joining the Union army. When the war was over, he came back West.

When the trapping business went sour and Fort Davy Crockett collapsed for want of interest, Grisham Duke worked as a scout during some of the Indian rackets. Pa built our rock and log ranch house in '67, and by then Old Man Duke was a true old-timer in a land where most men were happy to see their fiftieth birthday.

He finally learned to admit defeat to the high country snowstorms. He'd bring himself, his two horses, one gnarly rooster, and a half-dozen laying hens down to the valley to stay with us for weeks on end during the harshest months. My mother had been alive then. Pa and Old Man Duke had hit it right off, the more so because Duke had trapped with Grandpa Corrin in the olden days.

After supper we'd settle in front of the big stone fireplace, the fire burning off the bitter cold and the howling winds, while Grisham Duke spun us stories about how he'd helped build some of the earliest sutler stores in the region, and how he'd fought the Utes, and how he'd driven some of the ox teams that had dragged out the few pitted roads around the county.

The Homestead Act of '62 found him with a small grubstake and a will to finally settle down, and he'd picked this place before me to do it in, though heaven alone knew why. Pa had said it was the pure mean aggravation of him, refusing to give up to old age.

Duke spent his final Thanksgiving and Christmas holidays with us in 1879, the winter following the Indian rackets and so-called massacre down Meeker way. He'd come back to this homestead the day after Christmas to check on his buildings and shovel snow off his roofs so they wouldn't cave in. He hadn't come back to the ranch, and Pa rode up three days later to find Grisham Duke dead in his sleep. We'd had to wait till spring to bury him, and till then he'd lain in bed in the house before me, frozen stiff.

The rodents and magpies had taken over the Duke homestead for the seven years since the old man's death. Then last spring the Hearnes rode in on a small wagon to take possession of the place. Nobody seemed to know much about the Hearnes, other than that they'd bought a few cheap housekeeping items at the Tucker store in Windsor when moving in.

I rode up to see them shortly thereafter, in spite of Mr. Hearne's unfriendly attitude in the store that day. I'd been moving cattle in the region, and I wanted to invite them to our newly built church. But the woman had met me at the door with a frown on her face and hadn't even offered me a dipperful of water. When I'd invited her to join us at Sunday service, then to come by the ranch for dinner afterwards, she like to bit my head off. I reckoned I wasn't welcome, and I hadn't been back till now.

Bobby Hearne and I mounted his horse, but the poor thing could hardly move, it was so weak and misbegotten and spent from its journey. I climbed back off and walked alongside as we moved down the slanted road. Though we were still a spell distant, the dogs spotted us, and they broke into a ruckus. I looked up at Bobby to see that he was crying again. His jaw stuck out stubborn-like, but his eyes were sadder than a heifer's.

The harsh mountain winters and the blazing summer sun had turned Duke's snug little house into a shack. Now it was about the most miserable dwelling that I had ever seen inhabited by humans, and the closer you got the worse it looked.

It was small—only three rooms inside—and the batten boards on the outside walls were twisted and warped, leaving cracks wide enough for the rattlesnakes and prairie dogs to hold a hoedown in. Wooden shingles were missing in sections all over the roof, probably blown away years ago. A stovepipe protruded through the roof above the kitchen. The winds had been at that too, for it was tilted at a dangerous angle, supported only by some rusting wire. Most of the sash windows had the glass broken out and replaced by cardboard. The door at the front hung at a crazy angle as if one hinge was missing or broken, though another strand of heavy wire bore it up enough to close off the opening.

An old barn sat back from the house about a hundred yards, and it was also about to fall in. Old Man Duke's abandoned blacksmith shop sat at one end of the clearing, the roof gone, and the slanted door to a root cellar showed near a clump of service bushes in the back. On the far side of the barn was an outhouse with the familiar path worn down through the weeds.

Scrub oak, sagebrush, and service brush had declared war on the west side of the buildings, which were located on a slight incline facing south. Duke had had the good sense to build them with a southern exposure for winter, which was the only good thing about the place now. At least the house would be warm on those scant few days when the sun broke through to take the chill off the snowed-in countryside.

On the other hand, at least one person who lived here was far from lazy. Work had been done throughout the summer in the form of what had been a large garden and even larger corn patches near the barn, with old rotting pumpkin vines scattered around the field. A few stalks of corn still stood, awaiting the ravages of the winter snows.

Come to think of it, there seemed to be a powerful lot of cornfield there for a family of four. Mrs. Hearne must have done a lot of canning for her family in an attempt to keep the wolf from the door during the long, lean winter months.

"How many dogs you folks have?" I asked Bobby.

I could see two now, both mangy old things that had probably come for a stray bone and stayed.

Bobby had alighted from the horse and left it in the corral behind the barn, where a skinny little bay mare was rooting in a near-empty feed trough. Now we were sauntering around the side of the barn, casual-like, though the closer we got to the house the more he tensed up.

I found that the tension was catching, so I was trying to loosen him up some with small talk.

"Just them hounds," he said, jutting out a thumb. "Ma says we can't even keep them two fed."

At that moment I caught a quick glimpse through the barn door, which was slightly ajar. There was a man inside. He'd apparently seen me too, for he ducked away. It was dark in there, and when I blinked and looked again I couldn't see him.

We walked on past, and I said quietly to Bobby, "Who'd be in the barn this time of day?"

"Don't know," he muttered. "Maybe Jimmy."

I forgot about the barn as the kitchen door opened and Hearne himself staggered out onto the porch.

He was a middle-sized man with a sagging belly held back by a sleeveless undershirt. His arms had apparently been well muscled once, though they had long since gone to fat. He wore filthy twill trousers tied up with a rope, and his hair was so oily and dirty that it looked as if he'd pomaded it with bear grease. A reddish porcupine hank of hair that passed for beard and mustache covered most of his face. Above it, two little hog's eyes outlined in red tried to focus in the sunlight.

He had a double-barreled Winchester shotgun cradled in his arm: a newfangled piece of firepower that had cost a pretty penny. His head swung in a wide circle, and then he finally spotted me, stabilized himself, and brought up the shotgun.

"What you doin' on my property, you polecat?" His voice was thick with whiskey. "Get out of here, afore I take a notion to blow your fancy head off."

He was so drunk that I marveled how he stayed on his feet. He rocked back and forth on his heels, as if to bolster up my speculations, then he managed to focus again, this time on his son. "Bobby? Bobby, that you?"

"Yessir, Pa."

"What you doin' standing beside that pit viper, lad? Get on in the house."

"I brung him, Pa. To help Ma. Please let him go inside."

The old drunk barked out a string of curse words, then moved menacingly toward the boy. "You'd bring a stranger

35

into our family troubles? Ain't one hiding a day enough for ye?"

I stepped in front of Bobby and said in a friendly voice, "No harm intended, Mr. Hearne. I'd just like to help, if I can." I'd casually pulled my Colt out of my side holster. Apparently Hearne didn't even notice the motion, though now I had it held low and aimed, ready for use if I needed it.

Hearne's finger tensed on the shotgun trigger, though the barrel was wavering some. "Get out of here, I say."

I sighed and tightened my own trigger finger. I wasn't one to kill a man, as the events up on the mountain with the rustler had proved, but I seldom drew the line at winging one. There was a fair amount of flesh on Hearne to aim for and any number of ways to stop him cold without killing him, if it came to that.

On the other hand I wasn't even going to wing him unless I was forced to. Shooting a man is always a serious thing, whether he dies from it or not.

I said, "Bobby says his mother is hurt. I'm reckoning that you've been beating on her. Now if that's the truth of the matter and you don't let me get her some help, she might die, Mr. Hearne. And if she dies, I plan to see you hang for murder."

He stared at me with his little gimlet eyes, surprised, then he braced up. "What I've done to my woman is no business of yours. Get off my place, I say. Get, or I'll blast you to kingdom come!"

There would be no reasoning with him. He was crazy with the whiskey and probably irrational even in a sober state, considering his choice of lodgings. That finger of his was itching again—I could see it working the trigger.

He started walking slowly across the porch toward Bobby and me, as if savoring the moment. A wolfish grin appeared on his flaccid face.

I felt my own trigger finger tighten again. I glanced down at Bobby and saw the fear in his eyes as he looked at my Colt, then looked quickly away. I said out of the side of my mouth, "Bobby, I ain't going to kill your pa. I just mean to wing him so he don't kill me. Easy now."

Hearne was still coming across the porch, his shotgun aimed squarely at me.

I narrowed my eyes and took aim at his shooting hand. I was just ready to squeeze off my shot when something cracked like thunder. Suddenly Hearne's right leg vanished up to the kneecap, he fell sideways, then flat to his face, his shotgun exploded its load of buckshot into the porch roof, and splinters flew while the blast echoed off the hills.

I'd hit the dust when I heard the crack, pulling Bobby down beside me, and now I looked up and realized that Hearne had stepped onto a rotted board, then fell clear through the porch floor. He was all the way up to his hip now, pinned tighter than a roped steer. The shotgun landed outside his reach. Which didn't make a hill of beans, come to think of it, because he'd apparently hit his head on the heavy plank bench beside him as he fell. He was out like a coal-oil lantern in a Colorado blizzard.

"Reckon I'm not so useless after all, Courtney McCannon." Caroline's voice rang out, clear and hard.

Astonished, I turned to see her standing at the edge of the barn, the Remington cradled in her arms and all but smoking while she smiled that firm little smile she gets sometimes, the one that tells me I've run afoul of her expectations.

I realized then what had happened. Caroline had come down a ways on the buckboard, quiet-like, then she'd walked in and hid by the barn to watch the whole episode. And lucky for me she had, because her firing off that Remington had most likely kept me from having to drill old Mr. Hearne. On a sudden I wondered if he'd been winged by her.

She all but read my mind. "Don't worry—I just hit the rafters above him, and the noise from the gunshot threw him off balance."

"Reckon his own condition and that run-down porch did the rest," I said.

Bobby and I headed up the steps, then moved gingerly to where Hearne lay sprawled in front of the door.

I didn't want to waste any time on him, but I had to make sure he was out of our hair. I grabbed the shotgun, cracked the breech open, and found a shell in the other barrel. I pocketed it, handed the shotgun to Bobby, then rolled Hearne partway over on his belly and tied his hands behind him with a piece of rope that was hanging on a nail from the porch rafters. That done, I pulled his leg out of the hole and dragged him to one side of the front door, then offered up a silent prayer of thanks that the good Lord had a way of keeping His eye on me, even though His methods of helping out were often a mite odd.

I opened the front door carefully, not sure what to expect, but nothing scampered out at us, nobody fired any more shotguns. Bobby and I entered the house, Caroline right behind us. She pulled the door shut against the growing cold.

The house was dark. Cardboard covered all but two small windows. It was also cold inside, for any fire that had been lit in the small stone fireplace had long since gone out. The place smelled of corn whiskey, bacon grease, lye soap, and souring beans, but there was another smell too—the acrid, rusty odor of dried blood.

The Hearnes had kept most of Old Man Duke's handmade furniture. There was a rickety plank table with three straight-backed chairs lashed together with rawhide, and an ancient rocking chair with the seat stuffing foaming out. All the chairs had been turned over in some kind of ruckus.

The table had apparently once held a dozen or more tins of Van Camps Pork 'n' Beans, a half-dozen paper sacks of Arbuckles coffee, and any number of other store-bought supplies. Now the goods were scattered far and wide across the floor, and a ten-pound sack of flour had been torn wide open, to dust the hearth in winter white. The big old cast-iron pot that had hung in the fireplace had rolled across the floor, and I was careful not to step in the fermenting beans that had been spilled along its trail.

Bobby set the shotgun in a corner, then motioned for us to follow him. I ducked my head to step through a door into a low-ceilinged lean-to with a plank floor, the cracks filled with paper. A torn up Monkey Ward catalog and a pile of *Saturday Evening Posts* lay to one side of the bed, and I figured this was the source of the fancy caulking. At the far side of the room stood Duke's old iron bedstead, rusted now. Atop the springs was a straw pallet, and atop that pallet lay the crumpled-up form of a human being, covered by an old gray-brown army blanket.

"Ma?" Bobby's pain was stark in his voice. He stepped over to her side and peered down at her, though I could see he was scared of what he might find.

I pulled him back, then bent to look at her. Mrs. Hearne was a pitiful sight. The odd angle of her left arm told me it was likely broken. I had to brush back her matted brown hair to fully see her face. She was maybe thirty-five but was old beyond her years, with harsh lines set around her thin lips. Her many small scars and her crooked nose told me this wasn't the first time she'd been hurt. The woman's face was white, and her eyes were shut, as if in sleep. Her forehead was covered with a mat of dried blood. There was a large blue egg swelling up there, and there were angry-looking cuts and welts over her face and arms. She'd likely have some broken ribs and perhaps internal injuries besides. Her eyes were both puffed up and turning black and blue, and the angle of a bloody cut alongside her left eye told me that the "something" she'd been hit by was most likely her husband's fist.

I pulled down the blanket to see the rest of her. She seemed pitifully small—no more than five feet one and under a hundred pounds. Her bleached and blood-smeared flour-sack dress had small scraps of frayed white lace neatly sewn at the collar and sleeves. That made me sad, thinking about her trying to pretty it up like that. It was half torn off her, to show a ragged cotton shift underneath and heavy, brown cotton stockings.

Looking at her made my shoulders slump, and I felt a deep sense of shame that anyone who called himself human could do such a thing.

"Is my ma going to die?" Bobby asked. His voice sounded like a sad wind in timber.

"She's still breathing, though I can't rightly say how bad she's hurt," I replied. The horror of what had been done to her gnawed at my sense of decency and was about to explode into rage.

"She's going to need a doctor," said Caroline.

She'd been at my side as I examined the woman, and I was suddenly proud she was there. Her presence brought me up out of my gloom.

She turned to Bobby. "Boil me some water, young man. I'd like to clean these wounds and see just how bad your ma's hurt."

"Yes'm, Mrs. McCannon." The boy hurried back to the front of the house.

Caroline stood the Remington against the wall and leaned in close to me to say, "I saw a rider thunder out of here and head west just after I fired."

"Rider?" She had my full attention.

"The man was on a sorrel, though I didn't see the horse's forehead to see if it was starred. He came out of the back of the barn. He had on a faded black duster, and there was a sling on his arm. He took off out of here like a blast of buckshot out of that shotgun barrel."

An unpleasant realization was beginning to sink in. I went into the kitchen, where Bobby was trying to start a fire. Caroline followed me. I said, "Your brother own a sorrel with a white star on its forehead?"

Bobby's eyes took on a hunted look, as if he'd been found out at something. He nodded.

I gnawed on my cheek while I cogitated on that. "Reckon that was him in the barn," I said. "He likely had his mount hid there too." I scratched at my chin for a minute. Then I said, "You got any extra sides of beef hanging around the premises?"

Bobby looked down in shame. I figured then that he knew what was going on, though he could hardly be blamed for what his elders did. He said, "There's four sides hanging in the barn. Jimmy and Pa just butchered the last one."

I gave Caroline a disgusted look, which she shot right back at me, seeing how I'd told her everything that rustler had done.

But she waved her hand as if to fan smoke away and said, "We'll worry about that later, Court. Right now this woman needs some help. Come on, Bobby, I've changed my mind. Let's not worry about that fire right now. Let's get her to our house, where we can offer her some real help."

Caroline fetched clean blankets from the buckboard while Bobby and I went to get a battered old door from beside the empty chicken house. We fixed up the makeshift stretcher outside, then carried it back into the cold bedroom.

Bobby stood at the foot of the bed with tears in his eyes as Caroline sat down beside the woman on the pallet and stroked her forehead.

"Mrs. Hearne, can you hear me?" she asked.

I felt a flood of relief as the woman's eyelids fluttered open.

"Bobby?" Her voice was no more than a murmur, but she could at least talk a bit. "Bobby, are you here?"

The boy had leaned closer and into his mother's line of vision as her eyes opened up. Now he looked at Caroline, his own eyes wide with fear and hope all at the same time.

She nodded to indicate it was OK for him to talk to his mother.

"I'm here, Ma. Pa is—he's gone. Me and the McCannons are going to take you for help. Just . . . just . . ." He stumbled on the next word, then looked at Caroline again with a stricken expression in his eyes.

Caroline stroked the woman's forehead again. "I'm Caroline McCannon," she said. "We're going to take you back to our home. It may hurt a bit when we first lift you, but it won't be bad. Do you know how to pray?"

The woman's bleary eyes blinked in surprise, and she managed a slight nod.

"Then just keep your hand in the Lord's as we do this," Caroline said. "We'll be praying too."

It went easier than I'd expected. In short order we had Mrs. Hearne in the back of the buckboard and made comfortable amid the pillows and blankets atop the hay.

Once we got her settled, Caroline made a gesture to me, and I leaned closer. "She wants to say something to you."

I waited while the woman drew in a long, trembling breath, then looked up at me and said in a weak whisper, "Mr. McCannon. Th-thank you for coming." She had a near-worshipful look in her sad blue eyes that told me this was the first act of kindness she'd experienced in a good long while.

The look made me uncomfortable. I said, "You're welcome, ma'am. It ain't no more than I'd do for anyone."

As I climbed onto the buckboard, Bobby looked up at me and said, "What about my pa?"

"Let the coyotes have his blasted hide. Climb aboard here, son."

"Courtney McCannon!" Caroline's voice lashed out from the back.

Sheepishly I climbed back down, returned to the porch, untied the worthless varmint, then doused him with a bucket of cold water from the horse trough. He sat up sputtering, still drunk as a skunk. I felt like giving him a taste of the same medicine he'd fed his wife, but Caroline and the boy were watching, Mrs. Hearne needed tending, and I thought better of it.

We left him sitting there, half blind with liquor, half blind with meanness, not even knowing that we'd ridden off with his injured wife and youngest son.

4

"Plumb shame, that trouble you had t'other day," said Shorty Musket. He had a polecat grin spread out on his weather-creased face and a spark of bedevilment licking in his mud-brown eyes. His gray hair and bushy brows looked as if they'd weathered a tornado. His peg leg was jacked up on something behind the polished mahogany bar as he leaned forward to jaw at me, though up till now the palaver had been about everyone in the county except me.

I had a forkful of prime beef on its way to my mouth, and I didn't want to talk just then, so I nodded politely, then shoveled the steak on into my mouth and started chewing. Mrs. Rhoda Starr had been cooking here ever since the kitchen opened, and she was the best cook in the county, next to Caroline's mother.

Shorty was the proprietor and barkeep at Windsor's only hotel and saloon, the Elkhorn, which he'd built just the year before. He was another old-timer, who'd come to this country as a bullwhacker back in 1855 when the freight still came in by ox or mule train along the Oregon Trail to be dropped at the sutler store near Fort Steele. Shorty had hauled it on down to our parts. The Union Pacific Railroad came through Wyoming Territory in 1869, and after that a good number of men —ranchers among them—found extra income freighting supplies back down to our region, where the settlers had mostly starved for all but the basics till then.

For nigh unto twenty years altogether, Shorty moved freight to the small stores at the wide spots in the road called Lay and Hayden, Hahns Peak, and Steamboat, even to the White River Indian Agency, and subsequently to the town of Meeker, which sprang up in its place after the Utes had supposedly all been herded to the reservation down in Utah.

The Utes' eviction had followed their ambush and so-called massacre of the mean-spirited Indian agent Nathan Meeker along with his family and hired men. That had happened some seven years ago, though a handful of Utes still camped here and there along the Yampa River during the lean months, and some refused to so much as visit the Utah reservation.

Shorty lost his leg to a festering wound caused by a Ute arrow during the ruckus over Nathan Meeker. He hauled freight for a good many years thereafter, but the vinegar had gone out of him, and he'd taken to the hootch to help him get past his aches and pains.

He'd recently tired of the hard work and long hours on the road. The little town of Windsor was just budding out, and he found a spot due west of the confluence of the Yampa River and Fortification Creek where he built this plank and log emporium. He spruced up the rough-hewn barroom with this long mahogany bar and fancy-mirrored backbar he'd had shipped down from Laramie. He rounded up a half-dozen tables and a screen to section them off for hungry women and children and others who didn't care to sit at the bar. He had a fancy new cooking stove in the kitchen and a full dozen rooms —heated with their own potbellied stoves during the winter— for travelers and those of us who needed to stay in town overnight.

Windsor was some seventeen miles west of my ranch, and it was a growing wonder these days, though it had yet to hire any kind of lawman. The Banks family had settled the area some twenty years earlier. Others had slowly followed. I reckon that once a region is settled, others tend to follow, and in the past few years we'd had a flood of nigh unto ten new families settling in town, so that now we had a small post office, the Tucker general store, the new church, a livery stable, a combination bathhouse and barbershop, and a couple of other businesses that came and went, a saddlery among them.

But none of the establishments could compare to Shorty's Elkhorn Hotel and Saloon, an establishment that the city folks in Denver might have been proud to frequent—if they didn't have to listen to Shorty's gossiping tongue all day long.

I was sitting across the fancy mahogany bar from him, digging into a platterful of steak, potatoes, and eggs. It was just past three o'clock, Shorty's noon rush was long over, and I was his only customer, so I was getting the full benefit of his attention.

I'd brought the buggy into town an hour ago and rushed straight to the doc's, wanting him to come tend to Mrs. Hearne. But Doc Clayton had been busy sewing up the little Sweeney boy, who'd nigh unto ripped his leg off when that ornery old squaw horse of his suddenly leaned into a strand of barbed wire wrapped around a gatepost. The doc promised to ride back to the ranch with me when he was finished, but he had no idea how long that would be. I waited around in the anteroom of his little office long enough to feel foolish, then came here to separate my belly from my backbone with a hot meal.

Shorty was standing across the bar, waiting for me to answer his speculations, and now he repeated his comment. "Dagratted shame about your trouble, I say."

"What trouble was that?" I said, after I swallowed my mouthful and set to cutting off another bite of beef. I was plumb hungry. Plus I'd found out long ago that the less I talked and the more I listened, the more likely I was to learn something.

Shorty planted a knowing smirk on his face, as if he had possession of something I needed and wasn't about to let go. He walked down the bar to the coffee urn, pulled back the spigot, poured himself a hot cupful, then moved back up to stand across from me again. He picked up a liquor bottle from the backbar, uncorked it, tossed off a swallow of applejack, then used hot coffee as a chaser.

"That spider juice will rot your liver," I said. I took a drink of my own black coffee. I didn't rightly like a barroom and did my best to stay away from them, but in this country a man was lucky to find a place to get a square meal under any circumstances, and a teetotaler like myself could easily starve if he was to get judgmental.

"I'm talkin' about the trouble up in your high meadows a couple of days ago," Shorty said, leaning in close again, the smell of applejack strong on his breath.

"Came across a rustler," I said, leaning back a bit out of the way of his breath. I took another bite of steak.

Shorty nodded sagely. "Hear tell the dingbanged varmint shot your saddle mare."

It didn't surprise me that he knew so much. The boys had drawn their summer's wages as soon as we had all the stock moved down to winter range and the branding was done. They'd been here in town off and on since then, kicking up their heels, and I'd made no secret of my misadventure, so some of them were bound to talk.

"Shot her, all right," I said. "Best horse I ever owned too."

"I'd wager you'd like to get your hands on the worthless varmint what did it."

I took a long sip and finished off my Arbuckle's coffee. Due to the railroad up north and the fancy new packaging, it came in almost fresh these days. I lowered my eyes to look at the grounds in the bottom of my cup. "Had my sights on him. Let him get away."

Shorty's heavy gray eyebrows furrowed up. "Missed your shot?"

"I let him go."

Shorty's eyebrows dived into a scowl. "Mercy me! Consarned White River Ute shot your horse out from under you, and you plumb let him walk away?"

"Reckon I did. Only it was a white man, not an Indian, and he rode away. On a sorrel."

Shorty was struck speechless. He just stood there looking at me as if I'd sprouted buffalo horns. Then he muttered, "Good thing your pappy ain't alive to see this day." He turned and took another swig from the applejack, smacked his lips, scratched an armpit, then asked, "Who done it?"

46

"I'd rather not say."

"Someone from these parts?"

"Reckon I'd just rather not say. It doesn't rightly matter—it's not likely to happen again."

He spat and hit the brass cuspidor dead center. "Bad enough havin' to worry about them thievin' hungry redskins without havin' our own kind leechin' on us too."

Thinking to change the subject, I said, "Haven't seen many of the Ute up our way this fall. With game being so scarce, I'd have expected more of them."

One of the Utes' complaints was that there was hardly any game to be had near their new reservation at Fort Duchesne. This condition left them totally dependent on military supplies even during the best of times.

Shorty lowered his voice as if he were conspiring. "Yampawah and his dagnabbed thievin' band of renegades are back up here. Couple fellers seen 'em out along the Yampa makin' camp."

"I saw them too," I replied. "Yampawah and two others came by the ranch house a few days back. They had the courtesy to ask my permission to hunt on my northern rangeland."

"You give it to 'em?" His bleary eyes held scorn.

"Don't know why not. They've been hunting that land for as long as I can remember. Fact is, it used to be their land not so many years ago, and they're plumb welcome to share it."

I didn't bother to explain that it was common knowledge that Chief Yampawah and my pa had been friends, or as close to friends as an Indian and a white man could get. I tended to still honor Pa's friendships.

Shorty looked as me with disgust and spat again.

He hated the Utes. He'd been driving a freight wagon, delivering the goods that the U.S. government had promised to the starving Utes and which had been months overdue by then. The freight had been held up because some fools at the

47

Indian Agency in Washington, D.C., refused to release payment for shipping it. That added to a passel of other problems, then all of them together erupted into what folks still called the Meeker Massacre.

When the trouble started at the White River Agency, Major Thomas Thornburg left Fort Fred Steele, Wyoming, with three companies of cavalry and one company of infantry and headed south to help. They crossed the Yampa at Peck's Ford, not far from my bottomland. Then in spite of several friendly Utes' warnings, they traveled on over toward Milk Creek, where the renegade Utes had ambushed the troops the next day, killing Thornburg and eleven others and wounding nigh unto forty more.

Shorty'd had the bad fortune to walk straight into a side ruckus while on his way south to the Agency. No one had bothered to ride after him and tell him the freight was coming too late and the Utes were already on the warpath. Now there was nothing left of that leg but a stump and a sawed-off hunk of wood shaped something like a leg to hold it up.

Shorty was bunged up for sure. He stayed full of hootch, and everyone put up with his feistiness because of his hard luck and peg leg. At that moment I decided maybe that wasn't the right way to go about things. Reckon he was more than a mite foolish to blame a whole tribe of people for what a handful of renegades had done—and with more than a mite of provocation at that. I all but told him as much, but before I opened my mouth to utter the words, it struck me that I might as well turn around and whistle in the wind instead, for all the good it would do me.

Shorty stomped down the bar and into the kitchen, and I plowed into the rest of my vittles and thought some about Chief Yampawah and his band.

The Utes were mountain Indians. They still called themselves the Top of the Mountain People. Time was when they'd had full rein over most all of the Rockies, except toward the Eastern Plains, where the Arapahos and Cheyennes, their mortal enemies, had roamed. The early trappers, including my grandpa, had respected them for their skill in battle. The whole passel of them were bad medicine back then.

For centuries the Utes had fought—and beat—the Kiowas, Cheyennes, and Sioux. But then had come the end of the Civil War and a vast migration westward, and the Ute Indians had been confronted with a new kind of people, a new way of life, and a new brand of meanness they couldn't begin to understand.

The upshot of it was that Shorty and a bunch of others like him hated the Utes with a black hatred like nothing I'd ever seen. And the Utes—well, they'd been slowly moved off their hunting grounds and down into Utah, where their reliance on government provisions was compounded by the fact that those supplies were often late or stolen or otherwise diverted from the Utes' hungry bellies.

There'd been rumors for a long while that the men in Washington who gave out the freight contracts and the men who freighted in the goods were in cahoots, all of them so busy lining their own pockets that they wouldn't have helped a starving Indian if they'd tripped over one.

Shorty came back from the kitchen, carrying a plateful of steak and beans for himself. I was glad to see it; he was a mite under the weather for so early in the day. He sat down across from me, placed his plate a short distance from my own, then looked up and said, "You're a dagblamed fool."

I nodded, acknowledging the compliment, then I swamped up the last of my eggs with a slab of sourdough bread.

Shorty said, "I ain't going to be a whit surprised if you end up missin' more than a few beeves, you start lettin' the whole kit 'n' caboodle of the Ute Nation hunt on your lands."

I heard the door open behind me.

Shorty looked up, narrowed his eyes, and said, "Look. Looky here. Here comes a man right now who can talk some sense into your dagburned thick head."

I turned to see two men coming through the door. I recognized the lean, wiry man dressed in solid black wearing a silver-tooled belt to hold up his britches and a silver-tooled

Mexican hatband on his black Stetson. It was Moses Skettering of the M-Slash-S.

The brick-solid gent with him was a stranger, at least to me. But the boys had carried rumors thick and fast while they were kicking up their heels, and I'd heard that Skettering had hired himself a stock detective.

In spite of the fact that Skettering had been in these parts for some five years now and ran a ranch no more than twenty miles due northwest of my own, I didn't know the man well. He was somewhere in the neighborhood of forty, which put him about a decade ahead of me. Not that it meant a hill of beans. The man wasn't one to warm up to folks of any age. He kept to himself, I was told, and rumor had it that the wife who'd come West with him had long since gone back East. There was something dark about him, and it didn't all have to do with his coloring.

His black hair was cut short and shot through with gray, and his complexion was pasty beneath a slight summer's tan. His eyes were a darker gray, flinty, hard, and dead. He was short, almost as short as Shorty Musket, and bandy-legged from so many years in the saddle. Every time I saw him, he was sporting black whiskers on his chin, though the stubble never seemed to grow out into a full beard. His shoulders hunched some. He had the face of a ferret and the bitter appearance of a man who'd seen hard times and who hadn't weathered them well. Lines of malice had cut deep into his face.

Skettering was a Texan. I could tell by his way of speech, though he'd never shared his origins with anybody I knew. Rumor had it that he'd been in the Civil War like my pa, though he must have joined up when he was still a youngster, if that was the case. A good number of folks had come West after the war to start over again—or to forget, which made that the most likely of the various yarns I'd heard about this man.

Banty Brewster had got drunk with some of Skettering's cowhands. They told him that the blood and death of the war had gotten hold of Skettering's mind, made him dark and mean. But those boys had just quit Skettering's spread and were on their way down to the Two-Bar to work, so they might have been a mite prejudiced against their old boss.

As for me, I didn't know the man well enough to have an opinion one way or another about any of that.

The two men sauntered over to the table farthest from the bar, and I turned my attention to the man accompanying Skettering. He was a large, well-proportioned fellow, who seemed to move easily on his feet in spite of his size. He wore more black than Skettering himself, for there was no silver to spark up his outfit, and even the handle of the shooter he wore in the holster at his left side was black as an undertaker's bib, so that he appeared to suck up the light. His black leather jacket was fancy, with hand-stitching in the lapel. He had the sort of face the women call handsome, with a square-chiseled jawline and chestnut hair, trimmed neat into sideburns, his black hat tilted atop his head. He wore a trim gambler's mustache beneath a nose that looked like it had never seen the bad side of a fist. He glanced up on a sudden, perhaps sensing my gaze; his eyes were a clear hazel color and hard as a hangman's heart.

I nodded politely and went back to tending my own business. Old Shorty hoisted himself to his feet and hobbled over to their table, greeting Skettering friendly-like. The two men ordered steaks with sowbelly and beans and a bottle to keep them company while they waited. Shorty set the bottle and two glasses on the table, then headed for the kitchen to pass the food order along to Mrs. Starr.

Skettering turned to me, tilting his hat politely, and said, "Afternoon, McCannon." There was a whispery quality to his voice that put me in mind of a snake's hissing.

"Afternoon, Skettering." I nodded back.

The man with him was still taking my measure, but as Skettering spoke my name, he looked plumb pleased. He said, "You Courtney McCannon?"

"Yessir, reckon I am."

51

A friendly smile cracked his face, though it didn't warm the chill in his eyes. He said, "I'm Ben Blue. I had the pleasure of makin' the acquaintance of your charmin' wife a few days back when I stopped by your ranch to water my horse." His voice held the remnants of a deep Southern drawl.

As I stood and strode over, Blue took off his hat and laid it on the edge of the table, and I could see that he was somewhat older than he'd first seemed. His chestnut hair was flecked through with gray. He looked to be somewhere in his early fifties. That surprised me some. Reckon I'd expected a younger fellow, full of vinegar.

I said, "Caroline mentioned we'd had a stranger ride through. Pleased to make your acquaintance." I reached out to shake his hand.

With his left hand he brushed my handshake aside, saying, "Pardon my manners, but I've been told it isn't seemly for a man to shake hands with his left paw, and I'm afraid my right one doesn't work too well."

I let my hand drop to my side and glanced down to where his right hand lay hidden beneath the table. I hadn't noticed anything amiss when he'd come in, but then I'd been looking at the whole picture. I said, "Had some trouble?"

"No, no, it's an old wound, though not too pretty, I'm afraid." He gave me a cougar's grin that showed a bank of pearly white teeth.

To ease off the discomfort, I gestured toward the whiskey bottle and said, "I see you're both taking the chill off your bones. Got your branding done, Skettering?"

Skettering just studied me, but Blue smiled widely and said, "Set down for a spell, and I'll buy you a drink to repay you for your wife's hospitality."

I pulled my watch out of my pocket. It had been just under an hour since I'd left Doc Clayton's. "I got to hit the trail," I said, "but I appreciate the offer. Another time."

Blue nodded curtly, then tilted his whiskey glass and took a long swallow.

Shorty had come out of the kitchen and was back behind the bar, in a simmer as he listened to our every word. As I turned back toward the bar and fished in my pocket for a half eagle to pay him, he just sort of boiled over.

With hands waving wildly, he snorted, "Tell 'im, Skettering. Tell this lame-brained golliwog what them Injuns are up to. I swear and declare, this fool is letting them hunt on his rangeland, and all the while they're robbing the rest of us blind."

Skettering turned to me, his face pinching up some. He said, "That true what he says about Injuns huntin' your land?"

I nodded. "Chief Yampawah has hunted my land since my pa first settled it. His band used to have their hunting grounds there. No harm in it. The more venison they can butcher, the less need they'll have for cattle."

Skettering's face pinched up some more and took on a dark, choleric look. "Reckon you heard I been missin' beeves?"

"Yessir, I had heard you'd hired a stock detective. Though I've missed the particulars. I've been busy with the roundup and haven't been in town for a spell."

Skettering steeled up. In that whispery voice of his he said, "My boys been findin' Injun sign on my land, close to where my cattle have been taken."

"Can't say as I doubt your word," I said, "but I'd stake my life on the fact that the Indians leaving sign aren't with Yampawah. He has a hot temper when he's crossed, but he made a bargain a long time back with the ranchers in these parts, and he keeps his word."

Skettering drew in a long hiss of breath, and his eyes hooded over. He was too quiet, too steady, as he picked up his whiskey glass and drained it. Then he looked back at me, his eyes slits. He said, "I heard you lost some cattle too—and a saddle mare as well."

"Yessir, that's the truth. But the rustler wasn't an Indian, no matter what rumors been circulating. He was a white man, pure and simple."

Skettering looked surprised. "How do you know?"

"I saw him."

"Saw him? But—" He looked swiftly at Blue.

Blue's gaze shifted away from him.

Shorty broke in, "Don't sound right to me, not a blamed word of it. Saw the man, he says. Coulda shot 'im, he says—" He sputtered to a stop and started furiously polishing a glass he held in his hand.

Blue said easy-like, "Here now, gents, if McCannon says the rustler was a white man, he most likely was. Why would a man lie to protect someone who was rustling his cattle?" He smiled in my direction, but just as the smile took full shape I saw something dark slither through his eyes.

Shorty had refilled my coffee cup. I took a final sip, then set the cup on the bar. I was beginning to get a little riled with the company, not to mention with Shorty himself. He had all but called me a liar, and he'd come right out and branded me a fool. And now Skettering was insinuating some things that brought my dander up.

I picked my hat up off the bar and said, "I wish you luck with your problems, Skettering. I got to be heading home."

Skettering snarled, "Where's Yampawah now?"

"Reckon I wouldn't know." I put my hat on, then pulled on my fleece-lined coat and buttoned it partway up. As I adjusted my hat, I caught a glimpse of myself in the mirror behind the bar and was surprised enough by my appearance to look again. Reckon I didn't look at myself much at home, and I felt a sudden tuck of admiration for the figure I cut.

Not that I had that much to do with it. Caroline bought my clothes these days, so if I was looking a bit more prosperous than I truly was, she was the one to thank. My jaw was clean-shaven and the new Stetson that Caroline's mother had brought along from Denver was a rich, deep brown and creased just right. My elkskin coat had been hand-tailored by Mrs. Howard Murphy up in Hayden. I looked down at the Sunday boots I'd changed into before coming to town. They were also new, made from the hand-tooled leather just coming into fashion in Denver and ordered straight from Monkey Ward.

But just as I admired them, sudden trepidation hit. It didn't do to look too prosperous these days, with the other ranchers pulling in their belts just to stay alive. A prosperous man was a man who courted envy. Thinking about the problems that could bring, I vowed to put those boots back in the box and not take 'em out till spring.

Shorty groused, "Consarned shame ol' Major McCannon ain't still kickin'—"

"Well, Shorty," I replied, "reckon you're not the only one wishes my pa was still alive."

Skettering cut in, jabbing his stubby forefinger at me. "If you see Yampawah or any other Injuns, tell them if they so much as put a moccasin or hoofprint on my land, I'll shoot him and every other Injun in his band and cause such a she-bang that it'll wake up folks all the way to Washington."

I held my peace and said politely, "Yessir. If I see him, I sure will deliver that message."

Shorty still hadn't blown out all his wind. He was starting to have another conniption fit about the Indians, but I cut him short by turning and walking out the door—out into the crisp, clean afternoon air, and it was never more welcome.

5

I drove my buggy over to the Tucker store, loaded up some supplies Zebulon Tucker had gathered for me, then headed back to old Doc Clayton's house.

He'd sewn the Sweeney boy up right fine. The youngster and his mother were just leaving, the boy wincing and walking on crutches but on his feet again in spite of it. The doc got his medical kit together, kissed his slip of a wife good-bye, then accompanied me south towards the Yampa River road.

The doc was a short, rotund, cheery man who had just turned sixty, with a flat friendly face and a balding head covered with an ancient beaverskin hat. He was an old family friend, as comfortable with me as if he was kin. And he was tired after his bout with the Sweeney boy's leg, so he sat quietly alongside me, resting and enjoying the colors and the brisk autumn air.

The season had flamed the trees in russet and red and crested them in gold. Cattle grazed in the wide valley where Elkhead Creek ran southwest into the Yampa. The cattle had all been distant when I'd ridden into town, but now a few of them were close enough to the road for me to see their brands, and it surprised me to see the M-Slash-S.

Moses Skettering had apparently moved his herds a good deal lower than usual in anticipation of some harsh winter storms. They were on the westernmost side of Elkhead Creek, where its small clear stream dumped into the wider Yampa River. His Herefords were right across the river from where my own range began.

At first it riled me some to see him moving in so close, but after a bit of reflection I couldn't rightly say I blamed him for wanting to make use of the land. It was free range, open to anyone who got there first, and it was good grazing, considering what the drought had done to most of the rest of the rangeland that year.

The grass in this part of the Yampa River Valley was still somewhat green, curing on the stem. In hard times like these I saved my own part of this meadowland until late in winter. Boone Draw lay due north. It was a gap through which the winds blew, and that helped clear the ground of snow so that the stock could paw down to the feed underneath, even when the drifts in other places got too deep.

Seeing that open rangeland already in use set me to thinking about my finances again. From the looks of things, I was bound to need my own meadowland later in the winter. This season was going to make or break me, and losing or keeping the extra five hundred head of cattle that this meadowland might feed could make the difference in my keeping or losing the Lazy Double C ranch.

Last year grass-fat steers had been selling at $1.50 per hundred pounds on the hoof, and everybody had been worried sick at that. This year the price had fallen to $1.00 per hundred pounds on the Chicago market and as low as $2.00 a full head for some. The bottom had dropped clean out of the cattle business, that was for sure, and northwestern Colorado wasn't immune to the problem, not by a good, long shot.

The city stockyards weren't paying enough to bother shipping what cattle we had left, so the only thing we could do was try to nurse them through the rough spots and hope for better times. There were still strikes in all the big slaughter-houses—in Denver, Chicago, Kansas City—and more than one of them had gone belly up. And even if a rancher could find a buyer for his cattle, the railroads had jacked their rates up so high that a man couldn't afford to ship his stock by rail.

We'd had some bad luck the past two years, and that was a fact. But even at that we'd had it better than the ranchers up in Wyoming Territory—or out west in the rolling, sagebrushy hills of Utah and Nevada. All summer long we'd heard stories of cattle dying off from lack of feed and water, of ranchers going bust. The die-off from last year's blizzards had left cattlemen from Montana to Texas with stock losses of as much as 70 percent. Come last spring, the plains had been thick with carcasses of frozen cattle. And then had come the bleak, broiling droughts of summer.

We could blame the Chinooks for that. They'd arrived early—way too early. The hot winds had blown through the snow-laden mountains, had melted the drifts on the peaks, and set the waters to cascading in torrents onto the high mountain meadows and into the swift streams.

Last winter's blizzards had packed the snowdrifts deep in the high country. But not deep enough. Because the Chinooks had thawed the snows almost overnight, the lowlands had flooded. All the moisture except some from the highest snow-caps drained off the land rather than sinking in, and little more had come to the valleys and lowlands as the spring snowstorms hit and the regular thaws began. Compared to normal, the Elkhead had been just a small trickle running into the Yampa River.

Up in the mountains the grass had been deep and sweet and green, while down here in the valleys it had lain brown and parched everywhere except right here in the river bottom. Even the river itself was only half as deep as usual for this time of year.

The freight and stage road meandered close along the river, sometimes right beside its bank and sometimes as much as a half mile away, depending on the terrain. I stayed to it as I headed up to my ranch, bouncing along on the chuckholes, rocks, and ruts that had accumulated during the summer.

Old Doc Clayton was nodding off, managing to sleep a bit except when a bump awakened him. I kept mulling over my problems, gnawing away at Shorty's attempts to stir up trouble, and cogitating on the situation with Skettering and Blue.

Yet in spite of that undercurrent, my mind came back to the present often enough for me to enjoy the crispness of the changing season and the solitude of the ride. And in those moments I figured that if the good Lord could manage to lay out a spread like the glory in the valley around me, He might rightly manage to see me through whatever troubles the coming winter might bring.

It was coming on evening, and we were still some three miles east of the Elkhead Creek crossing, no more than five miles from my ranch buildings, when the crack of a gunshot set the horses to skittering, old Doc Clayton reared up out of his sleep, and I fought to get the team back under control. I just about had them settled too when another *Crack!* rang through the stillness and voices set to shouting.

I managed to rein in the horses, then stopped the buggy on the spot to listen.

Thwack! Another gunshot sounded, and right on its tail came a faint whooping and hollering from back in a thick stand of cottonwood trees.

Crack! Thwack! The shots came fast amid more whoops, then a woman screamed, long, in anger, and I'd have sworn I heard laughter.

Old Doc was blinking hard and trying to straighten his coat that had twisted up around him. "What in thunder is going on?"

"Sounds to me like some folks back in them trees are having a mighty good time at the expense of others," I said.

He was grumbly, for he'd awakened hard. He looked around, still discombobulated by what was happening, and I said to him, "Reckon you'd best stay here till I see what's up."

He had his own sidearm in a holster, so I kept my Colt .45 in place. Then I tied the buggy to a tree next to the road, grabbed my .30/06 Remington for good measure, and sprinted across the narrow meadow that separated the road from the thick stands of cottonwood and willow lining the riverbank.

When I got to the trees I slid in behind one, crept past it, then moved from tree to tree till I could see a good ways around me and all the way to the wide green water flowing between two leafy banks.

I spied an Indian camp set back near the deep green shallows—three elkhide tents pitched out in an open grassy spot between the huge, old knurled cottonwoods. Two rawboned Indian ponies were picketed off to my left. One snorted and threw up his head at my presence, eyed me with scorn, dismissed me as inconsequential, then went back to nudging at the dried grass.

"Wa-a-hoo!"

A man's shout was close enough to make me jump. I ducked behind a tree and just in time too, for at that moment a young squaw came darting through the trees, her black braids flying and her hide skirts a-flapping. Behind her, running for all he was worth, came a tall, skinny, bandy-legged cowhand, no more than twenty-one, with a scrap of blond beard trying to cover his chin and a hank of dirty yellow hair. The wide Texas hat atop his head was askew, and his face was liquor-flushed.

Neither of them saw me.

He lunged at the squaw and caught her, swooping her up under one arm as though she were a sack of potatoes.

She screamed and clawed at him, yelling Ute curse words and raking her fingernails down one side of his face to draw thin stripes of blood.

He yelped.

I was just stepping out from behind the tree, ready to join the ruckus, when he punched her as hard as he could, which wasn't all that hard, what with him being so close.

She whipped around like a fish on a hook and laid her teeth into his rib cage.

He howled and dropped her, grabbing at his ribs.

She darted a hand inside her bodice, came out with something that flashed silver, and brought it down on the cowhand's arm.

Blood spurted, and he yelled again as he grabbed his arm.

She scampered off into the trees, and I ducked back into hiding, leaving him sitting there cogitating on his cut-up arm and his newly learned lesson.

I heard other noises then. There was some whining and what sounded like babies crying and a man's loud, snarling voice over it all. I crept through the trees till I came to another small clearing just past the tepees.

Fresh deer hides and two fresh sides of venison were strung in the low tree branches, and there were pounding rocks on the ground, covered with what appeared to be berry juice and strips of raw meat. I reckoned the squaws had been turning the deer meat to jerky and getting ready to tan and cure the hides into fine buckskin.

Two older squaws were working over a campfire, tending to what appeared to be the start of a meal. A couple of papooses clung to their legs, and one held an even smaller infant hitched up on her hip, just as Caroline carried Little Johnny.

I recognized the thick-chested man who stood spread-eagle before them, rifle in hand, its butt resting on his hip and he swaying back and forth now and again, yapping and jawing and generally showing the effects of a bellyful of rotgut. It was Luke Coogan, foreman of the M-Slash-S.

He glared at the squaws and growled, "Which of you old hides is goin' to cook Luke Coogan somethin' to eat? Come on, now. Just drop them young'uns and get on over here with that food. I've a hankerin' to scalp them kids if ye don't get to hoppin'."

The squaws looked at him without understanding and continued their work, though I could see now that they were very much aware of him, their posture all tensed up, both watching him secretly from the corners of their eyes. I reckoned they were hoping that if they ignored him he'd turn tail and go away. But I knew they weren't going to have any such luck.

Coogan growled again, "C'mon, you old reprobates, get on over here." He grinned evilly, showing a gap where one front tooth should have been.

There was a rustling in the tree above me. I jerked my head upward and brought up my rifle, only to see a young

Indian lad, maybe six or seven, hiding up there in the branches and staring down at me. As our eyes met, his face froze in fear. I lowered my rifle and tried to smile at him, but under the circumstances I couldn't put much warmth in it. I was too steamed up at Coogan and that other rattler.

The boy's eyes got wider, and he slid down the back side of the tree like a squirrel, breaking a branch as he went. He scampered away into the undergrowth.

The snapping branch caused Coogan's head to spin around toward me.

I stepped into the clearing just as Coogan's blurred vision focused on me. I leveled my Remington at him and said, "Howdy, Coogan. You're makin' quite a ruckus. If I was you, I'd just drop that rifle. I reckon you need to do some thinking about how to treat womenfolk—Indian or not—a good deal more than you need some grub."

His expression of surprise turned to one of rage. "McCannon! This ain't none of your business, you—"

I interrupted his tirade. "Drop that rifle to the ground if you want to stay healthy."

He dropped it, grudgingly. Then he turned toward me and glared.

He was a runt in a way, no more than five and a half feet tall, but he looked as hard as an iron safe. His brown flannel shirt covered a barrel chest and arms the size of my own thighs. He'd lost his hat, and his brown hair was cropped short. His face, knotted up like a fist now, was set atop a neck thick as a full-grown log. He seemed a bit older than my own thirty-two years, and I'd heard he could lick a mountain lion with one hand tied behind his back, then swallow it whole. He had a reputation in town as a man who liked to start a ruckus.

As he peered at me from under his thick, grizzled brows, an ugly smile crept across his stumpy face, and I realized that those two squaws had plumb been forgotten. Luke Coogan had decided to fry other fish, and I was the trout he meant to fry.

A sudden shouting and scuffle erupted off to our left, diverting his stare. We both looked toward the noise, but I kept my firearm and one eye on Coogan even as he kept an eye on me.

The blond cowhand charged into the clearing, dragging another squaw, partly by her arm and partly by her hair. She wasn't much more than a child. I'd seen her before, and back then she'd seemed to be a happy little critter. Now she was silent and sullen. She had a defeated look on her face and a large welt across her cheek.

The cowhand stopped in his tracks when he saw me. He made as if to turn around and run back where he'd come from, then he thought better of it and dropped the squaw.

She bounded to her feet like a cat and moved to stand with the other squaws. One of the papooses set to wailing, and she went over close and began to stroke its hair, though all the time she stared at the cowhand, a look of black hatred on her face.

Coogan's eyes had lit up with evil delight. Some folks are like that. They feed on others' trouble, and I could see it in him. He was thinking about jumping me whether I held a Remington or not, just for the sport of it. I knew in that moment that he was the sort of man who'd attack a railroad loco-motive if he had a mind to and worry about the consequences later.

But much as he appeared to love trouble, I hated it. I had no intention of so much as scraping a knuckle on his worthless carcass.

I cocked my rifle and said to the both of them, "Boys, this happens to be my ranchland you're standing on. Aside from being a couple of squaw baiters, you're a couple of brainless polecats who don't have the sense to pour water out of your boots. Reckon if you didn't know it before, you'd bet-ter know it now. These squaws belong to Chief Yampawah and his band. That one you just left a welt on is his youngest daughter. Reckon if you've ever heard the name before, you know that Yampawah ain't likely to stop short of scalping you just on account of the damage you've already done to these squaws."

The skinny blond cowhand said, "I ain't skeered of no Injun." His voice was thick with liquor, and there was a sneer as deep as a dry gulch on his sallow face. But I noticed that his hand had crept up to hold onto his rib cage, and there was a mat of blood on his shirt there. That first squaw must have torn out a hunk of meat when she bit him.

I shook my head in frustration. "I'm asking you to move on from here before you end up losing your scalps or your livers over this matter."

"Heh," said Coogan. "You threatenin' to scalp us for havin' a little fun with some Ute squaws?"

"Boys," I said, "I reckon you've been drinking up your summer's wages, letting off some steam. But you're a couple of hotheaded fools. Yampawah and his braves will do the scalping. They'll hunt down the both of you, track you as easy as following a three-legged coyote, scalp you as quick as stealing eggs from a bird's nest, and I mean to say you're no match for them."

"Ain't no Injun can take me," said the blond varmint. His hand moved to hover just above his holstered six-shooter.

That bothered me some. Though I wasn't eager to let these men get away with what they'd been doing, on the other hand I wasn't anxious to drill them and go through the consequences. But I wasn't about to let them shoot me either.

The yellow-haired cowhand said, "Ain't no Injun lover goin' to tell me what to do—" His hand jerked downward for the six-shooter.

I brought up my Remington. But just as I started to squeeze off a shot, a rifle shot cracked behind us, we both ducked and spun, and a third party fired yet another shot, setting the splinters flying from the trees overhead.

We both stopped short, unsure who to fire on or what to do. And while I was discombobulated like that, the yellow-haired varmint suddenly braced and dived into me, throwing me back on my rump and knocking my Remington plumb out of my hands.

He rocked back on his heels, as surprised as I was that his tactic had worked. Then he grinned and aimed that six-shooter straight at me again.

I was just sitting there on the dead leaves, wondering what in blazes I was going to do, when Chief Yampawah stepped out of the trees and into the clearing with his Sharps buffalo gun aimed at the yellow-haired polecat who was fixing to shoot me.

The cowhand went white and lowered his gun.

I climbed to my feet and dusted off the seat of my pants. There weren't words big enough to thank Yampawah, so I just nodded howdy and let the silent message pass between us. Then I said, "Reckon you've been back in them trees long enough to pretty much see what's been going on."

"I have, Tall Gun." He'd called my pa that before me, and now the name was mine. It was his interpretation of the name McCannon, and though I didn't like it much I'd come to accept it as far better than what most Indians called white men.

"You have helped the Mountain People," Yampawah said and bowed his head solemnly. "The Mountain People will give you many thanks."

"Reckon the thanks are all mine," I said. "Reckon you plumb saved my hide."

6

Yampawah was a stubborn old Ute, and it showed in his chiseled face. His eyes were cold as brown river rocks. His jaw jutted out, firm as the cowcatcher on a locomotive. Two deep lines cut down from the sides of his mouth, and a deep frown had laid a permanent furrow between his eyes. His hair hung matted and long, the steel-gray frosting of age showing here and there against the raven black.

He was wearing a frayed white cotton shirt, bought in a store somewhere or stolen by someone. The Utes didn't have a white man's sense of thieving or personal possessions, and if something wasn't being used they were likely to find a use for it—or leastwise they had until the settlers caused them a ruckus or two over what was called their "thieving ways." Over Yampawah's shirt was a jacket made from buckskin, tanned till it was soft as moss. His trousers were army issue, probably also stolen. A knife gleamed in a sheath at his waist.

Flanking him on either side were two bronzed warriors as straight as hickory arrows. One of them was a young buck of about nineteen, with head held high and a flash of insult in his eyes. I'd heard him called Chased-by-Bears. The other was a brave about Yampawah's own age. I'd seen him with Yampawah almost every time I'd seen the chief. The white folks called the man Charley Crazy-Horse, for some reason I'd never understood. He was more or less Yampawah's sidekick, and he seemed sane enough to me, though a mite quiet most of the time.

The skinny cowhand was too drunk to have any sense left at all. As Yampawah stood, silent, taking in the scene, the cowhand suddenly brought up his gun and drew a bead on the stone-faced old chief.

Yampawah moved so fast I didn't even see it. Without

seeming to take aim, he drew off a shot and sent a bullet big enough to stop a buffalo smack into the man's upper arm.

The cowhand screamed, his elbow whipping outward from the impact. His six-shooter went flying, and his hand fell limply to his side, blood gushing down it like whiskey from a broken keg. His face had gone bone white, and he was gasping to draw air. He stared down at his mangled arm as though it belonged to someone else.

Coogan had been standing back as if waiting for an opening to make his own move. Now he started spitting out a steady stream of curses at the Utes, but he made no other move.

Yampawah said something to one of the older squaws.

She vanished back into the trees toward the tepees, then reappeared an instant later with a strip of rawhide and some rags. She set to work binding up the cowhand's hand and arm, one of the braves moving in close in case the man decided to attack her.

"Uh . . . ahem . . . excuse me, Courtney?" The voice was so timid I pretty near didn't hear it. But I did, and I turned. Doc Clayton stepped into the clearing. He'd drawn his sidearm, but he seemed uncertain as to what to do with it. His eyes narrowed with worry as he sized up the situation.

I shook my head. I'd plumb forgotten about him.

Yampawah drew himself up tight and looked the doc up and down.

Quickly I said, "Chief, this here is Doc Clayton, from Windsor. He's a powerful good medicine man."

"We've met," the doc said to me dryly. "They checked me out when they first rode in. Snuck up on the buggy and asked me what I was doing here. I told 'em about the ruckus back here in the trees."

"Sorry about leaving you to stew in the buggy," I said to him. "Didn't rightly get a chance to pry myself away from these drunken reprobates till just now."

"I've been watching from behind the trees for a spell," Doc said. "Figured I might be able to help." He stepped forward and knelt beside the squaw who was tending to the tow-headed cowhand.

The rest of us watched as they used the rawhide and rags to rig up a combination sling and tourniquet, though that squaw glared at the cowhand with a pure hatred that said clear as words that, if it was up to her, he'd be left to bleed to death and maybe have his throat slit besides.

While they were working, the old chief turned and looked full at me, drawing himself up in all his dignity. It reminded me that, no matter how long I'd known him, he was a Mountain Ute through and through and not likely to take much guff off of any white man. He said, "There are stories that we are stealing the ranchers' cattle."

I was surprised. Reckon word got around quick in these parts. I said, "There's trouble brewing, all right. I'm sorry to say that this ruckus here ain't going to help any."

A deep, flinty sadness came into his eyes. "The Big Cold will soon be here. My people were promised blankets and corn, buffalo robes and moccasins. We were promised beef for jerky. We were promised to be left in peace. The promises are broken again. When the Big Snows come, my people will have nothing."

I fell silent at that. There wasn't a blamed thing I could say, and the look in his eyes made me sick at heart.

"The lands towards the setting sun that were once rich in game have become barren. What the white man has not killed, the cold has taken."

"Reckon you're always welcome to hunt on my land," I said. But as soon as the words were out I wished I hadn't said them, for under the circumstances it only served to remind me that all this land had recently belonged to the Utes, that we were the trespassers here in spite of the treaties drummed up by the folks in Washington.

Yampawah nodded sagely. "I thank you, Tall Gun, but it would not be enough. Many Top of the Mountain People will starve this season. Because of this, some of the younger, more foolish braves have made raids to take cattle from ranchers who are close to the reservation. But none besides my clan have traveled this far east. And my people do not take cattle. Those ranchers who say we take their stock are full of the big wind."

"Reckon you don't even have to explain," I said, embarrassed. "Honest folks don't set much store by these tall tales anyway." I was uncomfortable at the turn the conversation had taken.

"There is a sadness in the air," said Yampawah. He seemed to be looking off into the distance. "My people have lost their courage. Their spirits have been broken. My warriors are tired, and my ponies are weak, and the squaws and papooses are hungry." His voice had taken on an almost eerie quality. "But as long as the grass is green and the rivers run, we will still call these mountains our home."

"Reckon this is your home."

Sudden contempt showed in his face, and he shook off his somber mood. He said, "We will not go back past the juniper hills towards the setting of the sun until we can take food to our people. But we will take only the deer and wapiti and the sage grouse and rabbit, and that only if the Great Spirit permits. And today I renew my treaty to you. I will not take your cattle, Tall Gun. And I have not yet taken the cattle of others."

I didn't miss that word *yet*. That was as close to a threat as I'd ever heard from old Yampawah.

I said, "Reckon as far as I'm concerned these mountains here are still your home. You're welcome to every bit of game my rangeland will provide."

He nodded solemnly. "You are a true friend to the Top of the Mountain People, Tall Gun. And we will be friends to you."

The doc and the squaw had more or less patched the drunk skinny cowhand back together by then, and he was hunkered down, his face drawn up in a wince that said the hootch was wearing off. Old Coogan was still standing, bowlegged and glaring at us as we talked. Yampawah's braves were stiff as the trees, their guns aimed at him. They were fairly itching for him to make a fool move.

Now, as Coogan heard me tell Yampawah again that he was welcome to hunt my rangeland, his mouth twisted up, and he spat out at me, "You no-account Injun lover, bringin' these savages here to thieve from us—"

I was suddenly of a mind to settle his hash right then and there, but I held back and said, "Reckon if I was you I'd learn some manners before someone lassos that evil tongue of yours and tears it clean out of your head."

That set Coogan to cursing again, and that in turn caused the braves to tense up and watch him even closer, and I could see they were hoping for him to finally draw down on them so they'd have an excuse to rip out his consarned liver.

I glanced at old Yampawah to see how he was taking it. He was looking down his nose at the varmint as though he'd found himself hip-deep in cow manure.

He turned and gave me a sudden dark look. "Now, you go."

Suddenly I realized what Yampawah had in mind for Skettering's two cowhands. That seemed to put the shoe on the other foot. If trouble had been brewing because of the men's attacking Yampawah's squaws, a full blizzard of it was bound to come along in the wake of the chief's killing two white men, no matter what they'd done to deserve it.

I said, "Sorry, Chief, but I reckon I'll have to take these two varmints along with me."

He looked at them and shook his head slowly, his eyes steady and full of hatred. "We will take them. They have dishonored our people."

On a sudden I was reminded of the Meeker Massacre. The renegade Utes had been provoked and had reacted by killing some fourteen white people and wounding another forty-four, old Shorty Musket among them.

What old Yampawah made me think of now was the aftermath, when rumors spread through the country like wildfire. Folks said the entire Ute Nation had taken up arms against every white settler on the western slope of the Rockies. Indians were said to be setting fires in the mountains, and down in the sage-covered hills the dead grasses along the river bottoms were said to be ablaze.

In truth they had only burned down the Thompson ranch buildings just out of Hayden, for though they might have hankered to burn every ranch and homestead in the country, they didn't. But in spite of that, the rumors carried all the way to Denver, and before anyone could put out that particular brushfire, old Governor Pitkin himself sent out the word that the Indians were off their reservations, out to burn to death every white person in the state, and they were to be treated as wild beasts to be hunted down and destroyed.

The Utes had the good sense to hightail it then. They took along some women and children from the White River Agency, including Meeker's wife and grown daughter, but not long thereafter they turned the captives over to a government commission on Plateau Creek. The Army finally palavered the Utes into delivering up four of their chiefs to be tried for instigating that incident, Yampawah among them.

They'd been tried, all right. And sentenced to do hard labor at Fort Leavenworth, Kansas. Chief Yampawah was the only one of the bunch who was actually put behind Fort Leavenworth's jail bars. They called him the ringleader of some of the orneriness after the "massacre," though he hadn't taken part in the event itself and no one could prove that he'd harmed a hair of anyone's head. But he was a powerful chief. The Army used him as a lesson to others, and he'd suffered for what others had done.

Most folks said Yampawah went plumb mean as a result of his prison time, for an Indian felt a jail cell a mite stronger than did a white man. Many an Indian had hanged himself rather than tolerate prison bars for even a short time. But Chief Yampawah had survived to become a hero to his clan. After a few months the government released him, and he returned to his people.

The whole uproar began to simmer down then, for the Bureau of Indian Affairs had found the excuse it was looking for to move the Utes again from the fertile western slopes of the Colorado Rockies to the juniper, cedar, and sage-clad hills and barren plains down in Utah.

Mean or not, Yampawah became the chief of all the White River Utes when Chief Ouray died not long thereafter. But by then the Utes had already been herded like so many pronghorn antelope out of the lush valleys and verdant mountains of Colorado's western slope and to the reservation at Fort Duchesne.

So things hadn't worked out too well for the Utes the last time they'd taken the bait of a bunch of white troublemakers, and they weren't likely to end up any better this time if old Yampawah had his way.

I set my jaw and said, "These two men are enemies to your people. But they are also my enemies. They're white men, Chief. They have to be punished by white men's laws. Reckon the best thing would be to take them up to the county seat and let Judge Warren decide what to do. I know the judge well, and he's a fair man. I figure he'll give them a fair trial, then convict them and jail their sorry hides."

Yampawah gave me a look of disbelief that would have withered one of the big old cottonwoods. His deep sunken eyes blazed with anger.

I said, "You have my word on it, Chief. They will go to trial. We'll tend to them in a way that won't end up hurting your people."

Old Coogan just stood there, sulking and listening to us jaw about him and the skinny gent. I still half expected them to make a move that would set the Indians loose on them, and the Indian braves were still poised, waiting.

Chief Yampawah heard me out, then looked at me a few times as if he was of a mind to argue. But finally he turned to the braves who still held their guns on the two cowhands and said, "Tall Gun has always spoken the truth to the Top of the Mountain People. And though my anger is great, I will not

72

have it harm my tribe. Charley Crazy-Horse will take the squaws and papooses to our lodge down the river. Chased-by-Bears and I will go with Tall Gun to take our enemies to the white man's council."

He turned and looked at me, and for a second I saw in that look all the cunning and all the pride and all the strength that these people had needed to weather the storms of their recent history in these parts. I saw a slight glinting threat of death there too as he said, "And if the way of Tall Gun does not work . . ."

The threat hung in the air. I chose not to challenge it. The braves were already hog-tying Coogan and his skinny, drunken sidekick. Chief Yampawah was looking away into the distance again, a resigned look on his face.

I felt my shoulders unbunch, and I realized that for the first time since I'd heard the rifle shots my trigger finger had unflexed.

7

It was coming on evening, and a chill was in the air. The lights were on in the ranch house and bunkhouse, and the blackening hills towering behind the buildings were outlined by light from a sun that had barely set, for the sky was still turning from smoky gold to dusky gray.

Caroline was waiting as we rode in, silhouetted by the honey-warm light pouring through our front door. As I climbed down from the buggy, she came down the steps and marched up to where we'd rolled to a stop beside the hitching post, just under a cluster of birch trees.

She gave Doc Clayton a welcome as he climbed down, then she turned to me and frowned. "It's about time you got home, Courtney McCannon. And what's this procession you've brought with you? It looks like P. T. Barnum's circus has come to town."

I looked back over my shoulder and saw things through her eyes. Skettering's two cowhands led the parade, as sorry looking a pair as I'd ever seen. Coogan wore a sulk on his mulish face. The skinny blond-haired gent rode beside him, hands tied to the saddle horn, his face still squirreled up from the pain in his arm. Behind the two cowhands came Chief Yampawah, sitting his horse like an ancient warrior, and beside him rode the brave called Chased-by-Bears, sitting his own horse as though he was of a mind to ride on into a rampage at that very moment.

I started to explain what had happened, but Caroline put a finger to my mouth. "Hush, Courtney, we'll sort it out later."

She turned to the doc. "Right now, you'll need to see our patient. Mrs. Hearne is getting along, but she's still in a good deal of pain. She'll . . ." She continued to explain the woman's condition as she took Doc in hand and led him away.

I got Yampawah and Chased-by-Bears settled, and Banty took over Skettering's cowhands. I put the Utes in the barn, and that only because it was getting fiercely cold at nights. Reckon I would have asked them to come right on into the ranch house and use one of our bedrooms, but they'd never accept such an invitation. To them, even having a barn over their heads was the next thing to having their legs caught in a wolf trap.

Banty locked Skettering's cowhands into a room in the bunkhouse and set several of our men to watch over them. A few of my hands had a burr under their saddles for Skettering's hands already, due to a run-in at the saloon in Windsor, and they were happy to make themselves useful. Once I had the situation arranged, I headed back to the house.

Doc Clayton was just finishing up his ministrations to Mrs. Hearne, who'd been put in an upstairs bedroom. I stayed in the parlor and waited until he and Caroline came down the stairs.

"How's she doing?"

The doc looked as though he wanted to spit horseshoe nails. "She'll live, though she'll be stiff and sore for a good long while. She has a couple of cracked ribs, but the rest of it is mostly on the surface. I believe the good Lord saw her through this one. But she's somewhat scarred up. This isn't the first time her husband has worked her over. In fact, I'd say this has been going on for years."

"Someone needs to take a horsewhip to that man," Caroline said. Her eyes sparkled with fury.

"I'll be happy to oblige," I said, "but first I'd like to get some hot vittles under my belt and a good night's sleep."

"Goodness," Caroline said, putting her hand to her mouth, her eyes suddenly wide with self-reproach. "Mother Johnson took Johnny and went to bed, and I've just gotten so used to her kindness, I didn't think. Let me rustle up something for you two. You must be next to starved."

The doc looked like he'd just heard an angel's voice. "Thank you, Caroline. I haven't been fed since early morning."

While we waited for her to rustle up grub, I took the doc out to the bunkhouse, and we took another look at the prisoners. We mostly wanted to make sure that the skinny cowhand—we learned that he called himself Rollin Bowles—was well enough to sit a horse and had sobered up some before we headed on the long ride up the Yampa and Elk Rivers to the county seat at Hahns Peak. Bowles's arm had stopped bleeding, though he was still in more than a mite of pain. But the doc said he'd be as well off in the saddle as on the ground by morning.

I shaved the cactus off my face and sponge-bathed myself clean while Caroline soaked in the tub in our newfangled bathroom. The hot water came direct from a heater attached to a big boiler we'd ordered last year from Monkey Ward, then installed in the basement with a pump to the well and all sorts of gadgetry.

When she came out, she'd dressed in a fluffy white cotton robe over a long blue flannel nightgown. Her feet were covered with white wool socks.

"Looks like you're planning to get cold tonight," I said, toweling the last of the lather from my cheek.

She stopped short and stared at me, a guarded look in her cool green eyes. "I thought I might sleep in Little Johnny's room."

"What on earth for?" She never slept in there except when the boy was sick, and he'd never been healthier than before his bedtime tonight. He'd been frisky as a colt.

She looked away, but not before I saw tears well into her eyes.

"What's wrong, darlin'?" I was alarmed. I thought maybe it was the baby. I stepped toward her, but she pushed me away.

I was silent, puzzled and a little hurt.

Then apparently she had better thoughts of her actions, for she turned to me and said, "Oh, Court. W-would you ever hit me?" There was a deep bruised look in her eyes.

The question surprised me so much that it took me a while to absorb her words. Then I said, "Why on earth would you ask me a question like that?"

"You get mad at me sometimes."

"What in blazes are you talking about?"

"When I ran the buggy into the ditch last year. You got that look on your face, and your fists clenched up, and you turned and stomped away. I didn't see you till well after supper time."

"And did I come in here knocking you around then? Well, did I?" She was beginning to get my dander up.

"No. But you were still mad."

"Maybe rightly so. But have I ever lifted a finger to you?"

"No. But—"

"But what? Do you think I'm cut from the same cloth as that polecat Hearne?"

"No. Of course not. But—well, have you ever hit a woman?"

My anger started to roil up, but I thought better of it and took a minute to get hold of myself. Then I swallowed hard and gave her a sad, droopy look, trying to cheer her up. "I never was around any women till you came along."

She managed a weak little smile. "Oh, Court, every unmarried female in four states had her cap set for you."

"Well, I'm plumb glad you know that. Now, can we go to bed?"

She climbed into bed.

I put out the light, and then slid in beside her. But when I tried to put my arms around her to calm her fears, she pulled away, stiff-like.

"I'm sorry, Court. I don't mean to take it out on you. But I just keep seeing that poor woman's beaten face and that slack-jawed, drunken fool she's married to—"

I sat straight up in bed and looked down at her. Her face was slightly lighted by a shaft of moonlight that filtered between the curtains.

"I'm not like him," I said, and I was surprised at the controlled anger in my voice. "Not even a little bit like him, not ever." For the first time in our marriage I thought about getting up and going to sleep in one of the spare rooms.

She seemed to know it. She took my hand. All the same, she kept at it. "But you wanted to beat him today?" This time it was more a question than an accusation.

"I did. And I still do. If I ever get my hands on him, I'll horsewhip him within an inch of his life. But I'd never lay my hands on a woman, and especially not the woman I love."

Again she was quiet for a long time, her back turned to me, and me not knowing what else to say to make her understand. But finally, in a meek little voice she said, "I just feel so helpless, carrying all this weight around. It's like being an invalid. I can't run, I can't ride anymore. I wish the baby would come, Court. I wish it was spring, and the cattle prices were back up, and I wish we were all safe and the baby was born and with us."

I reckon that surprised me more than her earlier words. "But you are safe," I said, feeling my anger vanish.

"No. There's something evil coming into this valley. I can feel it."

"Caroline. I'm not going to let anything happen to you or Little Johnny, or to that new life in your belly," I said. "Nothing. Even if it takes my own life to stop it from coming."

She sighed, long and deep, as if I'd just confirmed her worst fears. "But don't you see, Court—that's just it. If we lost you, the evil would still destroy us. How could I bear to live without you?"

I rolled over and captured her in my arms, then smoothed the strands of hair back from her forehead and looked down into her face. "Ah, woman. Why do you let your mind get in such a turmoil? We get up and more or less do our best with every passing day, and the good Lord has to see to the rest. If you can't trust in me, at least give Him a little more credit. He'll see us through."

She nestled into my arms then, and I held her tight, knowing I was holding a treasure I'd never be able to replace.

After a while, I kissed her. When she drew back, I stopped and let her have her space.

That sight up at the Hearne place hadn't been pretty, and I knew she still had the image inside her head. I myself wondered how a man could do such a thing to the woman he professed to love. It hurt me too to think of the bruises, the pain in the woman's eyes, the look of defeat, misery, constant humiliation and degradation, and fear.

We were both silent for a long time, and it wasn't one of the long, comfortable silences that made up such a large, solid part of our marriage. This one was troubled, both of us lost in our own miserable thoughts.

And just as I started to fall asleep, she spoke again. "Court?"

"Yes, darlin'."

"Where does the evil go? I mean, what if you had killed that rustler, or what if I had aimed to kill Hearne? Where would the evil in them go? I thought about plugging Hearne square in the heart. What if I had? Does the evil die with them, or does it just leave that body and go into somebody else?"

The question brought me back awake. I said, "I reckon there's more to both of them than just evil."

"But they do such evil things. And that makes them at least evil in some part. Where would that evil go, if they died? Would we have stopped something or started it?"

"I'm glad we didn't have to find out."

She hesitated, then said, "Is it ever right to kill a person?"

"The Good Book says, 'Thou shalt not kill.'"

"But that commandment means 'Thou shalt not murder.' There's a difference between wanton murder and killing to protect someone, even yourself."

"Yeah." It puzzled me that she was disturbed by such things. They had clawed at me on long, lonely nights for the better part of my life, but I'd never before realized that this part of her ran so deep.

"But you didn't shoot Hearne," I said. "And some of these things can only be answered by God Himself. Go to sleep. We've both got a long day coming up. Just leave those things to the good Lord, and I expect everything will work out fine."

Caroline was finally getting sleepy. She said, "I reckon He shows each of us what we have to do when the time comes, doesn't He?"

"I sure hope so."

"Well—good night, sweetheart. And Courtney?"

I suppressed a groan. "What?"

"I'm sorry about earlier. I know you'd never hurt me."

I brushed a kiss into her hair. "Don't concern yourself about it. I know that everything is hard on you these days. After the baby comes, things will get back to normal."

"I know. And I love you."

She finally fell asleep.

Morning came, after a too-short night. We rose early, and after a spot of breakfast the doc borrowed my rig and headed back toward Windsor while the rest of us varmints mounted up and moved east along the Yampa River road.

I had decided against Banty's riding with us. There was a passel of work to be done on the ranch before winter set in, and I reckoned I could handle the ride by myself. Still, the owlhoots, the chief, Chased-by-Bears, and I made quite a procession. Bowles sat in his saddle just fine, in spite of being tied to it. Coogan was bound up too, and he cursed nigh unto every step of the way.

As for me, well, I felt like a cocklebur that had been caught in a high wind. I was tired and peevish. I was falling behind in my ranch work, what with all my neighbors' escapades. I have to admit that I was somewhat perturbed at having to spend my day riding up to the county seat to hand over the two cowhands to the judge, though that was better than standing by and watching another Indian ruckus erupt. But I never liked to ride to Hahns Peak, even on a good day.

In my mind that cussed town was the most foolish, out-of-the-way place they could have thought up for a county seat. Trouble was, it had been a gold rush town, and it was still the biggest settlement in Routt County, remote though it was. Neither Hayden nor Steamboat Springs—not even Lay or the little knee-jerk hole-in-the-road town closest to us, called Windsor, was big enough to swat a fly with. None of the four settlements had more than a sprinkling of buildings huddled together.

But like it or not, I'd promised Yampawah that Sketter-ing's two cowhands would see justice. That meant handing them over to old Judge Warren, and that meant riding them up to Hahns Peak Village where he lived.

In spite of the two varmints bellyaching all the way, it was a pleasant ride. The Yampa River Valley was filled with wild grasses as high as our horses' bellies, frost-nipped to the color of wild timothy hay now. Some of the chokecherry bushes on the hillsides were still laden with berries, and there were a lot of wild currants and gooseberries on the river bottom. Cottontail rabbits scurried before our saddle horses as we scared them up from their shelters in the dead grass.

We rode east up the valley, between taller and taller hills. The mountains towered ahead, looming over them. There were high, hog-backed ridges thick with pine and aspen to our immediate south. The Flat Top Mountains occasionally loomed into view behind them, their tops covered by the early snow. The forest rolled up to our north and east, all the way to the end of the world.

When we came to the mountain they called Sleeping Giant, we turned north up the Elk River on the stage-freight road and toward Hahns Peak.

The gold-mining boom that had bred the town was over now. But several old mines were still producing, and there was still color in some of the creeks. The freight wagons had been hauling timber out of the nearby mountains too for the past couple of years. The wood was used for railroad ties on temporary spurs on the Union Pacific in Wyoming, or it was freighted to Denver, Leadville, Central City, or Black Hawk to be used as timbers in the mines or lumber for the new buildings that were still sprouting up in some areas like mushrooms.

The village sat near the southern flank of Hahns Peak itself, dead in the middle of a mountain meadow that in summer was sprinkled with white and yellow buttercups, Indian paintbrush, and huge blue and white columbine as fragile as summer snowflakes.

The air up here was crisper than it had been in the valley—a chilling warning of the changing seasons. The quakies, birch, and cottonwoods that spread over the lower part of the peak had dropped most of their leaves, and those that were left were the color of flames. First snows had already come and gone up here, harsher storms than those in the valley. The next snowfall would stay deep on the land until spring.

The town itself was a ragtag huddle of log, clapboard, and ramshackle buildings, most of them rough-hewn log cabins. There were several whitewashed clapboard frame houses; one of them belonged to the judge and Mrs. Warren.

Most of the houses at the edge of town were set up amid log corrals, outbuildings, and even a few small barns. This was a fast-built Western mining town, and the builders hadn't been particularly careful with their use of squares and levels, if they'd used any at all. The place looked almost as miserable as it had a couple of years before when it was called Bug Town, then Poverty Bar, by some of the disappointed gold-seekers who'd come and gone.

We stirred up quite a ruckus, the five of us: Chief Yampawah, Chased-by-Bears, Skettering's two cowhands trussed up like Thanksgiving turkeys, and myself. By the time we'd gotten within sight of town, we had a tail of half a dozen boys following along, some giggling, some sullen and looking up at us with suspicion in their wide eyes. Their assortment of dogs followed along too, yapping and barking and setting up a general commotion.

Folks appeared in the doorways of their houses, staring at us. A couple of them I knew and nodded to, and they politely nodded back, though I could tell they weren't all that eager to admit to knowing me when I was in such strange company. The few folks who were out and about on the main street stopped and stared.

We rode past the blacksmith shop, past the livery, past the hotel, the gambling hall, and the saloon. Our objective was the courthouse, a squat, three-gabled log building at the south end of Main Street. The jailhouse sat next door to it. It was a small log cabin, and Judge Warren's white frame house was right across the street behind a neat picket fence.

We reined up in front of the courthouse. The rest of the men stayed mounted while I walked across the street to get the judge.

At my knock, Mrs. Warren opened the door. She was a gray-haired, rosy-cheeked little woman who looked like a picture of Mrs. Santy Claus I'd seen once in the *Saturday Evening Post*. I took off my hat and nodded politely. "Afternoon, Mrs. Warren. The judge here?"

She had a cold. She dabbed at her nose with a handkerchief as she answered. "Why, Courtney McCannon! Whatever are you doing up here? Did you bring Caroline and that boy of yours with you?"

I said, "I'm sorry, ma'am, but I'm afraid we got a passel of trouble brewin'."

She peered around me to the street and saw the entourage of cowhands and Indians. She gasped. "Oh, my goodness! Isn't . . . isn't that Chief Yampawah?"

"Yes, ma'am, it surely is."

"Oh! Oh, my goodness! And the judge is gone—he's been in Denver for the better part of two weeks, helping to preside over the Packer murder trial, and then they asked him to stay on the bench for still another trial. Courtney, I—I am sorry. I don't expect he'll be back for some time. Are you . . . are you in danger? What have those foolish Indians done this time?"

83

"Nothing, ma'am. Mostly the trouble is what's been done to them. Those two cowhands were roustin' out their squaws, and it's got Chief Yampawah more than a mite mad."

"Oh, dear."

"Would you be kind enough to tell me who's in charge while the judge is gone?"

She nodded, saying, "I surely will. The man's name is Wally Schell. You don't know him yet, Courtney. He's an up-and-coming young lawyer from Leadville, a friend of one of the more prominent senators—you've heard of Otis Brown?"

"Yes, ma'am, I have."

She pursed her lips, looking pleased, and said, "Judge Warren is thinking of running for the state legislature. Senator Brown has offered to help him with his campaign. The senator was kind enough to suggest Wally Schell as a fill-in while the judge is gone. It seems to be working well. Wally's a fine young man and—"

"Where did you say I'd find him?"

"Oh, yes. He's over at the courthouse right this very minute." Her eyes kept darting to Yampawah and the others, then filling with a lick of delighted fear.

I said, "And is Sheriff Finsand around?"

"Yes, indeed, I do believe he's over there too."

"Thank you kindly," I said and started to turn away.

Remembering her manners, she said, "Now, Courtney, next time you get up this way, just you bring that wife and son of yours along and plan on spending some time visiting. We've got plenty of room for all of you anytime you decide to spend a few days. Land sakes, we never see you anymore."

I replied, "Thank you, ma'am. Maybe come spring we can take you up on your kind offer. By the way, could you tell me where the judge is staying in Denver?"

"He's at the Palace Hotel. Likely to be there another week or two."

"Thank you kindly." I nodded politely and backed out the door.

8

Yampawah and his brave sat their horses beside the cowhands, the whole passel of them getting restless by now and shooting each other the evil eye.

I walked over and told Yampawah to hold on, that I was going to get the lawmen. Then I walked through the front door of the courthouse and turned left into the judge's office.

The man sitting behind the judge's desk was middle-sized and smooth looking in an Eastern sort of way. He wore a black broadcloth suit with a little black string tie, and he was clean shaven except for a dark brown gambler's mustache. His hooded hazel eyes looked sleepy at first, but when I looked again I could see that they had more the look of a cat pretending to ignore a bird. His hair was dark brown, and his hairline receded some, maybe trying to make a match with his chin line, for the chin seemed to flatten off and taper to his neck rather than to square off as most chins do.

He sat facing the door, and he looked up, surprised, as I walked in. Sheriff Finsand's curly gray hair and thick shoulders were displayed in the chair opposite him. His back was to me. He had a gun and holster slung over the back of his chair.

The sheriff turned as I entered. Both men were holding hands of cards. There was a healthy pile of poker chips in front of each of them on the judge's desk, and stacks of law books, papers, and several yellow telegraph flimsies had been pushed to one side.

Sheriff Finsand laid his hand facedown when he saw me. He stood, looking me up and down, and stretched out his hand for a shake. He was a big fellow, wearing a plaid wool shirt and Levi's. His hard blue eyes peered out of a weather-chiseled face adorned with a short, well-trimmed gray beard. I'd always thought those blue eyes looked a little troubled behind that granite mask.

As he shook my hand, he said, "Howdy, McCannon. Ain't seen you around here for a good long spell."

"Howdy, Sheriff. Sorry to bother you folks, but we've had a mite of trouble down my way. Figured it ought to be cleared up as soon as possible."

The sheriff said, "Judge Warren isn't—" but Schell stood up and said, "I'm acting judge."

"I'm Courtney McCannon," I said. I held out my hand, and he gave it a halfhearted shake. His hand was soft as putty.

He said, "What seems to be the trouble?" The fellow was anxious to be doing some judging, all right.

I told them what had happened.

They raised their eyebrows some—both of them—when I told them old Yampawah was sitting on a horse right outside at that very minute, along with the two cowhands that had harassed his squaws. Schell stepped over and pulled the curtain aside, looking out. He frowned deeply, then turned back to me. "Did either of those two cowhands actually—ahem— have carnal knowledge of any of the squaws?"

"Most likely not," I said. "Reckon I interrupted 'em before they did any real damage."

"Were any of the Injuns harmed? Beaten? Shot?"

"Nossir. The only one shot was the lanky, yellow-haired cowhand riding the paint. Calls himself Rollin Bowles."

"And Yampawah shot him, you say?"

"Yessir," I replied, "that he did. And he could have killed him just as easy as winged him and still been within the law. The man had gone for his own gun and was drawing down on the chief."

Schell gave me a cool look. "I was under the impression that the Utes were confined to their reservation down at Fort Duchesne."

"Well, sir, that's not strictly true. They're supposed to stay on the reservation, but I reckon they more or less wander about as they please so long as they don't start too much of a ruckus—"

Schell cut me off. "We've heard up here that the Utes have been stealing some of the ranchers' cattle lately, mostly down around Windsor and Lay."

That surprised me. I'd only heard those rumors myself the day before. I blinked hard, then said, "I doubt if that's true. But if they're butchering cattle it's because they need the food. They've been having some mighty hard times since the weather went sour. Had some trouble with the supplies that were supposed to be handed out by the Indian Agency too. Reckon if they're starving due to the government's bone-headed ways, you couldn't blame them for picking off a stray here or there—"

"Starving?" The man snarled out the word like the idea made him mad.

"Yessir," I said, "reckon you aren't from these parts, or you'd know what's up." I waited for him to tell me where he hailed from, but he just sat there silent-like, so I went ahead and explained.

"Their government supplies aren't enough for them to live on, and they've been supplementing them with wild game. Trouble is, game's scarce now too because of the hard winter we had last year and the summer's drought. What complicates things is that most of the ranchers are afraid of the Utes after what happened to old Nathan Meeker. Most folks won't let them hunt on their rangeland.

"When Yampawah was a young chief, he and his people lived across the Flattops from where my pa started his ranch. My pa—Major McCannon—fought the Sioux and the Cheyenne when he was a young man, and I reckon you know the Utes and the Sioux and Cheyenne was always natural enemies. Yampawah and my pa got to respecting and liking one another. Reckon that's partly why Yampawah takes the trouble to ride all the way up to my rangeland to do his hunting—that and the fact that he gets plumb downright homesick for the land he grew up in."

"You actually invited Yampawah and his . . . um . . .

braves to come here and hunt?" He sounded horrified at the thought of it.

"Can't say I actually 'invited' them. They've more or less been hunting that region since long before I was born. Reckon they've got a standing invitation from the good Lord Himself is the way I see it. So long as they don't bother my stock—and they never have yet—they're welcome to all the wild game they can take."

"I see," said Schell snidely. The look on his face told me that he didn't see at all.

The sheriff piped up. "And Yampawah shot a white man?"

I nodded. "But I'll tell you again, I can't say as the white man didn't deserve it, seeing as how he was planning to plug Yampawah first."

Schell was looking self-righteous now. Something dark had gathered around his eyes that I didn't like. He turned to the sheriff and barked, "Charlie, I want you to go out there right now and arrest that savage."

The sheriff all but turned green. "Me?" he muttered. He looked around as if he was hoping there was someone else he could pass the order on to.

"You're the sheriff, aren't you?" pronounced Schell.

"But Wally, them Injuns are armed! That Yampawah is a killer!"

Funny, I'd always known that Finsand wasn't much of a man. But then he didn't need to be to keep the peace at Hahns Peak these days. The wide-open, whoop-and-holler days were over, and the folks were for the most part a bunch of hard-working, law-abiding family types. There was still a fight now and again in the logging camps or between the remaining miners, but they could and did handle their own affairs for the most part, and the sheriff was seldom called. In fact, I'd been told that the sheriff's job could have just as easily been handled by a lock-key and janitor. Finsand's guns were just for show.

Judge Warren, now—that was a different story altogether. He'd been the judge right through the rough-and-tumble days, when being a judge meant you had to have some sand in your craw. He could handle trouble, and no doubt about it. But Judge Warren wasn't here; he was over on the eastern slope helping to try a man who'd wintered up at Lake City with a handful of other people. They'd all been caught in a blizzard and snowed in, and Packer had "gone in with a handful and come out with a bellyful," so they said. Ate up every one of them so he could stay alive himself. The trial promised to be a long one. And standing in for the judge here in Hahns Peak was this mealy-mouthed, Eastern-polished dolt of an Indian hater.

I'd made a mistake by coming here, and on a sudden I knew it for sure. I said, "Now hold on. I brought Chief Yampawah up here on my word that something would be done about those two cowhands attacking his women. Yampawah shot Bowles because the man was fixing to shoot him. I say again that Yampawah was within his rights by any law of the land."

Schell drew himself up. "You saying you're a lawyer?"

"Nossir, but some things are self-evident."

"Perhaps. But I *am* a lawyer, and I don't have anybody's word on the matter except yours, which scarcely constitutes proof." There was a small, mean look on Schell's face, and his nostrils were pinched up tight.

Calmly I said, "Schell, if you arrest Yampawah you'd better be prepared to arrest the whole Ute Nation, because there ain't a man on the reservation—no matter how broken-backed they might seem—who won't pick up a gun to right things. I thought we'd learned that lesson back with old Nathan Meeker, and the Utes have their backs a whole lot tighter to the wall these days than old Meeker ever pushed them."

Schell said, "Nonsense."

I wasn't giving up. "Schell, those cowhands were in the wrong. Any decent man would have to agree. Now I ain't asking you to hang them. Just that you try them fair-like and stick them in the hoosegow long enough to teach them a lesson."

Schell looked at me with a weaselly kind of hatred, then snarled at Finsand, "Go out there and get those cowhands and bring them inside."

"And Yampawah?" Finsand was mighty nervous.

"Leave him be for right now. Let's see what the cowhands have to say. After I hear them out, then I'll decide what's best to do."

Sheriff Finsand managed to make a good show of bringing Bowles and Coogan into the office.

Coogan's hands were still trussed up with a rope while Bowles's arm was bandaged and the other had been tied to his side to keep him from making a sudden move. They shuffled around some at first, not knowing what to expect.

Schell put them right at ease in no time, though, when he said to Finsand, "Cut those men's hands loose!"

As soon as Finsand had obliged him, Schell said, "Now I'd like to hear you gentlemen's versions of what happened down on the Yampa River yesterday." He looked them over and smiled to encourage them.

Neither of them said a word.

Politely he asked, "Just what were the two of you doing on McCannon's rangeland?"

Coogan pumped up his nerve and said, "We ride for Moses Skettering. Over on the M-Slash-S."

"Yes, I'm familiar with the operation. Go on."

The smile of malice was nowhere to be found on Coogan's face today. He was as meek and mild and respectful as could be. The whiskey had long since worn off. He said, "The boss drove his cattle further south than usual, on account of the drought—"

"Yes, yes—"

"Found him a nice piece of open rangeland at the Elkhead River delta—"

"Get to the point."

"Well, we was cuttin' sign for strays, trailed 'em down to the river bottom, and we come right upon a consarned Injun camp!"

"Yes, I see . . ."

"Weren't no braves about. And them squaws was right friendly—they come right out and asked us to sit a spell and eat with 'em—"

I broke in, disgusted. "Schell, not one of Yampawah's squaws speaks a word of English."

Schell turned and blasted me. "Let the man tell what happened!"

"Well," said Coogan, and there was a trace of the old malice back now that he'd seen Schell speak up to me. "Them squaws wanted us to keep 'em company. They asked us to eat with 'em, said their menfolk were gone, though I can't say as I ever ate no Injun food. No tellin' what might be in it. But we was tired and was wantin' to find them cattle, and we thought them squaws mighta seed 'em, so we lit down and set a spell."

I wanted to step forward and knock the truth out of the lying varmint, but I kept my peace and bit on my lip.

Coogan was warming to his story now, and he pasted a put-upon look on his face. "Them squaws was plumb friendly-like, though I can't say as I ever hankered for no truck with 'em—too smelly for me. Anyways, they had their pounders and such out, poundin' what 'peared to be wild chokecherries into some kinda meat. I got my suspicions up right away and took a taste of that there meat—it was beef, sure as sin. Now Skettering's been missing more than a few head of cattle, and that set me to wonderin' where they'd got that beef."

"There were two fresh-killed deer hanging from the trees," I said. "Not a trace of a cow carcass in sight."

Schell gave me a haughty look. "Did you taste the meat?"

"Nossir, but—"

Schell cut me off. "I can see your problem," he said to Coogan. "We can get to that later. But right now, what I need to hear is exactly how was Mr. Bowles shot?"

"Oh, heh, that," said Coogan. "Well, we was just settin' there, trying to trip them squaws into sayin' somethin' about where they got that beef—and I'll admit they was hard to talk to—didn't know much more than a word or two what we could figger out—anyways all of a sudden McCannon here comes blastin' through the trees, pointin' that rifle of his at us and yellin' for us to get off'n his land."

Schell turned to me and said, "McCannon?"

I said, "These men weren't no more sitting peaceably with those squaws then old Yampawah is a square-tailed bobcat. Bowles tackled a squaw right before my eyes, and she wasn't a bit friendly about it either. She was fighting like a wildcat—took a hunk right out of his rib cage."

Schell glanced at Bowles, whose bandage was hidden by his shirt and coat. "Man don't look hurt to me," he said, "other than where he was shot by an Injun."

"Look at his skin there—you'll see a bite mark," I said, pointing. I was trying to make things work out right but reckon I'd already realized it was a pure waste of time.

Schell ignored my suggestion and turned back to Coogan. "Are any of McCannon's charges true?"

Coogan looked wounded. "Not a word of it. Can't see how it is that he wants to lie about us like that."

Schell turned to Bowles then. "I'd like to hear it from you—how you got shot."

Bowles was still surly, though he'd taken off his hat now and he held it in his good hand. He said, "It happened just like Coogan here told you."

I couldn't keep quiet. "Schell, this man was carrying a squaw into the bushes when I first saw him. I'm telling you again, he lost his hold on her, and she ran like greased lightning but not before she gnashed a hole in his ribs. If you choose to doubt my word, why don't you take a look and see for yourself?"

"I see no need to peer at another man's rib cage. Seems like a pure imposition, and it wouldn't prove a thing."

Finsand had apparently decided who he was going to back by then, for he piped up. "Even if he did have a bite mark, it could of happened any number of ways."

Bowles muttered, "Horse nipped me. McCannon seen it."

I snorted in disgust.

Coogan was beginning to like the way things were going. He'd been grinning maliciously at me behind Schell's back, but when Schell turned to him he washed his face of the grin and said right quick, "It appears to me that them Injuns is on the rampage again. Lucky for us we ain't both laid out slantin-dicular at the undertaker's."

I said, "That's the first piece of truth you've spoken since you came in here. Because if I hadn't talked Yampawah into riding you up here to the county seat for some justice, he'd most likely have dangled you from a tree right then and there, and been full within his rights to do it by any law of the land. I'm thinking now that I should have let it happen. Only trouble is, it probably wouldn't have been more than two days before a dozen or more innocent people would have died, Indians and whites alike, and all because of your drunken antics."

Schell looked at me with contempt. "I can't understand, Mr. McCannon, why a man of your means should want to take up with Injuns, and against his own kind at that."

I studied him measuredly before I answered. "These two cowhands ain't no more my kind than a skunk or a weasel. And it don't matter what color a man's skin is—he's either hurting or helping, and these two owlhoots were hurting us all."

"Is that supposed to mean something?"

"It is. It means the good Lord created every blamed one of us, and the color of a man's skin ain't what determines whether or not he's decent or if he's a hindrance or a help to his fellow man."

He looked at me hard for a minute, taking my measure, but he evidently decided not to try me on for size. He turned to Finsand and barked, "Sheriff, that settles it. I want you to go out there and arrest that Injun for shooting this man."

I wasn't about to let this foolishness grow any bigger. I admit that at that moment I was wishing I'd just let Yampawah do what he wanted with the cowhands, but it was a spell too late for that now, and it wouldn't have been right anyway. Easy-like, I said, "Afraid I can't let you do that."

Finsand started to reach for his gun, but I already had mine out by the time he got his fingers flexed.

Schell said, "McCannon, I realize you're a friend of Judge Warren's, but I'm in charge here now. I'll tell you right out, if you persist in this foolishness I'll issue a warrant for your arrest for interfering with justice."

I almost laughed out loud at that one. "You going to send Finsand to arrest me?"

"Make no mistake about it, I'll have all the firepower I need if it comes to that."

I'd had all the aggravation I could handle by then, so I ignored his threat. "Schell, I'm leaving here. You can keep these low-down squaw-hunters, but Yampawah and his brave are riding with me. Now I'd appreciate it if you'd just be smart enough to let well enough alone, and we can sort things out when the judge gets back. I don't reckon the sheriff here has any hankering to come ridin' after us. It would probably be just as well if you didn't encourage him, as I've no mind to have to shoot him or anyone else."

I backed out of the room with my gun on the four of them. Nobody made a move to stop me.

Yampawah knew. I didn't have to say a thing to him. He saw me backing out of there, gun in hand, and his face stormed up, and his fists drew up. He grabbed his rifle out of its boot, but I raised a hand to caution him.

I was careful to keep an eye on the door while I mounted my horse, then we lit a shuck out of town. We didn't slow down till we were all the way back down on the Elk River at a high spot where we could see riders coming if the sheriff was fool enough to follow Schell's lead.

I told Yampawah what had transpired, then asked him to lay low for a few days. "I'll contact the judge in Denver and tell him what's happened," I said. "A day or two, and he ought to have someone worth his salt up here to handle county business, or he'll be back himself."

Yampawah didn't say a word to me. After my little speech, he and Chased-by-Bears just looked at me as though they were sad to see me in such poor, deluded shape; then they rode off at a trot across the hills toward Saddle Mountain and California Park to the west.

I headed south, back to the Yampa River Valley. I was feeling about as foolish as I'd ever felt in my life.

It was late afternoon by the time we left Hahns Peak. It was a good five hours' ride back to the stage station at Hayden, and the wintery days were growing short, so I found myself doing most of my riding after sunset. A full moon shone, and frost lay heavy on the land. I could easily make out the high mountain pines, and after a while they gave way to cottonwoods, willows, and quakies, and then to meadowland as I entered the valley. The nip in the air helped to keep me awake even though my toes were cold in my leather boots.

When I got to the Hayden stage station, I awakened old Tom Owens so I could send Judge Warren a telegram. Then I rode the five or so miles on down to the ranch. It must have been nigh onto 3:00 A.M. when I got into the house, shucked out of my clothes, washed up, changed my long handles, then climbed quietly into bed beside Caroline. She awakened enough to give me a sleepy smile, then rolled over and went right back to sleep.

It was well after sunup when I woke up with the feeling that somebody was staring at me. I looked sleepily down at the foot of the bed. There stood Little Johnny, his blue-green eyes wide as saucers as he stared at me.

"Morning, Pa." A brush of a smile crossed his face as I sat up, then he said solemnly, "Cinnamon rolls for breakfast."

"Morning, Johnny." I was solemn as he was. Then with a chuckle I leaped out of bed and swooped him off his feet and toward the ceiling.

Just then Caroline came to the bedroom door. The smile on her face turned to a slight frown as she cautioned me. "Now, Court, do be careful."

But Johnny was laughing, which pleased me no end. Sometimes that boy worried me, he was so quiet. The moniker the cowhands had tied onto him, Little Cannon, didn't fit him at all. He was more like his ma than me. Quiet, smart as a whip, but not one to laugh easily. The past two years the ranch had about swallowed up my waking hours, what with all the problems we had. But what time I could make for Johnny, we always enjoyed each other.

Now the sunshine on his face and the late fall sunshine pouring through my bedroom window clean washed away the troubles of yesterday. I washed up and dressed and spent an extra half hour over breakfast, talking to my wife and son. Then I set about my own business. I still had a passel of work to do in order to get the corrals, the barns, and the hay and other supplies ready for the season of cold that would soon come to stay.

9

I called my ranch hands together and told them I'd had a run-in with the temporary law up in Hahns Peak. They seemed to find that a mite funny. I said if Sheriff Finsand came around for them to hog-tie him and bring him to me. They acted as if they hoped it would happen soon to break up the monotony of their work.

But the sheriff didn't show up. Truth to tell, I hadn't expected him to. The Indian camp down on the river had been moved while we were up at Hahns Peak, and I didn't see hide nor hair of Yampawah and his clan either. After a few days I plumb quit thinking about what had happened and went on about my business.

Caroline and I had opened our home to Mrs. Hearne and the youngest boy, Bobby. By the time they'd been with us for a week or more she'd healed up for the most part but still had great yellow-brown splotches of bruise on her face and arms. One of her bleached-out eyes was still a mite swollen, and she was quiet and meek as a church mouse. But Doc Clayton had been out from Windsor to tend her several times, and he'd given her a clean bill of health by then. Though she still had some pain from her broken ribs, she seemed to be mending up right well, and she insisted on helping around the house all she could.

Old Man Hearne had come to the house the third day she was there, when she'd still been in bed and in some pain. He'd flashed his new Winchester double-barreled shotgun and threatened to drill me if I didn't give back his wife. But she'd come to her bedroom window and showed some spunk when she made it right clear that she didn't intend to return home, leastwise not just then. In a flurry of curses he'd left, and he hadn't been back.

I'd warned my men to run him off the place if he showed up again—to go so far as to wing him if they had to. Not a one of them would have minded the chance, and some would have drilled him and planted him to boot. I'd had to discourage Banty and some others from visiting him with a horsewhip to beat some sense into his sorry hide the day they first saw what he'd done to his wife.

The morning the trouble started up again, we had an especially hearty breakfast of ham slabs and fried potatoes, soda biscuits and cinnamon rolls, and fried eggs fresh from the henhouse, cooked up by Mother Johnson with Mrs. Hearne's help.

Mrs. Hearne and Bobby had started joining us at all our meals at Caroline's insistence. She'd altered some of my old clothes to fit the boy and had given several of her simple dresses to the woman. Now the two Hearnes sat there at the breakfast table spit-shined and clean as a whistle, hanging their heads as if they felt ill at ease, asking us to pass things just a mite too timidly, like dogs with their tails tucked betwixt their legs. I reckoned that Old Man Hearne had done that to them.

All the same, I felt so bad for them that I plumb near wanted to howl like a coyote or shake them by their shoulders till they got some good sense. I knew they felt as if they were taking handouts from us, and I knew there was no worse feeling than having to beg. All the same, that wasn't the way Caroline and I saw it at all. We were plumb glad to be of help, and it was making our days a little sunnier to be able to. It was an awkward situation, but one I hoped would right itself as soon as they realized that all we wanted was to truly see them do well.

Caroline and I talked it over and decided that they were more than welcome to stay with us as long as they had a mind to. Even though Mother Johnson was staying with us, we still had all the room we needed and more.

My pa had added onto the original log and stone ranch house right after the Union Pacific started running the rails up in Wyoming Territory. The cattle business had been booming then, and he'd had the good sense to invest some money in the early mines over in Leadville and up on Independence Pass. I remembered when the mining stocks had first started paying off. My folks had taken the train to Denver to look over all the mining barons' houses in the ritzy part of the city. They'd traveled on to Leadville to visit the new opera house and had done the same there, so as to be able to build my ma a house second to none.

We had one now, a huge affair with two stories and seven bedrooms, including one that Ma had used many years ago as a sewing room and where Mrs. Hearne and her boy now slept. Rock fireplaces had been built into most every room as a hedge against the harsh winter cold, and there were bay windows, two balconies, and even a cupola at one corner with gingerbread trim and heavy shutters to be closed against the worst of the winter chill.

Pa had even gone so far as to build a carriage house, with a room above it for a stableman. We hadn't used it since my ma's death ten years before and hadn't used it much before then. Northwestern Colorado's roads weren't built for fancy carriages and such, though we had one parked in the carriage house all the same, gathering dust. The Hearnes could live above the carriage house and have their very own place, with just a little fixing up. We'd more or less decided that as soon as we had prepared the ranch for winter, that was just what we were going to suggest.

Mrs. Alice Nelson had been cooking for the cowhands for nigh unto a decade. Her husband was one of the older hands. But she was stoved up some with rheumatism and would welcome more help than Skunkweed chose to give her during the winter months. Skunkweed was a range cook, through and through. Put him at an indoors stove, and nigh unto everything he touched burned up. We gave him the job of tending the hay in the winter months. All in all, we could always use another good pair of hands.

Right here in our own household, Caroline was going to give birth in a few more months, and Little Johnny was a handful all by himself. Mother Johnson liked to travel back to Denver now and again to visit, and it would free up her time to have a second pair of hands around the place. Aside from all that, I plumb liked that Hearne boy. I would have liked to take a hand in teaching him how to ranch, how to take care of himself like a man.

I offered the job to Mrs. Hearne over breakfast one day, making sure to let her know how bad we needed her.

She just looked down at her hands, twisting her napkin, and said, "We'll see. I thank you, Mr. McCannon. I deeply appreciate the offer, more than you could know. But I've a family of my own. We'll just have to wait and see."

I was puzzled by her. Though she was meek and whipped, she seemed to have some formal schooling, and she was a right nice person, other than her broken spirit. I couldn't understand how she'd ended up with a man who misused her so badly, and I sure enough couldn't imagine her wanting to go back to him if she had any other choice at all.

After we'd eaten I went into my office to work on my books. I was still hoping to tighten my belt enough to make it through the winter without taking out a loan. What with all the ranchers going belly up, the banks were a mite too fast to foreclose these days. I didn't want to step into that bear trap unless it was the only possible way I could go.

It was coming on toward noon when Caroline came to the door and said, "Court?" It was an intense whisper.

I jerked up straight. "What is it?"

"Court, Jimmy Hearne just rode into the front yard. Could you come, please? I don't want to deal with him."

I'd already put my pen back in the inkwell. In two seconds I was at the front door, Caroline right beside me but back out of the way.

When I opened the door, Jimmy Hearne stood by the hitching rail in front of the porch. He was holding the reins of Bobby's old horse; a fancy new saddle was strapped to its swayed back. I reckoned he hadn't wanted to ride his sorrel down here in case I might recognize it.

In the harsh light of day Jimmy seemed to be teetering at that age where a boy turns into a man. I had seen more than one cowhand in the saddle at fourteen or fifteen years of age, and some were already mature men by then. But though Jimmy Hearne was a mite older than that, he seemed to be younger than any of them. I reckoned it came down to something inside a man.

As I looked at him, I thought for a moment about how I'd wanted to shoot him when I caught him rustling my cattle. I thought about the black hatred that had boiled up in me, and I was ashamed that I could have such a feeling for such a pitiful lad.

But young though he might seem, he already had a sullen look about him. He didn't bother with a polite greeting or a howdy. His ferret's face was drawn up just then in a poisonous sneer, and those blue eyes of his had a rheumy quality to them, like those of an old man. He turned his head and spat out a stick of wood he'd been chawing on, then said, "My ma here?"

I stepped out onto the porch, letting the screen door bang behind me but leaving the door itself ajar so that Caroline could hear. "Reckon you know your ma and your little brother Bobby have been staying with us."

Something ugly flashed in his eyes. "Pa sent me to bring 'em home."

I said, "They're welcome to leave anytime they want. Welcome to stay as long as they want too."

His eyes slitted up. "I want to see my ma."

I turned and spoke through the screen door. "Caroline, could you ask Mrs. Hearne to come on out here, please?"

While we waited, the Hearne boy and I just stood there and sized one another up. The way he looked at me, it seemed to me that he had a thing for me like a coyote has for a jackrabbit. Reckon I'd already figured out that most of his hatred sprang out of pure downright jealousy.

And I expect that made me a mite more sympathetic toward him than was good for me. I understood that my upbringing had been better than his was turning out to be. I reckoned that, in some upside-down way, his hatred for me evened things up for him, which more or less made it fair. As I say, I had a good deal still to learn back then.

He looked as if his fortunes had improved since our last meeting though. He was wearing a new pair of woolen trousers and a new red flannel shirt. His buckskin jacket was new too, and he sported a new hand-tooled holster with a pearl-handled six-shooter stuck into it that must have cost a pretty penny. Last time I'd ridden into town, Shorty Musket told me that Old Man Hearne was selling him barrels of homemade hootch to supplement what Musket got in from Rawlins. Reckon I figured then that maybe the boy's money had come from there. But I've got a mite more patience than I do good sense sometimes. I just wasn't ready to write that lad off as no-good just yet.

I said, "I been thinking some. Reckon I know why you fired on me up in the high country that day. I know how hard times can affect a man, and if it's all the same to you I'd just as soon let bygones be bygones, long as you don't plan to do it again."

He just stood there, looking at me as though I was a rodent and he was a trap.

I said, "Your ma was hurt bad, you know."

"Ain't none of your snoopy business!" He spat it out.

That irked me some. "Well, then," I said, "let me bring up something that is my business. I know I surprised you about to butcher one of my cows. Makes me feel right bad that you'd steal from me. But I reckon it makes me feel even worse to think about you folks back up there and the kind of winter we got coming on. If you could use a job, I could use another hand to feed cattle this winter. Reckon I could pay you off in food, butcher a cow or two to keep you folks going through the winter . . ."

Little flickers of fear were shooting through his eyes, and his gun hand had tensed. He said, "You're crazy, Mister."

"Not likely," I said mildly. "Just willing to give a man a chance to work for what he needs—"

"Don't need anything from the likes of you," he sneered. He had me puzzled. Fear still shot through his eyes, and he was so edgy that he seemed about to turn tail and run. At the same time, his gun hand hovered over that pearl-handled six-shooter, and I kept my eye on him, ready to duck in and grab my shotgun, which stood just inside the door, were it to become necessary.

His hand dropped away from the gun. He reached in his coat pocket, brought out another wood splinter, and stuck it in his mouth like a toothpick, arrogant-like.

I relaxed and said, "Let me tell you this much, boy. You don't want to make amends, so be it. But if you ever harm another head of my stock, you ever so much as look at another of my horses, I'll see you hang."

He glared at me, poisonous hatred in his eyes, and I felt rage starting to rise up in me too. I did my best to force it back down. I'd heard enough of Caroline's conversations with Mrs. Hearne to know that Old Man Hearne didn't save his beatings for just his wife. This lad before me had been tanned to rawhide most every day of his life, and I wasn't of a mind to carry on the tradition. At the same time, I wasn't of a mind to let him take all that out on me and mine.

Mrs. Hearne came through the door just then, patting a stray strand of gray hair into place. When she saw Jimmy, a little sob came out of her mouth, and she ran and threw her arms around him. She cried, "Jimmy! Oh, son, I been worried sick about you!"

He didn't return her hug, just acted kind of awkward and pulled her arms from around his shoulder. "Pa sent me to bring you home." He stood there, stiff and uncomfortable now.

She searched his eyes, looking for something, but he didn't show her any response, just stood there.

"Jimmy?"

He shifted and looked at her but didn't answer.

"Your pa been whipping at you?"

He still didn't speak, but his lips went thin, and his face drew up tight.

"Jimmy, where'd you get the money for all the new things? I told you—"

His eyes flashed as he snarled, "Shut up, Ma! Just shut your stupid mouth if you know what's good for you!"

I saw her stomach heave, even beneath her apron, as grief rolled through her like a wave. She put her hands over her face, and a sob escaped.

"Come on home, Ma," Jimmy said flatly. "You don't belong here with these high muckety-mucks. Likes of us got no call to be puttin' on airs, tryin' to be something you ain't. Come home. There's work needs to be done."

Resignation and weariness washed over her face. "All right," she replied. "Let me just get your little brother, and we'll be right along." She went back inside.

I followed her in, Caroline right behind me. "Mrs. Hearne, you know you're welcome to stay with us as long as you like. If you're worried about your husband harming that oldest boy of yours, I'll be happy to do whatever I can to help."

Tears filled her eyes, and she said, "Mr. McCannon, no-body in my whole life's ever been as good to me as you and Caroline have been. But Tom's my husband. It's the whiskey that's got him sick. I took vows, in sickness and in health— before God I took those vows—and I've got to go back. I always knew I'd have to. It's my cross to bear, Mr. McCannon, and I've got to bear it."

I felt so frustrated I was about to burst. "Ma'am, the way I see it, the good Lord's not the one responsible for us being in these kind of situations. He doesn't give us that much of a cross to bear. I don't suspect that's what the Good Book means at all. Don't you reckon that maybe He sent us your way because He wants you to live better than you have been?"

"That's blasphemous," she said, with the first hint of fire I'd seen in her. "I took my vows, and I'll keep them." She nodded her head stubbornly, then turned away.

There was a certain mulish pride in her carriage as she went up the stairs. And I knew there wasn't one solitary thing I could do just then to stop her.

10

It was a gray day, clouds hanging low. A chill had set into the land, and a few light snowstorms had come and gone, but the big snows Chief Yampawah talked about had yet to arrive.

I'd ridden to town for supplies again. Doc Clayton had a free hour, so I'd treated him to lunch at the Elkhorn Hotel and Saloon. Now we were sitting with our chairs propped back, enjoying cups of Arbuckles coffee and a good long talk about the general state of affairs with the worsening cattle market and how it was hitting our part of the state.

He said, "I know you, Court, and I know it shames you to be having such a hard time with the ranch. But I want you to know there isn't a rancher in these parts who isn't hurting as bad or worse than you are."

"I am plumb sorry to hear that."

"You've weathered things pretty well, considering. You'll come out of it. You've got your father's grit in you, Court, your father's very own. I'm not ashamed to say I miss the man."

Doc Clayton and my pa had become friends during the Civil War, Pa doing the killing and Doc doing the healing. Doc had come West at the same time as Pa, after the war was over and while the East was still in shambles. He set up practice in Denver City for a number of years, then he finally come to Windsor to get away from the chicanery of the fast city life. He built a comfortable one-story cottonwood log house for himself and his wife, had a couple of young'uns, and was as happy as a bug in springtime.

I said, "I can't help but wonder what Pa would be doing if he was still here. Feel sometimes like I'm doing things wrong, like there might be other ways . . ."

"Hogwash! You've handled that ranch as well as any man could. We've all just had some bad luck these past few years. Some bad, bad luck."

"It's been hard, all right," I agreed. "Reckon we've been lucky that all we've lost so far in these parts is livestock." I pointed at the Denver paper, which I'd been reading while I waited for him. He'd read it too—he mentioned it when he sat down at the table. The headlines warned us to get ready for another long winter and reminded us that last year better than two hundred folks had either frozen or starved to death on the plains in Nebraska and Kansas during the winter's storms.

"That's only the half of it, Court, only the half of it. Last time I was over in Denver I ran upon a banker I know from back in Nebraska. He told me that the Wilkie ranch lost over five thousand head last winter. Said that better than ten thousand cattle were found dead at spring thaw just between Garden City and Hayes Center over in Kansas. Ten thousand head! Good heavens, Court, ranchers from the Dakotas and down to Texas been going belly-up all year long. Just throwing up their hands and walking away from a hopeless situation. The J. M. Day spread in Kansas branded only one thousand calves last spring, down from five thousand the year before. Half the cattle left were crippled by the cold weather or by wolves and other predators."

"I only branded three hundred myself," I admitted. "Branded more'n a thousand the year before. My whole herd's down to under six thousand head now."

"The Kaye ranch down towards Utah is in bad shape too. Those folks come in the other day to buy some splints for breaks and such. Got to talking, and Mike Kaye says this summer's drought hurt them as much as last winter's blizzards."

I heard the doorway open. A draught of cold air swept into the room. The doc was facing the door, and a look of surprise and distaste appeared on his face. I turned, sloshing some of my coffee onto the blue-checked tablecloth in my curiosity to see who'd come in.

I was looking at Moses Skettering, Luke Coogan, and Ben Blue.

Skettering's eyes slitted up some, and his mouth cracked open in as near to a grin as I'd yet seen from him. He tipped his hat in our direction and said, "Afternoon, Doc, McCannon," in that dark, scratchy whisper of a voice.

Doc Clayton greeted him, and I nodded politely.

Coogan was the one I kept an eye on though. He had a mean look on his face, but he stared straight ahead, trying to pretend he didn't see me or know me.

But Blue? He looked dead at me and grinned like I was a long-lost friend. He tipped his black hat with his good hand—his crippled right one buried deep in his pocket—then he walked on past with Coogan and Skettering to settle at the far end of the bar.

Summer's work was done, and winter's hadn't yet turned heavy, so there were a few other folks there as well, drinking and visiting and a few playing poker. The old player piano in the back was chawing on a punched paper music roll so that there was a tinny, cheerful plunking in the background.

Clayton and I both fell silent. We watched as Shorty Musket hobbled up to them, set out three glasses, uncorked a bottle of Taos Lightning with his teeth, then spit the cork on the floor and set the bottle in front of them. The three paid us no mind. They tossed off a couple of shots of hootch apiece, then put their heads together in what appeared to be some serious palaver.

Shorty leaned into the group for a minute, trying to listen, but Blue brought up his head and glared, and Shorty got the message and hobbled on back down the bar to pick up his gossiping with old Jake Parton, another man who liked his hootch.

Clayton and I went back to our own conversation.

I'd told the doc about what had happened during my sojourn up to Hahns Peak, of course.

Now he said, "That man Coogan, he's the one?"

"Sure is."

The doc frowned into his empty cup and said, "Well, I expect that's hardly the end of the trouble from the looks of that centipede."

"Reckon it isn't," I replied. "Matter of fact, I wired Judge Warren and got a wire back from him just the other day. He'll be back from Denver by the end of the week. Wants me to try to hold things steady until then, but I reckon nothing else has come up anyway, at least not over that squaw-baiting matter. Heard Yampawah and his clan went down south towards Milk Creek for a spell. Staying away from that worthless Schell and his henchman sheriff, I expect."

Doc nodded. "If half of the white folks in this area had the good sense of that old Indian, this would be a whole lot better place to live. By the way, I heard the judge is planning to run for the state legislature. How's that coming along?"

"Don't know much about it," I replied, "but I'd sure like to see him get the job. Too many sidewinders running things now, if you ask me."

"Well, the judge is an honest man. We could do worse than to elect him." He scratched his chin. "Matter of fact, we've done worse a number of times."

"The judge just might make it. He has some powerful people on his side. His wife mentioned that Senator Otis Brown is helping him run his campaign."

"Brown?" Doc Clayton tensed up and frowned.

"Yessir. Something wrong?"

"You haven't heard?"

"Heard what?"

Doc Clayton sighed, and his shoulders slumped. "Well, you mean you really don't know. I expect you'd best hear it, and fast. You realize that Skettering's ranch isn't owned outright by Skettering?"

"Reckon I do know that. Mostly owned by investment companies. A few in Denver, but mostly from back East and over in England. Folks wanting to cash in on the cattle business without ever having sat a horse or seen a steer."

"That's true, Court. And I hate to be the one to bear bad tidings, but one of those Denver investors is none other than Senator Otis Brown. In fact, he owns a good-sized portion of Skettering's shares. You really didn't know?"

I felt like a horse had kicked me in the gut. "Nossir, I rightly didn't."

"You recall when the railroad bridge collapsed down by Leadville some five or so years back? The one that caused the Midland train wreck that killed all those folks?"

"Yessir."

"Company that built it belonged to Brown." At the look of shock on my face, he said, "Oh, it wasn't common knowledge, but I still have a lot of friends in Denver. A doctor is privy to all sorts of dirty secrets. I can tell you for a fact that it cost Brown a pretty penny to hush that all up and salvage his political career. In fact it about busted him. I've been told that Brown has dumped what was left of his family's money into the Skettering ranch, and he was expecting a fast and substantial return on that investment."

I thought about that. No one I knew was going to make any money ranching cattle this year, much less a whopping return. I didn't like the situation one bit.

"While we're at it, there's another thing or two you might as well know. That fellow Ben Blue?"

"Yessir?"

"He's no more a stock detective than I am. He's a hired killer. I have it from one of my friends, a Denver attorney, Matt Sterling."

"I recognize the name," I said. "Believe Pa knew him too. They both held shares in the same Leadville mines before Pa sold out and put the profits into land."

"Yes. I'd forgotten. Well, old Matt and I have been friends for years. He came over from Denver to hunt some elk up around Bears Ears with me while you were busy with the roundup. Matt brought the Union Pacific passenger car from Denver to Rawlins—fancy new machine with wine plush upholstery. I took a look in it when I picked him up in Rawlins

—I've a mind to take Emma on a trip to Denver on it some-time."

"I expect it costs a pretty penny," I said.

"Yes—well, back to the point. Matt pointed Blue out to me at the train station. He was excited that he'd ridden the train with a 'desperado.' Seems that Blue had boarded at Laramie, put his horse in the cattle car, then taken a seat at the end of the passenger car. Matt recognized him right away from Leadville—had seen him there at a saloon a time or two and heard what folks whispered through the grapevine about him. Word was that Blue used to do work for Sheriff Bart Duggan—you know, that so-called Leadville lawman who ran a pilfering gang that turned out to be ten times worse than any outlaw's? Matt heard that Blue shot several men in Leadville. Got away with it too. Claimed self-defense, and Duggan backed him up. And then when Duggan got in hot water, Blue lit a shuck out of town."

I pondered on that. Seemed to me there was a mite of distance between whatever Blue might have really done and the chain of rumors that had delivered the story to me. I said, "Wonder why Skettering brought him here."

"Well," Doc Clayton said, puffing up a little, important-like. "I have some theories on that."

He waited for me to say something, but I knew old doc well and knew he'd talk a whole lot faster and a whole lot more if I didn't seem too anxious. I sipped the last of my coffee and stretched. "Might good coffee today. Reckon I'll have another cup. How about you, Doc?"

That alarmed him, and he leaned in close and said, "Wait a minute. Wait till I explain. You know Shorty—I don't want him to hear so much as a breath of this. Back to Skettering. It seems to me that he'd like for folks to believe that the Indians are rustling his cattle."

"I'd say that's pretty evident. But what does that have to do with Ben Blue?"

"Courtney, Courtney. You've had your nose plowed so deep into that ranch that you've lost sight of what's happening in this county. There are some big changes in the wind, and I can't see as how any of them are for the better."

He proceeded to explain things to me, at least so far as they looked to him. The problem was with the folks who had invested in Skettering's ranch, he said again. When Senator Otis Brown and the rest of them first put up their money, there wasn't much chance you'd make less than 40, 50 percent return on your investment in the cattle business. Those had been boom years. But the bust had been on its way. What with the bad weather and bad luck, cattle profits turned sour just last year.

What it boiled down to was that Skettering had promised his investors the moon in order to get the money to start his ranch. Now it was time to pay up, and he couldn't deliver. The investors were talking about getting out of their contract with him. And if it came to that, he was bound to go belly-up.

"On top of that, I believe he's been padding his records," Doc Clayton said, leaning close to me and glancing down the room to where Skettering and his two hombres still sat jawing at the bar. "I believe he's been claiming far more cattle than the M-Slash-S has ever seen on its land."

I cogitated on that for a minute. No point in asking the doc where he got that kind of information, because he'd never tell me. But his words couldn't be taken lightly. If that was the case, then the investors in Skettering's ranch had been treated to a first-class swindle, and the weather and cattle market couldn't be blamed.

Doc was still talking low, so nobody could overhear him. "I expect he's padded his stock tally a thousand head here, a thousand head there, padded the records of his own land holdings and of the open rangeland available to him. Made it all look better than solid gold to those tinhorns back East and in Denver. Maybe a whole lot better than solid gold. Way I heard it, when he first started up he had those gullible investors shoving one another out of the way to buy up shares.

"Back then, profits in cattle were so high I suppose he didn't see how it could hurt. He might have gotten away with

112

it too if the bottom hadn't fallen out of the market. Make no mistake about it, no mistake at all. If what I've pieced together about this turns out to be true, then Skettering has some accounting and explaining coming up, and if you ask me he's desperate to cover his tracks."

I'd kept glancing at the backs of the three men at the bar as he talked. They were still knee-deep in their own conversation, but all the same it made me uncomfortable to be talking about such delicate things with them sitting so close. Still, old Doc had my curiosity up now. I asked, "How'd you figure all that out?"

He smiled slyly. "I keep my ears open. And you know it makes sense, Court. It plain makes sense." His face lit up in a grin. He glanced over at Skettering's back, then turned to me again and chuckled. "Moses Skettering would probably hang a man to keep him from knowing the truth. Think of it! All this fuddle over the Indians rustling his stock, and there wasn't any stock to begin with."

I shifted, uneasy. "Well, if that's the case, that don't exactly bode well for the Indians, does it?"

Doc Clayton turned serious. "There are certain kinds of men who'll do anything, anything at all, when they're teetering that close to the edge of ruination."

"So if all that proves true, why in blazes is Blue here? What hand is he playing in all this?"

The doc fell silent, and a somber mood seemed to take him. He reached in his vest and pulled out a stogie, bit off the tip, rolled the end in his mouth. Then he struck a kitchen match with his thumbnail and applied the flame to the freshly dampened end, frowning all the while. He drew long and hard, until the end took to glowing, then he said, "I don't know about that, Court. I don't rightly know what to make of Blue's being here. But I do know that wherever a man like that rides, serious trouble follows right behind. Serious trouble indeed."

"Well, Doc, I trust your judgment, make no mistake

about that. But I sure do hope you're wrong this time." I turned and signaled for Shorty to bring us more coffee.

Doc blinked, then said, "Don't look now, but Coogan has his eyes fixed on you. Looks like he's got a mad on."

I turned to look anyway, and as my eyes fell on Coogan, he caught my gaze and threw it back to me as a contemptuous challenge.

He appeared to be liquored up again. I knew that he was itching for a fight—probably wanted to pick up right where we'd left off when I'd delivered him to Schell and Sheriff Finsand at Hahns Peak.

I turned back around.

Doc Clayton was sitting real still, the smoke coiling up from his cigar. Quietly he said, "Seems we were right about that trouble."

I nodded. "Reckon a small parcel of it is standing at the bar this very minute, taking aim at me."

The doc and I both looked back at the bar at the same time, and that's all it took.

Coogan yelled loud and clear, "Hey there, Courtney McCannon! Been lovin' up any of them squaws lately?"

I looked down at my cup and tried to ignore him.

Then I heard a noise and turned to look again, not wanting him to bushwhack me. I saw him shambling over to a table near the bar, where John Calhoun and Sam Fitzpatrick sat playing poker. I had the feeling he was going to bring them into the trouble, and I was right, for he placed his palms on the table and leaned over them, then nodded toward me.

He snarled, "Reckon you don't know that your high-and-mighty Courtney McCannon is a squaw man. Keeps a few head on his ranch just for sport now and again. Found 'em myself, less'n you didn't hear."

The two men looked up at him as if he was about as pesky as a mosquito. Then they looked back down at their cards, and Fitzpatrick said, "Raise and see you a buck."

Coogan started to say something else to them, but Calhoun looked up with a mean expression on his face that stopped him short. "Get out of here, you saw-tailed rooster, or I'll pluck you and drop you in Shorty's pot."

That sent the reprobate swaying toward me, raising his hand and balling it into a fist.

Doc Clayton shook his head in disgust. He patted his vest to let me know that he was carrying that derringer he always packed. His black wool suit and vest gave him ample padding to hide the small shoulder holster and gun.

Pa had told me stories about the doc sawing off gangrened arms and legs while bullets were whizzing around him, about how Doc had once picked up a carbine and shot the head off a Graycoat who was fool enough to fire on the tent where he was tending the wounded.

The doc had the sand to stand up in a fight, and it was a good thing to know I wasn't alone, because Coogan was stomping toward me, and now Skettering and Blue had both turned around at the bar to watch, their hands hovering above their holstered guns just in case the trouble should get more serious than the tarring that Coogan was apparently hoping to give me.

My first instinct was to get up and walk out the door. But I'd walked away from this varmint up at Hahns Peak, and it seemed the man hadn't learned a blamed thing from it. Now, if I was going to get this matter straightened out, it seemed that I wasn't going to have the choice of refusing this fight. All the same, I just sat there, not reaching for my own sidearm, not saying a thing, just waiting to see what Coogan would do.

He sidled up to our table, the two of us still sitting. His breath smelled like a kerosene campfire. He said, "Still pryin' 'round in other folks' business, Courtney McCannon? Or did our new county judge teach you some manners?"

"Things being what they are," I said, as mildly as I could considering the way my temper was rising up, "I reckon we'd both be better off just to let things lie." I was remembering my promise to Judge Warren to keep things as level as possible till he got back.

Coogan rasped, "You're a low-bellied rattlesnake squaw-lover, McCannon—"

I'd had enough. "Ease off, Coogan," I said in a steely voice. "I'm in no hurry to give you the hiding you deserve for lying about me. Never knew a polecat that could tell a lie from the truth anyways—"

I cut my tantrum short. I could see from the expression on his face that I'd made a mistake in letting him get me riled. He was feeding on my anger as a buzzard feeds on a dead rabbit.

He sneered. "Well, I been anxious to settle the score with you. You got me sittin' up nights worried that you and them renegade redskins would be comin' after my scalp." He hee-hawed at that, slapping his knee and turning to see if anyone else thought he was funny.

Blue and Skettering just stood there, backs to the bar and elbows resting on it behind them, looking casual but with their hands still no more than inches above the butts of their guns. Blue's hard face wore a mirthless smile that I didn't like the looks of, while Skettering looked eager and blood-hungry, as if he'd sicced Coogan onto me and considered it sport, though he was trying some to mask his pleasure.

The player piano had rolled to a stop.

The room was deathly quiet.

All the men in the barroom had stopped what they were doing to watch us.

I knew most of them and didn't have to prove anything to any one of them. And I sure didn't intend to entertain them with a barroom fight. I braced myself, swallowing the anger that was rolling up again, and said to Coogan, "I'd be mighty obliged if you'd just move on back to the bar and forget this nonsense. Be happy to set the three of you up with a drink—"

I bit through the side of my tongue as that sidewinder kicked me on my right leg just below the knee. And before I had a chance to spring up and face him, he kicked the leg of my chair, knocking it out from under me so that the chair tipped backward and I went flying. Then he let fly too, as

116

soon as I hit the floor, with a boot that landed square in my rib cage. I heard something crack as I felt the pain in my side.

I rolled with the next kick as if I'd been pitched from the back of a bucking bronc—Doc Clayton leaping out of my way—and rolled up to my haunches, caught my balance, then sprang up at Coogan, whose mouth fell open in surprise.

He snarled, "Stay down, you blasted meddler!"

With a speed of a rattler's strike, he yanked a hunting knife out of his belt-sheath and came in low and fast, so fast that I knew Doc couldn't possibly have seen the knife and that no help would come from that direction.

I felt for my Colt, then saw it under the table where it had fallen free when I fell. All I had to use against that knife was my fists. I didn't move, just stood there and let him come at me with that thick, sharp blade aimed for my gizzard. Then at the last minute I swerved to one side and brought up my fist, hitting him square under his chin even as the knife slit though the side of my shirt.

He flew backwards, regained his balance, and came up short, stunned. He stood there, clenching his chin with one hand, the other still dangling that knife, shaking his head to try to clear it.

Blue yelled from the bar then, "Coogan! Get hold of yourself, you drunken fool. That's enough!"

Blue's belated interference struck me funny, on top of the fact that I'd caught Coogan with about the easiest punch there is to throw at a man. Reckon he'd just been overly impressed with the fact that he had that knife. I surprised myself by chuckling out loud, and even as the sound came out of my mouth I realized how crazy that must sound to those who were watching.

I was still mad that Coogan had blindsided me. But I also felt a sense of relief that everything was out in the open now. Skettering, Blue, and Coogan had finally come right out and branded themselves as my enemies. The only reason Blue had opened his mouth now was that he could see the weather changing and knew that Coogan was about to get himself beaten from here to Sunday.

For an instant the barroom was so quiet that I could hear the bar clock ticking. Someone cleared his throat. Coogan's gasps eased off as he caught his breath.

Then the fool lunged again, coming in low, still aiming to gut me and as hard to teach a lesson as a fallen log. He was in such a rage now that he was nigh unto frothing at the mouth as he began stabbing wildly.

In spite of the ugliness in the man's eyes, I nigh unto felt downright sorry for him. He was pasty and out of shape from too much hootch and off balance from all the whiskey he'd drunk that day. And from what I'd seen of the man so far, he was also stupid as a rattler, though no less dangerous, even at his best.

I got out of his way easily, sidestepping, then jumping aside again, but he wanted to carve a piece out of me so bad that his judgment had clean vanished and he just wouldn't give up.

Finally he came in wheezing, the knife jabbing thin air.

I'd had my fill of the stupidity, so I feinted the same right hook I'd used before. He was ready for it now, but I'd expected as much. He ducked straight into my left, and I knocked him backward and over a table. The knife went flying across the room to land on the floor near the card table, and Coogan crumpled to the floor and lay there, knocked plumb out.

Still coiled tight, expecting more trouble, I turned toward the bar, half expecting to see a gun or two leveled at me. But Skettering and Blue had their hands up now, palms flat and facing toward me and looks of pure innocence on their faces. I glanced around to see that Doc Clayton, an expression on his face like he was in a Sunday service, had his pistol pointed square at them.

Fitzpatrick yelled, "Good work, McCannon. Thanks for cleaning the vermin out of this saloon," and Calhoun and a couple of others yelled their congratulations.

I dusted myself off and gave them a tight little nod, but I can't say as I was much proud of myself. The man hadn't been a match for me, drunk or sober, and I hadn't wanted to tangle with him for all that. I'd known that one of us was bound to get hurt, and I hadn't been wrong about that. In spite of the fact that he was down and out, my rib cage was giving me fits. I'd broken a rib or two before, mostly busting broncs, and I wasn't any too pleased about this turn of events.

I picked up my Stetson from where it had landed on the floor, dusted it off, and said to Skettering, "Reckon you'd better take this varmint of yours on out of here and tend to him. And I reckon you and yours had best stay away from me and mine, because I'm starting to get a mite tired of your boys."

Skettering's eyes slitted up, but he kept his palms forward. "Your battle with Coogan is no fault of mine. Looks to me like you brought this bile on yourself by tryin' to put him in the jailhouse. And since it isn't my fight, I'll be happy to stay out of it. But I warn you, McCannon, right here in front of everybody. You keep bothering my boys, you're askin' for them to stand up to you, and there ain't no way I'm goin' to be able to stop them."

"Then I reckon I'll just have to stop them from time to time myself," I said.

Ben Blue just stood there, a sort of contemptuous look on his face as though he had no use for any of us.

I set my hat on my head, then turned to Doc Clayton. "C'mon, Doc. Reckon these fellers need to pick their garbage up and pack it home. And until it's gone, this room smells a mite strange to me."

Doc Clayton looked at me, looked at them, looked back at me, smiled widely, then put his gun back inside his vest and walked with me out the door.

11

I slept poorly that night, partly from trying to figure out the whirlwind of troubles that seemed to be coming my way and partly from the pain in my rib cage. Doc Clayton had bound my ribs up tight, but every time I rolled over or breathed a deep breath, the pain brought me back awake.

I climbed out of bed early the next morning to find that the windowpane was coated over with a miniature forest of frost. I shook the sash back and forth to jar some of the rime loose, then slid the window open to a blast of cold air. A fresh, thick blanket of snow had caked the whole world in white.

As the cold air came through the window, Caroline stirred and pulled the comforter up tighter around her neck, but she didn't wake up.

I shut the window, then changed my woolen pajamas for a pair of long handles, a pair of thick wool socks, my Levi's, boots, and a heavy flannel shirt. I stepped lightly through the doorway into Johnny's room.

He lay there, his tousled blond hair framing a face that was angelic in sleep. I sat on the featherbed beside him and said softly, "Hey, pard. Your pa's got something he wants to show you."

His eyes fluttered open once, then he closed them tightly and tried to stay asleep.

I said, "How'd you like to spend the morning sledding?"

His blue eyes popped open wide. "Did it snow, Pa?"

"Best snow I've ever seen."

He flew out of bed and to the window and stared at the frost with wonder in his eyes.

I said, "Jack Frost's been here, Son. Painted over your window with that little forest of ice trees."

He rubbed his eyes, then opened them wider. "Who's Jack Frost, Pa?"

"Tiny little critter, looks just like a man, 'cepting he carries around a frost paintbrush and paints ice-frosting over all the windows on cold nights."

"Can I see him, Pa? Where'd he go?"

I laughed. "Reckon he's long gone by now. Can't stay long next to anything warm, or he'll melt down to a puddle in no time. Reckon he ran away about sunup, like he most always does."

Johnny looked at me with those serious eyes of his and said, "You're fooling me, Pa."

I grinned. "Most likely."

He stepped on the cold floor between the rugs, then shivered and hopped back up on the bed. "Is Mama up? Did she see the snow?"

"Reckon not. I thought I'd let you tell her."

His eyes sparkled. "Let's go tell her right now, Pa."

I scooped him up, grabbing his slippers from the foot of the bed, and carried him into the next room.

Caroline's eyes were open. She looked at us as we came through the doorway, smiling sleepily and opening her arms wide.

Johnny dived into bed with her and said, "Guess what, Mama. It snowed."

Her eyes came awake too. Green eyes instead of blue, but the shape and expression in Johnny's was the same as her own. She said, "Already!" and there was just as much excitement in her voice as there had been in his. She turned to me, smiled, and said, "Well, now. The drought must finally really be over, thank the Lord."

"Amen," I agreed. "Time to get out the sled. You folks get dressed up warm. I'm going on down to the kitchen and see if I can't rustle up some flapjacks and bacon. Reckon we'll let Mother Johnson sleep in, if she's a mind to."

From the kitchen windows I could see up the eastern end of the valley as well as the hill behind the house. The snowfall had been at least a good two feet on the level, and the cottonwoods and willows drooped heavy with the snow. Not a footprint or a hoofprint showed anywhere in the new powdery blanket. It was a fresh world out there, a fresh season, and yesterday's troubles with Skettering and Coogan seemed small and manageable today in spite of the fire I felt in my ribs when I moved wrong.

The hill behind the house was perfect for sledding. I'd spent many a happy hour there as a youngster. Little Johnny would do the same, and soon he'd have a brother or sister to sled with him. One day I'd have grandchildren sledding down that hill.

There was something about the warmth inside the house and the blanket of white outside that made me feel safe, out of reach of the kind of petty, groveling, greedy evil that Skettering and his like had come to represent to me. As I heated up the griddle and set the bacon to sizzling, the pale sun shone through the snow-heavy branches; it would settle the top layer of snow today and melt it down some, but we'd have snow on the ground for days to come just from this snowfall alone.

After breakfast, Caroline and I pulled Johnny up the hill and sledded him down time and time again. She took over when my ribs began to ache too much and my breath started coming short. When he'd finally had enough, was so tired that he started to cry each time he tumbled off the sled, Caroline swooped him up and took him back to the house for some warmth and rest. I went on down to the big barn to check on the cowhands.

"Mornin', Mr. McCannon." Banty Brewster wiped his forehead with the back of his heavy sleeve and stopped pitching hay.

"Howdy, Banty."

He said, "Glad you come down. I was just fixin' to send somebody up to get you."

"What's the problem?"

"Someone broke into the tack room last night. Pried the hinges off the door and walked right on in. Them two new Denver saddles you just bought?"

"Yes?"

"Took 'em."

I breathed in and out. No point in getting my dander up if the fox was already out of the henhouse. I said, "I reckon you already checked around? Ought to be some footprints, what with all this fresh snow."

He looked disgruntled. "Don't you think I done thought of that, Mr. McCannon?"

I'd told him a thousand times if I'd told him once to call me Court, but he and a few of the other cowhands—mostly the ones who'd worked first for my pa, who had been a stickler for formality due to his high-ranking military days—refused to.

Banty grunted. "Whoever done it got in and out afore the snow fell. No tracks in the snow, and it covered up any tracks there mighta been cut into the ground before snowfall."

I'd already formed my own ideas about who it was. I said, "You tell Ledbetter yet?"

Hank Ledbetter was my foreman. Banty had acted as foreman during Pa's time, but Ledbetter was a good man, and I'd promoted him at Banty's request to handle the biggest part of the responsibilities now that Banty was feeling his age. Banty still handled a good many of the decisions around the ranch. Sometimes Banty was a bit too cantankerous on his own, but Ledbetter seemed to tame him down some. Together they could eat a polecat live and walk away to tell about it.

"Nossir, figgered to tell you first and see what you thought ought to be done."

"Well," I said, "any loss is hard in times like these, but I reckon it ain't going to make nor break us. Talk it over with Ledbetter and see what you two can figure out."

"Yessir." He shifted from one foot to the other as he always did when he had something to say, then he said it. "S'pect I'd just as well tell you and get it done with. This ain't the first time somethin' like this has happened. That's why we took to lockin' the place up to begin with."

"Why didn't you tell me?"

He looked down at his worn old boots and said, "S'pect I thought you'd laugh at me. Weren't nothing to worry about, anyways."

"What was taken?"

"You know them old hackamores we had hangin' on the wall for who knows how long?" His eyebrows peaked up, making him look forlorn. "And them old branding irons? The ones that you figgered was too rusted and burned out to use?"

"Branding irons?"

"Yessir, Mr. McCannon. Lazy Double C irons, sure as the day."

I don't mind telling you that I was perplexed by that. "What would anyone want with our old branding irons?"

He furled up those eyebrows again, pursed up his mouth, and then it crooked into a grin. "Heh. You got me on that one. 'Fraid I thought it was so peculiar that I weren't even goin' to mention it lest folks think I'd gone flat loco. Whoo-ee! Branding irons. Reckon someone's fixin' to rustle some cattle and brand 'em for us? Heh, heh."

I chuckled too, more to put him at ease than anything. Then I said, "Banty, just between you and me, I've got my suspicions it may have been that Jimmy Hearne. Might have come around when his ma was still here. Just wanted to stir things up. That boy's got a cocklebur under his saddle blanket about me. Maybe he saw those saddles first time around— figured how he might as well make himself some extra money. That lad has been up to a little bit of no good lately. Last time I saw him, he was dandied up fine, and his duds must of cost a pretty penny."

Banty said, "Why, that worthless black varmint—"

"Don't worry about it, Banty. It'll all come out in the wash. Just let the boys know we got a buzzard feeding on us, and tell them to keep their eyes open. If that boy ain't got no more brains than to come back a third time, let's put some buckshot in his britches."

"Yessir, Mr. McCannon. I surely will. I'll let the boys know too that they're to watch out for the coyote."

I went back to the house, thinking about the puzzle. Who in thunder would want to steal my old branding irons? My cattle, now that was something else again. It wouldn't be anything new at all for someone to steal a cow or two and brand them with his own sign. But stealing my branding irons? All the rest of that day the peculiar incident kept coming to mind.

But finally, at dinner time, with my family snug and warm in the ranch house and yet another snowfall blanketing the earth, I happily dived into a platterful of Mother Johnson's fried chicken. By the time I'd eaten my fill and Caroline and I had played a few games of checkers, I was plumb tuckered out. I stoked up the big old iron furnace in the basement, making sure it had plenty of coal to last till morning. By the time I'd checked all the windows and doors against the storm, my broken ribs were acting up again.

What with one thing then another, by the time Caroline and I hit the hay, I'd pushed the theft clean to the back of my mind.

12

The first blue norther of the winter came raging in the first week of December, blowing in a thick white veil of cold and death.

The cattle had smelled the storm coming all day. I'd ridden down with Banty and Skunkweed to scatter hay throughout the lower meadows, and all the time we were there they pawed at the earth and bawled more than usual, stirred up by the changing winds.

The ranch hands felt the storm coming too, and they busied themselves with odds and ends of work to ease their restlessness. There's always a sense of worry on a cattle ranch when a blizzard is on its way. Anything can happen.

Sure enough, by nightfall the subzero temperature had warmed some, and the winds had whistled in masses of ugly gray clouds that settled low to hide the mountains and even the hill behind us, smothering the land.

We all spent a quiet evening, Caroline and Johnny sitting in a corner under a gas lamp with picture books; Mother Johnson across from them knitting things for the baby; me beside the fireplace with a book on economics that I couldn't keep my mind on. We were all edgy.

But we were ready for the storm. As ready as we could get.

It started with a light snowfall, the flakes floating to the earth delicate-like, fooling us into contentment. By nine, the winds started howling, but no more than we were used to with any good storm. Little Johnny fell asleep in his mother's arms; the three of us grown-ups chatted for a while. Around ten o'clock, the winds were staying steady, and we all decided to go to bed.

I put out the fire in the fireplace and checked the furnace, while Caroline went around turning out the gas lamps.

Then I pulled the curtain back for another look outside. The square of window light showed a heavy wall of snow now. The big old elms in the yard were barely visible, and they were straining with the rising winds.

I stepped into the hallway and opened the door partway to have a look. The wind whipped a miniature blizzard into the hall, stinging my face. Quickly I shut the door.

Inside, the house stayed warm as toast. The storm might have been a thousand miles away except for the ceaseless whining of the wind.

After we'd gone to bed, Caroline went right to sleep, but I lay there in the dark and listened as the storm gathered and groaned. I started thinking about last winter's blizzards and what they'd done to my stock, not to mention all the other misery they'd brought. Cattle had frozen up along the drift fences and in gulches and creek bottoms, people had frozen out on the plains, people who hadn't had a chance against the biting winds that howled across the plains and mountains, those same winds that were wailing and licking around my ranch house right now.

Folks might already be freezing to death out on the plains. The thought sent a chill through me that the winter's cold couldn't match. A man could fight against Indians, gunmen, and outlaws; against hatred and jealousy and just plain stupidity. But the weather? That was the most worrisome thing to any stockman, for it was something that God alone could send or control.

Caroline and I slept close as we lived close, and that old bed was comfortable. Finally the tiredness got the best of my galloping mind. I slept hard, when I finally did sleep.

Around midnight, I woke up with the sudden feeling that something was wrong. I was lying flat on my back, and I was nigh unto paralyzed with foreboding. I couldn't shake it.

The wind had gained more strength. It was howling like a banshee wailing death. Sudden terror jarred me and brought me bolt upright in bed. The darkness of the room was dense and suffocating.

I rolled out of bed so as not to disturb Caroline and crept to the window. The brutal wind was whipping the snow into a whirling white fury, piling up deep drifts between the house and the barn. It was straining and tearing at the windowpane like a hostile demon spirit.

As I stood there, a branch just outside the window cracked with the weight of the wet new snow and fell to earth with a muffled thud.

There was going to be perdition to pay this winter.

I knew then that I had stock dying at that very moment, freezing to death, eyes blinded by the wind-driven snow, nostrils freezing shut so as to cut off their breath, legs collapsed beneath them from sheer exhaustion and the work of plowing through deep drifts toward a shelter they'd never find, the breath choked right out of them.

The worst of it was, there wasn't a blamed thing I could do to change things. I tried to pray, asking the good Lord to keep His hand on my cattle just as He'd kept His hand on King David's sheep. It was a long time before I could fall back asleep.

I awakened again a few hours later to look out the window at a pallid grayness that tried to pass for daybreak. The snow was still falling hard. We had ourselves a full-grown ring-tailed sidewinder of a blizzard.

Throughout the night the wind had lashed at the snow, drifting it up high against the fences and over the porch steps. It sifted under the doorways of the outbuildings, came up flush against the kitchen window in a giant drift, made white mounds of the haystacks, blanketed over the ice atop the creek, and leveled out the gulches and ditches up towards the scrub oak patch back of the barn.

From the kitchen window I could see that the drifts at the back of the smokehouse were especially high from the wind that whipped down and seesawed through the draw between the hills—that same draw that the road threaded through to run back up to the high country towards the Hearne place. The storm had been bad down here in the valley. It was bound to have been a whole lot worse up there, where on occasion the drifts could be as much as fifteen feet deep.

I thought about the Hearnes. It was likely that their little shack was buried plumb to the rafters. I vowed that as soon as I could I'd get up to check on them. Even if I had to snowshoe in to do it.

After a quick breakfast, I went outside. Even though the snow still fell, the boys had been busy. They'd cleared away some of the drifts to make a pathway from the bunkhouse to the barn. Chip Hutton and Al Perkins were whistling cheerfully as they shoveled a footpath to my own back door. They had already shoveled a path to the back house up past the machine shop a ways. They had their four-buckle overshoes snapped to the top and were otherwise bundled up against the cold.

I stopped a minute to jaw about the weather and thank them, then I went on down to the barn. Billy Bailey, Skunkweed, and Banty Brewster were inside, lanterns aglow, pitching hay to the penned-up stock and the milk cows who were in their stanchions on one side. The cows had to be watered, so they'd opened the barn doors and let them out in the corral, where we had watering tanks. Some cattle were drinking their fill and milling around the tanks, but most would soon find their way back into the shelter of the big barn after a short time in the cold.

I was pleased to see that the ranch cows were being tended, but my concerns were still with my range cattle. Only the hardy, native-bred range cattle stood a ghost of a chance in this kind of weather. I'd had enough foresight to bring most of my blooded Eastern stock in to the closest pasture, and when we'd felt the storm brewing I'd had the boys herd as many of them as would fit into the big old barn. The smell of ammonia and cow manure was strong in there. Mixed in was the smell of damp hay and old wood.

As big as that old barn was, it was impossible to make it airtight, and although it was a good deal warmer than it was outside, it was still drafty. But at least it broke the fury of the howling wind. As I moved here and there, trying to make myself generally useful, I kept running afoul of a half dozen cats who'd come in and were waiting for the boys to start milking, for they had picked up the habit of feeding the cats with a saucer or two of warm milk.

I wandered around, looking things over, and stopped short as I recognized a moldy smell. I didn't like that at all. I checked further and found that there was a good-sized wet place in the floor just to the left of the calf pens, near the end of the hayloft staircase. Looked like we had a leak in the roof up there. I hoped it wasn't getting into the haymow and ruining my hay. The Lord knew we had little enough of it under the circumstances. I'd have to get that roof patched up soon as the storm cleared.

I walked from the barn to the bunkhouse, then stopped on the porch to knock the snow from my hat and jacket and to stomp it from my boots. My gloves, jacket—even my Levi's— had caked over with snow just from my short time outside. Then I rapped on the door.

Ledbetter opened it. He was a wiry varmint with a hank of flame-red hair, a whip-thin body, and a hair-trigger temper —or so I'd been told. I'd never seen but the good side of him. He said, "Howdy there, Courtney. Cold enough for ya?"

I shivered and pulled off my gloves. "Plumb miserable."

The smell of frying bacon and fresh coffee came from the cookshack that had been connected to the sleeping quarters. It was spiced up with the smell of tobacco smoke and old leather thongs that the cowboys were using to patch up some bridles and hackamores hanging on the wall. They worked on them in the bunkhouse on stormy days, while they spun their tall tales and lied to each other about their prowess as cowboys and their flattering ways with women. It was a good deal warmer in there than the tack room down at the barn.

I stepped past the bunks and into the cookshack, where Mrs. Nelson had been busy before she'd left. Several of the hands were still eating their breakfast. I moved in close to the stone fireplace, which was packed with logs and full ablaze. I peeled off my gloves, stuck my hands out to the fire, and said, "Mornin', boys. Looks like you're planning to beat the early bird out."

"Ain't got the sense of a game-legged goose," groused Buck Weaver. "Else they'd of all cleared out'n this country afore this snow business began."

Banty and Billy Bailey had come in ahead of me. They had already washed up and were sitting at the long plank table, eating breakfast. Banty swallowed a mouthful of food, then said to Buck, "You could've flew South right along with them magpies, for all it'd matter to the most of us."

I could see that the snow hadn't frozen any vinegar or salt out of my boys.

Ledbetter was sitting back on a kitchen chair near the end of the table, drinking from a hot tin cup of coffee.

I poured one for myself and sat down across from him. I said, "It'll likely be noon or later before the weather breaks."

Banty grunted. "Wind's already easin' off some. Oughta be able to sled some hay down to the west pastures long about noon."

He really cared about the stock. I'd never seen a more gentle man at calving time. Reckon that's one reason that the grizzled little man had always held a special place in my pa's heart, and in mine as well.

"We're bound to have already lost some stock," I said. "You boys be careful—don't want to risk losing a cowhand or two to boot."

"We'd best get some men down right away to bust some watering holes in that river ice," said Ledbetter. He'd been sitting quiet-like, shoveling in grub. I agreed and poured myself another steaming hot cup of coffee.

Billy Bailey was in a grumpy mood. "Blasted dumb cattle. Think they'd be smart enough to do somethin' for themselves."

That brought a few whoops from the boys and some stories about cattle's thickheaded ways.

131

It was true. Range cattle had been known to do some mighty stupid things. On occasion they'd run for miles in a stampede until they were ready to drop. They'd run smack over anything in their way, just because of a lighting bolt and a clap of thunder or a cowboy's hat blowing off in their direction.

They also had a habit of piling up on top of one another at a drift fence in a ground blizzard. They were dumb critters all right, not a smart one in a trainload. Most didn't have the sense that God gave a jackrabbit.

The weather apparently had the boys spunked up, for in general they were cheerful and chuckling and bragging and baiting one another, but I could see beneath it all that they knew they were in for a brutal day's work. When they started pulling on their coats and slickers, I left them, and in the middle of all that boisterousness I forgot to mention the leak in the barn roof.

Before I went back to the house, I checked on all the outbuildings, looking to see if any of the roofs had sagged from the weight of the snow or if any leaks had developed. It was then that I remembered the leak in the barn roof and made a note to mention it to Hank Ledbetter later in the day. He was more or less the ranch's carpenter, and he'd be the one to get a few men together to fix the problem.

After I'd checked back in at the house and told Caroline where I'd be if she needed me, I went over to the stables, saddled up, and rode out with the boys to the watering holes in the river ice. The snow was almost knee deep to my saddle horse on the river bottom. My rib cage was still hurting, and the motion of riding aggravated it some. But I wasn't going to let that stop me from doing my work—though I'll admit it slowed me down a good bit.

It had been a bad storm, though we'd seen worse. Around noon the snow let up some, just as we'd predicted. Enough for us to get enough hayrack loads into the stock pastures, with four head of horses on the sled. I'd been especially worried about these cattle, and it was a relief to be able to get to them and see that they were fed.

The boys kept at it, hauling several loads and scattering hay across the snow and piling it in under the trees. That would hold these particular cattle for a day or so if need be.

The snow died off for only a couple of hours, then started up again. We rode on out to the west pasture in spite of it, to find that some of the weaker and helpless cattle had died in the night's blizzard. Their hides were encrusted with snow and frost where the fierce wind had driven it like buckshot into their sides. It looked as though some of them had suffocated, the fine snow and their breath freezing in their nostrils. Reckon that, with no protection, the poor critters never stood a chance.

We left the dead stock lie where they'd fallen. Ordinarily we'd have taken the hides before the bodies froze, but we wanted to beat the heavy snowfall and the darkness back to the ranch house.

By nightfall we had the better part of three new feet of snow on the level, with drifts as high as ten feet where the wind laid the snow up against the northernmost sides of the buildings. The sled trails to the haystacks were drifted over and would have to be broken out again tomorrow. I figured that by morning we'd be needing six head on an empty sled as opposed to four today, just to open up a trail.

I spent another restless evening, worrying and catnapping, getting up to go to the window every half hour or so, watching the snowfall and pacing. I finally rolled off into a decent sleep along about midnight.

The snow was still falling hard.

13

I woke up just before daylight to find that the winds had carried what was left of the storm on east. The temperature began to drop as the icy cold set in. A few clouds were on the eastern horizon, but with dawn approaching they would soon be gone. The last few stars twinkled in a frigid sky and looked so close that one could almost reach up and grab a handful.

I was the first one up, and the house was quiet. Outside, the world lay white and still. I stood there, chilled in spite of my heavy pajamas and thick wool robe, looking out the bedroom window. The elms, scrub oak, willows, and cottonwoods hung heavy with snow. Snow had filled the creek bed right up to the top of its banks. Except for the willows and a few cottonwood trees at the edges, it was hard to picture a stream buried down there somewhere. I dressed quietly so as to not disturb Caroline, then went down to the kitchen and rustled up some grub. I wanted to get up to the Hearne place first thing in order to see how they'd weathered the storm.

The clouds vanished with sunrise, blown on the wind, and the sky in the east turned from a rose-streaked, dusky purple to a bright crystal blue. The cold had beaded over the top of the snow with a frost that reflected a pale tint of the blue above. The ice crystals mirrored the morning sky almost as if they were made of blue glass.

The winds had scoured the draw between the hills of all but maybe a foot of snow, but when I got up into the high meadows the snow was belly deep. I took my horse back to the ranch, unsaddled him, and put him in the horse barn and pulled his bridle off. I gave him plenty of hay. All of us coddled our saddle horses. They took care of us, and we took care of them. I tied on my snowshoes, packed some supplies on my back, then headed out for the long walk up to the high country, leaving strange tracks sunk down into the fresh snow behind me.

It promised to be a long, hard walk in spite of the fact that I could shave off eight or so miles by avoiding the switchbacks the road took. But hard or not, I had to do it. There was something about Mrs. Hearne and the boy that I'd come to feel real personal about. Looking back, I'd have to say it had mostly to do with my good fortune compared to their own.

And I hated that awful, hangdog-yet-hateful look that Jimmy Hearne wore every time he saw me. Hated the way he covered it up with an arrogant shrug of his shoulders and that cocky attitude of his. Reckon that ate at me too. I felt as if that boy was unfinished business, and I still wanted to right the situation. I'd never felt that much downright sadness for anyone, man or boy, and it puzzled me how I could feel that way about someone who had tried to bushwhack me, who'd shot my best horse, who'd robbed my tack room (I was sure it had been Jimmy), and who'd generally fouled up my life six ways from Sunday. Ain't no accounting for feelings sometimes.

At times, when I'd think about those folks, they'd seem like a case of the itch. Other times, I'd feel as though I wanted to sit them all down and talk some sense into their heads. They had no business up in that mountain meadow in the middle of high winter. Even Old Man Duke—who weathered some mighty bad storms during his trapping days—had his mettle tested past tolerance during the harshest winter months.

I got to thinking about Grisham Duke again while I was walking through the deep snow. He'd been a tough old rooster who had fought the bad parts of nature with all the resources that he had, while he was proving up on his 320 acres of brush and rocks there on the south side of Slide Mountain. Down through the years he'd usually won the poker hand that Nature dealt him, even if it was by a slim margin, right up to the day the snows beat him.

Last winter had topped anything I remembered during Duke's lifetime. Fact was, folks said last winter had matched

135

or beaten anything that had hit these parts for a hundred years or more. This winter promised to be even worse, and now the Hearnes were up there in a place so isolated that even the jackrabbits and bobcats gave it wide berth.

I thought about that shack, about the roof and the teetering stovepipe, and I started walking faster. It suddenly struck me that they might already be buried in snow right up to the roof, and they might not even have the sense to have put in food, firewood, and water so they could weather the storm.

When I topped the ridge, I saw that my fears had been right. The shack was sure enough buried almost to the rafters. But a high pile of stovewood had been put in beside the house and shoveled clean, and smoke was rising from the stovepipe sticking through the slanted roof.

I thanked the good Lord. Maybe I had sized these folks up wrong. The snow around the ramshackle house and barn was pure and glistening in the sunlight, except where a sort of path had been plowed waist-high between the house and the outhouse. They hadn't been up and about much yet. I reckoned that maybe they had the good sense that God gave a gopher after all and had stayed holed up during the blizzard.

I was winded from the cold and from the weight of the heavy pack. I slipped it off, kicked off my snowshoes, and leaned them against the porch as I stopped beside the house to catch my breath. Then I stepped onto that sagging old porch —avoiding the hole that Old Man Hearne had broken through and hadn't bothered to mend—and I rapped smartly on the door.

When Mrs. Hearne opened the door she wore a puzzled expression, as if she couldn't imagine who on earth could be there. The instant she saw me, her face froze in fear. She tried to mask it, but I have to admit that I already knew that I'd made a mistake by coming.

Old Man Hearne stepped up behind her, bringing the reek of stale whiskey with him. He growled out, "McCannon! What in blazes are you doin' here meddlin'? Get on back where you come from, you snoopin' no-good!" He jutted his whiskery jaw out in menace and put a viselike grip on his wife's arm.

I said, "No harm intended. I wanted to check on you, see how you folks weathered the blizzard—"

"You sure got an all-fired interest in my business for some reason," the man muttered. His piggish little eyes were hot with rage.

"Nothing personal. Being neighborly is an old Colorado custom, and most of us in these parts check to see if our neighbors need help from time to time."

I have to admit that, whiskey stench or no, the warmth coming from inside that house felt inviting. In spite of my heavy, fleece-lined boots and the fact that the snowshoes had kept my feet mostly dry, it was a good deal colder up here than down in the valley, and a man could freeze to death with no trouble at all.

But I wasn't about to ask them if I could come in long enough to thaw out. Instead, I just said to the woman, "Caroline sent you a few things, ma'am. There's a quarter of a ham in there and some beefsteaks and some of her canning. She wanted you to have some of those rhubarb preserves you liked so well."

Mrs. Hearne looked ashamed of herself. She forced a smile to her face. Graciously she stepped forward to take the pack and said, "Why, thank you, Mr. McCan—" but Hearne yanked her arm hard, slinging her back into the room. He slammed the door shut so hard that snow avalanched down from the eaves and dusted me good.

I brushed the snow from my shoulders, took off my hat, and slapped it against my leg until it was clear of snow too, then I brushed off my pants and boots.

I was concerned about Mrs. Hearne and Bobby. They were having a hard enough time of it without having to do without food, and if it was left up to Old Man Hearne, I had a feeling they'd be having corn liquor for breakfast and bruises for supper all winter long. I left the sack of goods on the front porch, strapped on my snowshoes and pack again, then turned and sloughed back up the hill.

Once I topped the ridge, I took a few steps down the other side, then turned back so that I could see back down to the homestead without their seeing me. I reckon it was no more than five minutes before Mrs. Hearne came outside, picked up the gunnysack of goods I'd left there, and took it inside. That warmed me some. I turned and made the long, cold trek back down to the ranch.

It stayed cold for several days. The snow drifted and packed down hard on the roads and sled trails, such as they were. Three days after the blizzard, Tom Owens out of Hayden and some of the other mule skinners from the stage and freight stations hitched up three span of their big workhorses to their heavy wooden A-frame snowplows, took along their shovels, and reopened the main roads between Hahns Peak, Hayden, and Windsor.

On the third day after the stage started running again, about noon, Caroline called me out of my study and to the upstairs hall window. "Look, Court." She was nigh unto dancing with excitement. "I swear, if that isn't the strangest thing!"

The stage had pulled off the Yampa River road and onto our own snow-packed lane. It was a Concord, pulled by a feisty, high-stepping team of carriage horses. The luggage rack held two long sleigh runners, bound on and ready for attachment to the wheels should the snow set in quick. For the moment the wheels were unencumbered, turning on the packed snow, the two smaller in front and the large ones in back holding the compartment and the rear boot. The curtains in the passenger compartment were drawn open, telling me there was at least one passenger aboard.

As the stage drew closer, I recognized the driver in spite of his dark blue muffler and flop-eared cap. It was Rupert Harris, the stage driver out of Hayden. He had an old threadbare buffalo robe draped around his lap, and he looked plumb miserable from the cold.

We watched until the Concord was almost under the portico at the front of the house, then we ran downstairs and out onto the front porch. Mother Johnson and Johnny were already there.

As the stage drew to a halt, the door to the compartment opened timidly, then opened wider. A head with a gray Stetson popped out, the muffler around the neck a bright red tartan, and out stepped Judge Warren, sleek and silvered as you please in a pair of polished black boots and a heavy black dress coat. He was tall and lean, with a healthy silver mustache and a thick frost of hair that put me in mind of that writer whose picture and stories appeared some in the *Saturday Evening Post*—man named Mark Twain.

We were pleased and surprised all at once.

Rupert turned the stage and went on down to the bunkhouse to jaw with Banty and the boys, seeing as how they were all old friends, plus he needed to feed, water, and thaw out his horses.

Caroline and I pulled the judge inside the house, both of us talking all at once. Then, since it was close to noon, she set another plate, and we all sat down to a hearty midday meal.

Judge Warren told us a speck about his travels in Denver as we were eating, though he was careful to avoid the grisly matters dealing with the Packer trial itself. About halfway through the meal, he turned the talk to the telegram I'd sent to him at the Palace Hotel.

He said, "You know, Court, I had serious reservations about that lawyer Schell from the moment I first laid eyes on him." The judge was talking between bites of Mother Johnson's fried chicken. "He was just a bit too self-important for my taste, but I was in such a hurry to get over to Denver for the Packer trial, and Senator Brown had recommended him so highly—well, nothing much has happened around here for such a very long time, and I suppose I just figured that even if he wasn't right for the job, nothing would happen to test him. Looks like I should have followed my own judgment."

I was pleased to hear that he still had the good sense I knew him for. I said, "I reckon what's done is done. No one could have foreseen it."

He swallowed a hunk of mashed potatoes, then smiled warmly and said, "All the same, I wanted you to know that I sent Schell packing, and I plan to make it a point to let my colleagues on the bench know of his incompetence. A man who won't listen equally to both sides of an issue has no business being in the profession of law and certainly has no business acting as a judge."

I nodded, pleased. "Reckon that's the smartest thing you could have done. What about Yampawah? Is there a warrant out for his arrest?"

"Heaven bless us, no. Schell didn't even bother to draw up the papers." He frowned. "You know, Court, I'm not really sure how to go about straightening this matter out so nothing comes back on Yampawah and his folks. Seems like the story has gotten around the county some—of what happened up there. But I give you my word, I'll do something to see that the truth is told."

Caroline said, "Judge Warren, you haven't told us yet how your trials in Denver turned out."

He said, "Well, I wouldn't have missed it for all the world. The Packer trial didn't last all that long. Convicted him, I guess you heard, and left me with a passel of nightmares that still wake me up from time to time. Cannibalism isn't something we like to think our fellow man is capable of, if you'll pardon me for bringing up such an ugly topic in such pretty company as you ladies here.

"But tell you the truth, it was the second trial that mattered to me. The trial of Wolfram Carter, an Indian agent over on the east slope. That was a very important piece of litigation."

I said, "We read a bit about it in the *Rocky Mountain News*, though the news itself was a bit old by the time we got it. A Cheyenne by the name of Spotted Hands knifed him, wasn't that it?"

"Not quite," said the judge. "Spotted Hands claimed that the agent had been stealing the annuity goods from his tribe. Most of the Indians were passive about what was going on, but it seems that Spotted Hands's mother was ill and she died because of a lack of food. It set the Indian off. He took after Carter with a tomahawk, and Carter beat the man to a bloody pulp. Spotted Hands got his hands on a gun and went back and killed Carter in cold blood."

Mother Johnson said, "My, my."

I said, "The court found the Indian guilty?"

"Of course. He was guilty. Of murder. That wasn't the point as far as I was concerned. I was interested in the litigation because the agent seemed to have been lining his own pockets with the profits he was making from resale of the goods that rightfully belonged to the Indians. I didn't get involved in the trial expecting to get Spotted Hands off. Cold-blooded murder is never justified, and any man who resorts to such a way of settling his problems is likely to do the same thing again. No, the reason I got involved was to pry open the can of worms that keeps some of the Indian agents fat as river leeches, and the Carter trial surely did pry open that can."

"It is a disgrace," commented Caroline.

The judge dabbed politely at his mouth with one of our best linen napkins, then smiled. "I succeeded in my goal. I'm pleased to tell you that I've persuaded the governor to begin a full-scale investigation of the misappropriation of goods allocated to the reservations, and we expect that the investigation will extend all the way to the federal level."

"That's good news for sure, Judge," I commented. "But it may be happening a bit too late to do much good for the White River Utes—at least this year."

"Indeed?"

"Yessir. Chief Yampawah told me his people are in right bad shape—and mostly from depending on the government to keep their promises. Most of their supplies haven't showed up. A lot of it is still stashed in warehouses by the Union Pacific tracks up in Rawlins, for whatever reason only the good Lord knows. And I don't need to tell you how little wild game there is to be had in these parts after last winter's blizzards and the summer's droughts. Things are a good deal worse down their way, I'm told, or at least they were till the snow came. Now, I reckon things are about equally bad for them everywhere."

The judge looked sharply at me and clenched his jaw, his thin neck drawing taut for a moment at the strain. Then he said, "Court, just between you and me, do you believe there could be any truth to the rumor that Yampawah and his clan have been rustling cattle?"

I shook my head slowly, thinking, making sure of my answer. Then I replied, "Judge, I don't know about Yampawah himself, but I do know that the Utes out west have helped themselves to any stray cattle they could find ever since they've been on the reservation. But generally they've been smart enough to stick to unbranded stock, mavericks mostly. I'd hesitate to outright accuse them of rustling."

It was true. A good number of cattle always strayed away before anybody could put a brand on 'em. The ranchers hadn't liked losing cattle that way, but they hadn't gotten winded up about it either until the winter die-off and summer's drought had left them in such bad shape. Now, with every head of cattle being watched, there was trouble brewing.

We got word of it all the time. The ranchers that rode to Windsor or up to Hayden for supplies talked of little else, and they seemed open to following Skettering's lead: that is, they already tended to blame the Indians for everything bad that was happening to them, including the weather, when they could think of a way to do it.

The judge looked at me measuredly and said, "What about up here in the Yampa Valley, Court? I mean, specifically, what about the rumors that Yampawah and his band really were taking cattle from Moses Skettering? Could that have been the true reason those men were bothering the squaws?"

I weighed my words carefully. Doc Clayton had told me that Senator Brown had an interest in Skettering's ranch, and I have to admit I was thinking about how badly the judge seemed to need Brown's nomination for the state legislature if he was going to win the office. Reckon I was trying to figure if that nomination would mean enough to the judge to get him to bend toward Coogan's lies in order to please Skettering and Brown.

I said, "In the first place, Judge, even if the Indians were rustling, those men had no right to take it out on the squaws."

"True. True indeed."

"In the second instance, I'm going to have to say no. I asked Yampawah to his face if he'd been rustling beef. He told me he hadn't, and I believe him."

The judge looked displeased. "I have to remind you that once a pact's been broken, a lie isn't a moral wrong to an Indian. To their minds we've broken all the pacts we've made with them since Colorado was a territory, except for a few minor ones. Are you absolutely certain that Yampawah is telling you the truth about this?"

I was beginning to feel a mite irritated at this cross-examination. I reckon I let it show when I said, "Yes, Judge, I am sure I believe him. Can't imagine why I'd of said I was if I wasn't."

He held his hand up as if to stop me. "All right, Court, all right." He looked old at that moment and deeply worried. "It's just that I've been around so many bald-faced liars these past few weeks—I apologize for doubting your word. But you see, it's vitally important that my report be accurate."

"Report?"

"Oh, yes, Court, I forgot to mention that. I've asked the Bureau of Indian Affairs to send an investigator up here to help straighten out this business between Skettering's men and Yampawah's band. That seems to me to be a good first step toward getting this trouble straightened out. But I have to prepare a document for the request, and it's mighty important that it be exactly correct." His blue eyes twinkled. "Guess you could say I'm staking my future on your word. I can't imagine you being so testy as to not let me satisfy myself that you're not mistaken."

"Fair enough," I said. "Reckon I just figured that you and Sheriff Finsand—"

"Sheriff Finsand is about as worthless a lawman as ever was born. Not that it mattered for more years than I'd care to count. But with this trouble brewing now, we need someone with some ability and courage—and, not to sound immodest, mind you, I'm a bit too old for the job myself." He smiled. "Don't suppose you'd care to take it on?"

"Thank you kindly, Judge, but I'd just as soon hand wrestle a couple hundred grizzly bear."

"Well then, I expect the best way to clear this matter up is to have an investigator from the BIA come up here and look into things, since you don't want the job, Finsand can't handle the job, and I'm too old to be riding around the county asking all the varmints questions."

"Makes sense to me."

"But I'll tell you one thing right now, Court. I truly am sticking my neck out pretty far on this matter."

"How so?"

"Well, it's nip and tuck right now as to whether or not I get the nomination for the seat in the legislature. I need the help of the faction that Brown controls to make it, and I don't mind telling you I want that seat badly. I think day and night of how much good could be done from there."

I have to admit it made me feel a heap better to hear him come right out and say it. All my misgivings about him went up in smoke right then.

"Brown and his cohorts are opposed to the BIA controlling the Indians' affairs. They want the federal government out, which could be a very good thing except that the BIA has started trying to clean up its affairs of late. Brown and his colleagues are preparing a bill right now that would allow the states and the territories to govern the Indian affairs," the judge went on. "They aren't going to be pleased that I've called the BIA in on anything. And especially not into a matter that concerns Moses Skettering. Were you aware that Brown is a major shareholder in Skettering's ranch?"

"Yessir, I had heard that. But I don't reckon you might have so much trouble with Brown as you may think, Judge. When he finds out what Skettering's been up to, it may put the shoe on the other foot."

It was the judge's turn to be surprised as I told him all that Doc Clayton had told me, though I was careful not to tell the judge where I'd got my information. I figured I'd mention to Doc Clayton that I'd jawed about the matter with the judge, and then if the doc wanted to tell him more—such as where his information had come from—then it was up to him. I told the judge of the speculations that Skettering had padded his stock tallies in order to get Brown and the others to invest in the ranch in the first place.

When I'd finished, the judge was troubled. He said, "That does indeed put a different color on things, doesn't it?"

We'd finished our meal, and the judge and I were drinking coffee. Caroline and Mother Johnson were whisking away the dinner plates.

Now Mother Johnson said, "Surely you men have had enough of these problems for one day. Land-o-Goshen, you see each other about five full days out of the year, and all you do is talk about troubles, and those of other people at that! Now, Judge, I've been baking apple pies. Would you like a slice for dessert?"

Smiling, the judge said, "Two slices, ma'am, and two more to take home, if you don't mind. I can still taste those pies I judged last year at the county fair, and I was proud to hand you that blue ribbon."

"Just don't you worry," Mother Johnson said, as she picked up the near-empty chicken platter. "I've baked six whole pies, and I'd be pleased to send two of them up to Hahns Peak, just to prove that the blue ribbon was no mistake. Plus I'd like to show the folks in the county seat that I'm still in the running for the blue ribbon at next year's county fair."

"I expect you'll have to send up more than one or two pies if you plan for me to share them," the judge said. "I do believe that four whole pies would just make one good meal for my good wife and me, and I thank you kindly for the chance to tote them home."

That took the serious tone out of our conversation. The judge and I polished off some pie, then went into my study to drink more coffee and jaw about less edgy topics such as finances, and the cattle market, and other general matters that were troubling everyone in northwestern Colorado that year.

The judge stayed the night with us, and we talked long into the wee hours, catching up on everything. Rupert Harris put his horses in the barn and spent his own night in the bunkhouse, and I heard the boys jawing and laughing right up till I went to sleep.

Come morning, the two of them headed back up the freight road to Hayden, where the judge would transfer to another stage on to Hahns Peak. He left me a sight more peaceful-feeling than he'd found me, for I knew that whatever happened in Routt County would at least be handled in a decent and just fashion now that he was back.

Reckon I still hadn't quite figured out just how deep evil was already taking root. Nor had I accepted the fact that I was soon going to have to take a personal stand if it was ever to be rooted out. As I said, I still had a lot to learn back then. There was far worse yet to come.

14

The ranch kept my hands and me busy for a good long while, and I didn't get into Windsor again for nigh unto a month. The day the trouble started up again, I'd gone into town to pick up a wagonload of sacked oats and corn that I'd ordered a good three months before. Zebulon Tucker had sent word that it had finally been freighted down from the railroad depot at Rawlins.

I'd worked since sunup, then rode into town midafternoon. By the time I got there I was plumb hungry, so in spite of having to listen to Shorty Musket's poisonous tongue, I made my usual stop at the Elkhorn Hotel for some grub. Now I was sitting at the bar, polishing off a beefsteak and some hot biscuits and gravy.

Shorty was his usual talkative self, and he was no more pleasant than he'd been the last couple of times I'd been in. I reckon he didn't have to be, since this was the only place a man could get a square meal after a hard ride. And then there was the fact that he treated everybody the same—poorly—which meant he was as cantankerous to everybody else as he was to me. Reckon that fact made it a might easier to take him in stride.

He'd sidled up to me, and now he said, "Heared that worthless old Injun thief you call a friend is back in these parts."

That perked up my interest. "That right?"

Shorty was pleased at being able to get a reaction from me. With apparent relish, he licked his lips and said, "Sure is. One of Skettering's hands was in town yesterday. Said Skettering lost him some more beeves and found him some more Indian sign where they'd been butchered. Other feller said he'd talked to a couple of ranchers from down around

Lay, and they said Yampawah's consarned clan was headed back up here to the Yampa River Valley."

I said, "Did you hear how things are out west of Lay? They been having any more Indian trouble down that way, or down in Brown's Park?"

Shorty grinned importantly. "Plenty. Leastwise they been losin' cattle, whether or not to Injuns no one's for sure. You ask me, though, I'd say it's the redskins. Pretty near always is."

That was plumb bad news. The winter die-off from the first hard blizzard had been as high as we'd expected—nigh unto 10 percent. The weakest ones and the oldest ones had been hit hardest, to be sure, but still it was a heavy kill, and the hardest part of winter was still ahead of us. Tempers were short. More than one rancher was looking at going bust. It was a poor time for anyone to be rustling cattle or even having a reputation for it.

Shorty could see that his news bothered me. He swiped at a glass, a sly little smile crossing his face. Seemed he'd just finished his lunch before I came in, because he turned around to the backbar and picked up a few milk-white dishes and a fluted green glass bowl that was still half full of mashed potatoes and carried them all down to the end of the bar and shoved them through the window that opened into Mrs. Starr's tidy kitchen.

When he'd thumped his way back to me, he poured himself a whiskey, refilled my coffee cup, and said real friendly-like, "Mark my words, when the snow clears come spring and the blue stem sprouts again so's there's somethin' out there worth fightin' for besides the snow, there's going to be trouble all over these parts. Wouldn't surprise me a whit if'n we had an out-'n'-out range war."

I downed my coffee, then spoke. "Well, Shorty, I sure hope you're wrong. I'm praying that by then the trouble's all straightened out." I flipped him a half eagle, which he caught, bit on, and put in his pocket. Then I headed out the door for the Tucker store.

Zebulon Tucker had my buckboard loaded with my order and was busy piling some two dozen feed sacks atop one another when I went in. He walked back behind his counter and said, "How-de-do, Mr. McCannon. Nice weather we been having, hey?"

"That melt-off was a godsend," I agreed.

The Chinook had surprised us all by arriving not long after the last big snowstorm. Its warm winds melted most of the snow right off my land at the Elkhead River delta, opening up several miles of good, clear grazing land. If it snowed again I'd still be in trouble, but at least I'd had a small reprieve. "Come the next snow, I'm still going to be running short of feed again," I said. "I'd like to put in an order for as many more sacks as you can get freighted in."

"You and every other rancher around here, hey? Had two ranchers try to buy your feed right out from under me already. Truth is, Courtney, I've run short, and the driver down from Rawlins on this last wagon told me the oats and corn over on the plains are close to sold out already. Guess you picked the right time to stock up, hey?"

"Reckon you're right. When the weather turns bad again we're all going to have trouble keeping the stock fed."

"Well, you're welcome to whatever extra feed I got in stock, though it ain't more than these two dozen sacks. Got to take good care of our best customers, hey?"

I paid him for another order of sacked oats and corn, and told him I might pick up the two dozen he had on hand as well. I pretty much had my buckboard full, but I planned to send Banty or Skunkweed in to pick them up the next day if he still had them. I bought a few sacks of potatoes for the kitchen, so we could save the ones in the root cellar for when we couldn't get to town. Then I loaded a few other supplies on top of my overloaded wagon, jawed with Zeb for a mite longer about the shortages of feed, then I told him it was time for me to head on back to the ranch.

I'd just turned and started to open the door when I

glanced through his window. What I saw outside pulled me up short.

Skettering and Coogan had just ridden up and dismounted. They'd thrown their reins across the hitching post. Skettering was talking to Coogan as the blond-haired squaw baiter called Bowles pulled up beside them, driving a good-sized wagon.

I watched them through the window for a minute, Zeb standing behind me curiously polite. I could see why folks said Skettering was a soured and bitter man. If ever a man's appearance showed what he was inside, this one's did.

He wore black. I'd never seen him in anything else. As I watched, he pulled off that black Stetson and raked his fingers through his gray-shot black hair. I could see his eyes then. Flinty as usual, hard and dead. He started up the three short steps with that bandy-legged gait of his.

I pushed open the door and met him on the porch, saying, "Howdy, Skettering."

I'd surprised him. He stopped in his tracks for a moment, then he growled a greeting. "McCannon." He nodded curtly.

Coogan came right behind him, and though he seemed sober for once, I didn't bother speaking to him.

The varmint barreled up in front of me and stopped, looking right up into my face. "You too good to talk to the likes of me, Mr. Muckety-Muck?"

I said, "Howdy, Coogan. Now let me pass."

"Not likely," he said. He was itching for a fight again. His whipping over at Shorty's must have been eating at him some, and it hadn't taught him a confounded thing.

Easy-like I said, "Reckon I was wrong not to say hello. Now let me pass."

Coogan started to speak, but Skettering cut him off. "Let him go, Coogan."

Coogan stepped aside.

I said, "Thank you, Mr. Skettering. I surely appreciate the help." I moved on down to my buckboard.

But Skettering turned as he opened the door and shot back at me, "My men don't take no truck with any Injun lover, and I don't need one sidewinding up to me, neither. Just stay out of our way next time."

"Reckon I'll just do that," I said pleasantly. I turned to Coogan, then to Bowles, who was still sitting in the wagon seat. "Good day, boys."

They all stayed frozen in place and scowling like a bunch of skunks caught stealing eggs in the chicken house.

I climbed onto my wagon seat, picked up the lines, and shook them. The horses strained at the tugs, then we were off, me expecting trouble at any moment.

But as we turned the corner and headed toward the stage road, I looked back and saw that Coogan and Bowles had started to load feed sacks into their wagon, while Skettering was walking toward the Elkhorn Hotel and Saloon. I figured they'd bought up the other two dozen sacks from Tucker, and they were welcome to them. The Lord knew I had enough to last me if the freight came in on time, and since I'd driven off with a full buckboardload of grain, it was just as well that some was left for them, considering their miserable dispositions.

By the time I'd reached the river, it was coming on toward evening. The day's sunshine had thawed the top layer of the river ice. The smooth, cold water reflected the barren cottonwood trees along the bank and the rare blue sky above. The evening was crisp and clear, and the air was so pure and cold that it hurt my lungs to breathe. I pulled my scarf up over my mouth and nose.

Some five miles to the east of town I came to the place where Elkhead Creek ran into the Yampa River and formed a wide meadow. This rich, sweet grassland was the start of my winter range, and this was where the Chinooks had ridden through and melted the heaviest snow off my rangeland. From here on, the stage road passed through my land, and it was just some four to five miles past here that I'd come across Skettering's cowhands hurrahing the squaws.

I slapped the lines against the flanks of my horses and pushed them a little faster. It was coming on nightfall, and I was still a good ten miles from the ranch house. But the night was going to be a clear one, and the moon would be three-quarters—enough light to ride by if need be.

My main concern was with the growing cold. It was seeping into my boots, and my fingertips were numb in my gloves. The scarf around my nose was beginning to frost over from my breath.

I passed Skettering's cattle on the west side of the Elkhead River and north of the Yampa, just off my range and where he'd planted them for the winter. I crossed over the old cottonwood log bridge and rode another quarter mile. Then I topped a small rise and saw some unexpected cattle on my rangeland.

That surprised me. Then I figured that Banty and the boys had maybe second-guessed me and moved the cattle down here while I was in town. But I'd only passed about half the herd when something began to trouble me. I pulled in on the lines with a soft, "Whoa," and stopped the wagon.

I climbed out.

The Chinook winds hadn't been quite so generous here, and the snow was still packed a good deal. There was a bit of straw-colored grass poking through the snow where the cattle had taken up shelter, and the frozen trickle of a stream ran down the creek from the north.

What concerned me was that nobody had gone to the trouble of chopping it free of ice so the cattle could drink. That would have been a whole lot better than their eating snow, and if Banty had herded my cattle down here, that's the first thing he would have thought to do.

That riled me some. I walked over closer so that I was near enough to see the brands, and suddenly none of the whole thing made a bit of sense.

The brands were dirty.

The brand beneath was Skettering's M-Slash-S, while branded over the top of it was my own brand, the Lazy Double C. And beside that, the branding had been done so poorly that even an Eastern schoolboy who'd never seen the back end of a cow could have done a better job. It was about the most despicable brand of counterfeiting I had ever seen as a cowman, and not even a fool would have believed these were my cattle.

I stood there, my breath making smoke in the cold air, while I tried to figure it all out.

No way around it, these were Skettering's cattle. But why in thunder were they wearing my brand? And what the blue blazes were they doing this far east—on my range?

Was I looking at the work of another rustler?

But if a rustler had done this, why were the cattle left so that anyone who came by could see them from the road?

Then I glimpsed a flash from the corner of my eye, a glint of fading western sunlight on a rifle barrel.

I hit the snow just as a shot rang out, but I was cold, my reflexes were numbed, and a bullet drilled through my left shoulder, paralyzing my arm as if I'd been clubbed with a chunk of stovewood. I grabbed the shoulder, felt warmth gushing from a wound beneath my hand. I yanked my hand away. Blood spurted and poured down the inside of my shirt and out beneath my cowhide coat, clean into the snow where I lay. The bullet had torn a sizable chunk out of me.

Right atop the numbness, the pain seared through me like a hot poker. But I managed to keep my head. I flexed my right hand to make sure it worked, then pulled out my Colt. My hand slipped on the six-gun grips, which were slick and wet with blood. I wiped it clean on the snow, swiped it across my Levi's to dry it, then rolled over on one knee, pulled the hammer back, and brought it up to fire, though I was aware that a good enough time had passed since the bullet had hit me for the shooter to get away. Everything was moving slow, seeming about to wind to a stop. All the same, I brought up the gun, not even knowing where to shoot.

Suddenly there was a dark blur against the fading sun, a quick movement on the ridge above and north of me. I aimed at the movement and fired just as I heard a rifle's report. Snow flew up in a small geyser not six inches from me.

A loud, shrill whinny came from a thick copse of trees right beside me, startling me into rolling in that direction, gun in hand, expecting to face a second enemy. A horse stood there in the trees, tethered to a willow, all saddled up and ready to ride, but there was no rider.

I had gooseflesh all over me that had nothing to do with the cold. Though the horse wasn't a sorrel, it seemed to me that I'd gone through an experience enough similar to stand my teeth on edge. I was thinking that I'd been bushwhacked again by Jimmy Hearne, only this time he was bound to finish the job. I waited, torn between using my good hand to stop the blood flow and using it to hang onto the gun I needed if I was going to defend myself.

There was no motion except the horse's uneasy shifting, no noise except its nervous blowing. It had to belong to whoever was up there on that ridge.

That made sense. My arm still throbbed, but my mind had cleared some, and I could think well enough to figure that whoever it was must have been busy down here when he saw me coming. If he'd ridden that horse up the ridge, I'd have spotted him for sure. So he must have gone on foot, snaking up like a weasel along a rocky outcropping that jutted out a ways past the trees.

The wind had drifted the snow into a three-foot bank on my side of the stream. It was getting darker, and the moon was already high in the sky. I jackknifed over behind the snowbank just as a third shot sprayed snow where I'd been. Rifle fire echoed through the quiet valley. I got off another shot in the general direction of where the gunfire was coming from, but I was losing a lot of blood and feeling hazier by the minute. My Colt was no match for his rifle—I doubt if any of my shots reached halfway to him.

I had to get out of there.

But how?

Only one way. I had to get to that horse. I said a prayer. *Please, Lord, just let me live, oh, please, dear Lord . . .*

I desperately needed my .30/06, but it was still on the buckboard under the seat, and the team of horses, spooked by the racket of the gunfire, had run on down the road. I could see them in the distance, heading up the river road slow now, plodding along, though I expected their pace might pick up if there was any more gunplay.

I thought about my supplies in the back and worried that they'd bolt and spill the wagon, breaking open the sacks and spilling my winter feed. I doubted if they would run too far with that load, and I hoped that they would turn into the lane when they got to the ranch, as they always did. And even as I was thinking these thoughts they seemed foolish, as if some dark part of my mind was telling me not to care, that it was over and I didn't have to worry about making it through the winter after all.

I prayed that someone would come looking for me, if I was unable to get to the saddle horse. I was just far enough from home and hurt enough that it was unlikely I'd make it any other way.

The sun was far below the western horizon, and night was coming on hard and cold and fast, and it seemed a good deal darker than it should have been, what with that big shining three-quarter moon. The shadows were as long as they were going to get before the whole world turned dark, and I took full advantage of them.

I pulled myself along behind the snowbank, the pain in my shoulder taking my breath each time I moved, but then I'd made it! I was there in the trees, the horse right beside me, blowing and snorting and letting me know that he smelled my blood and didn't like it a bit.

I touched his side with my right hand, and he trembled with fear. But he was a well-trained horse, a bay with white stockings. He stayed still as a fence post when I'd finally pulled myself up, using first the stirrup then the saddle as handles. With my right hand I finally grabbed the saddle horn and lifted my foot into the stirrup. Then, with pain shooting through my left shoulder as though a bucket of hot lead had been poured on me, I swung up into the saddle.

I felt more blood trickling down through my long handles and onto my side. It took me a few minutes to clear my head and catch my breath from the climb up, but I managed to keep from blacking out. The blood had soaked my shirt through, and I felt it trickling down my side beneath my long handles. The instant the pain eased off the slightest bit, I reined the horse to the left and toward the road.

There was the thunderclap of another shot as we cleared the trees, but it was dark now, and the bushwhacker must have been aiming at only a rough target, because his shot was far wide of the mark. But it caused the horse to pitch and run, stumbling through the heavy, crusted snow where the wind had blown it into three-foot banks, running nonetheless, while another rifle shot hit wide of us.

I couldn't see clearly by then. I couldn't think. I gave the horse his head because I had to, I couldn't grip the reins tight enough to turn him. He took his head, lurching, then breaking into a dead run as another shot grazed his haunches.

That horse saved my life. It scrambled through a ditch, floundering in the snow, then we were up and on the other side, on the snow-packed stage road, passing my team and wagon, who were by then winded and in a steady trot. The horse was flying like the wind, as if the imps of hell were biting at his heels.

I kept the reins loose and hung onto the saddle horn with every mite of my dying strength, for I knew that if I fell from the saddle I would be as good as dead. Nobody was going to find me in time to save my life, for I was bound to either bleed or freeze to death long before sunup, and there was no guarantee my team on the buckboard would even find their way home.

The horse had a smooth gait, but still every time his hooves pounded the ground I felt agonizing pain tear at my shoulder so bad that I nearly passed out.

Then, as if a fog or a dream had swallowed me, I saw the lights of the ranch buildings ahead. I tried to call out, but there was no one there to call out to, and I couldn't make my voice work. My strength was gone. Everything was going dark—even the moon was swallowed up by darkness. A thick, heavy curtain seemed to be dropping around me.

With my last bit of strength, I neck-reined the horse, and he turned from the stage road into the lane. An eighth of a mile, then there it was at last—the house. The steps. And I was falling out of the saddle, hitting the snow-packed ground. The fiery pain in my shoulder flared up again, and there was a new pain, down low in my leg.

And then there was nothing left in the moon-filled, snow-filled night but the harsh sound of my own breathing. No feeling left but the searing, terrible pain.

The house loomed huge and cold above me, the few lights in its windows shining out to a cold world that in those moments was as far away from me as heaven seemed to be.

And then I was clawing my way up the steps onto the front porch, trying to call out for help but too weak to make a sound.

Dimly I heard voices inside and Little Johnny laughing at something. Then a distorted voice said, "Hush! Wait a minute. I thought I heard something . . ."

I heard Caroline say, "Oh, Mother, really, you're just imagining things."

"No, I'm sure I heard something—"

And then the door swung open, and Caroline stood there wreathed in light, a puzzled expression on her face as she stared out into the night.

I tried to say her name, but all that came out was a whisper as quiet as a child's breath.

But it was enough.

She looked down, and I'll never for the rest of my life forget the expression on her face as she saw me. Her hand flew to her mouth, stifling a scream, and she froze for an instant, then sobbed, "Court, oh, please, dear God, Courtney!" Then she wailed, "Help me, please, somebody—"

And I folded into the darkness and let the cold swallow me up.

15

Slowly I mended. By Christmas Eve I managed to help Caroline, Mother Johnson, and Johnny put the finishing touches on the tree, though I was still more than a mite stoved up. It hadn't helped matters that I'd broken my ankle when I fell from the saddle the night I was shot. My foot caught in the stirrup and twisted half off.

The Christmas tree was a fine ten-foot spruce, sledded in from the high country by my cowhands. It just barely fit in under the vaulted ceiling of our living room. It irritated me no end that I hadn't been able to take my family out to cut it.

I'd been mostly housebound since the shooting and restless as a flea on a hot griddle. Doc Clayton had ridden out the day after I'd been bushwhacked. He found that the bullet had drilled into my left shoulder all right, but it had slanted down to within a half inch of my heart and gone out my back and had done some powerful damage to my muscles—which was why it had more or less paralyzed me and why he ordered me to rest and recuperate instead of doing my fair share of the ranch work.

The paralysis was gone by the holiday, but my arm was still in a sling, and I was still half using a crutch to get around. I was clumsy as a newborn calf. But though I wasn't up to snuff, at least I was alive and with my family. We all thanked the good Lord for that.

My ma had furnished the parlor in satinwood Hepplewhite, and Caroline and Mother Johnson polished it for the holidays until it shone like glass in the light from the stone walk-in fireplace. The brass drawer handles on the chiffonier gleamed gold, as did the brass andirons and fire screen. The tall arched windows with their blue-bunting draperies framed the moonlit snowy night, while the lights from the bunkhouse and foreman's two-story home glowed warm in the background.

The boys had put up their own tree down in the bunkhouse, and I reckon they had a card game going or a tall-tale shindig in the works. Ledbetter and his wife and young'uns had their own tree too and had planned a meal for tomorrow that included her family from Hayden and anyone else who cared to show up. We were invited as well.

Yet for all the holiday joy, there was still a nip in the wind. I'd managed to tell Caroline some of what had happened before I plumb passed out the night I was shot. The day after, Ledbetter, Banty, and some other boys rose at daybreak to cut sign on the bushwhacker who'd drilled me.

They'd been up half the night unloading and storing the feed, for my team had brought the wagon up the lane to the barn not long after my borrowed horse carried me to the doorstep. The boys had tended to the animal, and it was down in the pole corral this very minute, while we decided just how and if it was to be returned.

And when I'd awakened late the next day to the doc's ministrations, I'd been pleased to learn that every single sack of feed grain had been tied right where Zeb Tucker had placed it, with nothing at all disturbed.

I also learned what the boys had found out. Seems that two horses had arrived at the spot where I'd been bushwhacked, but the boys managed to track only one lone horse north toward Skettering's ranch. Then the rider had cut west onto the stage-freight road that leads north to Rawlins. They'd lost him. Since I took one horse, that more or less proved that there were two men involved in the ambush.

The boys conjectured that after the riders had lost a horse to me, they rode double on the way back from Elkhead Creek to wherever they were headed. The deep cut of the tracks in the snow bolstered the suspicion that two had been mounted on the same poor steed.

The brand on the horse I'd borrowed was a registered brand from up in Wyoming, and some tracing showed that the brand belonged to the Swan Land & Cattle Company. That really didn't mean too much, for Skettering's men had horses with brands from all over the country, as did Ora Haley's riders and a dozen owlhoots who came and went. Folks bought and traded horses all the time, and many didn't bother to change the brands for a good long time if at all, so long as they had the papers to prove who rightly owned them.

Banty and Ledbetter found the cattle with the dirty brands right where I'd last seen them. They herded them back onto Skettering's valley rangeland, then Banty and Chip Hutton rode all the way north to Skettering's ranch to tell him that some varmint had branded his cattle over with my brand and then moved them onto my land.

The boys said he acted as if he thought they were all bald-faced liars or worse, and they grumbled about it for days, plumb sorry that they'd gone to all the trouble—though to tell the truth, they had in mind a chance to look him over too, or I reckon they truly wouldn't have bothered.

Doc Clayton spent a good deal of time with me while I was stoved up. Ledbetter was in and out too. He told me one thing that he'd kept to himself, and it plumb puzzled me: in addition to the horse that had carried the riders away, he'd found tracks from unshod ponies near where I'd come across the cattle. Said he knew that Yampawah and his band wouldn't have bushwhacked me, but he was speculating on whether or not there might be other Utes hunting up here.

I did some thinking before I told him it was unlikely. If there were Utes other than Yampawah and his clan around, surely someone would have seen them, and no one had said a word.

Still, we all had different suspicions as to who had ambushed me and why. Banty said it was Coogan, getting even. I couldn't see it, though, as he'd been in town when I'd left, and what with the heavy snow cover he couldn't have cut cross-country to beat me to the meadow.

As for me, I had my suspicions about that Hearne boy, but I didn't voice them to a soul. And that didn't rightly make

161

sense either. Why would he bushwhack me, and why would he be using my brand on Skettering's cattle?

Whoever it had been, one thing was for sure. Things were getting plumb ripe, and no doubt about it. That was one thing upon which we all agreed.

I had plenty of time while I was laid up to think about things. I reckon just being that close to death will do that to you—that is, get you to thinking about the important things— and I did some serious soul-searching during those long days and nights.

The Good Book says, "Thou shalt not kill." That's mostly what I cogitated upon. For I was in a full mind now to take my .30/06 and find the varmint who was behind all the troubles that had blown my way like an evil wind. I wanted to plug the man responsible once and for all, bury him six feet under, and put a stop to all the misery he was sending my direction. But even as I had those thoughts and those black, vile feelings, I kept hearing Pa reading the Good Book, "Thou shalt not kill."

I reckon only a man who rides the range, observes the seasons come and go, watches the births and deaths of his stock, sees the flowers, the birds, and all the other wild critters can truly appreciate the beauty and sanctity of life. And in all my born days, I'd never killed a thing needlessly. Least of all a man.

I'd had that drummed into me by my pa.

Pa had been born in the Carolinas, after his own pa had given up the wild life as a trapper down at Fort Davy Crockett and returned to his childhood home to marry and settle down. My pa had left home at an early age and traveled around a spell, then he'd signed up with the cavalry to fight the Indian wars on the eastern slope of Colorado Territory and up north in the Dakotas, fighting Sioux and Cheyenne. As I said before, reckon that's partly why he and Yampawah hit it off. They'd shared the same enemies.

But when it came to outright owning a man, Pa couldn't see it. Reckon I already mentioned that his antislavery frame of mind drove him to sign up on the Union side when the big war began, even though that meant he was fighting against his own cousins and other kinfolk. My pa showed true grit when he fully believed in something, right up to being ready to lay down his life for his principles.

I'd been born in Denver during the time of the Indian campaigns, some ten years before the war. At that time, Ma followed my pa from town to town and fort to fort until at last she got plumb tired of moving and took me to live with her family back in Kansas, where she'd first met him. About that time, Pa went to fight in the Civil War, and Ma didn't see him for well over a year. And finally the long, brutal war came to an end, and my pa came to Kansas and got us and brought us farther west.

Pa had killed more than his share of men. But something had happened to him during the war. Ma told me that he'd been wild in his youth and selfish to the core, though she hadn't realized it until after she'd married him. But he'd come back from the war a changed man. More serious, kinder, ready to settle down. He'd gotten so that he'd nigh unto get killed himself before he'd see anyone else get hurt, and he had those dark spells when he needed to be alone.

He never told Ma what had happened, only talked in general terms about the death and destruction and all the pain. And then he'd say that it didn't really matter anymore, that he'd put it all behind him and wanted to completely forget. But he couldn't. Whatever had happened to him wouldn't let him go. Ma told me he'd awaken in the night and get up to sit for long spells with a haunted look in his eyes, a man possessed with memories that seared his soul.

As I grew older, Pa mentioned the war to me from time to time, especially after Ma died. One day when I was about twelve, we were sitting on the bank of the Yampa with fishing rods in hand and the birds singing overhead in the trees, when he turned to me suddenly and said, "You know, son, of all God's laws there's only one I can't quite understand."

"What's that, Pa?"

"The commandment that says, 'Thou shalt not kill,'" he replied. "Reckon I could let a man shoot me and turn around and walk away—if I was able to walk. I've mellowed more than a little with age, but I'd never be able to let a man hurt one of my own and walk away. Reckon I believe that when it comes to protecting family, nobody could stand in my way, not even the Lord Himself."

It shocked me to hear him say that, for I had a deep faith in the Lord by then. My parents gave me a true Christian upbringing. I surely did know God's commandments, and I knew that, whatever else happened, the good Lord had to come first of all. It sounded like downright sacrilege to hear Pa talk that way, and it scared me.

"It's a funny thing," he went on, not realizing how he'd made me feel. "You can't break God's laws without paying the price, and a man can't kill another man without feeling some part of his own immortal soul shrivel up and die as well. But then—I don't rightly know. God puts us here and hands us a powerful big puzzle to solve. He sets us up against any number of two-legged varmints that would ruin the very world and kill everything good in it if we just let them alone to do their evil work.

"And there's evil aplenty to be done by them, mark my words. But the hard thing is—I find myself wonderin', has He thrown a ringer into the setup? I mean, did He fool us by settin' it up so's that there's no good way to stop them except by killin', yet killin' these vermin is wrong?"

A fish jumped just then and splashed back into the water, making little circles that fanned out in the mossy green. Pa was quiet for a time, lost in his own thoughts, and I didn't know how to answer him or even how to understand him yet, so I stayed quiet too.

Then he said, so softly I almost didn't hear him, "It doesn't make sense to me. It just doesn't make sense at all. God says, 'Thou shalt not kill,' and yet look at this world He puts us in, and the things we have to fix . . ."

I thought about that a lot when I was lying flat on my back. That black, boiling rage had come up in me again, and it seemed that to quench that rage I was going to have to kill whoever had pulled the trigger and done this to me, and whoever was behind all my other woes as well. But all the time, tangled up in my mind with my need for revenge was my pa's voice saying, "Can't kill another man without feeling some part of your own immortal soul shrivel up and die as well. 'Thou shalt not kill.'"

And right on top of that thought came another, arguing that whoever the man was who'd fired on me, he'd already cost me dearly and I owed him an equal amount of trouble back. The question now was, was I willing to give him that part of me as well—the part of my soul that would shrivel up and die if I shot him to death?

As that thought would come to me, I'd find myself thinking again about young Hearne and wondering where he fit into all this, for I was sure he was part of it somehow. And then I'd think about Coogan, and about Skettering, and about all the rest of the trouble that had come to the valley with the winter's winds.

I forced myself to make excuses for the Hearne boy. I told myself again that he'd tried to bushwhack me in the tall timber because of all the hard times he'd seen and because of all the beatings he'd taken from his pa. The boy was afraid, didn't know how to live in these parts without taking what belonged to others. And though his own troubles might have seared his conscience till he had none left, it had me making allowances for him and for what he'd done—even for his firing on me that day, for though he'd shot and killed old Brownie, he'd stopped short of actually plugging me.

But there was no way I could excuse whoever had fired on me from the ridge. Whoever that was, he'd done his level best to kill me and had almost finished the job. I was having trouble understanding how a man could do a thing like that. In fact, this whole dagburned thing was such a sackful of rattlers that a man could drive himself crazy as a bedbug just trying to understand it all.

"Court! Merry Christmas." Caroline interrupted my dark thoughts by bending to kiss me square on the top of my head. "Let's string and light the candles, then we'll have our evening meal."

We'd already adorned the tree with our collection of brightly colored ornaments, and over the days we'd added candied apples and red and green popcorn strings, with a popcorn ball here and there. We'd put red felt bows on the tree and some paper bells. Now we clipped on the candle holders with their different colored candles, and when that was done Caroline carried a taper around and lit each one carefully.

Our Christmas gifts had been wrapped up in pretty paper and tied with red ribbon and placed under the tree. Tomorrow would be bright with festivities. We'd serve a big breakfast for all who cared to eat with us, then, carrying gifts, we'd go to the Ledbetters and drink eggnog. But tonight we'd give thanks and have our family Christmas as we read the story of the Christ Child. We'd have our family meal and open our own private gifts to one another.

Johnny's eyes were sparkling. This was only his second Christmas, and the last one was a vague memory if that. I saw him sitting there, his face solemn as he gazed at the glittering tree. I loved him so much it was an ache in my heart. I thought about the ranch and how it was his future as well as mine and Caroline's. And then a dark, cold wind ran through me as I thought about what I might have to do if someone was actually trying to take it from me.

When all the candles were lit, Caroline doused the gas lamps one by one. Then we all sat back—the fireplace blazing on one side, the candle-lit tree by the back window—and looked out into the snow-filled night and at the high black hill beyond, the hill that led back up to the Hearnes' place. The moon was full, and the willows along the creek were heavy with frost and fresh snow.

Mother Johnson left us and went into the kitchen to put the finishing touches on our small dinner.

She and Caroline had taken over everything while I'd been bedridden. Caroline had even gone so far as to ask Ledbetter to butcher a half dozen of my better range steers and haul the meat down to the Ute reservation in Utah, and that without asking my permission. When she'd told me, she'd said that things were harder than ever for the Utes down there, whereas half our cattle were going to die from the cold anyway.

I hadn't argued. And she'd seen to it that one of the less temperamental cowhands took a proper Christmas basket up to the Hearnes in spite of everything, though he'd been advised to knock, leave it on their front porch, then leave, and that was advice he'd taken.

I hadn't told Caroline about my suspicions that the Hearne boy had been one of the varmints who shot me, but I suspected she knew. She also knew that neither of us, no matter what, would take out our enmity toward him on his mother and brother.

Mother Johnson carried the last steaming dish to the table, which was set in the dining alcove between the kitchen and the parlor, where we could see the Christmas tree. She said, "Come and get it!" and the three of us made tracks.

That old oak table was set with my ma's Irish linen tablecloth. We had her Irish crystal and the good silverware. We used the white and silver china that Mother Johnson had given to us as a wedding present, and I reckon she'd filled every dish in the cupboard with something good to eat. There were candles on the table too, enough to give us good light to see by.

Mother Johnson was about the best cook that God ever did put on this earth. On the table sat a roast turkey and sage chicken dumplings and dressing, and she'd made potatoes and peas and a flaming plum pudding for dessert.

We had the tree and the winterscape and the fireplace to warm us, along with our food. In spite of our troubles, we had plenty to be thankful for.

By way of saying grace, I read from the Good Book, from the second chapter of the book of Luke:

"And she brought forth her firstborn son, and wrapped him in swaddling clothes, and laid him in a manger; because there was no room for them in the inn. And there were in the same country shepherds abiding in the field, keeping watch over their flock by night. . . ."

After I had read the story of Christ's birth, we thanked the Lord for His blessings, then ate our meal by firelight and candle glow.

Mother Johnson's cheeks were rosy, and her grayed hair was caught up in a bun. She'd gone to the trouble of wearing her lavender satin dress. She was what Caroline would be when she reached that age—kind and warm and the most unselfish person I'd ever known.

If we'd let her, she'd have worked herself to death—not out of a sense of duty but because she wanted everything to be perfect for us. I loved her every bit as much as I had my own ma—reckon I'd more or less let Mother Johnson fill her place, as much as that was possible.

All those still living that I truly loved were with me that night. But every time I moved to pick up a fork or pass a dish, the throb in my shoulder reminded me that despite the love in this room on this special night, something dark and menacing was taking shape around us. And I couldn't help but wonder if this might be the last Christmas that we would spend so warm and secure, all of us together in this special place in this very special way.

16

The second blue norther of the year waited until just past the holidays, hovering and itching in the mountains to the north, veiling Bears Ears Peaks and Black Mountain while it gathered full strength. Then it came howling in a week after Christmas, roaring with those banshee winds, tearing at the ranch buildings, ripping at the stock, whipping fine snow into the cracks of the outbuildings and barns and gnashing at all that was warm and alive. The sky was a wall of white. You couldn't see but an arm's length in front of your face. It was hard to stand upright against the icy wind, and I knew the die-off from this storm would be far worse than the last.

We did what we could around the ranch, though it wasn't much. I was off my crutch by then and managed to help a bit. We forced our way against the whipping, snow-filled winds to feed what cattle we could, those only in the pastures closest to the ranch buildings. The others, out on the range, would once again have to fend for themselves.

For two full days the blizzard whipped and raged at everything, tearing branches from trees and driving head-high drifts against the buildings and drawing the breath from all but the strongest stock. When at last the blow died down enough for us to get out and about, my men tallied more than four hundred head of cattle piled up at the drift fences and smothered in the blizzard. And there were another hundred or so missing who weren't likely to survive.

We hauled hay out to the remaining stock and opened up the water holes again on the river. We brought in some of the smaller weaker cows on hayracks to keep them near the big barn so that we could tend to them. But my herds were growing smaller with every passing storm, and there was a long, long winter still ahead.

The judge came down from Hahns Peak again as soon as the weather broke. He'd been visiting his daughter in Denver for several weeks over the Christmas holiday, and it had taken a while for word of my ambush to get to him.

Caroline let him in, then called me from where I'd been going over the books again in my study, trying to find a way to make ends meet. We sat in the living room and talked about the bushwhacking incident as we enjoyed a hot cup of coffee.

After I'd spoken my piece on the subject, the judge said, "Well, Court, what, in your opinion, should we do about it? I understand you have no idea who shot you."

"Judge," I said, wincing as I turned toward him and pulled a tuck in my bad arm, "ain't no doubt about the fact that we need to get to the bottom of this, but I sure couldn't begin to tell you how to go about doing it."

He reached into his vest pocket—it was a green brocade —and pulled out a pipe. He reached into another pocket and brought out a pouch, opened it, and set to tamping the tobacco into his pipe. Then he said, "Thing that really puzzles me is that branding. You say you don't have the slightest idea of how Skettering's rebranded cattle got onto your land?"

"I've wracked my brain, and it makes no sense at all to me. None of it."

He looked at me judiciously for a moment, then went back to lighting his pipe. When he was finished, he said, "I'd rather not have to be the one to tell you this, but rumors are spreading that Yampawah's the one who herded those cattle onto your land. Some say that he did because he knows you'd let him get away with it."

"Did the folks that made up that story manage to spin another windy about why he went to all the trouble of branding them with my brand? Or of branding them at all, for that matter, seeing how he was most likely just going to butcher them anyway?"

The judge smiled at me, his eyes crinkling up in his wintry old face, then he went solemn again and said, "I'm afraid

170

they did. They say that you and Yampawah are scratching each other's backs. That he's using your ranch as a place to hide stolen cattle, and he gives you a percentage of them for your trouble."

I just looked at the judge and shook my head slowly, trying to swallow that. Then suddenly I saw it. I blinked hard and said, "So that's it!"

He took a long draw on his pipe, blew smoke up toward the ceiling, then smiled again and said, "You get the picture now, I see."

"That it's more of Skettering's work? You bet your boots I do."

"He's setting things up so that it looks like he's doing everyone a favor by making a move on you, Court. This way he has an excuse for his missing beeves and an excuse to take as much of what's yours as he can get his hands on in order to pacify his investors. It's a dirty scheme, but it might have worked if you hadn't stumbled across one of his men moving the dirty-branded cattle up into the upper pastures of your range."

"You seem to know quite a lot about this."

"I've had people looking into it," he said. Then he shut his mouth and looked pleased with himself.

"Got any idea which of his men it was? I saw Skettering, Coogan, and Bowles in town, so it couldn't have been none of them."

The judge said, "I guess it wouldn't surprise you to learn that Jimmy Hearne is tied up with Skettering."

"Reckon it wouldn't."

"But you will be surprised to learn that Luke Coogan rode into Hahns Peak Village a full day before you were shot to tell Sheriff Finsand that someone had taken some more of the M-Slash-S cattle and that they'd found Indian sign near to where the cattle had been taken."

"You reckon they faked it?"

"I do."

171

"Put some folks' backs to the wall, and they'll stoop to anything," I said.

"That's certainly true. But there's more news," he added. "We had a couple of other visitors up at Hahns Peak just before this last storm hit—at the county land office."

"Yessir?"

"Jimmy Hearne and his father came up to file homestead rights on the old Grisham Duke place. The claim was filed in Mr. Hearne's name."

I thought about that, then said, "Well, I reckon if Hearne gets that whole three hundred and twenty acres it's not going to matter to me one way or another. Those saddle-backed ridges around that meadow keep it separated off from my summer range anyways."

"Ah, but it *will* make a difference to you, Court."

"How's that?"

"Doc Clayton has heard that Hearne is getting that land for Skettering—that he's planning to turn it over for Skettering's use right away, legal or not. And I can tell you for a fact that the Hearnes have recently gotten money from somewhere. They must have spent close to three hundred dollars up there the day they filed. They dropped most of it in a poker game, but every merchant in town got a small share."

I twisted up my face. "And I been worrying about them up there starving."

The judge took a long draw on his pipe, as though he was steeling himself for something else unpleasant, then he said, "The thing is, Court, that while I was going through the homestead papers I found some other recent filings. Schell's signature was on them, and he didn't bother to tell me about them. One is an application by Rollin Bowles for the mountain meadowland just to the east of the Hearnes'—"

"That's my summer rangeland!"

The judge nodded solemnly. "Yes, Court, I know it is. The other application is for your rangeland too. It was issued to one Lucas Homer Coogan for the land on the east side of the Elkhead River delta."

"Fire and brimstone. That's my *winter* range." I felt my throat dry up, and that was all I could say.

"Skettering is putting a tight squeeze on you, Court. Make no mistake about that."

"Have you told Senator Brown what Skettering is up to with the cattle count?"

The judge frowned deeply at that. "Not yet. I can't quite be sure at this point if that's the best thing to do."

"Why in thunder not?"

The judge hedged around, then said, "Well, Court, there's more to this than you might think."

I felt a sudden deep surge of mistrust. I wondered if he wasn't stalling because he didn't want to put Brown in a bad mood that might reflect on his own ambitions to get into the state legislature. I hid my thoughts behind a poker face and said, "So you reckon that Skettering is using that Hearne boy against me?"

"That seems to be about the size of it, doesn't it?"

"Moses Skettering ought to be hung," I said. "What kind of polecat would use a poor miserable kid like that to do his dirty work? That boy's filled with poison from the beatings his pa gives him. It ain't right to use up someone who never stood a chance."

"There's more to *that* story than you might know too, Court."

"How's that?"

"While I was in Denver this last time, I checked them out with the Kansas City constabulary. The Hearnes didn't come West just because Old Man Hearne got laid off in the stockyards, though that's part of it. Court, Jimmy Hearne killed a man—stabbed him to death in a saloon brawl. The constables couldn't prove it in a court of law, but they know it was him. Whatever it is that's brought him to this point, whatever made him this way, I believe your sympathies are misplaced."

I pondered that for a moment. "Caroline tells me that

I've a habit of giving folks too much free rein. Reckon in this instance she might be right."

"That Hearne boy bears watching, but Moses Skettering is behind all this, no doubt about it. And he's in deep trouble —I've looked into that too. He's up to his neck with his stockholders. He's either going to cover his tracks, or he's going to lose everything he has. Otis Brown is no man to trifle with, and when he learns that Skettering has cheated and double-crossed him there's going to be the piper to pay, one way or another."

"Then why don't you just tell him?"

The judge shook his head. "Not yet."

"Why in blazes not?"

The judge looked at me, blew out some pipe smoke as though he was losing his patience, and then his face went hard. "All in due time, Court. All in due time. At any rate, let's put that aside for the moment. I brought a visitor with me, someone you need to meet. I left him visiting with Mother Johnson in the kitchen while I came and told you about the land problems. I wanted our conversation to be private, and he was half starved, so it seemed best that I talk and he eat. Now, I'll leave it to you how much of all this you choose to tell him."

"Who is it?"

"The man from the Bureau of Indian Affairs. He's out of Denver, and he's been in these parts for almost a week. I met him at the stage station in Hayden to bring him here. And before you get your dander up, I want to tell you that a few of those fellows truly care about what they're doing. They'd like to stop the thieving from the Indians, but they have a good deal of corruption to wade through before they can do it. This man's name is Kenny Payne. I've been told by people I trust that he's a good man and honest. Give him a chance, and he just might do us some good."

"Reckon I'll just keep things simple and tell him everything."

"Then you're not covering up for Yampawah? Not at all?" He skewered me with a sudden gaze.

"Judge, if you wasn't a friend of mine—"

"All right, Court, all right. It's just because we're friends that I know how deeply your loyalties run, and I still need to be absolutely certain."

He went out and came back in less than a minute, saying to the man beside him, "Come on in, Payne."

The man who came through the door was nigh unto twice my size, and he'd have made about four of the judge. He had light brown hair and a clean-shaven face, sad gray eyes with a lick of flint in them, and a cowhand's stride. He wore a nickel-plated hogleg on his hip—something I didn't normally allow in the house—and he looked like he'd ridden some hard range.

The judge introduced us, and while we were shaking hands the judge said, "When you got shot, I put through an emergency request. It seemed to me like things were boiling up fast. The BIA agreed with me."

Payne sat in one of the leather armchairs, holding his hat on his knees, sitting on its edge as though it was uncomfortable. I figured he most likely spent the better part of his time in a saddle. His was a tough job that kept him on the move, especially in these hard times. Probably slept with one eye open too.

He had a friendly tone of voice, though there was a lot of reserve in it. He said, "The passes between here and Denver are closed now, so I brought a train out of Cheyenne, then rode down from Rawlins to Windsor on the stage. I got snowed in there for a few days. But I managed to ask a few questions, and I got to visit with Moses Skettering."

"He talked to Shorty Musket too," the judge said.

Payne nodded. "True. He's quite a character. If you listened to his blarney long enough, you'd start believing the Utes could divide themselves in two and be in four places all at once, starting trouble in every one of them. Lost his leg in the Indian ruckus, I understand. Down at the White River Agency?"

"It was during the ambush at Milk Creek," I replied. "It left Shorty plumb gnarled up and mad."

Payne was proving to be a sharp one. I liked the man already. I asked him, "What's your opinion on Skettering's missing cattle?"

Payne said, "From what I can see so far, I have to agree with the judge here. Skettering's setting up a smoke screen for some reason, and you seem to be part of his plans."

"Do you reckon it's possible that Yampawah and his band could have been anywhere's near to Elkhead when I was bushwhacked?"

Payne shook his head. "Ain't possible at all. I spoke to half a dozen folks in the past two days who say that Yampawah's been down around the Meeker settlement for several weeks or more. Caused quite a ruckus down there too—got to drinking, then gambling on some pony races. Lost most of his things and got in a fistfight with a cowhand who squawked about it to high heaven. From what I hear, that Yampawah must be a feisty old Indian. Lookin' forward to meetin' him."

"Well," I said, "he's a strange bird. Likes that hootch and those ponies as well as any other Indian, but when it comes right down to brass tacks he's got a good deal of dignity. He's rightfully skittish of folks, like a bull elk or a bear or beaver when there's trappers or hunters around. And he'd take a scalp if he'd a mind to. He sure enough would have killed Coogan and Bowles that day if I hadn't mixed into things. But he's not a spiteful man, nor is he sly. Somehow I couldn't see him mixed up in this mess."

"You care to tell me why not?"

"He's too good a hunter for one thing, and the Indians would always rather have wild game than beef if they can get it."

Payne said, "Well, I suspect that after what happened up at Hahns Peak he was right to get out of the county for a while. Seems that so far he's shown some common sense in this matter, all except for leaving the reservation to begin with."

It looked to me like Payne was going to be impartial or, if partial, at least biased in favor of keeping things right for the Indians. There was a good chance he might just be the man to help us get this thing straightened out.

I said, "So you believe that Yampawah shot Bowles in self-defense?"

The faintest flicker of a smile passed across his face. A glint of skepticism showed in those flinty gray eyes. "I know Judge Warren to be an honest man. He's told me that you are too. But aside from that, what's happening here is nothing new. I'm risking my skin to even talk about it, but if something isn't done we're going to have some more Indian bloodshed, mark my words. I reckon that a good two-thirds of the annuity goods that have been promised by the treaty with the Indians—not just the Utes, but the Sioux, Cheyenne, Kiowas, even the Apaches and Navajos down in Arizona Territory—are being skimmed off and resold in order to line white men's pockets.

"About all it takes to get a contract as an Indian agent these days is a promise to split the takings with the government man who gives you the contract. I was never so happy in my life as when the judge here insisted on starting an investigation into the Indian Agency's affairs. I'd had such a bellyful that I was about to take things into my own hands and start using my gun."

The judge frowned. "My colleagues in Denver tell me that things are getting under way at the higher levels but we're meeting with a lot of resistance. The people at the top who are lining their pockets are powerful, wealthy men, and they're not going to give up their takings easily and certainly not during these hard times."

Payne said, "It doesn't bother me to tell you that a couple of senators—believe you know them, Judge; Latham Morris and Otis Brown?—they're dragging their feet. Inside word is that they made some plans of their own. Brown has money

177

tied up in Skettering's ranch. Guess you knew that. They've already put things into motion to try to get Skettering the cattle contract for the Ute reservation."

The judge's winter-whitened face turned as ashen as his hair. The news astonished me too.

The judge said, "Brown? Morris?" His voice was tight. "But—but they're always carping about the federal government having their fingers in the state's pie. They're the ones who talk loudest and fight hardest every time the federal government does anything that might infringe on states' rights! They're constantly grandstanding about the Indians' affairs being administered at the federal level. I-I simply can't believe it!"

But I could see he believed every word of it and was troubled by what he'd learned.

The smile on Kenny Payne's face was twisted, as if he'd had a bellyful of something rancid and had held it for as long as he'd a mind to.

He said, "I doubt if they're griping so loud now that they've figured out how to get themselves a cut of the pie that's being passed out. Those fellows are blowing some of the same smoke screen that Skettering is, Judge. I know that you're a smart old fellow and can usually hold your own, but you're out of the mainstream of things in the government, both federal and state. And mind my words, one's as bad as the other when there's crooked money to be made. You'd be surprised at how fast some of those fellows patch up their differences. I guess one reason I'd like to help you get things straightened out over here is that I'd like to see you win that seat in the legislature that you've been hankerin' for. It'd be nice to have a few more honest men running things."

"Thank you," the judge said. He thought for a moment. "Well. Brown and Morris. That indeed puts a different complexion on things. Well, well, well . . ."

Payne nodded. "They've been using you, Judge. Not your fault—how could you have known what pit vipers they really are? But we've got to start cleanin' things up some-where, and so far as I can see it might as well be here."

I asked Payne, "Just what is it that you plan to do?"

He shook his head. "I'm not sure how best to handle things yet. Come sunup tomorrow morning I'm going to ride back up to Skettering's ranch. Want to ask him a few more questions. I'll decide after I hear what he has to say. I'll just make it look like I'm checking into the rumors that the Ute have been rustling cattle. That ought to open him up to me."

I said, "Reckon you'd best spend the night here with us and let us treat the two of you to a good hot dinner. There's another storm brewing, and aside from that the beds and board at the hotel in Windsor aren't near so good as here at the McCannons'. I'll let you pay me back in a good, stiff game of poker."

Payne cracked a grin. "I'll be happy to take you up on that if you'll throw in a good hot bath."

"My pleasure. It's goin' to be nice having you here. Can't tell you how hard it's been, being stoved up and without good company for so long."

17

We were going into the hard months of winter. From January to the last of March is usually northwestern Colorado's worst time for winter storms and freezing weather. During those months the winds whistled almost constantly up through the Yampa River Valley and down Elkhead Creek. They whipped around the tops of Black Mountain and the other peaks to the north of us and swallowed the Flat Tops to our south. The sky lay dark with fat, ugly clouds for days on end. The days themselves were gray and dreary, always spitting some snow or sleet from the scudding skies, the unending wind whipping the frozen moisture around like bird shot. Somehow the wind never seemed to clear away the clouds. One batch would blow on south, and another would come right on its heels to snag on the mountaintops and lie down low in an icy fog on the river bottom.

The temperature dropped to well below zero and stayed there, hitting forty below for nigh unto six days in a row at one stretch. The cold was terrible, with the chill seeping through our mackinaws and other heavy clothing, even when we were in the barn. Our saddle horses were coated with light frost on their flanks; icicles hung from their nostrils if we were on the trail any length of time. We covered our ears with stocking caps, and they still froze. When we were working, our hands and feet were numb most of the day, and some of the cowboys dismounted and led their horses by the reins in order to stay out of the icy wind.

The Yampa River froze thicker and harder. We were chopping holes in the ice for almost a mile stretch every morning, so our thirsty cattle could drink. The creek behind the house was solid ice. I was doing what I could, though my arm was still stoved up some and I still wasn't back up to snuff.

We were hand-feeding from the hayrack every head of cattle we could find. The snow had a way of thawing on top in the warmer afternoons, then freezing into a hard crust. There was no way the cattle could nuzzle through to the wild timothy and Johnsongrass that lay buried underneath it all. We were going through our hay and feed grain a lot faster than I'd planned. And still, in spite of the fact that the boys were working harder against the weather than I'd ever have believed possible, we were losing cattle every day.

Most of them died from the cold—they were helpless, and their legs and feet bled from the grinding caused by the hard, granulated snow. It nigh unto broke my heart to see it, and I did my best for every one of them, but sometimes Nature just has a way of calling the odds.

The coyotes would gather at night near the stock bedding grounds, and at every opportunity they would jump a weak yearling or range cow. Cottontails and jackrabbits were scarce food for the starving predators. The hungry coyotes grew so bold that on occasion they would even come into the ranch yard and fight with our dogs, trying to get to the chicken house or even to take the dogs themselves. More than once I was awakened to snarling and yelping and had to grab my shotgun and go on down and settle things.

After a month of this, my rangeland was littered with frozen cattle carcasses, and I knew there would be worse to come before spring. We left the frozen cattle where they lay, hoping to lure the coyotes away from the living stock, but the varmints liked the fresh red meat and the warm red blood. So I kept my cowboys out patrolling the stock as much as possible, tramping around on snowshoes, rifles ready against the marauders, themselves freezing half to death.

The boys' nerves were ragged, and they'd grown to hate the cold, but at last count we'd taken thirty-six coyote hides. They were worth about a dollar apiece, and the cowhands appreciated the extra pocket money. As for me, my own resources were dwindling fast, for the scarcity of grain and the added trouble of shipping in that weather brought the cost of feed up close to the price of gold, or so it seemed to me.

I was wearing thin in every way. The only thing that kept me going was Caroline, with her belly getting rounder every day. That young'un was soon to be born and no mistake about it.

Mother Johnson was a strength. She wore a smile and worked herself to the bone to make things comfortable for Caroline, and Little Johnny kept my chin up, too. But for all that, I found most of my strength in long nights spent reading the Bible and in my times of prayer.

I hadn't heard from the judge or from the BIA man, Kenny Payne. They were both busy with their own affairs and would let me know if they got a handle on the varmints who had tried to do me in. I more than had my own hands full— although I'll admit that if I'd been able to ride I'd have been right along with Payne, trying to get to the bottom of why Hearne—if that's who it had been—had bushwhacked me.

Every morning when I woke up, the pain in my shoulder was still so bad that I had to hand-pull myself out of bed. I thought a lot about Jimmy Hearne, his standing up there on the ridge, trying once more to kill me. Whatever pity I had felt for the lad had turned into solid black hatred. Every day that I was hampered in my work by the pain in my body, the poison bit deeper into my soul.

I was hard bit by my helplessness. Even one more pair of hands could have helped feed more cattle, and all I could do was limp around the ranch buildings or ride as far as a horse could go in the snow on my rangeland, and ride easy at that. I sat in the saddle many a time, stiff as a barn board and freezing after doing my level best to do my share, and had to watch my men finish up the heaviest work.

With every new storm, the grass and brush was buried a little deeper, and the odds of survival grew a little slimmer for every head of stock I owned.

The Utes, being mountain Indians, had lasted nigh unto three-hundred-fifty winters before a white man so much as set foot in these mountains and valleys. Reckon that's why it didn't surprise me much when Chip Hutton rode in after tending to some cattle down the valley and mentioned to me in passing that old Yampawah and some of his tribe had set up camp again down by the river.

Truth is, it didn't surprise me at all. But it sure did worry me some.

Yampawah and his clan should have holed up on the reservation in this kind of weather. They must have traveled the river valleys in from the canyon country near their reserve in Utah and stayed in the shelter and windbreak of the brush and cottonwoods during the harsh blizzard and cold of the last storm. I figured game had to be plumb scarce and things really bad down that way to cause them to ride up-country more than a hundred miles in the dead of winter and bring their squaws and papooses along. Yampawah must have been awfully desperate to pull a fool stunt like that in this kind of weather.

All the same, they had plenty of wood on the river bottom for their campfires. The snowfall was lighter there, and firewood could easily be dug out. And there were a few rabbits and grouse holed up under the willows, which were easy to catch in the deep snow. I reckoned that would keep them more or less fed for a while.

And then a day after they'd arrived, along about mid-February, the sky turned to heavy lead, and the clouds scudded up from the west, and we knew that another blizzard was blowing in, this one from down around Utah way.

There was a stillness in the air. The icy clouds hanging over the valley told me that the storm brewing was something that even Yampawah and his people most likely hadn't expected. Utes or not, no man had seen a winter like this. No one could have predicted the savagery of these storms.

When I was a lad I had heard old-timers talk about the 100-year storms of northwest Colorado, when the blizzards stalked and killed and the rivers rampaged and flooded the valleys from snowmelt in the spring. Old Man Duke had told us of a time when the whole Yampa River Valley had been two miles wide with floodwater during spring runoff after a bad winter and deep snows in the high country. One early party of explorers had mapped the valley out as a lake, and folks reckoned they'd just come across the region during flood time.

It began to look as if this might be one of those winters again. And if that was the case, we didn't have much of a spring to look forward to either, what with the river's expected flooding and the rangeland there all but wiped out for the season.

These troubles and others were on my mind the next morning when Chip Hutton come to my kitchen door as I was pouring myself a cup of coffee. I hadn't really talked with him since he'd spotted Yampawah and his band. He'd wanted to tell me he was riding down to the lower range to check the cattle there, but I invited him in, sat him at the kitchen table, and handed him a steaming cupful. Then I said, "I got a burr under my saddle, Chip. Maybe you can scratch it for me. What do you reckon Yampawah and his people are doing up here this time of year?"

Hutton had taken off his gloves. He brushed his hands together to put some circulation back into them, and now he was holding the coffee cup close-like to gather the warmth. He said, "Your guess is 'bout as good as my own, Boss. All I know is what he said he was doin' up here. Said he heard you was having some trouble. Said you were a friend of the Top of the Mountain People, and he'd come to help."

That downright puzzled me.

It must have taken Yampawah several days of hard traveling to get back up here, and where would he have heard such a rumor anyway? They might have been down on the White River near the Meeker settlement when the last storm blew in instead of on the reservation. Folks traveled back and forth to the J.W. Hugus store there, and rumors could have spread. I had no way of knowing.

It didn't matter anyway, because they were down on the river below my ranch now, and that did bother me. It could easily mean trouble with Skettering and his bunch, once they heard the Indians were back.

"When you ride that way, tell the old varmint I'd like to talk to him," I said. "Tell him I'll ride down in a day or two, or—if he'd rather—he's welcome to ride up here."

But a heavy snowfall began that night, and what with the new work around the ranch itself, I put off my visit to Yampawah.

I had to ride through the storm into town to get more feed, but Zeb Tucker had only a partial shipment for me. The train had been held up by a Wyoming ground blizzard for half a week, and by the time they got to Rawlins they'd nigh sold off all their feed.

The Union Pacific was the only shipper running. On top of that, the freight sleds down from their Rawlins warehouse were only getting through once, maybe twice, a month now, with a full three-span on the front end to pull the weight through the snow. Tucker told me that the Union Pacific itself had been snowbound a half-dozen times already, mostly from ground blizzards and deep drifts in the cuts. The stage that came across the mountains from Denver hadn't been running since the first snow had choked up the passes back before Thanksgiving.

The only news we were getting from outside was from the mule skinners on the freight outfits that came down from Rawlins, bringing whatever supplies they could get through. We got the newspapers still, from Cheyenne and Denver and even Kansas City if we'd a mind for them, but they were as much as a month old by the time they reached us now. Even at that, we could tell that things all over the country were as bad as last year and bound to get worse.

There were ruinous stock die-offs everywhere: on the eastern slopes of the Rockies, up in Montana and the Dakotas, all across Wyoming Territory, through the plains of Kansas and the Indian Nation, and down into Texas. It was as if the fury of a white-breathed angel of death had been turned loose against the stockmen all across the country, and at times when I prayed I felt as if I was squaring off against a freezing wall and God Himself had deserted me and every other stockman afoot.

A good number of people were freezing to death as well, getting lost in blizzards, wandering around in circles, blind as a bat in the wind and snow. The papers carried more than one story of folks dying a hundred yards or less from their ranch buildings and homesteads, not knowing where they were in the heavy, confusing whiteouts.

The snowfall had started light, but it kept up for two long days. On the third afternoon it picked up speed with a howling wind that set the snowflakes cutting at an angle into a man's face like buckshot from a 16-gauge shotgun, and I knew another full-on blizzard was in the making.

I sent Chip and a couple of the boys back down to the river to fetch old Yampawah and his wild bunch. I reckoned there was plenty of room for them to weather out the storm inside some of my ranch buildings. The horse barn hayloft was big enough for a lot of men to sleep in. There wasn't too much hay left in it anyway. There was no reason for those Indians to be out there in the cold as long as they didn't burn my ranch down with a careless fire.

Besides, I wanted to talk to that old Indian. There was something going on inside that head of his, or my name wasn't Courtney McCannon.

The Utes came straggling in, plastered with snow, just as the evening shadows cut across the valley. The snowfall was already so thick that I couldn't see them till they were plumb up in the yard. Yampawah was in the lead, pulling on a spotted pony that was as lean as an Arkansas razorback hog.

The old chief's head was bare and frosty. He wore a faded blanket that looked as if it had been stolen from a bawdy house somewhere—all red with bright gold flowers embroidered onto it, and the Lord alone knew where he'd really got it. He had two of his squaws tramping alongside him, one

186

wearing his big old buffalo-hide coat and the other wrapped in blankets until she looked like a circus clown. They wore deer-skin leggings with the hair turned in, tied over their moccasins and halfway up to their knees to help them stay warm.

Charley Crazy-Horse was right behind Yampawah, leading another pony that wasn't long for this world. It was so skinny that its ribs were sticking out of its rough winter coat of hair and so weak that it could scarcely walk. Chased-by-Bears and another brave were with the party, along with a passel of squaws and papooses, maybe ten in all. They had six travois, pulled along by horses with a bit more meat on them than the first two ponies. The travois held their elkhide tepees and other pitiful belongings.

My cow barn was a sturdy building, one of the biggest structures in the county. In spite of the fact that we had it packed with as many cattle as it could hold, we made room for the Indians' horses inside.

We took the Utes over to the horse barn and left their travois alongside it. They dug out what they needed for the night, then we showed them where they could make their beds in the hay in the loft. I figured they'd stay at least a mite warmer there.

Charley Crazy-Horse didn't like my hayloft. He brought in his elkhide tent and set it up on the floor near the windward side of the barn. Which didn't make a whit of difference to me or the boys. If they wanted to live like Indians, I reckon that's what they were, and that was surely their privilege.

As soon as they were settled, Caroline, Mother Johnson, Alice Nelson, and Virginia Ledbetter showed up, followed by several of the men, sheepish looks on their faces, carrying our big chuck wagon cook pots full of beef stew, and pans of fresh-baked cornbread, and a hot coffeepot. A couple of the boys hauled in big old barrels and built fires inside them, careful to keep them well away from the wooden walls and the hay.

Banty, Ledbetter, Chip Hutton, and I stayed and ate with the Indians, sitting Indian-style there in the warm, dry hay. After the boys had packed it in, they went back to the bunkhouse, while Ledbetter went on home. They knew I wanted to palaver with Yampawah.

Seems that Chief Yampawah had a thing or two he wanted to say to me too, for as soon as he'd wolfed down one more plate of cornbread and stew, he set his tin plate down, sat back and looked dead at me, folded his arms, and waited.

I said, "Well, Chief, looks like we're in for a regular tail twister of a storm."

Yampawah wasn't one to mince words, and he wasn't feeling like talking about the weather. He ignored my words and went right to the point. "I have lived long among the white men, a great trial that has not been of my choosing. I have learned much of their ways. But I feel bad medicine. Many things are happening that I do not understand."

"Reckon I'd be happy to explain as much as I can, though I have to admit I'm a mite perplexed myself."

He nodded solemnly. "Then I will ask you." He paused, thinking, then chose his words with care. "We rode with you, as you wished, to the white man's councils. Is that not so?"

"Reckon it is." I knew he was talking about our ride up to Hahns Peak.

"We found betrayal. That is as it has always been. The men who insulted my squaws have gone free, and this is also as it has always been."

I couldn't meet his eyes. It was the pure truth, and I knew it, and I was ashamed for the folks who'd done it, but all the same it was beyond my power to fix it, even though I'd tried.

Chief Yampawah gazed hard at me with his flinty eyes, and there was a spark of fire in them now. He said, "You are stubborn, Tall Gun. You will never listen, and because of this you have brought bad medicine on our people and upon yourself. Your enemies have counted coup on you, and you did not kill them to regain your honor. And now I have come back because they have also tried to kill you."

"I was shot," I admitted. "But I reckon you're a mite late. I'm mostly mended up by now."

He snorted in contempt, and his words were harsh and short. "They will kill you. You must stop them first."

I said, "Chief, I have to admit I made a mistake by riding you and Skettering's worthless cowhands all the way up to Hahns Peak that day. But Schell—that varmint that caused all the trouble—he's gone, sent packing. All the same, you're right about there being some bad medicine in these parts right now. But there are some good men around too. We'll get things straightened out. I give you my word on it. Just sit tight and don't do anything reckless or foolish."

Yampawah said sadly, "You have given me your word before, Tall Gun. I know you do not mean to lie, but you do not have the medicine to make your words come true."

I said, "Judge Warren will—"

But Yampawah raised a hand to hush me. "You did not have the medicine to put the men who harmed our squaws in the white man's prison as you said. You do not even have strong enough medicine to protect yourself against the evil ones from your own tribe."

I said, "You're biting off a hunk of trouble if you get into this, Chief."

Suddenly a deep, ancient anger flared up in his eyes. "I will repay the men who harmed my squaws and who harmed you."

"Chief," I warned, "if you get into the fracas, you're going to be stepping right into a trap."

I thought about it minute, then I figured things couldn't get much worse unless Yampawah carried out his threats, which he was likely to do if he didn't come to his senses. But I knew that most times he was a sensible old Indian, except when he was riled up. So I told him some of what Skettering had been up to and explained why Skettering had reason to want to blame the Indians for his so-called stock losses and why it would behoove us all to let the BIA handle matters.

When I was done talking, Yampawah gave me a leathery smile and said, "So we now share enemies, even as I once did with your father. But this time I will capture the enemy, Tall Gun, and I will count coup for both of us."

That frustrated me no end. I hadn't made that old Indian see daylight at all. I said, "Yampawah, I'm asking you as a friend. Stay out of it. There's nothing you can do that won't make matters worse."

He nodded with a slow, solemn dignity edged in bitterness. Then he said, "Trouble has followed like the wind at my back all my life. It has blown me forward, making me the winner of many races, and it has made me strong. I belong to the Top of the Mountain People. When the white man came, our troubles came. We could defeat the Sioux, the Crow, the Cheyenne—but the white man . . ."

He looked at me with a look as near to hatred as he'd ever given me, and for an instant I could see what it was that made other folks hereabouts wary of him. I felt a lick of fear crawl up my back.

"The white man," he repeated, "is like no other enemy. With a white man, a Ute never knows what the next wind will bring. And you, Tall Gun . . ." The hatred faded out of his eyes and was replaced by the look of patient, bitter persistence that usually lay there. He said, "You are an honest man. But you cannot see as clearly as the Ute."

That riled me some.

A new sadness licked across his face as he saw my reaction. He said, "My spirit carries me far. In my spirit dreams I see the world beneath me and the Top of the Mountain People. The clouds and the eagles and the shadows of death. My people know. We know that there are evil white men who steal the food and blankets and horses and cattle that the honest white men have promised to us. And we know that their pockets are heavy with gold while our people lie starving and freezing. But we cannot count coup on them, for there are other white men between them and us—men like you, Tall

Gun. Men with truth in their words and goodness in their hearts but with weak medicine."

I couldn't answer him.

Old Yampawah was talking to me more than he ever had before. Most likely more than he ever would again. Reckon his belly was full, and it was warm in the barn, and I figured he was feeling a mite safe for a change.

We'd lit a kerosene lantern against the darkness, set it in a small tin tub so it couldn't ignite the hay even if it was knocked over. A few of the squaws sat in the background listening to us talk, maybe understanding some of what we said. But most of the Indians had succumbed to their full bellies and the warmth and had made themselves pallets up in the hayloft, where they'd fallen asleep. They were a worn-out people at the best of times, their spirits flickering like a campfire in a heavy wind.

The wind suddenly howled outside, long and mournful and low, and suddenly the chief's head jerked to one side, and his eyes narrowed up as he froze, listening.

He turned to me. He had a strange light in his eyes, a hollow pathway to another world. He said, "I hear the spirits singing. They sing of death." I was just about to get spooked by him when he abruptly relaxed and said, "But the winds fly on past. Death will not come tonight."

I was happy to hear it, I can tell you that.

Yampawah said, "We are brothers, Tall Gun. Our skins are different, but we are brothers."

I was plumb pleased by his words. I said, "Thank you kindly."

He was brooding again, though, and didn't even hear me. He said, "You are not like the cutthroat Cheyenne who take and waste and pillage. You are not like the Sioux or the Crow. You are not like so many of the other white men, nor was your father. You came to our mountains, but you did not take them. You used our land, but you shared it with us too. The others—they share nothing."

191

"Reckon the best advice is in the Good Book," I said. "Do unto others . . ." I let the words taper off. I wasn't so sure those words came from the Bible after all, but they held some good advice for all that.

Yampawah fell silent again. He was staring at the darkness that lay beyond the outer edges of the lantern light, staring as if he were looking into the vast, black cavern of the future.

It struck me that there was something about him at that moment—something so downright dignified—that I was having trouble imagining this to be the same old renegade who was known to gamble on the ponies at the races and get drunk for a week if he lost the bet. Reckon I was seeing Yampawah as he'd once been, in a former glory when he had indeed been a chief, a glory that was gone not only for Yampawah but for all the Indians in the land. I felt an ache in my heart, and it was joined by another howling gust of wind.

Softly Yampawah said, "I hear the winds. They sing again of death." Then he stared past me off into the shadows and into a future too dark to comprehend.

I didn't say any more, just sat and watched him for a spell, feeling the menacing edge of the shadows drawing closer as the coal oil in the lantern began to burn out. Then I stood up, walked over to the makeshift stoves, the metal barrels that held fire. I picked up a couple of sticks of dead cottonwood and put them on the fires. Banty had already told me he'd come and check on them in an hour or so to make sure they were put out. By then the inside of the barn would be more or less warm enough to stay that way the better part of the night.

I stood and looked at old Yampawah, but his head was sagging, and he appeared to have fallen asleep. I turned and headed out the barn door.

The wind blew hard, and the snow swirled around me, stirring up a mighty bad storm.

On a sudden I ached to wrap my arms around my wife and my boy, to hold them tight against me, to be in the warmth of my own house, secure against the wind and the coming blizzard and whatever else that violent winter had in store.

In spite of the pain in my ankle, I sprinted across the yard in a walk so fast that it might as well have been a run. But once inside the house, I looked back through the windowpane, back to the barn. And sadness settled down over me like the snow that blanketed my yard. Reckon I knew that some things had already changed and could never be brought back again.

18

By morning, the storm had done its worst, then blown on over.

Yampawah and his clan packed up early and left, though I offered to let him stay the winter if he'd a mind to. He wouldn't tell me where he was going, but he did make a solemn promise to stay out of Skettering's matters at least until the snow had melted again.

That set my mind at ease, and by midmorning I was involved in other worries, mostly about the new stock die-off and my crippled herd. Gradually Yampawah and that particular set of problems worked its way to the back of my mind as I set about the work of keeping my ranch together.

By a week after that I was feeling somewhat better and doing most of my fair share of the work. I was putting in some long hours, trying to make up for lost time, and I was down at the barn, fixing up a broken harness flank-strap in the tack room when Ledbetter came bursting in the door.

He looked at me with those bleached-denim eyes of his, lifted up his hat, and ran his fingers through his carrot-top hair, nervous-like. I saw that his hand held a tremor, and I set my work down and paid full mind to him.

His face was white as frozen beef jerky, and his voice held a shiver as he said, "Court, you'd better get out here and have a look at what Chip Hutton just brought in."

I followed him out the barn door.

A big drab-brown workhorse stood there, still hitched to a bobsled. Chip had stepped down from the sled and stood beside it.

There was a tattered old blanket pulled over whatever it was that lay in the sled box. My first thought was that it must be a yearling that had met with some strange end, what with everybody acting so mysterious and all.

Then Ledbetter said, "Hutton found him out in Little Mud Gulch, about twelve miles south of where our pasture meets Skettering's. He ain't a pretty sight, Court—"

He'd said it just as I pulled back the blanket and found out for myself.

The head had rolled over to one side before he'd frozen, so that I could see one side of his face as well as the back of his head. The sight hit me in the gut like a sledgehammer, and I had to put my hand on the side of the sled for a minute to steady myself.

Someone had struck him in the back of his head with something sharp that fractured his skull. Probably ambushed, was the way it looked to me. In all probability he never knew what hit him, and he must have died instantly. His face was mottled purple and black on its down side, and smears of blood were frozen to his face and matted his hair. Even though the features were distorted by death, there was no mistaking the face.

It was Kenny Payne, the BIA man.

Ledbetter said, "Looks like somebody done him in with a hatchet."

"Or a tomahawk," said Hutton. When Ledbetter scowled at him, he said, "Well, there ain't no way to tell the difference, is there?"

I mulled that over, then said, "I reckon there ain't at that." I laid the blanket down across his face again, thinking all the while of Yampawah last night, hearing the wind spirits singing of death. I fought back a chill that had nothing to do with the weather. "How'd you happen to come across him, Chip?"

Hutton was shaken, but he held himself together, I'll give him that. He said, "I was trackin' some strays that had wandered up the gulch toward the high country, toward Slide Mountain, I reckon to get shelter from the wind. They were bound to starve to death up there. I come across Payne along about five miles to the west of the Hearne homestead, layin' up against the sagebrush on a steep knoll, in plain sight and easy to see. One of the boys had this sled down at the river, getting a load of firewood. I rode down to get help, and we took this rig and went back over there. We dragged and carried Payne off the steep slope, got him back down to the bobsled, and we brought him in."

"No sight of his horse or pack?"

"None. Just him, layin' there in the snow."

"Covered over?"

"Just drifts. He'd either missed the blizzard or last night's winds blew most of the snow off him."

"Was he completely froze up?"

"Plumb stiff already."

"No way to tell how long he's been dead then," I said. "Reckon he was gunshot too?" I didn't have the heart just then to examine the rest of the man's body.

"Nossir, I'd say not. Didn't see no holes in him nor in his clothes. Didn't go so far as to try to pry his clothes off him though."

"No need to, Chip. You did the right thing." To the both of them I said, "We'll have to let the judge know about this right away. He'll want to be the one to notify the BIA."

"There's goin' to be some big grief to pay on this one," said Hutton.

"And half of Georgia to boot," Ledbetter agreed.

Hutton said, "Rough time of the year to rout the soldiers out."

I froze in place when I heard that, thinking about it, then turned to him, saying, "You reckon that's the way things'll go?"

Ledbetter answered for him. "This man was lookin' into the so-called rustling by the Utes. Now he shows up dead—tomahawk or hatchet, it don't rightly matter when you get right down to it—and I reckon I don't need to tell you what it looks like."

"He was more of a mind to investigate the chicanery against the Utes," I said. "Truth was, he was looking into any number of things."

"How many folks knew that?" Ledbetter asked.

I took his point. Payne himself had said he was going to make it look like he was checking into the rumors that the Utes had been rustling cattle, in order to get Skettering and others to open up to him. I'd honored his wish for silence and hadn't even discussed the matter with my own cowhands. Beside me, only Judge Warren and Payne himself knew that his true reason for being here was to straighten out the problems with the annuity goods that had been promised to the Indians by the U.S. Government treaties.

He'd wanted to find out where the skimming was taking place, who was taking part in it, and who the thieves were paying off in the government. In short, he'd drawn off against not only the thieves who lined their pockets with Indian goods but also against the government men who gave out the contracts—Senator Otis Brown among them.

Payne had said his first step would be to talk to Moses Skettering. Senator Otis Brown had money tied up in Skettering's ranch, and he had his own idea about what should happen with the government contracts. In fact, he wanted to get Skettering the cattle contract for the Ute reservation.

I remembered the twisted smile on Kenny Payne's face, the one that made him look like he'd had a bellyful of something rancid and had held it as long as he'd a mind to. I remembered his saying that certain state officials were as bad as the ones in the federal government, when there was crooked money to be made.

Payne had meant to begin cleaning the stables and start by talking to Skettering. That thought kept coming to my mind. The last time I'd seen him, he'd left my ranch at sunup the morning after he arrived, on his way to Skettering's. I thought about Doc Clayton telling me that Ben Blue was a hired killer, hired by Skettering for any number of reasons.

But Payne had ridden off weeks ago. I hadn't heard hide nor hair of him since, or of Judge Warren. All the same, Payne had said he was risking his skin in order to stop the

197

bloodshed he knew was coming if the troubles didn't get set straight. He sure had been.

And now there were only two of us left who knew the true reason he'd been here. What with all the rumors that had been stirred up about the Utes rustling beef, it was bound to look to most others as if the rustling was what had brought him here, especially since he'd probably come right out and said as much to any number of people. Chip Hutton was right: the way things stood, soldiers could be down from Fort Steele to take things up with the Utes.

Thinking about that, I had to shake my head to clear it. Stupidly I said, "Yampawah couldn't have picked a worse time to come back up here. Looks like he's set to take the blame on this one all right."

Hutton said, "Well, what are they doin' back up here this time of year? I ain't never seen 'em around here in midwinter before. And particular during the likes of the blizzards we've had this year."

"They grew up here, bad winters and all," I reminded him.

But Ledbetter was off on the same train of thought. He said, "They've been around here for several days. By Ned, they *could* have done this." He sounded as if he didn't really want to believe it but halfway did in spite of himself.

"Yes," I said, "Yampawah could have done this or worse. But I'm here to tell you that he didn't. I'd lay my life on the fact that this here is the work of Ben Blue."

"*Blue?*" Hutton sounded as if he'd never in a thousand years have come up with that one on his own.

I'd warned my boys to watch themselves around Ben Blue, that he was bad medicine, but I hadn't told them what Doc Clayton had said about his being a hired killer. Reckon I thought some of them might get high-spirited and take a mind to try him on for size, especially after I'd been shot. I'd been worried that they'd take out after the wrong man, since I'd thought Jimmy Hearne played a part in the bushwhacking. Now I wondered if I'd done the right thing.

I said, "Ben Blue is a hired killer. And if that's the case, there's no reason for him to be brought in here except to kill, is there?"

Ledbetter frowned. "I heard Blue is a stock detective. And even if he was of a mind to kill, why would he pick off an investigator for the BIA?"

I reckoned right then that keeping my lip buttoned was about to do more harm than good, so I told the two of them everything. I started with what Doc Clayton had told me about Blue working in Leadville, then went on to tell them about Skettering's fancy bookwork when it came to counting cattle. By the time I was done, both of them just stood there, looking as though they had been blindsided by a two-by-four.

Ledbetter said, "Why you been keeping this under your hat, Court? We'd of found some way to stop 'em."

I said, "Reckon I didn't want no killing, boys. Hotter this situation gets, the more likely it is that someone's going to get lead poisoning. I reckon if it's at all possible, we're still going to let the authorities handle this one."

Chip Hutton made a scornful hissing noise. "You mean Sheriff Finsand?"

"I mean Judge Warren. He can get other men and deputize them if he needs to."

"I'd go after Blue in a minute, badge or no badge," Hutton said with a swagger.

"Then I reckon you can see why I was hard put to tell you about his reputation."

Ledbetter was thinking things over hard, and I could see he was working himself up. He said, "It's going to end up the same, no matter who gets notified. If you tell Judge Warren, as soon as he tells the BIA, they're going to send up soldiers from the Meeker garrison or down from Fort Steele. First thing any of 'em is going to do is the easy thing, which is to roust out Yampawah and his clan. Either way you look at it, that skunk Skettering will get just what he wants."

I'd never before seen Ledbetter so perturbed in my life.

"Either way you look at it," he went on, "we've got an Indian ruckus on our hands. Mad as all the Utes are—reservation or not—they're going to do something if the soldiers go after Yampawah. That old Indian has a mite of respect from his tribe. And last time that happened, they was burning buildings from here to the San Juans—"

"They burnt down the Thompsons' ranch buildings," I said, trying to settle him down some. "The rest of the burnings turned out to be just rumor, if you'll kindle your memory some."

"All the same, the Thompson buildings were just up-river, and I have a wife and family here . . ."

Ledbetter was talking himself into a pure-on fit of worry.

I said, "I have a family here myself, and I reckon they'll be just fine. So will your own. Looks to me like the thing to do is find out who killed Kenny Payne."

"I'm beginning to wonder," Ledbetter said, stirring himself up again. "It could have been Yampawah's braves—we don't have any proof they didn't. And if that's the case, they've got to be stopped—"

"You know for sure they axed him?" I shot back.

A little bit of the fire went out of him. "Can't say as I do."

"Then you're going to add more than a mite of fuel to the flames if you go around saying they did it. Look, I'm going to have to notify the judge," I said. "Hopefully he'll have the good sense to tell the men in the BIA that Payne was most likely killed by someone other than the Indians."

"And if the people at the BIA don't believe the judge and call in the soldiers?"

"We need to settle Blue and Skettering's hides right now and straighten this out ourselves," Chip Hutton said. "Me and some of the other boys would be proud to back you up on this."

I hesitated and looked out across the snow-caked land, past the big house and the outbuildings, past the creek with its snow-bent trees, up the hill to where a square iron fence marked off my parents' gravestones. The sky above it was a cloudless vault of blue. The willows beside the fence were weighted heavy with snow, protecting the wrought iron and the headstones and the frigid earth that lay beneath it—and the wooden coffins that lay cold and lifeless under the snow and the frozen soil.

I thought about my pa. I wondered what he would have done with this situation.

He'd have picked up a gun. Of that I was suddenly sure. He'd have thought long and hard about it, but if he was as sure that Ben Blue and Moses Skettering were behind this as I was, he'd have gone the limit in the end.

Yet, *Thou shalt not kill . . .*

The words came back to me, but with them came the rest of it. My pa had killed more than one man—many more than one. But he'd made me vow never to follow that part of his trail.

"Once you start it, the killing never stops," he'd told me. "And once you take a man's life, no matter how bad he deserves it, he still beats you just by forcing your hand to the act. The sharp blades of remorse cut into your immortal soul for all eternity, Courtney. Mark my words. There are reasons for all of God's laws—you'll learn that some day. And when God says, 'Thou shalt not kill,' He says it because life is the most sacred thing He gives us, and you don't tamper with it without paying the full price."

I turned my head away from the gravestones, stepped over and pulled back the blanket again, and looked at what was left of Kenny Payne.

Someone had tampered with Payne's life, and right then I was certain it had been Ben Blue. I wondered how many men Blue had killed, and why. Did *he* feel the sharp blades of remorse cutting into his immortal soul when he thought about them, or was it like butchering cattle to him, just one more varmint under the knife? I drew the blanket up to cover Payne's body again. I'd liked and respected the man, and I felt a sadness cut into me.

201

Hutton and Ledbetter stood there, quiet, watching me. Several other of the boys had gathered around too, staying to one side, silent and waiting to see what I'd do.

I straightened up and spoke to them. "Boys, I'm riding up to Hayden to send a wire to the judge. I'd appreciate it if you'd put this body in the smokehouse and let it stay froze till we see what the judge wants done with it."

Hutton muttered, "Thought we already let the judge handle things once. Thought that was how Payne got kilt to begin with."

Ledbetter just looked at me, and for the first time in my life I saw a touch of disrespect in those weathered blue eyes. Quietly he said, "Well, Court, I suspect it's your ranch—and it's likely to be your hide."

He turned to the others, who hadn't been close enough to hear what he'd said. He barked to them, "C'mon, boys, time's a-wastin'. We got cattle to feed and fences to mend, and I plan to see it done before dark."

I saddled my mare, mounted her, and rode for the telegraph station at Hayden.

19

The judge's return telegram came within the hour. The operator, Sam Taylor, took the message off the line, wrote it down, and handed it to me. It was short and printed on a yellow telegraph flimsy:

HAVE CONTACTED BIA IN DENVER—stop—
ADVISED ONE WEEK DELAY WHILE
WASHINGTON NOTIFIED—stop—WILL
CONTACT YOU AS SOON AS LEARN
DECISION ON ACTION.

It was signed "Judge Lester Warren, District Court, Hahns Peak Village, Seat of Routt County, State of Colorado."

Two days after I'd ridden into Hayden to send the judge a telegram, my daughter was born. It happened on a night when the frost and snow were silver-blue in the light of a hunter's moon. Caroline awakened me at 3:00 A.M., I called Mother Johnson, and she shooed me out and left me to boil and carry water, to go ask Virginia Ledbetter to come and help, and to look in on Little Johnny from time to time, though that didn't last long since I soon awakened him.

The delivery was a hard one. Mother Johnson and Virginia Ledbetter hushed and fussed about while I sat with Johnny in the next room, feeling foolish and about as worthless as Adam's off-ox.

I was a mite perturbed that they wouldn't let me help, though I did manage to pace the floor and pray and worry. I'd pulled more calves than either of them had seen babies, and I reckoned they needed me in there. But Caroline had made Mother Johnson promise that she wouldn't let me see her all bloody and in pain. Reckon she was afraid it would be too disturbing, so they kept me out and nothing for me to do but go along with it.

Several times her moans and cries pulled me through the door, but they shooed me right back out again, saying that with the way Caroline felt about things and all, I was bound to make matters worse than they were.

At last Mother Johnson came to the doorway. She was fairly beaming. "Caroline wants you to come in now. It's a girl, Court, a six-pound seven-ounce miracle."

I rushed in.

Caroline was haggard and tired, but the glow on her face gave her a beauty I'd only seen once before, and that was when Johnny was born. No more than two hours after I'd awakened, I was called into the bedroom to see a tiny angel with pale brown hair wrapped in swaddling clothes and lying in Caroline's arms, its little face so pinched up it was beautiful.

Mother Johnson stood proudly beside the two of them, her hair damp from sweat, but a smile as big as the moon on her face.

Caroline whispered, "Look, Court. She's just exactly what I wanted."

I chuckled at that, knowing that she'd have said the same thing if it had been a boy.

We sat Johnny on the bed beside her, me explaining to him that this tiny little critter was the sister he had wanted, that it was just going to be a matter of time before she'd be filled out enough to go sledding with him, but in the meantime he had to be mighty careful with her.

He was pleased at that, saying, "She's like a flower, ain't she, Pa? Ma told me. You planted the seed, and now she's like a blossom. Ain't that right, Pa?" He was as excited as I'd ever seen him.

I answered him, "That's exactly right, Son."

We named the child Marjorie Elizabeth McCannon. My mother had made me promise that if ever I had a girl child, I'd name her after my grandmother Marjorie; Caroline, for her part, wanted the baby named after her own mother—Elizabeth Johnson. It was a mighty big name for such a little tyke, but that's what we named her, all the same.

That blessed event kept me busy for a few days, what with helping tend to Caroline and handling Johnny. He was plumb proud of that new addition to our family, and he had a mind to treat Little Meg—which was what Caroline chose to call the baby—like she was a fancy grown-up's toy he couldn't get his hands on except when we kept him tamed down some. He'd have had her out sledding and busting broncos if given half a chance.

Virginia Ledbetter helped with the cooking and cleaning, and that freed me up to tend to the basics of the ranch, but I spent those few days wrapped in the wonder of a new life come to this earth, and one I'd taken a part in creating at that.

My daughter was nigh unto a full week old when trouble came again, sure and swift as a lightning bolt, and no time to think about what to do, no time to consider right or wrong before the onslaught forced our hand.

Billy Bailey was a salty young'un out of Rawlins, who'd been with us for the better part of two years, in spite of the fact that he was barely out of his teens. He and Banty Brewster had been in charge of feeding the cattle down at the Elkhead River delta. They'd ridden out with a big load of hay long before sunup, Bailey driving the team and Banty riding alongside in case he needed to herd some strays. No more than an hour past daylight, I was down at the stables tending to an Appaloosa with some saddle sores when I heard a commotion outside.

I stepped out the stable door just as Banty rode in like a whirlwind, jumped from his horse, and hollered, "They got Bailey—back-shot 'im—the blasted no-count vultures, shoot a man like that, warn't hardly more'n a boy—" He choked up then and couldn't talk.

I grabbed him and shook him once. "Give it to me straight. *Who* shot him?" I felt his shoulders heave beneath my hands.

"D-didn't see him, Court. Just heard the report, and then there was Bailey, falling out of the hayrack . . ."

My men were already whipping into action, checking their side arms and rifles, checking ammunition, getting their horses ready to mount. It took me no more than five swift minutes to buckle on my Colt, grab up my Remington, swing a saddle on my own horse, and swing astride her. Then we were on our way, riding as hard as the frozen ground would let us run.

We'd no more than come around the river's bend so that we could see the delta than we knew what had happened.

Skettering was moving his cattle across the ice-bound river and onto my rangeland. This was the only good land I had left, the place where the wind whipped down through Boone Draw and kept the tall, stem-cured brown grass more or less blown clean. I'd been saving that rangeland for the harshest months of winter. I'd just moved some thirty head of my own cattle onto it two weeks before and was planning to bring in several hundred more before the week ended.

Skettering and his men saw us coming. Two cowhands standing guard brought their Winchesters and shotguns up and ready. The others stopped for a quick look our way, then went back to their work, hazing the herd across the ice, whooping and waving their hats to keep them moving, riding back to the draw now and again to round up a stray. With every passing minute more of his cattle were on my land. I guessed maybe a hundred fifty head all told were grazing the bluestem grass that poked out above the light snow cover. My own cattle were milling among them.

As we drew near, Coogan and Bowles rode into my cattle and started to drive them back and off my land. No doubt about it, Skettering was bucking to push things all the way, and it was time to fish or cut bait.

I reined in. Now I lifted my hand to signal my boys to stop too. I rode into the midst of my cattle, and their bodies surged around me, warming me, their bawling and confusion adding to my own bedevilment.

Coogan and Bowles reined in and stopped to watch me.

I'd spotted Bailey. He was still alive, though hurt bad. He'd crawled over to lie beneath a large cottonwood at the right side of the hayrack. Brewster had unhooked the team and tied them to the hayrack before he headed to the ranch. Their reins dangled to the ground as they fussed and pawed and tried to get free.

Bailey's rifle was thrown out a short way from the hayrack, as if he'd had it cradled under his arm when he fell. I reached down and swept it up, then rode over to him and swung down. I already knew that he was in a bad way, even before I rolled him over and took a good look at the wound. The shot had gone clean through the back of his shoulder then come out the front. His long face was pale, his sandy hair was damp from sweat. He was bleeding badly, and I went to work padding up the wound with my kerchief and whatever else I could find.

Always before when I'd seen a person hurt it had opened a wound in me too, and now that feeling came again. But right atop it a feeling of coldness washed in over that grief and swept it away. I suddenly felt almost as if I'd turned to stone. And I was flooded through with a deadly sense of resolve that I'd never known before.

I leaned in over the boy. "Who shot you, Billy?"

His face drew up like a fist from the pain of trying to talk. He stammered, "I—I don't know, Court. The polecat back-shot me—I didn't see him—"

"Good enough, pardner. You hush up now. We can get to the bottom of it after we get you patched up some."

While I knelt there trying to tend to that poor, scared cowhand, I could see the pure truth. Skettering had declared war on me and no two ways about it. I'd walked away from the ill wind he was blowing my way as much as I could. From now on I was going to face the hard truth.

I saw movement out of the corner of my eye. A rider had trotted his horse closer to where I stood, then stopped to watch me. I blinked hard when I saw that it was Jimmy

Hearne, sitting astride that sorrel with the white star on its forehead, the same horse I'd seen him riding in the high country the day he'd shot old Brownie.

Don't know why that surprised me. Even though I'd come to the conclusion that he was tied in with Skettering, I hadn't realized he was actually riding for him. I saw it then. They were so sure they had the upper hand that they weren't bothering to hide their tracks at all anymore.

Skettering's other men had stopped work now, reining their horses in, their mounts prancing, heads high with tight reins. I reached in under Bailey's shoulders and dragged him, fast-like, into the thicket behind the meadow, saying, "Looks like we got some unfinished business, pardner. Hold tight. I'll be back in a spell." I propped his rifle beside him for good measure.

I ran back to my mount and stepped into my stirrup, swung astride, then reined her toward Moses Skettering. He just sat his own horse, his face dark with whatever wicked thoughts lodged in him as he waited for me.

I rode closer to him, easy and steady, and everyone turned to watch as they waited to see what was going to happen. Only the cattle, milling about and bawling, were unconcerned about the storm brewing.

I reined up alongside him, laying my hand lightly on my thigh and close to the butt of my Colt as I said, "Mornin', Skettering. Reckon you must already know that one of my boys got back-shot. Wonder if you could kindly tell me what happened?"

For a brief instant his haggard face drew up into something like a wolfish grin, then went stony again as he said, "Don't know nothing about it."

I felt my jaw go tight. I said, "Reckon you might not know either that this is my rangeland. Fact is, this land you're on is a deeded preemption belonging to me. Lazy Double C has been grazing this land for nigh onto twenty years—"

"So you say. Law says it belongs to Luke Coogan. He filed claim on it no more than a week ago."

I felt a black wind race through me. "That claim won't hold up in court."

The grin was real this time, and it was mean to the core. He said, "Ride on up and see that judge friend of yours then. Fight it in the courts all you want to, but get off this land. I got Coogan's permission to use it, and I'm blamed well going to!"

I said, "Skettering, seems to me there's been trouble enough already—"

A shot cracked, then echoed through the valley. I jerked back and fought with my horse as it skittered in a half circle. Then another shot came, even as I brought my mount up short and whipped around. My gun was drawn, but I wasn't sure where to aim.

A shotgun blast ricocheted thunder off the hills, overshadowing the echo of the other gunshots, and Al Perkins's horse reared onto its hind legs, neighing long and shrill. Then it danced backward and to one side, trying to pitch Perkins from the saddle. A streamer of red appeared across its flank where buckshot pellets had seared it.

Perkins held on, firing his own pistol toward one of Skettering's men, who was galloping away, a shotgun cradled loosely under one arm.

I tried to get off a shot at the varmint, but I couldn't get a clear line of fire. All of my men had their guns drawn, and though we could see who'd pulled the shotgun, I still had no idea who'd fired the rifle shots or where they'd come from.

I glanced back around to see that Skettering was just sitting there watching it all. He was paying me no more mind than if I'd been a knot on a log. He had a peculiar look on his face that matched his stillness, a look of gloating mixed with hate. Then his flinty eyes glanced sideways.

I followed his quick look to see Ben Blue, astride his horse, trotting along the edge of the cattle. It looked like he was maneuvering to draw a bead on Banty Brewster, and old Banty was just sitting there, his back to Blue, his gun limp in his hand. But as I watched, Banty seemed to sense something and began to turn.

I brought my Colt up, took aim at Blue's left arm, but just as I went to pull the trigger something slammed me around, there was a hot sensation in my hand, and my gun fell to the ground.

I whipped around to see Jimmy Hearne three horse-lengths away, his gun aimed dead at me and a savage grin on his face. In that flash of time I could read the light in his eyes, and I knew he was recollecting the day I'd shot him, the day he'd been rustling my cattle, and he was relishing his chance to get even. And then I realized what he'd been up to. They'd no doubt planned to blame that rustling on Yampawah too, maybe even get me to help tie my own noose.

I rolled from my horse and hit the ground under the cattle, the dull sound of their milling hooves all around me. I heard Hearne's pistol cut loose and another shotgun blast, but I was out of his sight, trying to keep from getting crushed, scrambling atop the cow manure and the melting snow.

A strange thought passed through my mind. If I survived this, Caroline would have to throw me a change of clothes out on the porch when I got home and burn the ones I wore.

There was pain in my hand, but I flexed it, and it moved fine. It was just smarting from the recoil as the gun flew from my grip. I'd got lucky. Jimmy Hearne had hit the gun rather than the hand itself.

It was then that I sensed something more hair-raising than any gunshot. There was a new feeling in the air, something raw and so full of fear that I could truly smell it, like the blood and raw ammonia of a fresh-butchered cow.

Suddenly I knew what it was. The gunfire had spooked the herd. They were getting set to stampede. I felt the tension fairly crackling in the air. The only thing that was keeping them from stampeding was their confusion, what with Skettering's cattle coming into my own small herd. If they all got to moving in the same direction, they were going to break loose like an ice floe in a spring gusher.

I tried to stand, but a sudden pressure stopped me. I felt horse hair and the rough leather of a saddle. I looked up just as a spurred boot kicked out at me. I heard a growling laugh and saw Skettering bring his rifle butt around. I dodged, but the butt took me in the side, the weight of the horse behind it, and it pitched me back to the cold earth.

I rolled, to take one of Skettering's horse's hooves right into my sore shoulder. Pain cut through me like a cleaver.

Another gunshot rang out. I rolled aside, beneath a pair of hooves, and missed them to roll out the other side, reaching for the skinning knife I kept sheathed inside my boot, even as I realized it was powerful little help against the flood of evil that had been unleashed upon me.

And then the thunder hit.

Rifle shots echoed back and forth, a horse screamed. A man screamed too, but in rage rather than pain. Men shouted, cursed, and the cattle were surging around me. I managed to roll myself out from under their hooves to the side of the herd. I stood, finally, to see Chip Hutton huddled on the ground no more than ten yards from me, his hand on his arm where he'd been shot.

I saw my horse standing at the edge of the timber that edged the meadow. I raced as fast as my legs would carry me, then grabbed my Remington .30/06 out of the scabbard and tried to leap atop the critter, but at my touch the horse lunged away from me. He felt it too, the raw power in the herd around him, and he was plumb spooked.

Just then Banty rode up to Hutton and slid off his horse. He fell to his knees to look at Hutton's wound just as Blue came up behind him to try again, eyes narrowed, gun aimed. He wanted Banty bad, probably because Banty had seen who'd shot Bailey, and it seemed to me that he had a stomach for back-shooting rather than facing a man.

I reckoned then that Blue himself had been the one to shoot Billy Bailey, but I had no time to think more than that, for Blue was taking aim, and as he drew off at Banty I whipped my own firearm up. I got off my shot too fast and missed him, but the bullet brought him around to face me and made him hold off on shooting Banty.

Another rifle shot cracked. I spun around to see Coogan coming up, getting ready to fire again, aiming beyond me. I wheeled back. Banty was running. A shot cracked out, and then Banty was running slower, limping. Coogan had hit him but not killed him—not yet.

The men who were still mounted were fighting against the surging cattle, the fear growing stronger, and the surging herd drew Coogan's and Blue's attention away from Banty and me for the moment. I tried to get to Banty, but a thick wall of cattle brought me to a stop.

Then a different noise pulled me around. Jimmy Hearne was riding down hard on me, his six-shooter ready to take aim.

Al Perkins came in from the side at a dead run, his horse's flank red with blood from the shotgun blast, and he smashed that horse smack into Hearne's mount, shouldering it sideways.

Hearne fell off the far side, just as Skettering rode in behind Perkins and brought his rifle butt across the back of Perkins's head, knocking him reeling so that he barely stayed in the saddle.

We were getting the worst of this battle, and no two ways about it. If the tide didn't turn pretty quick, all my boys would be hurt or dead, the McCannon name would be disgraced forever, and all my pa's work and sweat and tears would have been for nothing and my own as well. At that moment not one of our lives was worth a plugged nickel.

And as that thought hit me, a sudden powerful surge like first breakup of a log-jammed creek pushed me backwards. The power of it broke me loose and to the edge of the clearing, sending me running backward, having all I could do to stay afoot.

One loco critter was all it ever took, a lead cow who could turn the herd. The cattle were all facing the same direction now—west—and they were milling and rubbing against one another, lowing, moving faster, and suddenly like a flood tide their energy was massed into a thick, forward surge.

I heard a shout, looked over at Skettering, saw him spin about, his face registering shock as two dozen steers bore down on him. He spurred his horse. It bucked and bolted forward and off to the side and pitched itself out of the way of the red flood, for the cattle were running now, slow but picking up speed, and anything in their way was caught up in the torrent.

My own horse was still mixed in with the herd. Its eyes were wide with terror as it was jostled past me. I felt something hot and touched my shoulder to find that the old wound had been reopened, and I was losing blood. But that thought was washed from my mind as the herd swerved toward me.

I managed to roll to one side and tumble into a watery ditch. Then I scrambled up and out the other side and skedaddled into a clump of cottonwoods. Once behind them, I caught my breath and watched the wall of cattle moving past, faster then faster, the men's shouts vanishing behind the thunder of hoofbeats.

Skettering rode high in his saddle, off to the other side of the raging clay-red stream. The thunder was rumbling past me and down through the valley now. I saw him raise his pistol and fire into the air, although I couldn't hear the report above the pounding of hooves. But the lead cattle heard, for they veered again, away from him.

He reined his horse around so abruptly that the bit nearly broke its jaw, his own face set in rage. He waved for his men to follow as he rode back across the river, his horse skidding on the river ice where the cattle's hooves had beaten through the snow cover as they crossed earlier.

His cowhands rode in behind him, all of them heading northwest toward their ranch, riding with the herd, no doubt hoping to let their cattle wear themselves down or be stopped by the deep snow to the west or by the heavy timber a half mile downstream. A good number of my own cattle were mixed in with that stampede, but I wasn't of a mind just then to question the good Lord's answer to the silent prayers I'd been muttering. If it cost me a few head to get out of this predicament, so be it and amen.

As sudden as it had started, the roar of cattle was gone around the bend, leaving only a quaking in the earth beneath our feet.

Ledbetter's face was white as he rode up to me. "You OK, Boss? By vexation and thunder, that arm of yours appears to be hurt again. It looks bad."

I grimaced as I tried to move it but said, "I'll be all right. How's Banty? Hutton? Did they get Perkins too?"

Ledbetter jerked his head to the side and said, "Look for yourself."

Perkins rode up, leading my horse. He dismounted and stood beside me.

I said, "I thought they'd done for you."

He replied with a boost that helped me into the saddle. "Knocked me a-loop for a spell, but I'm tough as rawhide," he said. "Skettering and his henchmen ain't going to be the ones to cash in old Al."

Ledbetter's face set hard. "Court, you'd best know right now. Hutton's hurt bad."

"I know. I saw it." On a sudden, I felt weak and dizzy.

Perkins was looking at me strangely, his eyes trailing down my side and to the ground. I followed his gaze to see blood dripping all the way down my leg and onto the shoulder of the saddle horse. I felt my side. It was damp too. I held out my hand. It was smeared with blood. I figured I'd been hit after all, without so much as knowing it.

Perkins said to Ledbetter, "We'd best get the boss in to the doc. They got Banty too. They winged him, and then he got stomped by the cattle—"

I said, "Bailey's worst off. He's over behind that clump of cottonwoods."

"I seen him. He was still alive."

"Go get him, then you get him and Chip Hutton and Banty into town to the doc. I'll make it back to the ranch."

"Don't go acting loco, Court—"

"Go on. The doc can't work on but one of us at a time anyways, and Caroline can tend to me for a while. Have some of the boys see if they can find my revolver out there in the mud and cow manure, and then when the doc is finished working on the others, bring him on out to take a look at me."

Ledbetter decided not to argue. "Up to you, I expect. Whatever we do, we'd best get moving. If we don't get Bailey and Chip Hutton to the doc pretty soon, we're going to be delivering them to their Maker instead."

For a minute I couldn't do anything but sit that horse and breathe deep. I was feeling weaker by the minute, but I was just as perturbed that things had turned into such a stirred-up mess. I turned to Perkins. "We drill any of them?"

His voice was bitter. "Not a one. They caught us off guard, Boss. While we was fixin' to palaver, they was fixin' to dig our graves."

Ledbetter looked at me steadily, and I saw accusation in his eyes. "After we take Chip and Banty to the doc's, you want me to get a couple of the boys together and ride after Skettering? We could take his hide if we'd a mind to—"

"Much obliged, but I reckon it's not really your fight," I said tightly. "Even if I was to lose every head of cattle I own and every acre of rangeland, there's no shred of a reason for any one of you getting killed."

Perkins snorted. "You're wrong about that, Boss. But even if you was right, it don't change the fact that something's goin' to have to be done and soon, or Skettering's varmints are going to turn this valley into a graveyard, and we're going to be the ones planted in it. Us and maybe Yampawah and his hungry bunch."

"We're going to do something, all right." I heard the grimness in my own voice. "But we're goin' to make good and sure that it's the right thing before we do it. Now let's get those boys in to the doc's."

20

I woke up the next morning in my own bed with the sun filtering through the drawn muslin curtains. Caroline had done her best with me, but a fever had set in, and I'd gone out like a campfire in a gully washer no more than an hour after I'd returned to the ranch house.

Doc Clayton was sitting in the leather wing chair beside me. His eyes were shut. His face was pale from exhaustion, and his mouth sagged open as he made a little snore. His brown wool vest was wrinkled and unbuttoned, his white cotton shirt sleeves were rolled up, and he had a Navajo blanket thrown across his lap. His thinning brown hair stuck up in places like dry grass.

I leaned on my arm, trying to sit up. Pain shot through my shoulder, and I moaned. My hand shot to the shoulder, and I touched a swathe of bandages.

Doc's eyes flew open, and he was at full military attention, glowering down at me before I'd even halfway settled myself again. He barked, "Court, if you don't quit punishing that shoulder you're bound and for sure to lose the use of that arm."

I suddenly remembered everything, clearer than it appeared to me while it was happening.

I had three cowhands hurt because of Skettering's gang: Banty, Chip Hutton, and the Bailey boy—and the last two hurt bad. I remembered feverish dreams, with old Yampawah's voice hovering behind all my recollections, talking once again of the wind-song of death.

"How are my boys?" I muttered. In spite of myself, I shivered long and hard.

"They're stove up some, but no worse than yourself. Pull that blanket up," Doc growled. "I spent six hours of pure hard work trying to mend up that arm of yours. I don't plan to see you break those stitches open again, and I sure don't plan to let you up and take a chill and die of pneumonia. Get that blanket up. Here, blast it, let me do it!"

His eyes were bloodshot, and I knew he was drained. He leaned over me, talking as he yanked the blanket up around my chin. His breath smelled of stale pipe tobacco.

I touched my bandage. "What happened? Was I gunshot?"

"Looks to me like hoof-whipped is more like it. Seems that one of those heifers kicked your shoulder hard enough to split the skin."

I remembered Skettering's horse's hooves digging into my sore shoulder. I felt a wash of relief to hear that I hadn't been shot, but a wash of savage anger came next that Skettering had done this to me.

Little Johnny had evidently heard Doc rumbling, for he poked his head through the doorway just then.

I forced a smile to my face and said, "Howdy, son."

He stood there, eyes wide, taking things in. He tried to smile back at me, but his lip trembled some. "Mornin', Pa." He sounded sad. He said, "I heard you yellin' last night. Ma said you was hurt on account of the cattle."

He came toward me, and I reached my good arm out toward him, pulling the blanket from my shoulders as I moved. His eyes widened as he saw the bandages.

At that moment the doc swept Johnny up, saying, "It looks a heap worse than it is, little fellow. Your pa's going to be OK."

Then Johnny saw Caroline coming into the room and reached for her. She was a vision in pink calico, with a white ribbon in her dark hair. She took Johnny from Doc, her arms full with him. He was a chunk for a two-year-old, and she was still mending from the baby's birth.

She sat down across the room on the Boston rocker and hugged him tight. She nuzzled his cheek and said, "Just don't you worry. Seems like we have some angels who take care of your father from time to time." She looked at the doc and smiled. "Right now one of those angels' names appears to be Doc Clayton."

He seemed embarrassed, then looked at the floor.

She let Johnny go, giving him a light swat on his backside. "Now just you run back down to the kitchen and help Grandmom fry up those eggs. Land sakes, I thought you said you were hungry!"

He was reluctant to leave. He sidled toward the door, then stopped. "Is Pa going to eat with us?"

Caroline shook her head and frowned. "Not this morning."

But I was already swinging my long-handled legs over the side of the featherbed. I said, "You bet your boots I am. Tell Grandmom to put on another rasher of bacon."

Doc stood up, saying, "Whoa, boy. You're not getting out of that bed yet."

"Doc, I remember the last time I got stove up, I laid in this bed a week and was housebound for a month. By the time I got up I was so stiff and sore that I like to never got moving again. I'll take it slow and easy, but I've a mind to move around. There are things that have to be done, and I ain't likely to do them from this bed."

I ignored the surge of pain in my shoulder and the weakness that washed over me as I reached over to the chair and grabbed my Levi's.

Caroline shook her head. "He never learns a thing." She was wearing a frown as she went out the door after Johnny.

Doc left the room too, and I set to shaving the cactus from my face and washing up. As I dressed, I tried to decide what needed to be done. Being a cattleman, I have to admit I was used to a heap of bad wind blowing in my direction and coming from a lot of different places at that. But having my own body bunged up again was the final straw.

The more I thought about it, the more it seemed that things had been going from bad to worse ever since I'd been bushwhacked up in the tall timber that day. After that, I'd been shoulder-shot when driving my load of oats and corn home from the Tucker store. Having that lame shoulder dragging me down all the time had been about my worst problem up until the moment they'd brought Payne in on that bobsled. And then Banty had come riding in with the bad news about Bailey.

Now I'd be a monkey's uncle if I didn't have the same old problem of a lame shoulder back again, on top of all the rest. I was plumb perturbed as I thought about all that had happened. But I wasn't about to lie down with it. A man could die in bed.

As everything came back, I knew with cold, dead certainty that something was going to have to be done about Skettering and his gang. I turned to look at myself in the mirror and saw that knowledge come into my face—it turned dark, as if someone had switched off the light behind it.

And I reckon I knew too that whatever was going to be done would be on my shoulders and mine alone. No matter what happened, not one more of my men was going to be hurt! Not if I could help it. They were hired hands and good ones, and my trouble with Skettering was not their battle—although I knew that any one of them would fight to the finish for me.

As yet I didn't know exactly where that left me. Hadn't had time to mull it over and figure it out, but I was about to.

Breakfast was harder to handle than I'd expected it to be, but I wasn't about to get back in that bed. I reckon most of my problem was that I felt plumb foolish for more or less letting the same thing happen to me twice, both times getting bushwhacked and not doing what was needed to prevent it on account of my so-called principles.

I was plumb fed up with Skettering's bunch. But more than that, I was fed up with myself. It seemed to me that I was becoming more of a coward than a man of principle. And for all that, I still didn't have a handle on what needed doing next.

Throughout breakfast, Caroline kept that frown on her face. When she'd look at me, I saw that something was gnawing at her. Reckon I was figuring it was just her irritation at my foolishness in letting myself get hurt again, since she nagged me all the way through the meal about going back to bed. But right after she'd poured the doc his final cup of coffee, it came out.

Smoothing her hair like she always did when she was troubled, she said, "Doc, I never knew Court's father well—"

"Not many folks did," Doc replied. "He was a hard man to know." He took a sip of coffee and nodded his approval once again to Mother Johnson, who smiled.

I was surprised to hear her bring up my father. I shoveled a bite of flapjack into my mouth and listened to what was on her mind.

Caroline was looking down at her plate, using her fork to push a small slab of bacon around. Reckon I hadn't noticed till then that she wasn't eating. She said, "Doc, tell me. Do you think that Major McCannon was a cruel man?"

"Cruel? The major?"

"Well . . . you know, I was only around him the two years before he died, but looking back I can't remember ever having seen him smile. There was something about him that was . . . well . . . maybe not cruel . . . maybe more like . . . tormented."

"Tormented?"

Caroline fussed. "It's hard to say exactly—"

He interrupted. "Yes, well, I think I know what you mean. But I can tell you from firsthand experience, there wasn't so much as a lick of cruelty in Major McCannon. Not so much as a lick."

Caroline stammered, "It's just that I heard so much about how fierce he was during the Indian campaigns, and then he spent so much time with the Utes after he came back from the big war . . ."

I was still surprised at the turn the conversation had taken. I don't think we'd truly talked about Pa for a year or more, though he was mentioned from time to time in passing.

Caroline and I had been married only two years before my pa's death, and she had never known my mother at all.

We all fell silent, me shoveling in food, Little Johnny at the side of the table playing, the baby in a crib in the corner sleeping, and the rest lost in their thoughts. Caroline kept looking straight down at her plate, with her frown growing deeper.

Finally Mother Johnson broke the silence. "Caroline! My land, why don't you just tell them?"

I said, "Tell us what?"

Caroline stood up, sweeping her long skirt to one side. She went to the high oak chiffonier, pulled open one of its wide drawers, and took out a thin stack of tintypes. She sat back down and moved her plate and glass to one side. Then, holding the cardboard-backed photographs close to her, she said to the doc, "You know, Court and I lived here on the ranch with the major for a spell before he died. He was always polite to me, always considerate, and the gentlest man alive. But he was so unhappy. I could never understand it."

"He loved that wife of his about as much as Court loves you," Doc said, "but for all that, he was never a happy man after he came back from the big war."

I was curious as to why this mattered at this moment, and I wondered what she was doing with those tintypes. But I knew better than to rush my wife into anything.

Doc took a long sip of coffee. "When I first knew him, he'd just come back East and joined the Union army. He had a passel of guilt about the way his kinfolks had made their money. He was a hard-boiled antislaver, serious as sin about the battle we were about to fight and yet shamed sometimes that he was fighting against his own boyhood friends and cousins. But for all that, he was feisty and laughed a good deal."

"It's hard to think of him ever being like that," Caroline said.

The doc nodded. "I didn't meet up with him again until after the papers were signed at Appomattox and he'd decided to come back West. By then he was a different person. Terribly unhappy—you're right about that. But your mother, Court—well, that woman was the shining light of the major's life. I understand that in their younger days he was too rambunctious to treat her as good as she deserved, but he did his best to make up for it later. When she died, he just turned into a shadow."

Caroline's green eyes had kindled with interest. "Do you think that was it then? I mean, do some men really just wither up and fade away when they lose the woman they love?"

A dark memory crossed the doc's face. "It was that, but it was something more too. Something happened between the time I knew him in Virginia and the time he came back West. Something pretty horrible, I'd say, to have changed him that much. But then sometimes war does that to a man.

"Look at Moses Skettering. Fought for the Graycoats, they say. Some folks hereabouts say that's what turned him into the black-hearted devil that he is. Too much suffering—whether his own or that which he inflicted on others is hard to say—but too much suffering just the same. Seems that it withered up his humanity, turned him into not much more than a shell filled up with hatred for his fellow man."

"I've only met Moses Skettering in passing," Caroline said. "I really don't know much about the man."

"Reckon that's because whatever time you spend in Windsor has revolved around the church since it was built, and Skettering isn't one to go to church," I said.

"I haven't even been to town all winter," Caroline said dismally.

"Then it's lucky for us the parson doesn't mind driving out once in a while," Mother Johnson said, her lips pursed in disapproval. She understood that Caroline hadn't been able to ride through the snow and mud during the last months of her pregnancy, and since then she'd been housebound by caring for the baby, who was too small to make the cold, windy trip into town this time of year.

All the same, Mother Johnson believed in church three times a week. In Denver that was easy to do. Out here she felt guilty at our distance from town. Reckon she thought that was the same thing as distance from the good Lord Himself.

"Skettering's a miserable man," the doc said. "Filled full of hatred. He managed to hide it when he was first settling in here. But I've got a keen eye, and I'd seen it from time and time, even before he lit into Court."

"He's going to push things to the limit, isn't he?" Caroline said, turning to me.

I saw sick worry in her eyes that nigh broke my heart. I'd wanted to keep the whole thing from her, but considering the way Skettering and his varmints kept knocking me around six ways from Sunday, I'd figured she had to know what the snake was up to.

"Reckon yesterday was the limit," I said, looking down and away from her eyes.

She paused, thinking, then she laid the tintypes on the table and said, "Mom and I were looking for some of your and Johnny's baby things in the trunks up in the attic. We got to rummaging around, and we found these."

She handed me one. I recognized it. In fact, I'd shown it to Caroline when we'd first been married, so I knew she'd seen it before too. My pa stood there in his Union blues, his major's insignia on his shoulders, his brown Vandyke beard and mustache perfectly trimmed as always. Several tough and tired-looking Bluecoats stood beside him, carbines aimed at about a dozen men in tattered uniforms, a couple in civilian clothing, standing in a straggling line, waiting to be herded into the open door of a boxcar. There was a scribble beneath the picture that read, "Major William Brevard McCannon with prisoners of war, after the Battle of Richmond."

I knew the picture well. When I was a boy, I'd spent hours going through Pa's things, reliving an imaginary version of the war. I handed the tintype to the doc, then turned to Caroline, puzzled, and said, "Reckon I don't see just why this matters right now."

She handed me a second tintype, saying, "Look closer at this one then."

It was similar to the first, but this picture had been taken from a side angle, so that you could see the prisoners' faces, and one man—a gray-coated officer—stood in front of them beside my pa.

Caroline said, "You know, Court, I had the strangest feeling that day when Ben Blue rode in to water his horse. I felt that I'd seen him somewhere before. Look, look here." She pointed to the gray-coated officer with her forefinger. "Look at that face."

I felt a shock like a razor whip.

Looking straight out of the photograph was Ben Blue, an expression of subdued rage mixed with deep, deep sadness on his face. He was younger by some twenty years, ragged and unshaven though wearing that Johnny Reb officer's uniform. He was lean and haggard-looking, but it was he.

Caroline turned the tintype over. Written on the back was the legend, "Union Major William B. McCannon with Confederate Lt. Benjamin Buchanan, after the capture of Buchanan's forces at Richmond."

Doc took the picture, looked at it, and said, "Well, I'll be dogged, if that doesn't beat all—"

Caroline said, "I'm right, aren't I? It's him."

I nodded, while the doc said again, "If that isn't the strangest thing—"

Caroline said, "Doesn't that make you wonder why this 'Ben Blue,' as he now calls himself, is really here?"

Doc said, "You thinking it has something to do with the major?"

Flatly I said, "My pa's been dead for a good long time, Caroline. If Blue, or Buchanan, or whatever you want to call him, could have found out where he was, he'd surely have found that out as well."

I glanced at the doc. He'd turned to look at me. His lips were pursed up tight as if he wasn't planning to say a word. His face was whiter and more tired than when I'd first waked him up.

I said, "What do you think, Doc? This fit in with any-thing you might know?"

Caroline interrupted, "It's too much of a coincidence, isn't it? I mean, what else could he be doing here?"

The doc started to say something, stopped himself, said instead, "I couldn't tell you. But I do know a few people, and I promise you this, I'll make it a point to find out what I can. In the meantime I'd well be careful to watch my back, Court. That trouble at the delta yesterday is bound to be just the beginning. As for Blue?" He shook his head in consternation. "Whatever he was during the war, I can full well tell you what he is now. He's a hired killer. And it seems to me that unless someone takes this bull by the horns, him and Skettering are in this valley to stay."

21

When trouble comes, it comes in bunches, and I'd fought only the first skirmish in that particular war.

The roads had dried up some, and along about three o'clock of that same day, just after the doc had departed for home, a sleek black buggy turned off the river stage road and made for our ranch house.

I'd finally given in to Caroline and Mother Johnson and gone upstairs to rest for a spell. But I couldn't get Skettering, Blue, and Hearne off my mind long enough to fall asleep, and in spite of Doc's reassuring words, I was still concerned about Banty and Billy Bailey.

When Caroline came and told me company was on the way, I stood at the bedroom window, watching the buggy come down the muddy lane. I'd gone downstairs by the time it drew to a stop in front of the ranch house.

Out climbed Judge Warren.

Right behind him came a man who was as round as a watermelon, with a head that appeared to be cut a mite too small for his body in spite of its several rolling chins. He reminded me of the egg in the Humpty-Dumpty story in one of Johnny's picture books. His legs were stubby and short.

But he was a dandy dresser, I'll give him that. I could see the sparkle of his gold watch chain dangling from a fob on his vest. He'd clothed himself in a good brown wool suit and an expensive greatcoat. He wore a red plaid muffler that he'd wrapped around his ears and his neck, though it did nothing to conceal all of his chins. Atop his head he'd chunked on an old-fashioned stovepipe hat.

When Caroline and I greeted the two of them at the door, I could see that the man's cheeks were fat and ruddy from the cold. His eyes looked small because of the fat in his face, and they were as hard and as black as a fresh-mined chunk of coal.

"Court," said the judge, "I'm pleased to be able to introduce you to Senator Otis Brown."

I'd already suspected as much, so I shook his hand mildly, told him that I was pleased to meet him. But I wasn't strictly speaking the truth. Brown was already looking at me as if he figured that everything bad that had ever happened in the whole blasted county was bound to be my fault, and I reckon that brought my hackles up some.

All the same, I managed to get past the formalities. When we were inside and seated, I tried to stay calm as he drank my company sherry wine from my mother's favorite Irish crystal decanter and glasses while explaining to me just why it was that I shouldn't have been born in the first place.

He started off by explaining that he'd been concerned by the death of BIA agent Kenny Payne and had needed to do some business with Judge Warren up at Hahns Peak anyway. He'd been tending to those matters when he heard about my boys' and Skettering's trouble down at the delta. He followed that up with some boasting about what an important man he was and how much his image meant—mostly to himself, I reckoned. Then he finally got around to saying what was on his mind.

"Mis-ter McCannon," he started off, "it has been a solidly accepted fact ever since the first trouble began with these Utes in this part of our state that the individual who thinks he's doing the most good for these poor backward redskins is often as not the one stirring up the most trouble, albeit unintentionally. *Harumph.* I understand that was a factor in your trouble with Moses Skettering and perhaps the reason why some of your men and his ended up having a shoot-out yesterday down at Elkhead Creek. Am I wrong about that?"

He took a sip of sherry to whet his tongue.

I took a deep breath and reined in my anger. Just as I started to reply, his tongue set to wagging again.

"I've made it no secret that I own considerable interests in the ranch that Moses Skettering runs—and calls his own, I might add, though with no right to do so. *Ahem.* It was brought to our attention when we rode through Hayden—and were stopped, I might also add, by that rude telegraph operator at the stage depot there—that this trouble yesterday was more than a mere ruckus between a few unruly cowhands. The man said he'd heard your trouble with Skettering was turning into a full-on range war."

"I expect you might say that."

"I was told that the trouble had something to do with my very own cattle—that is, with the cattle that belong to the M-Slash-S, which, as I said, I partly own. Is that correct?"

I said, "Reckon it had a mite more to do with the men than with the cattle—"

But he cut me short, waving a fat little paw and leaving a trail of smoke from his cigar. "While I was in this part of the state, I'd planned to look into matters concerning the theft of my cattle by certain renegade Injuns. Now it seems that I've made a timely—yes, timely—arrival, for it seems that matters do appear to be getting worse."

The judge had slumped down in the armchair with a disgruntled look on his face. Caroline caught my eye and rolled her own toward the heavens.

I bit my lip and kept my peace.

Brown said, "In spite of the fact that I have financial interests in the M-Slash-S, I want to tell you that what we're after here is justice—yes, justice—and I'm here to see that justice is done." He raised his glass as if to make a toast to himself, then gulped it all down. His eyes told me that he was a shrewd man, though you would never know him for anything but a buffoon from the way he talked.

Caroline offered him a refill. He smiled and asked for only half a glass.

Getting his wind up again, he said, "The judge has been kind enough to inform me that all might not be completely well with my holdings at the ranch."

The judge looked at me as if to apologize for ever having said a word.

Brown continued, "Yes, indeed. Now, I'd like to get the full matter straightened out." He leaned in close, and I could smell the cigar smoke and alcohol on his breath. His voice dropped, so that Caroline also had to lean forward to hear what he was saying.

"The fact is, the judge tells me that Mr. Skettering has been falsifying his records in order to defraud his investors, which of course includes me. So you can see that I do, indeed, have reason to be concerned over my holdings, aside from the trouble with the Injuns."

He cleared his throat, then barreled ahead in a louder voice. "However—*harumph*—I might say that is a harsh accusation and particularly when coming from an advocate of the law such as the judge here. I have a great deal of respect for Judge Warren"—he was talking about the man as if he weren't even there—"and I feel the accusation has to be taken seriously. All the same, I take every man's complaints with a grain of salt, for there's no telling what ax he may have to grind."

I thought he was finished and started once again to say something, but he had only been catching his breath.

"I might add that I have indeed had a most tedious journey. I am, frankly, exhausted. But make no mistake about it, I plan to find out just what has occurred between you and the man who manages my ranch. I swan, I can't believe that I have walked in on the tail of an actual shoot-out! And I was figuring that the folks up in these parts were becoming more civilized now that we had the Injun situation more or less under control."

Caroline's eyes blazed green fire at that, and I could see her biting on her lip to keep from speaking her mind.

The senator leaned in even closer to me. His beady black eyes snapped. He said, "I am told that you and yours are, if I might say it, more or less trying to pin the blame on Moses Skettering for all that has gone wrong here, including the Injun thefts. Well?"

He'd stopped so abruptly that he'd caught me off guard. He was drawn up in an accusing posture, and I couldn't think of a blamed thing to say in that instant.

Caroline was fairly steaming. "That is the most unfair string of words that have ever been uttered in this household."

I recovered then and said, "She's right, Senator. That's not exactly the way things have been happening—" But before I could even finish, Brown was running off at the mouth again.

"I would have sworn that I'd never live so long as to see the day that Coloradans would socially backslide so far as to actually gunfight over cattle. *Harumph.* Sir, would you be so kind as to tell me in your own words just exactly what did happen here? Were there indeed three men injured?"

"Four, including Court," Caroline snapped.

"Now, little lady, just settle down there." He brushed a hand in her direction as though he were brushing aside a fly. "This is man's business." He turned back to me.

Startled, I blurted out, "They're trying to steal my rangeland, Senator—"

But once again he was thinking about himself rather than listening. He plowed on like a freight train barreling downgrade with no brakes. "That Injun has me concerned. That one who calls himself the Chief of Mountain People or some such nonsense, the one who'd been stealing livestock from my ranch—what was his name again?" He turned toward Judge Warren.

The judge said, "Chief Yampawah, and I don't recall saying that he was stealing anyone's livestock."

"Yes, well—" he turned back to me "—was he involved in the shoot-out?"

I was shaking my head in disbelief. I felt as if I had a bellyful of sour apples, just listening to his talk. I said, "Senator, didn't you just tell me that the judge said Skettering was padding his cattle tally?"

"What?"

"Falsifying his records, I believe is the way you put it. Lying, in other words, about how many cattle he had to begin with and how many he has now. Lying about the Indians rustling his nonexistent cattle, for that matter."

He bristled at that. "We mustn't be hasty to accuse an innocent man. And what of this dispute about my ranchland? I received a telegram some weeks ago to the effect that the land in that part of the delta had been proved up by a man name of Luke Coogan, who had given Skettering permission to run his cattle there through winter's hardest months."

I was worn out from the pain in my shoulder and another pain that had nothing to do with the comfort of my chair. I said, "I got three cowhands hurt on account of this business and half a dozen more who're still searching for my stampeded cattle. I'm proud that you chose to visit us, Senator, but where were you when the man who runs your spread was back-shooting my men and stealing my land? Just what people are you serving anyway?"

The judge saw how upset I was. He looked up from under those thorny white eyebrows of his and said, "Now, Court, do try to understand. The senator can't be expected to know all the particulars—"

Brown puffed up and said, "I serve the people of the state of Colorado, Mis-ter McCannon. You can put that in the bank. *Harumph!* I will get this matter settled, mark my words. We'll be riding on to Windsor to spend the night at the Elkhorn Hotel and Saloon. And then we'll ride out to the M-Slash-S to talk to Mr. Skettering himself. I can see that you're taking a hard line with this. Unfortunate. You'd be a good deal better off if you chose to cooperate.

"Frankly, it will depend upon what Mr. Skettering tells me whether or not I recommend to my friends in the BIA that they send in soldiers from the Meeker garrison to arrest the chief. That's what the folks in Washington want to do about the matter. I'll be quite frank about that. And perhaps they're right, though the judge here has persuaded me to look further into matters before I offer my position on the situation."

"Yampawah had nothing to do with any of this, and I'd stake my life on the fact that he wasn't behind the killing of Kenny Payne."

"So you say. From what I understand, he's nothing but a troublemaker and should have stayed in Leavenworth after the ruckus at White River. Why he's loose I have no idea, and if you had a bone in your head you'd be glad to see the end of him. I expect that once he's gone and the cattle thefts stop, the rest of the trouble will die down too."

He looked at me as if he expected me to be pleased. His cheeks puffed up as he smiled, but his eyes stayed black and dead.

I said, "You're barking up the wrong tree, Senator, and from what I can see at this minute you're bound to make matters worse instead of better."

But he didn't seem to hear a word I'd said. He turned to the judge. "I'm sure that with Judge Warren's help we can find a solution to this problem. Yes, indeed. A solution that is acceptable to all concerned." He turned to Caroline again, as if he were addressing a servant. "Now, Mrs. McCannon, if you'll just pour me another glass of that excellent sherry of yours for a road-warmer—yes, that's quite enough, thank you—we'll be on our way." He swallowed the sherry in one lick, then took a puff on the still-lit butt of his cigar and ground it out in the saucer that Caroline had provided for him to use as an ashtray.

When Senator Otis Brown stood to put on his coat and hat, I felt a wash of relief. When he'd gone out the door and climbed in the carriage, Caroline and I came back in the house, looking at one another in angry bewilderment.

The judge picked that moment to knock on the door, then stick in his head. Apparently he'd made some excuse, climbed back out of the carriage, and come to have a private word with us.

He said, "Court, I'm sure sorry about this development. I got word that the BIA in Washington was talking about calling out the soldiers from the Meeker garrison, so I encour-

232

aged Brown to come on over and stick his nose into things, thinking I could persuade him to call them off. I can see now that I've made a mistake, but I still think I can keep it in hand.

"I deeply apologize to you for his being here—and especially to you, Miss Caroline, for his despicable behavior. I promise you that as soon as we visit Skettering's ranch, I plan to get him on the passenger train at Rawlins and back to Denver as soon as I possibly can. After that I'll deal with the BIA directly to undo whatever harm he might put in motion."

I said, "Judge, I'll be happy to have the boys throw a rope on him and drag him up to the depot in Rawlins this very minute. Just say the word."

The judge shook his head quickly. "He may be long-winded, Court, but he's a powerful man. I put up with him for one reason only. If he says the word, I'll never be nominated, much less win the election. As much as I hate having to do it, I have to keep the man happy, see to it that he leaves here with at least a feeling of some sort of satisfaction."

He glanced out the window as if to make sure the senator was still in the carriage, then he said, "Things are worse than they seem, Court. Just between the two of us, I've learned that Brown is in league with the most crooked factions in the state and federal governments. Kenny Payne was right. And Brown is still planning to get the cattle contracts for the Indian reservations awarded to the M-Slash-S. There's big money for him in this, Court, and money he badly needs. I guess I don't have to tell you what it all means for the Utes."

"Well, things never get so bad but what they can't get worse," I said.

The judge looked out the window again. This time, looking over his shoulder, I could see the curtain in the buggy pulled back and Brown looking toward us, an impatient expression on his face.

Judge Warren emitted a mild oath, then said, "To tell you the truth, I think that Brown already knew Skettering was cheating him. He didn't act a bit surprised. I don't think it matters to him, so long as he can dip his fingers into this new pot." He sighed. "Hold things steady, Court. I'll need your help while I figure out a way to get Brown out of my hair and get his greedy fingers out of the Indians' supplies."

"I'll do the best I can."

Judge Warren said, "Thank you, Court. As soon as I get rid of Brown, I plan to get matters straightened out with regard to Coogan's claim on your land. It's illegal—I know it is because I drew up the original preemption for your father, and he earned it fair and square."

"Your biggest problem is going to be the death of Kenny Payne."

"I plan to let the soldiers handle it, Court. That seems best to me, so long as they understand that they can't just blame things wholesale on Yampawah's tribe." He sighed again, as though he was plumb wore out. "Well . . . I'd best get out there and keep my eye on Brown. No telling what that man might stir up before I can get him out of here."

He walked to the door, then turned back to me and tipped his hat. I could see the worried look on his face as he climbed into the buggy, and then it rolled away.

22

Billy Bailey died that night. He'd come home to mend, after the doc treated his wound in town. But infection set in, and before he knew how sick he was, he was dead.

I rode up to Hayden's stage station the next morning and tried to notify his folks in Rawlins by telegram, but they'd moved on to parts unknown. Two of the cowhands had already put his coffin on a spring wagon by the time I got back, ready to set out for Rawlins. Now they pulled the simple wooden coffin back off, and we decided to bury him on the ranch.

I sent word to Pastor Teagarden in Windsor, asking him to come out for the burial. I felt a strong need to talk to him anyway, but it was impossible for me to make the trip into town just then, what with all that was going on. He rode out the next day on his little bay mare.

Several others, including many of Billy's cowboy friends from Windsor and Hayden, joined us in paying our final respects as we buried him in the family cemetery on the hill north of the ranch buildings. I sure hated to see him go. It left a lump in my throat and an ache in my heart, and as I listened to the preacher I felt more than a few tears run down my cheeks.

During the service I noticed that Caroline was especially white-faced and tight-lipped, but then a lot of folks had been that way around me lately.

During the short committal by Parson Teagarden, I stood beside her, with her bracing me up as much as I was warming her. There was a light snow falling from the scudding clouds, even though it was getting close to spring. Then, just as the final prayer was carried away on the crisp snow-laden wind, she leaned up tighter against me and whispered, "Court, we need to talk."

"I'm listening."

"No, we need to talk privately. Later, when we get home."

We walked over to the small buckboard we'd used as a hearse. The parson joined us for the short rough ride back down the hill.

Virginia Ledbetter and Alice Nelson had put together a feed for all the boys, so we joined them down at the bunkhouse, Caroline included, and filled our tin plates with fried chicken, mashed potatoes, hot biscuits, beans, and hot apple pie. I had a bunch of angelic cowhands for a while down there —no smoking or chewing or rough talk while the parson was there. It was pretty hard on them, as they weren't used to it.

Because of losing Billy there was a sadness about the meal—but a good deal of friendly ribbing and a sense of friendship too. I'd expected to see that look of accusation that Ledbetter had given me in more than one pair of eyes, but every last man came up and offered his help and told me how plumb sorry he was for the way things had turned out and how he understood my predicament.

Which is more than I could say for Caroline. We left the parson down with the boys and walked back up to the house, where Mother Johnson had been tending to the young'uns.

The minute we'd unwrapped our scarves and hung our coats in the hall closet, Caroline turned and gave me that stern look of hers and said, "I asked the parson to come up here before he leaves so we can have a moment of private prayer with him."

That surprised me some. "Reckon that's OK with me."

"Court, I told you we needed to talk."

She took me by the hand and led me into the parlor. I'd left a fire blazing in the fireplace, but it had worn down to mostly embers by then, though the room was still warm enough, what with the furnace turned on high and filled with coal.

She settled into one of the rockers beside the fire and motioned me into the other one.

I settled down too and put out my hands to unthaw, then looked at her and said, "Yes'm. What's on your mind?"

She looked square at me then, and the look on her face was a surprise to me. It was the look she used when she was plumb fed up with Johnny and was ready to tan his britches.

"Courtney McCannon, you've a dead cowhand buried up on that hill now, and I want to know what you intend to do about it." Her jaw stuck out, color had risen in her creamy cheeks, and her eyes flashed green.

I felt a helpless feeling wash over me. "What do you reckon I ought to do?"

"You have to stop that man." It didn't take much figuring to know she meant Moses Skettering.

"Reckon that sooner or later I'm going to have to drill him," I said, looking hard into the dying embers.

"Yes, and that worries me more than anything else. I can see it stealing over you, Courtney. Something dark and mean, and sometimes when I look into your eyes these days you're looking into a distant land. That look just gives me the chills."

"I've walked away from things long enough," I said. "I'm beginning to feel like an outright coward."

"You're no such thing. But neither are you a cold-blooded killer. There has to be another way, Courtney. We have to find it. That's why I want to talk to the parson and pray about it."

"Reckon I already know what the parson will say—same as what it says in the Good Book. 'Thou shalt not kill.'"

"God never says we have to passively accept evil. Fact is, He says we're to go out as warriors and fight it."

"The facts are plain, Caroline. The Good Book says, 'Thou shalt not kill.'"

"Why do you have to think in terms of *killing* him?"

"If you knew the polecat, you'd know I'm not likely to stop him in any other way."

"Maybe you can't, Courtney. But God can."

I felt sudden bitterness well up inside me. "Reckon that

kind of help came along a mite too late to help Kenny Payne and Billy Bailey."

"You see what I mean, Courtney? You're changing right before my eyes."

"Reckon I'd better do something different," I said. "Or every last one of us could end up buried on that hill."

I looked out the window then to the iron fence high on the hill that marked the gravestones of the handful of people buried there, my ma and pa among them. Suddenly I felt my throat close up, and I stood, excused myself, and walked out of the room. I had tears welling up in my eyes, and at that moment I didn't want Caroline to see them. They felt like a sign of my weakness and helplessness against the troubles in the world.

The parson came not long thereafter. We prayed and visited, and we offered him a light supper, but he was still full of vittles from the bunkhouse and eager to be on the road, so the opportunity to talk deeply on the subject of killing never came around. Since it was so near nightfall, Banty and Buck Weaver rode into town with him, planning to spend the night there.

Caroline and the others fell asleep early. But I was too restless to sleep, so I went to the kitchen window and pulled back the curtains. The bunkhouse showed lights, and I could hear laughter and palaver in what promised to be a long, empty night.

I pulled on my jacket and walked back down there. The boys had broke out the hootch and were drinking in memory of Billy Bailey. As I walked in, tension filled the air that shouldn't have been there. I could feel it. I saw it on their faces, but nobody would come right out and say anything.

Finally I got right down to brass tacks. "All right. What's the matter here?"

Perkins scratched around at his unshaven chin as though he didn't want to say it, then said it anyway. "Boss, we've been having a few drinks for the memory of Bailey. We've been talkin', wonderin' what's to be done about the Skettering bunch. Me and the boys here are all for riding up and paying 'em some retribution, give 'em a sample of lead and gunpowder. Them same skunks killed that there Payne feller too, and ain't nobody doing a blasted thing about it."

Old Ed Nelson had pretty much stayed out of things, as he always did. A man lives in these parts as long as he had, he's likely to have seen and done a little of everything and not be likely to get too easily stirred up. But now he agreed. "Perkins is right, Court. What the blazes we doin' sittin' here like skeered rabbits waitin' for those no-good varmints to sneak up on us again and drop us in their pot?"

I stepped over and poured myself a cup of coffee, then said, "Sorry to keep you all in the dark. As you know, the judge was here yesterday, and he brought that no-good Senator Brown with him. The judge says the BIA is about to call in the soldiers to straighten out the Payne killing. Senator Otis Brown wants to hang Yampawah and the rest of the Indians and call the matter finished. But the judge has better sense. He's going to get Brown straightened out, then go to work on the Skettering trouble. Figures he still might have to call in soldiers, but he's fixing to send them after the men who bushwhacked us instead. He's more or less asked me to lay low till he can get the saddle on things."

"We don't need the judge," Nelson said. In all the years I'd known him, I'd never seen him so riled up. "This is Lazy Double C business, and we can manage it ourselves."

I didn't like their mood. "Look, boys, if we ride on Skettering just now, we're going to play right into his hands. He's trying to rile me up enough to get me to make a stupid play. He wants my good rangeland, make no mistake about it. And there's something else going on besides, something I don't have a clear handle on yet—"

"That man needs a good dose of lead," said Chip Hutton. He was still on the mend from when he'd been knocked off his horse during the ruckus down at the delta. He'd been in a foul mood ever since.

I finished off my coffee and stood up. "Sorry, boys. I reckon we're going to have to let things ride for a day or two.

Might be able to straighten things out without anybody else getting hurt, and that would suit me just fine."

"Well," Nelson said, looking at me sidewise, "if your pa was still running things, I don't expect that's what he'd say."

I felt anger and shame well up in me, but I managed to keep a lid on it. I knew that everybody was looking forward to washing the sour taste of defeat out of their mouths. I said, "Reckon it ain't like it was twenty or more years ago around here. If you go out gunning for someone now, you're likely to be the one who ends up in the hoosegow or decorating a cottonwood. Seems to me that's a worse way to die than taking a bullet."

"Could be at that," Perkins agreed. He looked at the other men, frowning as if to say they were wasting their time by trying to reason with me. He said to me, "Have a drink, Boss?" They all knew I was a teetotaler. He was politely asking me to leave.

"Reckon I'd best get back up to the house," I said. I pulled on my coat. They had that potbellied stove of theirs going full blast, and I'd been seated too close to it for comfort.

Quietly Ed Nelson said, "Hope that shoulder of your'n holds up, Boss. We're right sorry you got hurt." There was a double meaning in his words.

I nodded politely and thanked him for the comment, then I headed on out the door.

23

Next morning when I went to make my rounds just after sunup, I was pleased to find the men busy and cheerful. There was an expectation in the air that fairly sizzled. I figured they'd talked things over and settled down some. I was hoping they'd decided to leave the retribution to the soldiers from the White River garrison.

A golden shimmer of sunlight played on the snow. The sky was pure, pale blue and not a trace of clouds to be seen. A swift, dry wind was coming from the southwest. The snow on the lower slopes was beginning to melt.

We spent the morning at the odds and ends of ranch work that make up a cowhand's life during the winter months, along with fighting the weather and saving stock. We mended harness, cleaned out the cow barn, and did some repairs to wagon wheels and to the chuck wagon—to get it ready for spring roundup even though that was still a good month or more away. A couple of the boys had irrigation shovels and were channeling some of the meltwater away from the corrals. Everybody stayed busy, and the resentment that had filled the air the night before seemed itself to have melted in the light of day.

By late morning I knew for certain that the strong, warm wind that had been building from the southwest since just after daybreak was a true Chinook—a wind that melted the snow in its path like a hot breath. It had already started to thaw the icy crust atop the snow on even the upper hillsides.

A Chinook could be a blessing or a curse. It could raise the temperature by as much as fifty degrees in a single day, turning a miserable bout of winter into virtual spring. But the hot dry winds could also set a person's nerves on edge and cause an itchy sense of discontent. If the melt-off was too sudden, it could bring ice breakups and floods. In two or three days, with temperatures staying above freezing at night, a Chinook could thaw every bit of the heavy snow cover, leaving the pasturelands saturated with water and mud.

I was put upon to decide whether I was glad to see the winds or was perturbed by them. It crossed my mind that we could have used a good Chinook a month ago when my cattle were starving and freezing on the feed grounds. But I was hoping—praying, if the truth be known—that the Chinook didn't stay long. I remembered what had happened the year before, when the price we'd paid for a short spell of warmth had been far too dear.

When the winds came last spring—later than this, to be sure—they'd melted the ice almost overnight, thawed the snow to slush, filled rivers and creeks to the banks and caused them to flood. A slow melt-off always saturated the soil and nourished good summer's crops and wild grasses and hay, even if there was little rain in the spring and summer months. With a Chinook, though, the snow melted so fast that the runoff cascaded down the hills and roared into the Yampa River, flooding the river bottom for miles. Last year our precious water had flowed down the flooding Yampa, then into the Grand River and on to Mexico, leaving most of the land beneath us parched and useless.

And then almost no rain had come during the summer months. No doubt about it, last year's winds brought us a searing drought that had helped put me in my financial trouble, for they had dried up half the feed and grass and caused me to have to more than double my usual grain bill. We all knew we wouldn't make it through another summer like the last.

So when the warm gusting wind began to taper off in midafternoon and I knew we were in for another cold spell, I was relieved.

By evening the winds had ridden on north, and a new crop of icicles was forming from the ranch building eaves. A fresh skim of ice had begun to gather on the watering troughs, though it was thin enough that the horses could easily nuzzle through. There was a good half foot of meltwater running on top of the ice in the creek bed. I figured it would be gone around midnight when the new freeze-up set in for good.

During the early hours of the day I spent my time in and out of the house, energized by the warm winds. I was working hard, but I didn't have my mind on what I was doing. I kept thinking about my pa and Ben Blue—or the Johnny Reb lieutenant Buchanan, as the tintypes called him. Twice I went into my office, opened up the right-hand drawer of my desk, and thumbed through the photographs of Pa with his Confederate prisoners, including Ben Blue, or Buchanan. But think and worry as I might, I couldn't make much sense of it all.

Twenty or more years had passed since the end of the Civil War. Pa had been dead for more than five years. I wondered if Ben Blue had come here looking for him. But if Blue was driven by revenge, why had he waited until now?

I thought about the times I'd seen the man in town, before the shoot-out at the Elkhead delta. He'd always been more than ordinarily friendly to me, though I had to admit I'd had the feeling all along that something was wrong about his being here. Now I was dead certain that something was powerfully wrong.

My shoulder throbbed some that day, for I worked it harder than I had since I'd been hurt. But things weren't nearly as bad as Doc Clayton had thought, and I was mending fine for all that. I was thankful to the Almighty Lord for getting me back up on my feet faster than last time.

And I was grateful too for that new little bundle of life in the house. Looking down at that baby or holding her in my arms was as good as any medicine I've ever had. It put a thaw in my own soul—except for those dark places where the fury toward Skettering lay bottled up, fermenting and waiting to break loose.

And there was some guilt locked away back in there too, mostly for Billy Bailey's being dead. Reckon it didn't matter much what other folks thought of the way I'd handled my troubles. I felt enough shame for the lot of us.

Ledbetter and I worked in the barn together that afternoon, and we found ourselves talking a little about what had happened. He'd thawed some too by then and wasn't quite so hot to ride on Skettering and his men as he'd been right after Bailey's burial. Reckon he'd got some sense into his head, for he seemed satisfied to wait until the judge got matters straightened out legal-like.

We'd stopped taking chances. We'd posted men to the north of the creek junction in case Skettering made another move to rake up trouble, and we had cowhands keeping their eyes peeled wherever they were. But nobody had seen hide nor hair of Skettering or of any of his men. He seemed to be lying low. All the same, I had a good notion that he was far from finished with me. But what with those winds and that new baby and all the rest that was on my mind, I had a hard time that day worrying about anything else.

By 8:00 P.M. we were all of us tuckered out. By 9:00 most everyone on the ranch had gone to bed. I was sleeping with Little Johnny in his big old warm bed. The wound in my shoulder still had me awkward, and I thrashed some when I rolled over in the night. Caroline needed her rest, and I didn't want to disturb her, and Johnny had insisted I bunk with him rather than sleeping in my office or a spare room.

Johnny's room was right above the porch at the back of the house, facing the hill. Reckon that's why I heard the pounding on the kitchen door right away. The dogs had wakened me a while before, barking and snarling. I'd figured that a wild animal of some sort had come into the yard, maybe a skunk or a groundhog. I didn't pay them much mind.

But at the banging I came awake and rolled out of bed instantly, then cracked open the window. Perkins stood there, looking up at me. I kept my voice low. "Pipe down—I'm on my way!"

As I pulled on my Levi's, I could see through the window to the endless black hills behind me and to the black vault of sky with its cold-seeming stars. An old range hand like myself knows the stars. I'd spent many a night under them, and I knew it had to be somewhere along about 3:00 in the morning.

Quiet as I could, I ran down the stairs and pulled open the door. A gust of cold air stung me. Perkins's eyes were red-rimmed from interrupted sleep, and his clothing was only halfway on. He was buttoning his coat, and his face was stark with worry. Even before he said a word, I saw the soot on his face.

"It's the barn, Court! Come on!" He spun around and hightailed it back across the yard.

I smelled smoke then. I grabbed my heavy coat off the rack and ran out the door, around the side of the house, right behind him.

Ed Nelson was hobbling out of the bunkhouse, trying to pull his boots all the way on as he came, hopping on one foot and half bent over. He spotted me and yelled, "Them blasted sidewinders have fired the barn, Courtney. Blast their evil hides!"

As I rounded the bunkhouse, I could see the dark outline of the barn against the blacker night. Half a dozen men were already running here and there around the huge old structure, and I could hear the flames crackling, could feel the reflected heat in the air. There was a gaping black hole where the barn's huge front door stood open. Cattle were coming out of it, shuffling and lowing and getting wedged together. A blasphemous cowhand separated two of them, cursing for all he was worth as he hazed them out the door.

Thin smoke streamers coiled up from the west end of the barn, pale against the black sky. Even thicker snakes of smoke came out the window of the hayloft. I saw the first fire as small licks of flame bit through the roof. I heard the timbers crack, and my heart knotted into a fist in my chest.

Ledbetter ran up, out of breath. "It's the hayloft, Court. They fired the hay! Chip Hutton got up to take a leak and saw the snake-eyed varmint that did it leap astraddle his horse and take off at a dead run. Lucky for us Chip smelled the smoke and rousted me and the boys out that very same minute. But

I'm tellin' you, the varmint who did this can't be too far away."

"You send anyone after him?"

"I decided not to spare the men."

"You did the right thing," I said. "Reckon we all know more or less who it was anyways, no matter who struck the match."

Ledbetter nodded and turned back to the barn.

I lit a shuck too and ducked past the cattle and through the side door. I was sickened by what I saw.

The light inside the barn was feeble and red. Small flames ate at the hay in the loft above my head, licking and curling in evil flickers of light. The rafters were almost hidden by a heavy gray mist of smoke. The boys had a bucket line going, hastily scooping up water from the watering troughs. Two men stood braced on the ladder, passing pails up to two more men near the hayloft window, who took the buckets and swiftly sloshed the water onto the flames. One cowhand was manning the pump down at the trough. Still another was up there in the hayloft—maybe more than one—beating at the fire with a wet horse blanket.

I yelled up to them, "If you can't whip that fire out, boys, give yourselves plenty of time to get shed of this place!"

Chip Hutton yelled back down in a raspy voice, "We ain't quittin' till the blamed thing is out."

I couldn't get into the hayloft without interrupting the men's work, so I turned to helping move the cattle. They were plumb loco from the crackle of flames above their heads and from the strangling, billowing smoke. They milled together, pushing and crowding at the sides of the pens so hard I was afraid they'd clean knock the walls down. The men had two of the larger pens emptied already. I pulled open the gate to a third one and set the cattle to moving in the direction of the outside door.

We moved fast. Even if we couldn't save the barn, we were going to save those cattle. The longer I worked, the more I clenched my teeth at the thought of Skettering and his henchmen doing this to me. I kept thinking of revenge as much as saving the cattle, my anger forcing me to work harder.

The smoke grew thicker. The air was hard to breathe, but I worked faster, hazing the cattle towards the door. In no more than half an hour we had the cattle out and into the outside corrals, shoving and fighting at us, butting, pushing, and crowding us with their horns and heads, and all the while the black smoke kept getting thicker down in the stalls and stanchions and holding pens. It blinded us, filled up our lungs, and choked us, until we were milling and stumbling about almost as badly as the cattle themselves.

Just as I swung the last pen open to haze the final bunch toward the door, a whoop came from overhead. It was followed by a happy shout, and then everyone was hoo-rawing and laughing and coughing all at once, and I heard someone yell, "We got 'er out, boys! Ever' last speck!"

Chip Hutton came scrambling down the ladder, a grin showing through the caked soot on his face. He dropped to the floor beside me and said, "I never seen nothing like it! The dagblamed fire ran across the top of the hay like a prairie fire, but it couldn't take full hold. The hay was wet, by heavens. Big hole in the worthless roof! That's the only reason the whole blasted barn didn't burn to the ground."

I suddenly remembered the hole I'd seen in the roof. What with everything else that had been happening, I'd plumb forgotten to tell Ledbetter about it. Thank the good Lord for my poor memory!

I climbed up the ladder with Chip, and he showed me what had happened. Whoever had set the fire hadn't noticed the hole overhead. The day's thaw had melted the snow on the roof and set it running in a small torrent through the opening to soak the bottom layer of hay and to drench the wood beneath and around it. It appeared that the flames had flared across the top of the hay right quickly, but when it burned down to the soggy underside, it had died down. That fact had given my boys time to douse the flames, even with their meager bucket brigade.

We were all red and raw and scraped, a few of us burned some and smelling like rabbits smoked with the hide on. But after we took count, we saw that none of us was too bad off. As for my cattle, they appeared to be in better shape than we were.

We moved into the bunkhouse. Mrs. Nelson was up, making breakfast and hot coffee, and she immediately set the boys to washing at the pump in the washhouse that was next to the kitchen. My eyes were blurred and raw, but I took a moment and thanked the good Lord for the way things had turned out.

Even as I was standing there with my eyes shut, offering up thanks, I heard Ed Nelson pipe up, "That's it for the barn. Appears we got lucky. It also appears that we need to send a couple of men back to watch for live embers."

Chip Hutton and Buck Weaver volunteered.

Nelson said, "As for the rest of us, I'd say we need to get on with the job of finding and stringing up whatever sidewinders set 'er afire!"

The boys went to cussing and threatening at that. I stood back and watched them, and soon they were making plans to ride up to Skettering's ranch come dawn to settle his hash once and for all. They were like a corral full of loco bulls bellowing and pawing the dirt, none of them thinking clearly, only feeling black, raw rage at what they'd just been through.

The men were still lined up, waiting their turn at the washroom sink. I stepped outside, filled my raw lungs with the fresh cold air, and let the smoke work its way out of my bloodshot eyes.

The first pale crack of light was sweeping down the river valley from up towards Hayden. The sky held the promise of a clear morning. I turned and looked at the northernmost skyline, toward Skettering's ranch. I felt something cold as a snake's blood coil up inside me, but I stopped it aborning. My eyes dropped from the northernmost peaks to my own ranch house. There was no lamplight showing in the windows yet. That was a good sign. The barn was a ways from the house, and though we'd made some noise, we apparently hadn't awakened anybody with our ruckus.

I stepped over to the horse trough. The boys had used the old stale water in their bucket brigade, but they had pumped it full again with fresh cold water from the well. I dipped my hands into it, washing them off. The icy water turned smoky, as if I'd spilled a bottle of ink in it. I stepped over to a clean patch of snow, cupped up a double handful and used it to wash my face. The cold soothed my eyes, and I pressed the snow to them, holding it there for a few moments. I was ready to head for the house and get the coffeepot started and stoke up the coal fire. I wanted to take a hot sudsy bath.

I stepped back inside the bunkhouse and motioned for Ledbetter to follow me outside. When he did, I said, "I'm turning these boys over to you. If they get out of hand, come and get me. I don't want so much as a one of them riding off this ranch today. Other than that, let them talk it out of their systems, and I'll see you after I catch up on my sleep. We'll decide then what to do, once we all have clear heads."

"Yessir, Courtney. Reckon they're just feeling their oats, and they'll settle down soon."

"If they don't, there's going to be another funeral coming up, and I reckon it won't be Skettering's," I said. "First thing that polecat is going to expect us to do is come riding for him and his outlaws, and they'll sure as sin be ready and eager to accommodate whatever trouble we bring their way."

"I ain't going to let anything happen," Ledbetter said. But there was a strange look in his eyes that I couldn't quite read.

As I walked back toward the house, I thought about it. I wasn't sure if the look was disrespect, anger, or just pure plain fatigue.

24

Reckon the good Lord was still taking care of me, turning me toward the house just then. The valley lay partly shrouded in a hazy morning fog that had rolled in from the river, and as I looked again at the ranch house, I saw a ribbon of smoke curling up from the parlor chimney. I figured that someone had got up and started a fire for bathing and breakfast.

The house was brooding and solemn and silent against the hill; the foundations were misted by the river fog. The windows were still dark, the house's turrets and cupolas seemed solid as stone. My pa had done a good job when he built it. I glanced east at the growing daylight, then back at the house. Smoke twisted up from the chimney and blended into the fading gray dawn.

A light came on inside. A strange sort of light. It came from the window of the upstairs hallway, flickering orange and saffron. As it licked at the inside of another window, I felt my guts lurch and my throat choke up with fear.

I yelled at the top of my lungs for help and set out at a dead run, calling for Caroline and shouting for the boys, and I had just hit the front porch when flame burst through the roof, a tongue of fire flaring upward toward the sky. Smoke poured out behind it in great, twisting black billows.

I crashed in the door, raced up the stairs. At the top I was stopped by a solid wall of flame. Timbers crashed somewhere, making an awful noise, and I saw that the fire was already gnawing through the framework.

Sobbing, half retching from the smoke I'd swallowed, more than half blinded, I rolled through the pitching, writhing wall of fire, then straight on through and out the hall window, and I knew that, all the time I'd been fighting to save my barn and my cattle, a more evil threat had been coiling its fiery way into my hearth and my family's very being.

I found myself on the porch roof. Broken glass lay all around, and flames crawled out the window behind me, trying to take hold in the shingles of the roof as the morning breeze fed their fury.

There were smoke-misted outlines of men below me now, calling up to me and thronging about. I heard the sound of more breaking glass, then someone yelled, "Get them folks out of there," but I didn't bother to see who was shouting. I was scrambling across the slanted porch roof toward Johnny's bedroom window.

I heard loud sobbing. I realized it was me, weeping and praying all together, and then I was bringing my boot up and kicking in the window to Johnny's room, and then I fell through it and into an inferno.

I tried to call to him, but my throat was too raspy from the smoke I'd swallowed, and instead I choked and gagged on the hot surges of fumes. I felt the fire's edge as it ate at the flocked wallpaper. I was close to his bed. Smoke filled my eyes, my throat, heat tore at me so hard that I wanted to scream.

I was at the bed now, reaching down—I recoiled as my hand touched a searing brass bedpost, then I reached blindly forward and stuck my hands straight into an ugly wall of flames and realized that the mattress was ablaze.

"Johnny!"

I was shivering now, as if I were in a river of ice instead of flame, and I kept saying my son's name over and over, a prayer in itself, and I knew I was drenched in my own sweat, the heat washing over me as I felt myself sagging, falling against the fiery walls, grasping for the bed and again grabbing the hot bedpost.

Then, "Pa!"

I heard his voice behind me, screaming in terror, and I stumbled once again, bracing myself by pushing on the burning mattress.

He cried out again. "Pa! Pa, I can't see—it hurts, Pa! It hurts!"

I whipped around, grabbing blindly for his voice, reaching past the wall of flame and into a space in the corner of the room. Suddenly I had him in my arms, and he was crying, sobbing, his voice rasping and coughing from the smoke even as he managed to say, "It hurts, Pa . . ." He held the old teddy bear I'd had as a boy—I'd passed it on to him. It was on fire.

I tore it from him, beating at his bedshirt as I somehow carried him back to the window and found my way through the licking flames and scouring smoke.

And then there were hands reaching through the window, helping me, and they'd taken Johnny from me. He was gone again, and I was being pulled outside too.

They helped me from the porch roof. Someone pressed snow into my blistered face, and I could hear Johnny coughing and crying all at the same time, and Ledbetter said, "The boy will be all right, Court. You got him in time. Burnt some, but nothing bad. Maybe a little smoke poisoning in his lungs."

I pulled away from the snow pack, and I could see again. A force greater than my own strength pulled me up, and I found myself climbing, scaling the trellises. And then I was atop the porch roof once more, up the railing and the latticework that held Caroline's morning glory vines in spring, and I was moving alongside the windows, feeling the blasts of the flames again.

Someone shouted, "Court, you blamed fool—you'll kill yourself. We'll get 'em."

But I was already through our broken bedroom window and inside, looking for Caroline and the baby.

The flames hadn't taken hold here yet as they had in Johnny's room, but I could hear a steady crackling rushing toward me down the hall. The world was a black, evil wall of smoke.

I was startled by Al Perkins's voice nearby, saying, "Who in ruination . . . Court?" Then I saw his dim outline, and

Caroline's soot-stained face took form beside his own, her eyes wide with terror, her arms filled with the baby.

I tried to force words out of my scratchy throat as I heard Al say, "I got her, Court," and then I was gagging from the smoke, and Perkins was guiding Caroline with Little Meg to the window, and I was feeling my way along behind them.

When we were out on the roof, Caroline looked at me with deep fear in her eyes. "Where's Johnny?"

"He's all right," I said, and then I felt myself sag with relief as the boys began helping her to the ground.

They took the baby from her arms, and someone gasped, "Oh, thank God—" And then, from below, I saw Caroline looking up at me, her eyes awash with tears and pain. "Courtney! My mother!"

The boys were reaching up again, helping Perkins down, but I turned, leaning against the hot exterior wall as I made my way along the roof toward Mother Johnson's room. I heard the boys shout, and then the crackling flames were licking high again in front of me.

They had organized a bucket brigade from the creek and had set up a ladder to the porch roof, with two men up there dousing the flames through the windows, almost as they had done at the barn. The part of the house where Mother Johnson slept was still a ragged wall of fire.

I lunged forward to find myself stopped by two pairs of hands just inside in the smoke-filled hallway. I heard Ed Nelson saying, "Court, you're a piebald fool. We got her out already, but you ain't going to be so lucky if you don't get some sense into your head."

I'd been moving in pure panic, feeling my way along, my eyes finally stung sightless by the smoke and the heat. A hand turned me back around. I felt myself pushed into the cool air and knew I was back through the window, and then someone gave me a push, throwing me off balance, and I slid off the porch roof into a snowbank.

I touched my face. It was one massive rasp of blistered

pain, and my eyes felt as though someone had thrown acid in them. I scooped up a handful of snow and held it to my face.

Then I heard Virginia Ledbetter's voice, crying and saying, "Oh, Caroline, oh, no, oh, I am so sorry—" And she was weeping, and I was on my feet, feeling my way around the house and toward them, and then I heard her husband saying, "Thank the good Lord Almighty, the little critter doesn't have so much as a burn on her. But it looks like we're going to lose the house."

Half an hour later my eyes had stopped streaming, and enough of the pain was gone so that I could think of other things. I stood and watched as the boys put out the last flickers of flame. I watched as the boiling smoke turned to thin streamers and then began to die into small tatters and puffs.

The west wing was gone, the top two floors of the cupola that had held Johnny's room were burned to a cinder. But though the white exterior was sooty and burned, the better part of the house remained. Only the good Lord Himself knows how the boys managed to save it. And as I stood there watching, I was thinking about my family, about my son and my wife and my firstborn daughter, that tiny, mysterious bundle of God's joyful life. Through His grace we had all survived the catastrophe.

Ledbetter came to stand beside me. "I am plumb terrible sorry, Court. Sorry as can be."

His wife had taken Caroline and the children down to their house. She'd not only taken in Mother Johnson but offered to make up a spare room for the four of us till we could get our roof fixed and the burned places boarded up.

"I'm deeply obliged," I said. "If it hadn't been for you and the boys, I'd have lost everything including my family."

Ledbetter was embarrassed by the thanks. He said, "Come on down to the house, Court. You could do with a bite to eat and some ointment on your face and hands."

I said, "I'll be along directly."

He shifted from one foot to the other. "What are you planning to do?"

"Don't rightly know yet."

He shifted again, nervous to say his piece. But he spoke up all the same. "This may not be the time to bring it up, but we'd best take the bull by the horns. Don't know how Skettering pulled this off, but we both know he done it, and if the man's gone this far, he ain't goin' to stop now."

I said easy-like, "I still mean to handle this thing my own way, Hank. In the meantime, I'd still appreciate it if you and the boys would stay strictly out of it, you understand?"

His face furled up into a frown. "Suspect I do. Suspect you're going to let Moses Skettering take away everything you have, the lives of your family included, before you get up enough grit to stop him." He shot me a look of pure disgust, then turned and stomped toward his house.

I went around to the back of the smokehouse and heaved, cleaning my stomach of the smoke I'd swallowed. Then I watched the boys walk through the house, making sure the last of the fire was truly out.

Strange thing. As I stood there, I felt the pain inside me dry up, to be replaced by something as cold as river ice. A steel spring had been wound tight inside me for a long time now, and I felt as if it was about to break and cause me to fly apart.

Thou shalt not kill. I heard the words in my head, but I buried them beneath my rage. And I knew for certain in that moment that I was going to stop Moses Skettering one way or another, even if it cost me my immortal soul.

When I'd pulled myself together some, I walked down to the Ledbetters' and checked on my family. The baby was asleep on a small cot in the bedroom, innocent and unconcerned as a kitten. Virginia had mixed up some tea for Caroline and Johnny, using an old Indian remedy that calmed them. She'd helped them bathe, tended to their burns, and dressed Caroline in one of her simple cotton dresses. Caroline had a large swath of blisters on the left side of her face, cutting across the cheek, and she'd been burned across her neck and shoulder. Virginia had dressed and tended to that, and now she insisted on putting a gooey, smelly ointment on my own blistered hands and face.

She tried to get me to stay and rest, but I told her and Caroline that I needed to ride into Hayden to notify Judge Warren of what had transpired and see what sort of help he could send our way.

I went down to the stables, saddled my sturdiest horse, checked my rifle and my Colt, buttoned up the heavy spare coat I'd had in the tack room, tied a thick wool scarf around my neck, and pulled my hat down low against the chill. Then I swung into the saddle and rode out of there alone, the men watching me, some of them looking at me as if I were a whipped dog with my tail tucked betwixt my legs, off to beg for help again where none had yet been found.

I didn't say a word to anyone, didn't feel like talking. I just reined my horse towards the Yampa River road, trotted down the lane to it, then rode east toward Hayden.

The Chinook had melted part of the snow in the high mountain meadows, and in some places a horse and rider could get through without too much trouble. But in other places the going was rough, for the underbase of the snow was destabilized from the fast melt-off and prone to sliding away with you.

About a mile east of my ranch buildings I doubled back across the meadow and rode up onto the hill due north of my house. I soon found a trail tramped into the snow where riders from the Hearne place had come and gone to a point where they could dismount and watch my buildings without being seen.

I found two sets of fresh hoofprints, and some boot prints beside them, as if the riders had dismounted and stood for a spell, tramping around. It had snowed the day before, so I knew they had come down sometime late last night, well after the Chinook had died and the ground had started to freeze up again.

256

They hadn't bothered to try to hide their trail. Reckon they hadn't expected anybody to be alive who cared enough to bother tracking them.

I rode on north till I was at the far top of the hill. Then I reined in and turned around.

The valley lay below, the river a brown ribbon between banks of cottonwood trees and willows at the far side of the road and fields. The Flat Tops and Pyramid Peak lay on the far horizon beyond the river. The fog had lifted, and the valley looked serene, the sort of place where a family could be safe and warm while waiting for spring breakup.

There was a grassy meadow on the far side of the river. Closer was the stage-freight road, then another wide meadow with a lane transecting it north and south, coming toward me and my ranch buildings. The big barn that had been set afire lay to the southernmost edge of the complex, nearest the river road.

The Ledbetters' house sat across the lane from it, a white frame put up by my pa so that his foreman could live in as good a house as most folks had in town. The house looked warm. Smoke curled up from two chimneys, and for a minute I thought better of what I was about to do. I wanted to go back into that house and be safe and warm with my friends and family.

As I watched, Hank Ledbetter came out the kitchen door and strode off toward the barn. Other folks were out and about as well, and some of the boys were moving the cattle on out to pasture.

The barn hadn't been too badly damaged. There was a jagged break in the roof where some blackened rafters showed through, but they'd saved most of what was left of my hay and feed, and the roof could be repaired. We had a good stockpile of lumber stored before snowfall in order to build a new cookshack. We could use that for mending until the sawmill on Black Mountain opened up come spring.

A fit of melancholy swept through me like a cold wind. On a sudden I realized that I was saying good-bye to all that lay in the valley beneath me. I was taking leave of my childhood, of my family, and my innocence, and maybe even bidding farewell to the good Lord Himself, though the very thought of that brought a shudder to my soul. But I didn't know any other course of action I could take. It was time for me to take matters in hand.

Still, I was reluctant to turn and ride away. I gazed off to my east and west. My range cattle were strung all up and down the valley. The swift, warm thaw had opened up some grazing land, and I saw my hayrack moving down the stage road to the west. I was right proud of my boys as I watched the ranch coming to life. After all that had happened to them during the night, they'd all gone right back to the business of running cattle as soon as the trouble died down.

Down at the bottom of the hill was the creek. Just to the far side of it was my ranch house. There was a blackened, gaping hole in the side, looking like the cavity of death that Skettering had meant it to be. From up here, the damage looked minimal. I reckoned it would be easy enough for Caroline to oversee repairs if I wasn't around to do it.

I turned in my saddle and looked straight across the hill to my left to bid one final farewell. There, under the late morning sun, was the small, iron-fenced cemetery where my parents lay buried. I thought about the way I had let them down by not stopping this situation in its tracks and about all the work that they'd put into the ranch below me. I thought about Pa and wondered what he would have done if faced with the decisions I had to make. I felt my jaw clench tight and my hands tense into fists. I shook the reins, and my horse turned to the right. I started up the draw toward the Hearne place.

When Mrs. Hearne opened the door she smiled warmly, then froze, probably puzzled by my burns or by the angry look on my face—a look I didn't try to mask. She said, "Why, Mr. McCannon! Whatever is wrong? Are you hurt?"

"Not too badly, ma'am. I'm sorry to bother you, but I got to see that oldest boy of yours."

Her cheeks flushed, and it wasn't from the cold. She stammered, "I . . . uh . . . I haven't seen him this mornin'. He's—he's riding for Moses Skettering now. I haven't—oh, I *will* tell you. He and another man rode through here last night, stopped just for a minute—then they went right on back to Skettering's ranch."

"Would that fellow with him happen to go by the name of Ben Blue?"

"Mr. Blue? Oh, my, no. It was that rough one, the one they call Luke Coogan." She shot me a look composed of curiosity and shame, as if she already suspected they must have done something. Then a different look flashed through her eyes, and she exclaimed, "Wish my boy would find some other folks to ride with. Maybe you'd have something for him—"

I cut her short. "Thank you, ma'am." Then I turned, swung astride my horse, and set out to the west, following the snow-packed trail that led in the direction of Moses Skettering's M-Slash-S ranch.

25

The trail took me along the rim of the mountain. It was an old cow trail, and I was somewhat familiar with it. It had been plowed out some by horses riding through, either coming or going—I couldn't tell—but it looked as if it had been used some off and on all winter. I had to skirt a few deep, unstable snowdrifts as I rode downslope in a series of wide switchbacks that snaked in and out of the tall timber. At one point I lost my bearings and reined in to study the lay of the land.

I was on a tall sandstone bluff. Behind me were the snow-capped Elkhead Mountains, sloping upward from the foothills, then towering to the pale blue sky. I turned back to gaze westward. A series of sagebrushy, snow-laden plateaus tapered off to the flatland beyond. This was Skettering's primary rangeland.

It was cross-hatched with arroyos and gullies, and the hills surprised you now and again by jutting up steep and sudden. There was no belly-deep grass here as there was in my valley—only stirrup-high sagebrush that in summer was scattered through with Johnsongrass and wheat grass, sparse picking to be sure but cattle feed nonetheless.

Leastwise it had been until last summer's drought, which had left it nigh unto worthless. In spite of the heavy winter snowfall, I could see that the scrub oak and service brush and some of the quakies were still parched and brittle and close to dead.

When I had my bearings, I took up the trail again, riding slow and steady, my mind on what was before me and a growing dread in my belly. All the same, I knew I'd been pushed as far as I could go. I'd always been taught that the Christian way was to respect my fellow man, to help a neighbor every chance I got, and walk away from trouble. Now I could see that something was wrong with that line of thinking, for it had caused me to turn the other cheek so long that I had nearly let my family die in a blaze of pain. I had to rethink what this Christian business was all about, but the more I tried to untangle my thoughts, the more knotted up they became.

After a good two hours of riding, the trail took me down through a long gulch, then back up a steep hill, and along the edge of more tall timber. The sheer mountainside towered straight up behind me now, with only a narrow ledge set here and there into the tall blue spruce sentinels. A jigsaw swath seeded with saplings and scrub oak cut through the trees where an avalanche had once plowed down all the timber.

I was more than ever careful of my horse's footing, for I knew that the snowpack towering above it could be set loose easy, due to the undermelt caused by the Chinook. At one treacherous point, I dismounted and led my horse up a small rise. From there I could see that a little valley opened up before me. I came around a patch of trees, and there it was, no more than a hundred yards beneath me and partway sheltered by a sandrock overhang. Skettering's M-Slash-S ranch.

I led my horse into a concealing copse of trees, then crept forward and stretched out on my belly atop the wind-cleared sandrock to survey the buildings. I wanted to know who was there and what they were up to.

It had been years since I'd ridden up to this area. This was the first time I'd seen this particular spread, for it was fairly new. The main house was a one-story, rough cottonwood log structure, big enough to have maybe two or three good-sized rooms, with a sandstone fireplace at one end and a plank porch along the front and side. There was a small rough log barn, and just below the cliff where I lay was a bunkhouse, sheltered up against the rock wall. It had a cookshack attached, which displayed another sandstone fireplace. Smoke crawled up from the chimney.

There were several cedar-post corrals, one of them attached to what appeared to be the stables. In one corral, Jimmy Hearne's sorrel was scratching an itch by rubbing up against one of the cedar posts. Several other horses stood at the far side near the stable doors, nuzzling into a hay pile or standing half asleep. Two other horses were tethered in front of the bunkhouse, saddled and ready to ride.

I moved around to see that Skettering's buckboard and wagon sat at the far side of the ranch house, both piled deep with snow. A door swung open, surprising me in the mountain silence. I slid back from the edge with a start, then peered back over the rim.

Ben Blue strode onto the front porch. He stood there clapping his gloved hands together, then slapped them on the thighs of his Levi's, warming them against the cold.

I snaked my hand down and laid it lightly on the butt of my holstered Colt. I watched every move he made.

I pulled the Colt out and aimed it, my trigger finger ready. A cold wind froze my heart, and a dark voice whispered for me to squeeze that trigger and drop him on the spot. I could have shot him right then. At the same time something held me back, telling me to wait, reminding me that I'd come for Jimmy Hearne and Luke Coogan to take them back alive or dead to face the judge.

Skettering came out to stand beside Blue. A hate-filled expression formed on that soul-shriveled face as he spoke to Blue. I tilted my aim so that any shot I fired would take him clean in the middle of his forehead. That voice whispered again that this man was a back-shooter, he'd sent folks to bushwhack me more than once, he'd tried to steal my ranchland. That voice said I had every right to claim his life, to drop him and Blue both where they stood, then turn and ride back to my own business and have done with the lot of them. In that minute, I wanted so badly to shoot them both that I felt my guts tighten up.

They palavered for a minute, their voices too far away to hear, then Blue stepped over to one of the saddled horses, swung astride, and set off down the snow-packed wagon road that led toward Windsor. Skettering stood watching him ride away, that mean look still on his face. Then he stepped off the porch and walked over to the bunkhouse, went inside, and the door swung shut behind him.

I waited. My hands were getting cold, and my ears and nose were numb, but I wanted to be sure of my moves before I made them.

After a short spell a man came out of the barn. He had a kerchief pulled up high around his chin and a hat pulled low against the cold, but I recognized him as Rollin Bowles. He started rolling a barrel of what I took to be oats or corn over to one of the wagons. He hoisted it into the back, unmindful of the snow, then he trudged back into the barn.

The door of the bunkhouse opened then, and Jimmy Hearne came out and walked down a short path to an outhouse. A few minutes later he came back. When he opened the bunkhouse door and went in, I could smell hot coffee and frying bacon. My guts rolled over again, this time from hunger.

Bowles was back outside now, working a light covering of snow off a haystack located near the barn. When he had it partway cleared off, he grabbed a pitchfork and started pitching hay into the rack of a wagon in the stackyard. A sloppy worker, that one.

Still I watched.

I wanted to know how many men were down there, where they were, and what they were doing before I moved in. That same steely anger was still coiled tight inside me; it wasn't letting up so much as an inch. I was going to either take Coogan and Hearne or kill them, and I didn't care which, but I wasn't going to ride in like a fool either.

A sudden noise froze me. In order to shelter myself from the ranch buildings, I'd left myself wide open to anyone up here on the ridge. I reckoned some varmint had moved back in the brush or timber, maybe an elk or deer, but it could have been a two-legged polecat too. I inched slowly to one side and crouched in under the shelter of a large balsam.

Brush cracked. Something big was breaking through the undergrowth. I braced myself, my heart hammering against my chest, my trigger finger trembling. There was still more rustling back there in the thicket, then something came crashing through the undergrowth and into the open space.

A grizzly!

The bear must have just left hibernation, for it was hungry, mean, and desperate. It also dragged one hind leg, leaving a trail of blood in the snow. I swung around when I heard more brush breaking and a horse blowing back in the timber.

The bear saw me move. It stopped short, turned, then raised up on its hind legs, ready to charge, its fangs dripping and sharp as knife blades. It was hurt, and hurt bad, and there's no more dangerous animal than a wounded grizzly.

Then I heard a man's voice, so close that it startled me. "Whoa, now, steady there." A rifle clap smashed the stillness.

Luke Coogan broke through the underbrush and into the clearing. He was mounted on a claybank, and he held a Sharps buffalo gun aimed crosswise of me. He had a smirk on his face.

The grizzly fell to all fours, turned on its heels, and took off across the clearing, trying to get away.

Coogan watched as the bear met the tall timber and disappeared back into the avalanche clearing. He was waiting for a clear shot. He hadn't even seen my horse yet, but he would at any minute.

I took aim at him, but I hesitated at shooting a man in cold blood like that.

Evidently the sun glinted off my gun barrel, and Coogan saw it. He froze up, then spun to look dead at me, his Sharps aimed at me now. The expression on his face turned from one of smirking pleasure to one of outright relish.

He sneered. "Well, lookee here! If it ain't the great McCannon hisself!" He frowned a second, puzzled, then said, "Jimmy Hearne said—well, I thought you were long dead." His grin returned and broadened. "Well—heh—if you ain't yet, you soon enough will be." He squinted and looked closer at me. "What's them blisters on your face? You been fryin' your own breakfast?"

Holding my gun steady, I said, "Drop that buffalo gun, Coogan."

He kept looking at me. In his eyes was such an unholy glee that for the first time I understood. Destruction could worm its way so deeply into people's souls that they didn't care if they themselves were destroyed, just so long as they could destroy others. It was the same expression I'd seen so many times in Skettering's eyes. And Blue's. It was an unholy record of hatred against all that was good and worth having in this world.

The gun in my hand might have been a toy for all the mind he paid to it, though I still had a bead on him and he knew it. He just sat on his horse, peering down at me from under those thick, grizzled eyebrows, that malicious smile creeping across his face again. For the first time I noticed that the saddle on his horse was a good Denver rig, worth a pretty penny. I knew, because I'd paid for it.

It was one of the saddles that the Hearne boy had taken from my tack room, right after he stole the branding irons.

I felt my trigger finger tighten on the metal.

Coogan's grin widened. He made his eyes go wide with mock fear as he held up his hands, the Sharps still in the right one, though pointed toward the sky now. "Well, now, McCannon, looks as if'n you got me." His grin widened. "Heh. You blasted fool. Don't you know you got a yellow reputation a mile wide? I know you ain't going to use that gun, so whyn't you just go on and drop it now—save me the trouble of sitting here skeered to death—" He moved like a whip, cross-drawing his pistol and firing while he was still jawing at me.

I saw it coming and got off a shot just as he did. The reports echoed together. But he'd surprised me again, and my shot clean missed him. He fired again, and my Colt spun out of my hand as I ducked and rolled in the snow, thinking that I was indeed a fool, a cowpuncher trying to move against a bunch of hard-core gunslingers whose only business was death.

With three paces Coogan's horse was above me, and I could see him leaning out and over me, his face so full of gloating that it had fair turned green. His lantern jaw hung slack and hungry, his thick body was stiff with malicious satisfaction.

A grin came to his face. "So you thought you was hard-scrabble tough, did you? Wanted to gnaw a piece out'n old Luke Coogan?" His gun was aimed at my forehead now, and it didn't waver as much as a tenth of an inch either way. "You think you whipped me at the Elkhorn saloon that day? You blamed fool. Only reason you walked away alive was because there were witnesses."

Abruptly a dark look crossed his face. Swaggering, he said, "Get up, you. I owe you a few things. Got me a mind to ride you down to the ranch house an' show the boys what I done ketched today."

I stood. He bore around and behind me, his gun held steady on me, and then he brought the rifle up and prodded me along on foot through the snow trail he'd tromped out on his way up, along a short switchback that took us down to the ranch.

26

Coogan marched me into the ranch house as his prize. The inside was at least warm, for the fireplace at the end of the large main room was ablaze with logs, and I was soon plumb uncomfortable in my heavy sheepskin-lined coat. But no one made a move to take it from me, and I wasn't about to volunteer it. The room was a combination living and eating room, long and sparsely filled with rough furnishings. One wall was used to hang tack such as bridles and saddles and other leather goods that might go brittle in the cold.

Skettering's polecats soon gathered, every one of them cocky as a strutting rooster. They looked me over as if I was a head of beef on the block and commented on my ignorance and cowardice and general lack of good sense.

I fought them as they tied me up, but there were too blasted many of them, and soon they'd trussed up my hands and feet, then dangled me by the wrists from a rope strung over a narrow cottonwood rafter. The ceiling was low, and they played out the rope a few feet so the toes of my boots touched the rough plank floor just enough to take some of the pressure off my arms. The pain in my shoulder flared up, but it wasn't anything near so fierce as the white-hot hatred in my guts or the shame that swallowed me whole.

Jimmy Hearne sashayed over to stand in front of me. The look of malicious satisfaction on his face was matched by that of Skettering, who sat on a wooden chair at the kitchen table watching them harass me. At that moment Hearne was as big a man as he'd ever be, and in my mind that made him about the size of a barn rat.

He had a big, sharp Bowie knife in his hand, and he took to baiting me with it. Coogan, Bowles, and a couple of other mangy-looking varmints I didn't know sat back grinning, swigging on whiskey bottles, and egging him on. They were all taking advantage of the occasion to get themselves drunk.

Hearne sneered, and the look on his face was odd. He still had that appearance of youth about him, though those rheumy blue eyes seemed older than ever. I reckon misery can do that to a man, whether he's getting it or inflicting it, just as a dusty wind can turn a green bush into a withered-up tumbleweed.

I thought again about how I'd wanted to shoot Jimmy Hearne when I first caught him rustling my cattle. I thought about the black hatred that had boiled up in me when he'd shot Brownie, and I knew now that there was no shame in those feelings, that there was no longer anything pitiful about this lad. His ferret face drew up in that same poisonous sneer I'd first seen the day he'd come to take his ma back to her miserable life. I could see his pa in him, the same meanness and spitefulness, and I reckoned he'd already taken heavy to the liquor, also just like his pa.

He seemed to see the contempt in my eyes, for he drew himself up and snarled, "Had to come a-prying into our affairs, didn't you, Mr. High Muckety-muck? Couldn't leave well enough alone after I told you to. Had to keep on a-snoopin' like an old Injun squaw. Look where it's got you now, you lame-brained fool. You'd been better off if I'da been able to get a clean shot at you that day you ketched me with your cattle, instead of having to drop your horse instead."

His knife-flick caught in the leather of my coat. He jerked it upward, and the leather split open.

I forced myself to swallow the fear rising in my throat. His sour whiskey breath was in my face.

He and the others meant to take the starch plumb out of me, no two ways about it. Most of all they wanted me to beg for my life. Reckon the whiskey-soaked, double-dealing varmints were trying to force me down to their level, and I reckon I wasn't going to let them do it, for I sealed my lips tight and wouldn't utter so much as a word.

Funny thing about men who let their souls shrivel up. Seems they always aim to undo anyone or anything that's managed to stay unshriveled.

Hearne stepped back, studying me with a look on his face as though he'd swallowed a crawful of his own poison. He said, "You're so high and mighty you just couldn't stay out'n things, could you?"

He stepped forward again and laid the knife's sharp blade against my neck. All he had to do was draw his right hand across in one swift movement, and my throat would be slit. He pressed the blade in. I felt the razor-sharp edge break skin and a thin trickle of warmth run down into my shirt.

He was watching my eyes, searching for the first glimmer of fear, looking for something to feed on, but I kept them masked, steady. He moved back, disappointed.

Coogan sat to one side, his eyes agleam with pleasure as he watched Hearne working on me. Skettering himself still kept distant from us all, watching with the contempt of someone who's seen so much death that it's become a familiar monotony. But now and again a shade of a smile crossed his face. He was the only one that wasn't tippling heavily from the jugs of rotgut whiskey.

Bowles slammed an empty jug to the floor and said to Skettering, "You got any more of Old Man Hearne's spider juice?"

I could see that Bowles's gun hand was mangled up some from where Yampawah had shot him that day he'd been hoorawing the squaws. I hadn't noticed before, but Yampawah had apparently made a left-handed gunslinger out of this yellow-haired varmint.

Skettering gestured, and Bowles stepped over and opened a cupboard door to rummage around inside. As he moved, he asked Skettering in a slurred voice, "When's Blue comin' back?"

"Couple a days."

"Rode up to Hahns Peak to get the job done and over with?"

I reckon Skettering already saw me as a goner by then, for he answered as if I wasn't even there. "That's right. Brown said to hurry things up before they got out of hand."

Hahns Peak! That blindsided me. Why had Blue ridden up to Hahns Peak, and what was it that Brown thought was getting out of hand?

There was something in the wind that went beyond their raw hatred of me. Maybe something that took in the judge and all those I'd left behind at the ranch. I'd been thinking that if only I could stop these varmints, my family and friends would be safe. An ice-cold shiver ran down my back.

I had to get away from these sidewinders. I should have ridden up to the judge's as I'd told Caroline I was going to, but that choice was no longer mine to make. There were six men here—Coogan, Bowles, Hearne, Skettering, and the two ranch hands I didn't know. Every man was armed, and they all wanted to see me torn apart and dead.

Funny thing, though—in that minute I realized that I wasn't afraid of one of them, not for all that they'd done to me. Reckon I'd gone cold at that point when I'd stood above my ranch buildings and looked down at the ruin they brought about every time they laid their hands to my life. The feeling of rock-hard coldness that had settled in then had stayed with me. One way or another, as long as these vultures were around, life wasn't going to be worth living anyway, so I might as well take it to the limit.

Truth to be told, these varmints had turned into a job to be done, something as necessary as branding steers, or picking up the winterkill from all over my rangeland come spring, or shooting the renegade coyotes that mauled my newborn calves.

Hearne sidled up again. I tried to shut off his words, but this time he got my full attention.

"Too bad about that woman of your'n, McCannon. Guess she must of been fried when your house burned. I set up there on the bluff and watched you fools scurrying around down at the barn like a bunch of ants in a stirred-up anthill, while all the time the real trouble was in your own house. I'll be skinned if you weren't right funny."

I felt my guts roll over at the words, and my breath came quick.

His eyes slitted up. He knew he'd drawn blood. He leaned in closer and licked at his lower lip. "I fired the upstairs hallway first—it was easy as anything to get in, what with you and all your men down at the barn savin' your cattle." He searched my eyes, looking for the pain he was trying to kindle in my soul.

I held steady and said in a matter-of-fact voice, "I don't understand that, Jimmy. I had you figured for better stock. I thought you'd want to take matters up with me man-to-man, rather than sneaking up in the night like a skunk and going after my wife and kids."

His face curled up. "That was Blue's idea, not mine. He said to set the house afire. Said he wanted to see that wife of your'n burnt dead."

I recoiled as if I'd been slapped, at the vileness and hatred in the idea.

He grinned as he saw my reaction. He said, "It was easy as anything, settin' them curtains afire. A little jug of coal oil done the rest. Sorry I had to skedaddle before the end. Guess it musta been quite a fire, judgin' from those blisters on your hands and face. Wish we coulda stuck around for the whole show, but Coogan said we'd better ride—"

Coogan jumped to his feet, his fists balled up. "Shut up. I told you before, keep your trap shut about me and anything I do, or you're likely to find your tongue cut out and stuffed down your yappin' throat."

Hearne turned on him, eyes ablaze. "I ain't taking all the blame. You done it too—"

Coogan came across the room in two swift strides, brought his hand back, and cracked Hearne across the mouth so hard that I heard bone break and the blood spurted.

In that split second of confusion, I coiled up my legs, kicked out full force, and caught Coogan square in his rib cage. His chest caved in as he howled with pain and reeled backward, doubling up, his hands flying to protect what was left of his ribs.

Jimmy Hearne was atop Coogan the instant he hit the floor. The evil he'd been aiming at me had found a new target.

Bowles got off a shot at me—the bullet whacked straight into the plank wall at my back.

I managed to use the momentum from my impact with Coogan to start swinging till I'd hit the wall behind me. I managed to catch my heel in an outjut of log that allowed me to grab up and get hold of the rope that held me tied to the rafter.

I was trying to catch my balance as Bowles barreled into me, howling like a stuck pig. His impact coupled with my dead weight splintered the cottonwood beam over my head. It held for just an instant, then it clean cracked through, spilling me to the floor. The rope slipped clear of the broken beam.

My hands and feet were still tied, but Bowles had fallen to the floor too. We'd landed next to Skettering, Coogan, and Hearne.

Coogan threw Hearne from atop him, both he and Skettering jumped the boy, and now they were trying to subdue him, but it was like trying to tackle a wildcat. The three of them were in a tangle of arms and legs and stale sweat and whiskey-fouled breath, and the whole ball of them came rolling into Bowles, knocking him off balance even as he managed to climb to his feet and bring up his gun.

He stumbled backward, and the six-shooter flew out of his hand, but he didn't go after it. Instead he jumped on me, snarling and cursing and tearing at me. I brought my trussed hands up and over his head, clamped his throat between my wrists like a vise, and wrenched his head sharply to one side, trying to snap his wretched neck. He gagged and thrashed about, breaking my hold and about yanking my arms out of their pits as he did it. When he reared back, both hands to his throat, I reached out and grabbed for his gun and got it.

272

I was taking aim at Bowles when something knocked me aside. I stared up and saw Skettering, a look of gnashing hatred on his face as he took aim and fired two deafening shots directly into Jimmy Hearne's face and chest. The terrified expression on the boy's face froze there, as death took him swiftly and he fell prostrate to the floor.

There was still confusion, everybody moving and shuffling around. I'd ended up near the table. I rolled under it, then pulled myself along the wall, my breath coming short and a sudden fire of pain in my shoulder. Weakness ran through me, but I managed to get across to the other side and reached up to turn the doorknob, then I rolled through and was skittering across the wide porch and down the four steps.

I heard curses behind me and the pounding of boot heels, and then I'd rolled off the porch and back into the crawl space beneath the rotten porch planks.

Someone fell to his knees at the bottom of the steps and got off a wild shot, but I'd already pulled myself back into the black, damp cold. The light outlined him, though, and I still had Bowles's gun. I got a quick glimpse of a face—I thought it was Bowles—then the varmint's head was in and under the floorboards, and licks of flame were coming from his gun barrel. Bullets thudded into the rock foundation behind me.

And now I was firing too, at the flame and the wedge of his body outlined in the sunlight at the edge of the crawl space. I heard the smack of my bullet entering flesh, then a grunt of pain and a low groan. Bowles scampered backward, and there was some palavering out there. I reckoned they were regrouping so as to take me down once and for all.

I squirmed back as far against the rock foundation as I could get, then curled up and fell to work with the skinning knife I carried in my boot, hacking at the ropes that still bound my hands and feet. I could hear Skettering and Coogan talking somewhere near the porch.

"That no-good Hearne boy had two good chances at him and missed him both times!" Skettering's voice was filled with ridicule.

"Heh," said Coogan, "he ain't the only one that missed. That black varmint's got more lives than a bobcat. But we got him fair to rights this time. I expect Blue will get rid of the judge, and we'll get McCannon planted, and then things ought to be clear and quiet around here for a spell."

Skettering said, "You want to crawl in there after him?"

"Thankee, no. Don't know why the blazes I didn't kill him inside the house. I fired square at him."

"Shouldn't have listened to Blue about setting that fire," Skettering said. "It was a blamed waste of time. We still got the rattler to deal with, only now he's coiled back up under my own ranch house. Sometimes I think I ain't ever going to get rid of the snake."

I thought about that, and I sent up a prayer of thanks that the good Lord had kept His hand on me through all they'd sent my way.

There was a sound like spitting, then Coogan said, "That fire was foolish all right. But it seemed right important to Blue that the house be burnt down. It ain't easy to say no to a man like that'n, less'n he's riding off and leaving the country. I sure wouldn't want him trailing me nowhere."

I'd kept my eye peeled for when they made their move. Now Coogan leaned down once, then was gone, as though he was afraid of being a target. I knew he couldn't see me back there in the darkness.

"Can't see nothing back there. Hurry up. Say, wonder why the senator changed his mind and got hisself in such an all-fired hurry?"

"You'd best stay out of that end of things. They don't concern you," Skettering said in a tight voice.

"No need to get your dander up. I expect you're right. It ain't no concern of mine. And it ain't doin' neither one of us any good to stand here and beat our gums. How about you, Moses? Whyn't *you* go on in there after him?"

There was a long pause, then Skettering said, "Bring out that shotgun. We'll just spray buckshot back in there until we've turned him into crow feed."

With a final jerk I cut through the last strand of rope, and I was free. It was good to get the blood circulating in my wrists and ankles again. I eased up off where I'd been leaning on my bad shoulder and looked around.

The porch was a wide one, running the full width of the house. On three sides there was daylight, and I'd seen men's feet moving to the sides from time to time. I reckoned they were all keeping an eye out for me. Along to the back of me was a wedge of blackness, and I figured it for the sandstone foundation of the house. But somewhere off in that blackness I saw a faint glimmer of light, and that set me to wondering.

I dragged myself over to find that the light leaked through a small chink in the rocks. I pried at the caulking that held the stones together. It was dried adobe mud, and it had been softened some by the dampness. I set my knife to it, and it crumbled away by the handful. I lifted out a wide, flat rock and was looking into a deep, black hole.

A dim shaft of sunlight slanted in from above, and the smell down there was familiar. I sniffed like a rabbit and knew I'd found the musty, earthen scent of a potato cellar.

A door slammed shut above me. Quickly I removed two more rocks and had a hole large enough to squeeze through.

Footsteps creaked across the porch, then Skettering said, "Got that shotgun?"

I'd maneuvered myself around so that my feet were dangling through the hole. I dropped about four feet atop some potatoes in a plank bin. A few rolled out, and I held my breath, but evidently the sound didn't carry. I was in a cellar under the house. I glanced back at the hole I'd arrived through and could see the narrow wedge of sunlight from the front of the porch. Both barrels of a shotgun glinted as they slid into the edge of the crawl space, right beside the steps.

I dropped all the way into the potato bin just as the shotgun blast sprayed the crawl space with a deafening roar and enough buckshot to kill a dozen rattlers and a prairie dog. Another blast deafened me, and I hunkered down, then waited.

I could still hear their voices, but barely.

Skettering said, "Must already be dead. Go in there and see."

"Thankee, no. If that varmint's still kickin', I'd sooner stick my neck in a hangman's noose."

"If I ever take a mind to tell Sheriff Finsand what all you've been up to, that might be arranged," Skettering said. "Crawl on in there."

"No sirree bob. Here, let's load 'er up again."

I threw my legs over the side of the bin and to the packed-earth floor. I could see a bit better now. The leak of sunlight was coming through a plank door slanted into the earth above me. An earthen ramp and a wooden stairway led up to the door, which angled in over my head. There was a small gap between two of the planks.

The shotgun blasted again, and I ducked without thinking as rock shards flew through the hole I'd opened up. I crawled up the sloped, rotted stairway and pushed upward on the overhead door. It was held down from the outside, most likely by something heavy laid across it to weight it down during a windstorm.

No way out.

But then, straining, I shoved again at the plank where the sunlight leaked through, felt the springiness of the rotten wood, and felt it start to move. The plank was almost rotted through from exposure to the rains and snows of the past. I heaved into it again with all I had, and it gave way. I reached my hand through the ragged hole and fumbled around. A thick board lay on top. I heaved it off and was pushing the door up and open, climbing up through it, just as I heard the third blast of buckshot that was supposed to have sent my hide to kingdom come.

27

I came out behind the house, then stood flat against the wall, looking for a way back up to where I'd left my horse on the sandrock ridge.

The land rolled off flat to the south and west, all snow and sagebrush. Due east was a sheer rock wall that would take hours to climb and me stuck like a fly on a wall for them to pick off while I was trying. The only way was to get around to the front of the house, then light a shuck for the hill that Coogan had brought me down.

I moved along the side of the house, my heart pounding, expecting to run into somebody at any moment. But I made it to the front corner, then leaned in against the wall and listened. I could hear them talking again, though they were a mite distant.

Coogan sputtered, "Ain't heard nary a sound from back in there. Hold on—"

"I tell you, he's already dead." The voice belonged to Bowles. He'd evidently moved around front too.

"I ain't makin' no wagers on it," said Coogan. "We'd likely of heard something."

Skettering said, "Well, hang it all, if you're too yellow to crawl in there and see, then get on over to the barn and bring out the tracking dogs."

I checked Bowles's pistol. It was empty—the shot I'd fired at Bowles apparently had been the last one in the chamber. Once the dogs were loose, I was done for. I had to get away without their seeing me, make it up that ridge to my horse— and to my rifle, which was still in my saddle-scabbard. As for my Colt, I figured I'd let it lie this time and let old Zeb Tucker sell me a new one. That shooter was plumb bad luck any-way—either that or it just didn't fit my hand, for this was the second time this winter that it had been shot away from me.

277

I tossed Bowles's gun aside as the worthless hunk of metal it was without bullets. My hand was numb from the grip I'd had on it.

I edged around until I could see the snow-covered ridge. The trail up was slick with mud due to the spring thaw. But it didn't seem so steep as it had seemed from above. I figured I could make it if they didn't see me first and pick me off.

I looked harder, then decided I'd try to crawl as the crow flies, straight up and between the sagebrush and trees. If I took the trail itself with its several switchbacks, I was going to be out in the open from time to time, with no brush for cover. Either way I'd be exposed as I crossed the open meadow for about thirty yards, stuck out there against the snow like a knot on a log. All they'd have to do was to get me in their sights and pull the trigger.

But as I moved off in that direction, I spotted a ray of hope. A gully zagged down from the ridge off to my right. I hadn't seen it before because its banks were hid by the terrain. It was filled with a heavy growth of sagebrush and had a few cedars, small quakies, and some service brush and scrub oak scattered in it. *A good place for small game to hide*, I thought. And I was the game. All the same, if the good Lord rode with me, I'd make it.

I could hear the tracking dogs now, yelping hungrily, excited, coming from the direction of the kennel in the barn. It was now or never. I took off at a dead run.

I stayed to the south of the house till I had to cross over to the ravine. I'd almost made the brush cover when they spotted me.

Buckshot blasted, spraying up snow just behind me. The noise crashed, then echoed off the mountain peaks. I stayed low, running humped over, scrambling up the gulch now, and the dogs barked and snarled. Coogan and Skettering, shouting and cursing, were running along behind.

I dove through the brush, and the branches tore at my clothes, scratched my hands and face. But I was moving like lightning and was already two-thirds of the way up to my horse and the trail that I had ridden in on.

All of a sudden an outcropping of sandrock appeared, and a small, sharp ledge jutted out above me and blocked off the ravine. I could get past it, but to do so I'd have to climb up and out of the ravine and show myself fully to the men behind me.

I stopped, my heart pumping and my breath coming in short gasps. I was soaked through beneath my heavy coat, shirt, and vest, soaked through with my own sweat. I knew I was trapped. Panic ripped through me, tightened my throat.

I desperately looked around for a way out. Directly above, a rock outcropping projected from the ledge, a low overhang that created a small cave of sorts back under the sandstone. I moved toward it, hoping to somehow make a final standoff there.

The brush just below me cracked and broke, and then I heard Skettering. "Coogan! Keep going—you almost got him. There! Right up there by that scrub brush."

The dogs came lunging, barking up the slope, growling and snarling, closing in for the kill.

I doubled down and started to ease in under the rocky ledge. Then I sensed something tremble back in there, and a low growl froze my blood. And then I could see it, back there in the shadows, deep in beneath the overhang, next to the wall.

It was the wounded grizzly, sure as thunder, looking big as a house back in the den where it had been hiding. It was the same bear all right. I realized now that it was a large critter, probably a female, with a hump on her back and eyes rolling in near-blind rage. Saliva dripped from her open mouth, and her teeth looked as sharp as a badger's claws. The brute came up out of her crouch, and I could see the bullet wounds in her leg and side where the bristly black hairs were stained dark with blood.

She made ready to jump me, mouth slavering and rounded

pupils full of the hot beastly hatred I'd seen so recently in Hearne's eyes—and in Skettering's and Coogan's as well.

Slowly, keeping my eyes on the beast, I bent down to pick up a narrow sandstone slab that the rains had washed out of the outcropping. It was poor protection, to be sure, but it was the only weapon in sight other than the small knife I'd stuck back in my boot, and that wasn't going to do me much good now. At least if the bear charged me, perhaps I could distract her by throwing the slab at her.

Coogan broke through the brush below. I was bent over, still picking up the rock, and as I looked up he gloated, "Well, now, if'n we ain't got 'im cornered—"

The grizzly roared out of that hole like a runaway locomotive, me still bending, and it flew right over me and lashed out for Coogan, taking him dead-center and nigh unto breaking him in half. His terrified scream ricocheted off the mountains.

Man and bear hit the ground and rolled until they were stopped by the scrub oaks and quakie trees at the edge of the bluff. And when they'd stopped, I saw that the grizzly was still in a frenzy and had its jaw buried deep in Coogan's throat, tearing at it, and its sharp claws had already left great, bloody rips in his hide.

The dogs went crazy, barking and yelping. They tore up the slope and laid into the bear, working themselves into a frenzy as filled with blood lust as the grizzly itself. But the bear's claws kept them at bay, for those giant paws ripped tufts of hair and blood with every swipe that connected. One dog was knocked completely off the ledge and down into the ravine below.

And all the while the brute went at Coogan, lying there with that Sharps rifle still frozen in his hand, though I knew he was already dead.

I still gripped the sandstone rock I'd picked up when the grizzly leaped out of his hiding place. When the bear turned on the dogs, I threw it, knowing even as I did that it was a hiccup in a blizzard in the face of such wild fury. The dogs' howls of blood lust and yelps of pain echoed above me in the hills, then began to die into a loco tangle of yowling and snarling.

Skettering's voice called from below me. "Coogan! You get him? What's going on up there? Coogan! You hear me?"

Skettering would have a gun. I still had to get away.

I moved upslope, leaving the racket of the dogs and the bear behind me. I had almost made it to the top of the sandstone outcropping when I slipped. I caught hold of a gnarled juniper that had grown out of the side of the ravine, got my balance, and started climbing again.

Then a rifle cracked, and I looked over my shoulder to see Skettering and his two cowhands standing at the bottom of the slope, still not up to where the grizzly had taken Coogan. They were looking my direction and firing, seeing me now but only me, and not knowing of that giant black ball of death that was tearing up their dogs. I scrambled for all I was worth, trying to reach the top of the ridge.

Crack! Another shot stirred up snow to my right.

I was praying. I knew the gunfire was going to hit me at any minute. I was too good a target for them to miss much longer. I could see over the top now and was ready to climb over when another rifle shot came, barely missing me.

And then I felt a rumble beneath my feet. Reckon I thought at first I'd been hit and everything was shaking inside me, but then the rumbling grew louder, and the mountain above me gave off a low, terrifying roar, and a nameless fear gripped and smothered me.

I grabbed another juniper and pulled myself up far enough to see my horse, still tethered in the trees above. The quaking intensified, and the rumble above me grew deeper. My horse set to whinnying, then bucking and rearing back to get away from the shuddering earth.

I saw a wall of snow cascading down the mountain high above us, coming with a speed faster than a freight train.

Avalanche!

The white, powdery wall was a good fifty to seventy-five feet high, tearing out giant trees by their roots, picking up huge boulders and ancient deadfalls of downed timber, carrying them along in its churning turbulence as if they were matchsticks, and heading straight toward me as a huge white wall of death.

I slid back downslope and ducked in under that sandstone shelf and listened to the mountain fall down around me. I knew now that the gunfire had knocked this freezing white horror loose. What with the warm Chinooks melting the snow cover's underbase, it had just been waiting for something to jar it free.

Within a minute the wind-blast and roar of the thundering snow was so intense that I clapped my hands over my ears to shut out the fury of the sound. Snow sifted through the air above me as the cutting edge approached. I shoved deep back under the outcropping where the wounded grizzly had been holed up. The smell of blood and wild animal scent was all around me, but though the snow might bury me alive here, at least it wouldn't carry me back into that rock-rimmed valley where Skettering's brand of death lay waiting.

I thought briefly about Skettering down below, and then it was on me and I was thinking of nothing but prayer as terror such as I'd never known before ripped through me and the snow roared and cascaded down and jumped the outcropping, spraying off the bluff, and the rock ledge above me shook like a giant's hand was tearing at it.

Something crashed, and I looked out to see that a full-grown blue spruce had caught on the ledge and was prying at the sandrock overhead with the force of a thousand tons of nitroglycerin behind it. With a dynamite blast of noise, the tree snapped in half beneath the avalanche, and the shreds of wood and needled branches roared with the snow on down the mountain into the valley below. The tornado winds ripping at my shaken shelter now roared around me, and suddenly it was black, and I was buried, as the white muffled mass roared past and left a trail that swallowed up the light and the air that let me breathe.

Slowly the ground beneath me stabilized. The roar died down, the ringing in my ears softened some. The world seemed to settle around me. Suddenly something dropped outside with a thud, and I realized it was the thick layer of snow that had stuck to the door of my hideout. I could suddenly see sunlight again, filtering through the thick powder of snow in the air.

I waited, shivering, my heart thudding through my rib cage, plumb afraid to move. Reckon I was afraid I'd shake something loose, and the whole blamed nightmare would start again.

I must have hunkered there a full ten minutes, making sure that it was all over, before I pushed my way out and up and through the heavy layer of powdered snow and debris that lay all around me and the overhanging ledge.

Outside my shelter, fine snow was still filtering through the air, and the sunlight was making tiny rainbows in it as it hung in the now quiet atmosphere like a haze all around me. This soft frozen mist was settling gently down atop the high avalanche drift below—a thick cover of snow so deep that it had plumb buried the valley beneath me.

Only the eaves of Skettering's main house and the roof of the barn jutted up above the snow, with all the twisted logs and rocks mixed in. The ranch buildings—what was left of them—were buried. Splinters and torn trees, huge boulders and rocks, planks, cedar posts, and corral poles—all were sifted throughout the snow like a broken up shipwreck on a solid sea of white.

In an instant I took all that in, then turned to look at the opening of the ravine below me where I'd last seen Skettering and his men. The avalanche filled the ravine to the brim and spilled out into the meadows, covering over or grinding away every trace of Coogan, the dogs, and the pain-crazed bear.

So Skettering was gone too. He had to be. Whether he'd been buried in the slide or had made it back down towards the ranch, the man was entombed in a grave of pure snow white.

A muffled whinny cut through the air above me. I crawled out and up through the soft powder. Then I could see above me, and I understood that by God's grace the avalanche had funneled through a chute that a former, ages-old avalanche had taken, tearing out the timber to either side of the swath but missing the woods where my horse was tethered. We'd both survived only because we were at the edge of that chute, and only the outside edge of the fury had hit us, while the central fierceness of the slide had hit Skettering's buildings full force.

My horse was still tied to the small aspen where I had left him, buried up to his belly in the loose snow that had sloughed off from the main slide, but he was still standing, still alive, and nervous as a preacher in a saloon.

I said a prayer of thanks, then I started the long steep climb up to him through the deep, sugar-fine snow that was still settling down through the air around me like a white mantle of blessing.

28

I dug out my horse and led him deep into the timber and away from the slide trough, then upslope to an old game trail. We crossed high above timberline, above where the snow had cut loose and started its downhill rampage. When we'd got to the other side and past the high banks the slide had left in its wake, I mounted, found the trail, and rode back down into the timber.

I slept a little in the saddle on the way back. I didn't stop at the Hearnes' homestead. Mrs. Hearne would know soon enough that her boy was dead. And as for the rest of it, it was plumb beyond me what to do to better her and the younger boy's plight unless she somehow found the grit to try to help herself.

It was shortly past dark when I rode between the hills and down the draw to the north of my ranch. The big old house looked forlorn and forsaken below me, not a light showing anywhere. The full moon was a milk-glass bowl with ghostly tatters of cloud veiling it. The moonlight revealed the gaping maw where the fire had gutted the upstairs wing, showed it black, empty, and lonesome as death itself.

But there were lights in the bunkhouse windows, and nigh unto every window in the bottom floor of Ledbetter's big two-story home was ablaze. Caroline and the young'uns were no doubt still at the Ledbetters', probably worrying about me and fussing about when I would get home but staying busy for all that. It was hard to believe that it had been less than a full day since my world had rolled upside down.

As I rode down the draw, someone stepped out the kitchen door and onto the bunkhouse porch, lit a lantern, then went back inside. The dogs heard me and started barking.

I'd be glad for the warmth of the house and a hot cup of coffee and a short night's rest. With nightfall, the chill had set in and seemed to seep into my stiff joints. I was weary through my very bones. But there wouldn't be much rest for me for a while. Not till I knew what Ben Blue and Senator Otis Brown were doing—and why Blue had ridden to Hahns Peak.

Skunkweed was at the stables, tending to a frostbitten horse. He helped me unsaddle my weary mount, feed, and water him. Then I let Skunkweed rub him down and give him a box of oats, while I told the old cowhand what had happened.

When I'd finished talking, I said, "I'm going to sleep for a short spell and get some grub. Reckon the fastest mount is the pinto. Saddle him in about two hours, and if I'm not here on my own, come wake me up."

"Yessir, Court, but I reckon this could wait till morning. Leastwise, one of us boys would be mighty proud to ride up to Hayden and send a telegram to warn the judge that something's afoot."

"Telegraph office in Hahns Peak closes about three in the afternoon," I said. "The judge wouldn't get a telegram till tomorrow at best, and with hard riding I could be there by dawn."

"You'll kill yourself before this is over and save your foes the trouble," Skunkweed grumbled. "You ought to send someone else."

"I'll think about it," I said. "But wake me up, all the same."

I went over to the Ledbetters'. Their children and my own had all been put to bed, and Caroline and Virginia were sitting in matching wingback chairs, doing mending from a big wicker basket full of clothing, while Ledbetter sat stretched out in front of the blazing fireplace with his boots off, his stocking feet near the flames, reading the *Denver Post*.

I told them what had happened. Caroline's face was drawn and white when I was done, and I knew from the green fire in her eyes that when we were alone I was going to get a tongue-lashing for my recklessness. But the look of contempt that I'd seen for so long in Ledbetter's eyes was replaced by one of shock, then wavering belief, then surprised admiration.

Reckon that irked me for all that, considering that I'd nigh unto gotten my fool hide killed and the good Lord alone had pulled me out of it and had to send a grizzly and an avalanche to boot. I felt a sadness like a howling prairie wind when I thought about those men lying dead beneath the thick, heavy snow. In spite of the fact that they would have killed me, and gladly, each man's death somehow diminished my own life.

I finally washed up some in the water closet, then went upstairs and lay atop my borrowed bed with only my boots off and dropped into a black, weary sleep.

Skunkweed didn't wake me up till near midnight, giving me four hours' sleep in all. I didn't grumble at him, for I knew he'd done the right thing. He helped me carry the supplies I'd need and packed them in my saddlebags, among them a borrowed six-shooter and my heaviest, fleece-lined poncho.

As I rode along the dark stage-freight road, I did a heap of thinking about the trouble that had plagued this valley, and I figured some things out. Ben Blue—that is, Lieutenant Ben Buchanan—had shown up in these parts just about the time that the judge had contacted Kenny Payne to look into the crooked dealings at the Indian Agencies. Skettering had tried to pass Blue off as a stock detective, but now I figured that someone else had really hired the man—Senator Otis Brown.

No wonder the senator hadn't been too worried about Skettering's crooked bookkeeping when it came to land and cattle. Compared with what Brown himself was organizing, Skettering's work was no more than a schoolboy's hand in a cookie jar, for it seemed now that the whole thing boiled down to the government contracts for the supplies to the Indians. Whoever held those controlled a fortune, and one trickled away through theft so often that folks had grown to expect it. Ben Blue and the senator were in cahoots, no doubt about it.

And it looked to me as if the only folks in the way were Judge Warren and me.

I slept some in the saddle again, my horse staying on the road with a loose rein.

After passing the Sleeping Giant and turning north up Elk River toward Hahns Peak, I stopped and made a fire, careful to shelter it from any prying eyes, even though the darkness seemed cold and empty and I reckoned I was the only fool in a thousand miles beneath the star-blazed night. I brewed myself a pot of coffee, ate some of my hardtack, then melted water for my horse and fed her oats. When I was done I kicked the fire out and was back in the saddle and on my way in a short time.

By the stars it was right at 3:00 A.M. when I rode into Hahns Peak Village. Up here high in the mountains the stars hung so big and low that I felt as if I could reach right up and grab one, burn myself on its cold glitter. The air was crisp, with frost sparkling in the pale starlight. The moon had disappeared southwest of Wolf Mountain an hour or so before.

The warm Chinook winds of the last week had left only small snowbanks, which had been piled at the edge of the street. Most of the roads were open but still muddy in places beneath the frosty crust that had frozen over the top. The main street was again dry after a long cold winter. It was rutted with wagon tracks and hoof marks.

The town might have been a graveyard with house-shaped tombstones, sheltered by the mine-pocked peak looming off to the north. All was dark and quiet. No barking or yapping greeted me. I reckoned that the night was so brisk that even the dogs had been invited inside. The only movement came from the threads of smoke rising up from the chimneys and stovepipes of the flimsy houses. All the horses had been stabled for the night, apparently in private barns or in the big livery barn across the street from the hotel.

The clip-clop of my horse's hooves made an eerie echo as I rode down Main Street and past the dead-eyed windows. The only light came from the high, narrow windows in the lobby of the hotel where a gas lamp burned, and one lonely light shone in a second-story window.

I rode the full length of town to the judge's house. There was one light burning there too, in the kitchen window, which surprised me some.

I dismounted, then stepped onto the porch and rapped lightly at the door so as not to awaken anybody who wasn't already awake.

Mrs. Warren pulled aside the window curtain, saw it was me, then opened the door. Her gray hair was tied up in a bun at the back of her head and covered with a hairnet. Her eyebrows were knitted into a perplexed frown. She wore a thick gray wool nightcloak and heavy slippers. Warmth seeped out the door as she said, "Courtney! Land sakes alive, whatever are you doing out there? Come in here before you catch your death of cold."

As she closed the door behind me, I said, "Ma'am, I'm sorry to bother you like this so early in the mornin'—"

"My gracious! What in land sakes happened to you?"

"I had a little accident, ma'am." I touched one of my burns—it was still hot with pain. But I wasn't ready yet to explain to anyone about the fire and all the rest. That could come later—with the morning.

"My goodness, Courtney. Well, it's good to finally see you anyway. We've been expecting you to show up at any time."

"Expecting me?"

"Why, yes. My goodness, we knew you'd be along to help that Indian friend of yours."

Stupidly I said, "Indian friend?"

"Why, yes, Chief Yampawah. As soon as the soldiers brought him in, I said to the judge, 'I'll just bet you anything that Courtney McCannon is up here within one day.'" She smiled, wrinkles lifting her forehead, then she frowned quickly as she sneezed and brought a big linen kerchief to her nose.

"Yampawah? The soldiers brought him in?" Then, re-

289

membering myself, I said, "Ma'am, excuse me, but can you tell me if Senator Brown is staying with you folks?"

"Why, no, he's at the hotel—"

I said, "Thank God for that. Ma'am, I know it's an awkward time, but I need to see the judge right away."

She frowned again, then said, "Now, Courtney, you must be half frozen. Why don't I make you a hot cup of tea? I was just brewing water for my own. I've been up most of the night with this cold—I just can't seem to shake one like I used to." She was already moving around, getting out another cup and saucer. "I'll be so happy when we move down to Denver and away from these terrible winters—"

I said, "Ma'am, I'd appreciate anything hot right now, but I do need to see the judge right away."

"Now, Courtney, the judge had a hard day. And he has to drive Senator Brown up to Encampment this morning, so he can catch the stage to Laramie—"

"Laramie?"

"Why, yes. Land sakes, Courtney, I've never seen you like this. My heavens, are you all right? You must be coming down with something too. I don't believe I'd be surprised, what with all this terrible weather. Cream or sugar?"

"Ma'am—"

"You'd best get out of that coat and climb into bed yourself, instead of awakening the judge. Land sakes, you look like death's been riding on your coattails."

"Reckon he rode along ahead of me, ma'am."

"What's that?" She stopped in mid-motion with the teapot in her hand and cocked her head, listening harder.

Judge Warren stepped into the kitchen just then, pulling the belt of his red plaid robe tight over thick gray long handles. "I thought I heard voices. What is this, Violet? What in thunder is going on? Were you planning to keep our visitor all to yourself?" He smiled warmly, shook my hand, then peered closely at my face. "What happened? Looks like somebody took a hot poker to you."

"That's close, but time enough for that later."

He blinked, then gave me a puzzled look. All the same, he said, "Anyway, good to see you, Court," and let it be. He sat down at the table across from me.

Mrs. Warren huffed. "Well, as long as you're up, you'd best have a cup of tea too."

The judge said, "Thank you, Violet, I believe I will. And I believe I'll warm it up with a taste of brandy."

"Drinking at this time of mornin'," she bristled. Then she swept through the doorway and came right back with a silver tray holding crystal glasses and a crystal brandy decanter.

The judge offered to pour me a drink, but I declined. I laid my coat, gloves, scarf, and hat on a wooden chair in a corner as he poured a drink for himself, then his wife.

She didn't complain as she took a dainty sip. She fanned the air in front of her face as it went down though and coughed, then said, "Perhaps a little medicinal nip will help with this cold."

The judge looked me over. "Violet said we'd be seeing you, though I didn't expect you to make the ride at night."

"Judge, I didn't know that Yampawah had been arrested until I stepped into this room. What happened?"

He chewed on his lip, frowning. "I'm terribly sorry, Court. It seems that when Senator Brown got back to Denver he sent a wire to the Meeker garrison and told them to arrest Yampawah for the murder of Kenny Payne. He'd assured me he'd do no such thing, and I didn't know a thing about it until two soldiers showed up yesterday afternoon with Yampawah, Chased-by-Bears, and Charley Crazy-Horse in irons. I put them in the jailhouse—didn't have much choice.

"Seems Brown and Skettering had a good long talk while we were in Windsor that day we visited your ranch, and I wasn't privy to the conversation. I believe now that the two of them must have been cooking this up all along, and Brown lied in his boots to keep me from knowing until the damage had already been done."

"You say they arrested him for killing the BIA man?"

"That's right."

"Just what is Brown planning to use for proof?"

The judge shook his head in frustration. "It seems that Skettering claims Yampawah came to his ranch and threatened him and his men, that Payne came along no more than an hour afterward, and when he learned of Yampawah's behavior, he rode off after the old chief. Next day your boys found Payne dead and froze stiff. That's Skettering's story, whether it's the truth or not, and it'll likely stand up in court. Considering the mood everyone's in, that's as good as saying that he saw Yampawah kill Payne." He swallowed his brandy at one gulp, then refilled his glass.

"Are you going to be the one to try Yampawah?"

He shook his head. "I refused. I've already told Brown and anyone else who'll listen that this whole thing is a farce. But Brown and his crooked friends won't stop now. I expect they'll take the chief to the Meeker garrison and try him by military tribunal. And after the rackets in '79, what with the Army still agitated because of the Utes setting on Major Thornburg and his troops, I don't need to tell you that the Army lawyers are going to take Skettering's word over Yampawah's."

I said, "Skettering's dead."

The judge said, "I can't for the life of me—" He whipped around to stare at me. "What's that you say?"

"Judge, Moses Skettering is deader than a hunk of last year's beef jerky."

I told them the whole story then, from the fires at my ranch to my ride to Skettering's place, and right on through the rest of it.

When I'd done, Mrs. Warren had finished off a full tumbler of brandy, and she kept saying, "Oh my, oh my goodness," while the judge just sat there, his face knotted up like a fist and fury blazing in his eyes.

While I had him in the right frame of mind, I told him I'd overheard Skettering's ranch hands mention that something was afoot with regard to him, the senator, and Ben Blue. I explained how I figured that Blue meant to kill him, maybe bushwhack him, because with him and me out of the way they'd have free rein over the whole northwestern part of the state.

The judge said, "That explains a lot, Court. Such as why Brown was so insistent that I be the one to drive him up to the Encampment stage station in the morning. He said we had more to talk about, that my nomination was all set but that there were some last minute details that were confidential—why, that walleyed, witch-bridled polecat—"

I said, "I'll be happy to ride along, Judge. Out of sight, of course. My guess is that Blue will ride behind and bushwhack you, just as he's done me a couple of times. With me riding shotgun, we could stop him in his tracks."

"Blue said he'd rode up to file on some land. Hadn't gotten around to it yet by yesterday evening though. Plumb strange. He and Brown are a mite close for new acquaintances. I had noticed that."

"They're setting you up for the kill."

The judge pondered that, then said, "Yes, well, I have my own sidearm, thank you, and I'm not so old but what I can't take care of myself. What worries me more than Blue is that Sheriff Finsand is still in charge of the jail, and the more I see of him these days the less I trust him. Right now he'd rather fight Yampawah than cross me. But with Yampawah and his two braves in the hoosegow and all the rest that's going on, the minute I ride out of town there's no telling what might transpire."

"Wouldn't he be afraid of the consequences when you get back?"

The judge looked disgusted. "Not if he's in cahoots with Blue and doesn't expect me to *make* it back. All those fools do these days is play cards together every time Blue rides up here."

That surprised me. "He comes up often?"

"Once a week or so. I reckon Blue has had all the time he'd need to twist around what's left of Finsand's decency. I wouldn't trust any one of those varmints farther than I could spit backwards."

"Reckon I'll be pleased to keep an eye on Yampawah and his boys," I said, though I had misgivings about letting the judge ride off alone with Brown—and Ben Blue following. "What do you plan to do when you get back?"

"By Ned, this is still my jurisdiction! I'm going to write out a writ of release for Yampawah and his braves right now. But I don't want Brown to know anything about it until that old Indian has a chance to get far away from here. If that blowhard senator knows anything, he'll double-cross me again. The minute he reaches Denver he'll be looking to throw a plank in the works."

"Sounds like you've got your hands full there."

He nodded. "Court, I'd appreciate it if you'd take the writ over to Finsand right after we leave town. He won't cross you either, I can promise you that. Take Yampawah and his boys and ride down the other way, get them back to the reservation, where they've got some access to the troops at Fort Duchesne. I can work directly with them to keep the Meeker soldiers off their property till this has been straightened out through the BIA in Washington."

"Reckon it'll work?"

"Don't see why not. With Brown out of the way before the writ is served, I can leave everyone—Finsand and the soldiers, too—under the impression that Yampawah's release is Brown's idea. That way no one will come riding after us, and Brown won't even know about it until he arrives in Denver. Then, with Skettering dead—I can barely believe that!—his chief witness is gone. Then let Brown try to stir up what he will, that crooked devil—"

My eyes had filled with grit. I suddenly felt my chin sag to my chest and couldn't seem to pull it back up until I felt Mrs. Warren shaking my shoulder and saying, "My land, Courtney McCannon, you must be tired! You'd best get to bed if you're going to be doing anything later this morning."

The judge said, "I'll put your horse in the barn and see that it's cared for. You go on upstairs and get some rest. I'll wake you up in a few hours when the writ is ready and just before Brown and I are ready to set out for Encampment. Violet? Will you show Courtney the spare room?"

29

Judge Warren was right about Finsand. After I'd watched the judge and Brown ride out of town in that sleek black buggy the judge owned, I went directly over to the jailhouse. Finsand had a game of poker going with a blue-coated soldier who was so young that he still had peach fuzz on his face. From the looks of things, the sheriff was fleecing him good.

Finsand didn't look too happy when he saw me coming through the door. He took the writ from me and read it, his face screwing up into a scowl, then handed it to the soldier.

When the boy was done reading, he looked at Finsand. "Wait a minute. I have to get my commanding officer—"

But Finsand said, "Can't keep that old Injun no matter who says to now. Your military command told me that you didn't even have the papers for his arrest to begin with. Sergeant said you were waiting for them to arrive at the Meeker garrison. Anyhow, this is the judge's jurisdiction, and with the judge signin' this paper, I have to let the Injuns go. I don't have no choice, though I swear by heaven I wish I did have." He was nigh unto whining by then.

When Yampawah came out of the cell, worn and weary, his face told me nothing.

The sheriff puffed up his heavy chest and said, "Well, Injun, looks like you get to go free to kill some more white folks—" I looked hard at Finsand, and he shut up, pasted a hard look on his tight-lipped face, and opened the cell that held Charley Crazy-Horse and Chased-by-Bears.

When we got outside, I said to Yampawah, "Reckon you don't even know what hit you, do you, Chief?"

He gave me a cold look and drew himself up in defiance. "I was camped with my people up the valley, two days from your ranch. The soldiers came. I did not know what they wanted with me, but I did not want my people to be harmed.

296

I did not fight. I chose to test your white man's poisonous medicine, Tall Gun."

I grinned. "Reckon you're getting somewhat smarter in your old age, Chief. A lawman was killed, a man who came here to look into the charges that you'd been rustling beef. A very powerful white man set you up to hang for his death. But another white man—one with good, strong medicine—well, he set you free. Upshot of all this is, the same evil white men who tried to do you in are now planning to do in the man who helped you out. I say we need to stop them."

I didn't have to ask him twice.

Their ponies had been left at the livery stable. The young dark-haired liveryman was sleeping late and woke up grouchy.

I said, "Any other riders take out of here this morning?"

"Only one. Ben Blue. Gave me a half eagle to have his horse watered, fed, and saddled last night, then rode out."

"Much obliged," I said. I flipped the liveryman a full eagle to help us feed and water the Utes' horses and to pay for their room and board.

It seemed odd that Blue had ridden out so early. I began to wonder if he didn't plan to catch the judge in Encampment or on the way back, when the senator was clean out of the picture.

We rode north, up the Hahns Peak–Encampment wagon road, moving at a run at first, then slowing down to a fast trot as we got closer to catching up with the judge's buggy or with Ben Blue, whoever came first.

We could see the buggy tracks as clear as day, cut atop the newly thawing mud. There were countless jackrabbit tracks on the deep snowbanks alongside the road, but other than that the land here was pristine. A hawk circled overhead looking for breakfast, then made a harsh little cry that trailed off into silence as he suddenly dived toward the earth. There wasn't another sign of man or beast to be seen anywhere, and the hawk dipped back up after a moment and flew away, something in its beak, behind the hills.

It was cold enough for the horses' breath to come out in little white puffs. The sky was icy blue. Hahns Peak towered up ahead of us, a sugar-white cone decorated with green pine, filling the skyline now. The pine forest was dappled here and there with fir, spruce, barren aspen, and birch that made a snow-filled carpet all the way up the mountain to timberline.

We rode around the peak, then north toward King Solomon Creek, then cut across to Whiskey Park and the Encampment trail. The only sound was the occasional squeak of saddle leather, for the three Indians were so quiet I began to wonder if they hadn't turned into cigar store displays.

We caught up with the judge's buggy about a half mile downslope of the peak and trailed it, careful not to be seen, while we looked for signs of Ben Blue.

We kept our eyes peeled for hoofprints, either on the muddy road or in the snow to either side of it—but Blue apparently hadn't been this way. Leastwise not this morning. There were switchbacks and hills and places where the timber obscured the road for long spells. But we managed most of the time to keep the buggy in sight.

I was worried some about the peak itself. The western flank was far enough away so that a man with a rifle would have to be awful lucky to make his shot but not so far away that it was impossible. And I reckon that by then I'd heard enough about Ben Blue to expect anything.

Except what happened.

Chief Yampawah, watching closely, saw my eyes searching the peak. He said, "He will not be there, Tall Gun. That would be the foolish way." Then his face took on a serene look as he gazed at the mountain. He said, "This is a magnificent mountain, is it not?"

"Sure is."

His voice took on that faraway quality it sometimes had. "When the Great Spirit grew weary of the flatlands of the prairies, He created the mountains so that He might use them as stepping-stones to descend to earth."

I always felt my hair sort of stand on end when he began to talk like that, but this time the words struck me nicely. Still, I didn't comment. I'd tried before to tell Yampawah about my own spiritual beliefs, and the more I listened to him the more I realized that we had a good deal in common.

Trouble was, when it came to talking about Jesus Christ as God, Yampawah turned to granite. He'd had a crawful of white folks who had tried to shove their religion down his throat at the end of a gun barrel, and because of them he didn't have the first idea what I was talking about when I spoke of Christ as a messenger of life and love.

Now he was off in his own world. He said, "After the Great Spirit created the mountain, He then made the Top of the Mountain People, so that we might live in the mountains He created—"

He jerked his horse to a stop, putting up a hand to signal a halt. The rest of us froze along with him and looked hard in the direction he indicated.

We'd come atop a rise, and below us we could see the judge's buggy. But his horses were snorting now and rearing as if they had been spooked by something, and the judge was having a hard time controlling the spirited team.

We kicked our mounts into motion and trotted down the slope and around the bend, reining in just in time to keep from being seen. And by the time we got back into a place where we could see the ruckus, the horses had panicked and thrown the buggy clean off the road, where it was mired in a deep, soft snowbank.

Both the judge and Senator Brown climbed out as we watched. They bent to look at the wheels and otherwise survey their problem.

Silently I motioned for Yampawah to dismount and for the other braves to stand guard on the road behind us. We grabbed our rifles and, moving through the deep snow in the shelter of the timber, crept close enough to hear the men's sharp, angry voices, though we were still too far away to make out what they were saying.

Eyes narrowed, looking around me, rifle ready, I said quiet-like to Yampawah, "If you ask me, this most likely is a mite too much for coincidence—"

The words had no more come out of my mouth than a wink of sunlight glinted in the trees on a ridge above the buggy.

I shielded my eyes, looked, and again saw the sunlight winking on a gun barrel! Ben Blue—it had to be Blue—had somehow circled around and was up there in those trees. How in thunder had he got up there?

I motioned for Yampawah to duck in beneath the timber, hoping Blue hadn't already spotted us, and the old Indian followed me. We slogged in and around the timber, keeping out of sight of the rifleman. The snow was deep here and soft. How on earth had Blue gotten through it? I'd have sworn those woods were impassable—particularly on horseback!

We were getting closer to the buggy, which was directly downslope from us now. Judge Warren and Senator Brown were still standing in the frosty morning, arguing about something, most likely how best to get the buggy out.

Then on a sudden, Brown raised his voice and his hand ducked inside his vest and came out with a good-sized pistol, aimed square at Judge Warren.

My trigger finger went taut as I swung up my rifle, the barrel aimed for Brown's chest, and I sensed rather than saw that Yampawah's gun was aimed too.

But the judge hadn't so much as flinched at the sight of Brown's weapon. His face stormed up, and, quicker than I could see, he'd drawn a little derringer out of his own hidden holster, and now he held it aimed dead at Brown in a Mexican standoff.

A sudden *zing* sliced the air. The judge's gun went flying, and he reeled back and fell into the snowbank.

A low, sarcastic laugh came from the thick timber just above us, and then Ben Blue himself came walking out of the trees not ten yards past us, though he didn't see us yet. He was moving deftly atop the snow—on snowshoes! Apparently he'd tied his horse in a thicket someplace and come along on foot.

Reckon I'd underestimated his resourcefulness. He must have left long before sunup, taking advantage of the crusted snow to snowshoe north and across the westernmost foot of the peak in order to dry-gulch the judge in this forsaken spot.

The judge sat up, dazed. Apparently the shot had only stunned him. That puzzled me too. Why, if Blue had gone to all the trouble of getting here sight unseen, hadn't he already shot the judge dead?

Brown answered my silent question by shouting, "Hurry on down here, Blue. There may very well be other riders on this road. Let's get this buggy turned over right away!"

He addressed the judge then, his voice ringing clearly in the cold silent air. "Now then, you meddling old fool, I'm going to have the personal pleasure of putting you under. And make no mistake about it, it will be pure pleasure to silence that troublemaking mouth of yours once and for all."

Blue scampered down the slope, snow flying in his wake, and skidded to a stop to stand beside the two men and the buggy, a diabolic smirk on his face.

I had my rifle trained on Blue, while Yampawah's was on Brown.

In that Southern accent of his Blue said, "Well, suh, Senator, if you choose to do the job yourself, it's fine with me. But my payment will remain the same."

"I should have known that anyone who'd let Indian women and children die of disease and starvation just to line their own pockets would be capable of any type of cold-blooded murder." The judge's words were filled with contempt.

Blue smiled like a lizard, slow and lazy. "We can make your departure painful if you like and still have it look like an accident. Why don't you just let things go easy with you, suh? Now lean in here and help me tip this buggy over. We'll soon have it upside down with you on the bottom. Dagnabbit! These no-count horses aren't makin' the job any easier."

"Brown," the judge said sternly, "whether I'm dead or alive, you're finished. Skettering will never testify against Yampawah, and his books are about to be opened to inspection by the whole blamed world."

Brown stiffened and hollered, "You pompous old windbag, Skettering will do anything I tell him to. I own that man, lock, stock, and barrel."

"*Owned* him, Brown. Skettering's dead."

"Why, you old reprobate, you expect me to believe that? Hurry it up, Blue. The judge is getting wily here, and I don't plan to listen to this troublemaking old liar a word longer."

"I could use a little help," Blue said.

He leaned his shoulder to the buggy, pushing, and Brown turned to the task as well, though it didn't seem that he was applying much pressure.

As soon as they'd turned their backs to us, we stepped into view of the judge, our rifles still aimed, Yampawah scowling.

The judge turned plumb white when he saw us, but I held up a cautioning finger to him as we dropped a bead on the two men, who were both grunting and now had the buggy halfway up on its side, about to roll.

Easy-like, I said, "Howdy, gentlemen."

They whipped around and stared at us as if we were two ghosts stepped fresh from the grave. The buggy wheels bounced back to the ground.

It took the senator a moment to compose himself. Then, fists balled up and in a fury, he turned on Blue. "Ben, you lop-eared son of Satan, this is your job. I'm paying you to— confound it all, you let these fools creep up on us. Now *do* something!"

But Blue was already doing something. Quicker than a rattler striking, he spun around and dived in under the buggy bed—out of sight and rolling—while Brown was still blustering. He rolled to a stop with his rifle barrel poking out. Then it crawled around to face me, and I dived too, just as it belched out flame and smoke.

Yampawah lunged for the bushes too, and we were stunned for a second, like setting hens, but luckily Blue couldn't see too well from under there, for if his aim had been straight we'd have been dead men.

For a split instant the world seemed to stop in its tracks. Then Yampawah and I bolted at the same time for a large boulder alongside the road.

The judge was out of Blue's line of fire—so long as Blue stayed under the buggy—and he had Brown by the collar and was dragging him toward the ditch. Both of them were scuffling, and then Brown was tripping and sliding down into the mud. When they came up, the judge was holding Brown's own pistol on him and Brown just stood there, hangdog and whipped, with yellow fire blazing in his malice-filled eyes.

I looked back to the real trouble, just as Blue fired another rifle shot.

When it missed, he yelled out, "Hey, McCannon. What you shooting at me for?"

That made me take a step back, and if my hands hadn't been filled with my rifle, I'd have scratched my head. Shooting at *him*? What in thunder? Was the man plumb loco, or was I?

He spoke again, and this time his voice was friendly but cold all at the same time. "Courtney McCannon in the flesh. Well, suh, I swan, I never really thought I'd live long enough to see the day." He chuckled, and it made my blood run cold. He said, "Thoughts of that pappy of yours—and then of you, suh, after he died—well, you McCannons have kept me going through many, many a long night."

I fell to my stomach, still sheltered by the boulder, and tried to draw a bead on him. I could see the metal of his rifle, gleaming in the morning sunlight where the tip of it stuck out, but he was well sheltered where the buggy was half tipped by its slide into the ditch.

He said, "Yes, suh, thought we'd seen the last of you when Coogan an' that Hearne boy set fire to your house, but your hide's a good deal tougher than it seems."

An unholy curiosity kept me listening to what he was saying, even though I already knew I was either listening to a madman who'd dropped plumb off the edge or he was just using the time to reload or crawl around to get off a better shot. But it wouldn't take him this long to reload. Not near this long.

His voice took on a hollow quality as it rang out like a preacher's. "The sins of the fathers will be visited on the sons. Isn't that what your Good Book says? And the wages of sin is death? I'm only doing what I have to, Courtney. I believe you can see that. No reason for everyone to be afraid of me, even though there's blood on my hands. Not a man here who doesn't have blood on his hands, is there? The judge, he'd hang a man soon as look at him. Brown there, well, he'll be sleeping with the ghosts of starved Injuns for the rest of his born days and well into eternity besides.

"And as for you? You're the son of the father that the Good Book talks about, and the Lord knows your father had plenty of blood on his hands—enough to cover your own and all your children's as well."

He fell silent, but my skin was crawling. I said, "What in blazes are you up to, Blue? What quarrel do you have with me?"

"I wanted to kill that brown-haired woman of yours, Courtney. As sure as your pappy killed my Louisa." His voice cracked. "Did your pappy tell you about her? About how pretty she was, how we was just newly wed and talking about having our first son, when he left her in that house to crackle like pork rind?" He suddenly laughed long and low.

"Blue!" Brown shouted. He had regained some spunk. "The judge has got me! You get out here and do the job I've paid you to do."

Blue's voice growled back with a deep, furious rage. "Hang the judge, and hang you too, Brown. I'd never have taken your cursed job if it hadn't been for—" his voice changed again into something low and crafty and totally focused on me "—if it hadn't of been for McCannon here.

304

Suh—" he was talking to me again "—it's a fact that your pappy burnt my house to the ground and killed my bride of only one short week. Then when me and my troops rode after him he beat me again and put me in prison to give me a good long while to ponder on what he'd done to me. That's where I saw what I had to do. I'll kill every McCannon on the face of this earth before I'm through, suh, and though I'd wanted to start with that fancy wife of yours, I'll have to change my plans and start with you."

I had to ask the question. I said, "Blue. My pa's been dead for nigh onto five years. Why'd you wait till now to come looking for us?"

Wearily he said, "A man's life gets away from him at times. Up till six years ago I was in military prison. After that, something just seemed to come along to stop me every time. But when I learned that the judge was a friend and distant neighbor of the dishonorable McCannon family, and Moses Skettering and Brown needed to plant you two and get you out of the way of their business—" his voice tightened up "—well, suh, it was all cut out for me then, and I knew it was time."

A sudden bullet zinged into the mud at our feet, and then his gun was belching flame and smoke, and Yampawah and I were firing back, trying to send our bullets true but stopped by the awkward angle of the upturned buggy.

Blue's gun barked again, and I fired, then Yampawah fired, and I finally got off a shot that hit home. Blue howled with pain, the sound trailing off into a groan.

Yampawah scrambled down the ditch and up to the buggy and fired another shot under it, just to be sure.

There was silence.

I'd shot him. I'd finished him. And I felt a vast relief to be done with him. But at the same time a feeling like a dark wind came blowing through my mind. Someone or something was laughing back in that eternal darkness, an evil skull-head with a grin on its face that would surely haunt me through all eternity, telling me that Blue had won more in death than he had in life. I had stepped into the same evil turmoil of personal vengeance and hatred that had driven Ben Buchanan Blue for the last two decades. And my pa had been right. The death of Ben Blue also killed something vital within me.

But even as that thought came, a new wave of relief swept through me, and I thought again about all those mighty men in the Bible who'd had to stand their ground against evil, who'd fought to the end, the good Lord seeing them all the way through. And I knew that my soul wasn't in jeopardy after all, that the Lord had allowed me to triumph, and there was a great deal more to the business of fighting evil in this world than I'd ever understand.

The Lord hadn't called on us to be cowards. Caroline was right. We were soldiers—in a mighty battle—and all of a sudden I had the sense that—rather than losing my immortal soul—I had just won something honorable and good and true.

Still, it all boiled down to the fact that Blue was dead. Yampawah dragged his body out from under the buggy, and I was looking at a man who had once been handsome but who had withered up even in life from the death and destruction of a war that should have never happened, brother against brother, a tear-stained, bloodstained blot on the pages of all our lives that stayed with us still.

As Yampawah dragged the body forward, the glove slid off Blue's right hand, that hand he'd hidden from the world. It lay there limp, shriveled, and fire-scarred. And I knew then he'd been in the house when it had burned, that he had tried to save his bride, that he had maybe even watched her die.

I turned away and wept.

30

We were at my ranch house, two weeks later. Judge Warren tamped tobacco into his pipe with his forefinger, looked at me with his gray brows making hawk's wings above his sharp old eyes, and said, "No, Court, we'll never know for sure if your father realized the woman was in the house when he ordered his troops to set fire to it. But according to what I've been able to dig out, it wouldn't have mattered to him anyway. The Confederates had laid up in there—at Lieutenant Buchanan's orders I might add—and were cutting your father's men to ribbons. There was no possibility of retreat, no other way than to flush them out. If he'd done otherwise, he'd have lost every single man in his command."

"And that's what tortured my pa all the rest of his born days?"

"It tore him in half, Court—the fact that he'd set fire to a woman, even though he hadn't realized it at the time. He wasn't the sort of man to make excuses for himself, no matter if what he'd done was justified."

I shook my head sadly, looking into the fire in the fireplace, seeing images of a thousand memories and recollections in there. "So he spent the rest of his life punishing himself for doing something he more or less had to do." It was a problem that had been bothering me too lately, as I tried to swallow the ashes of Ben Blue's death and all the rest that had happened and tried to come to terms with it.

The judge bit on the stem of his pipe, then replied, "There seldom is good reason for punishing oneself, is there? You see people punishing themselves every day of their lives for things that they couldn't have stopped happening even if they'd anticipated them. There are regrets in every part of *my* life. There are trials I've presided over that I'd like to have seen turn out different—and they could have, had I known ahead of time what I knew later. But—hey, there, Court. You letting me sit here and talk to myself?"

"Sorry." I had indeed gotten lost in my own thoughts. Mostly I was thinking about what might have happened if I'd pulled the trigger on Jimmy Hearne when they'd first used him to get at me up in the tall timber that day.

The judge was saying, "If we could go back and do things over, I believe that every one of us would do at least some things differently. But in the meantime all we can do is the best we can with what we have to work with. Yes, the best we can, and if we learn to trust the Lord and look to Him for guidance, He'll see us through."

To shake off my own guilty thoughts, I said, "You reckon they'll ever get to the bottom of what Skettering was up to?"

The judge chuckled at that. "I doubt if they'll even recover the records—crooked or not—by the time the snow's melted off them. Plumb covered that house to the rafters, just like you said."

I thought about that too. I didn't feel good or bad about that bunch. Skettering had more or less brought his fate on himself, and I reckoned that avalanche could be called an act of God. They'd all been buried all right. Not one of them survived. And I reckoned that if they'd had a choice, they'd far rather have been in the worst prison in the land than where they were now.

Senator Otis Brown had resigned and was being investigated for corruption. And it looked as if the thefts from the Indian Agencies were going to be a mite easier to prove than Skettering's crimes, for there were people aplenty trying to talk now in order to save their own skins. Brown would undoubtedly see the inside of a prison, if the judge and his colleagues had anything to say about it, and their power in the government was growing every day now that the senator and his no-good crew were out of their hair.

"I expect Brown to be indicted by midsummer," the judge was saying now. "That crook still has a good number of powerful friends who are going to go down with him. And now that he's no longer able to hornswoggle things, I have my nomination to the senate. I'll soon be in a position to begin straightening out the rest of the corruption."

He puffed silently at his pipe for a moment, as both of us followed our own thoughts. Then he said, "By the way, Court, I've just learned that Skettering's remaining cattle are going to be auctioned off as soon as they can round them up this spring. If I were you, I'd buy them up. Times are changing, and your winter die-off was bad. You're going to need to re-build your herds."

That piqued me some—and shamed me too as I thought about my still precarious financial situation. "I need to build up my herd for sure, Judge. I just don't have the money to buy any cattle, and I ain't likely to have any more money come spring. It's been a hard couple of years."

I lifted my coffee cup and took a sip, then looked beyond the judge and out the window. The snow was falling again, softly. By morning we'd have a new foot on the ground. But the snow didn't matter now. It was just another spring squall that had drifted up the Yampa River from somewhere out towards Utah, and it would melt off with tomorrow's warm spring sunlight. The judge and Mrs. Warren would be staying overnight; the Mrs. and Caroline were in the kitchen making our dinner.

With a secretive smile on his face, the judge said, "Violet and I have a little extra put back. I'd be pleased to let you borrow it if need be."

"Thank you kindly, but I don't intend to borrow any more money. My pa fought long and hard to stay out of debt, and he left me this ranch free and clear. I reckon that if the good Lord's willing, I can hang on for another six months. Beyond that—well, I just can't say."

"They're changing the rules for assignment of the cattle contracts for the Indian Agencies," the judge said, smiling

309

wider now. "They're giving the Indians a bit more say-so about how the contracts are let out. Yampawah has asked that you be given the contract for the Ute reservation. I've seconded the suggestion. I don't know why that cagey old Indian respects you so much, but he said that you and the Top of the Mountain People could trust one another, and he'd be right pleased to see you get the contract."

I was so surprised and touched that I couldn't say a word.

"I sent a wire to Washington," the judge went on, his grin as wide as the river now. "They've already approved you. No matter what the cattle market does this year, you're going to need all the beef you can get your hands on."

That news set me back some, I can tell you. Feeling foolish and pleased all at the same time, I tried to thank him, but my tongue kept getting in the way of my teeth.

The judge was chuckling out loud.

Caroline and Mrs. Warren came to the kitchen door then, a look of curiosity on Caroline's face, Mrs. Warren smiling knowingly.

Caroline was wearing a high-collared dress that all but hid the ugly scars that remained from the fire, save for the few slight ones on her cheek. She'd wear those scars the rest of her life, but she was a strong woman, and she'd pulled herself together right well, overseeing the boarding up of the burned section of the house with a vengeance, though I knew she wanted badly to rebuild what we'd lost.

She tilted a spatula toward me. "Court? What is it? Mrs. Warren said you had something to tell me."

I replied, "We can rebuild the house and barn, Caroline, and spruce them up some besides."

She pursed her lips firmly and said, "Now, Court, you can't be serious. With all the debts we've got and the winter-kill . . ."

"We've just been awarded the cattle contract for the Ute reservation."

She gasped, then said, "Oh . . . oh, my . . ."

She turned, delicate-like, and handed the wooden spatula to Mrs. Warren. Then she turned back to me and broke into tears.

I went to her, put my arms around her, and when she looked up at me I could see that she was crying for joy.

She said, "Oh . . . oh, I'm so sorry, Court, it's just that it's been so hard for so long—" And then she buried her face in my shoulder that had been stoved up for so long but which was now completely mended.

Little Johnny came running into the room, excited, saying, "Look! This train runs—it goes on the floor!"

And as he set the wooden toy on the carpet, I said, "Thank the judge and Mrs. Warren for the gift."

He did, and the judge took a long draw on his pipe, knowing that the gift I'd meant wasn't just the toy train they'd brought along. They had also brought some pretty dresses for the baby, and she looked like a beautiful china doll. I was almost afraid to pick her up from her day crib in the corner. I was afraid she would break in two.

Caroline pulled herself back together, patting her cheeks with a lace kerchief, apologizing and thanking the Warrens too. Then she turned to me. "Court, you know what we were talking about last night? Do you think that now we might be able to—"

They'd found Old Man Hearne frozen to death the week before. He'd been on the way back from Windsor, dead drunk, and had apparently passed out and fallen from his wagon. Mrs. Hearne and little Bobby had already gone back to her family in Chicago, where Mrs. Hearne planned to work in the packing sheds. Caroline had told me when they'd left that she'd like to be able to do something to help them—maybe send them something from time to time to help out.

Now I grinned, feeling good too. "I reckon we could probably work something out."

Caroline smiled, and joy cut through her such as I hadn't seen since the day the baby was born. She'd heal. We all would.

It had been a cruel, ruinous winter, but spring was here. Within days, the new snow would melt off. The bluebells and paintbrush and buttercups would peek up through the tall grass on the hill back of our house, and the grass would grow tall and green again. Within a month, the dandelions would make a carpet of yellow all down the Yampa River Valley, while up in the tall timber the columbines would raise their delicate blue and white petals to the warm winds.

We'd rebuild the damage to the house and the barn, and we'd rebuild our wounded souls. One day this bloody season would be nothing but a lonesome memory of the time when I learned that no matter where evil appears or how it takes hold, with the help and guidance of the good Lord you have to do your part to root it out and destroy it before it destroys you.